MULE TRAIN

Huw Francis

TP

ThunderPoint Publishing Limited

First Published in Great Britain in 2013 by
ThunderPoint Publishing Limited
Summit House
4-5 Mitchell Street
Edinburgh
Scotland EH6 7BD

Map Copyright © Globe Turner

ISBN: 978-0-9575689-1-4

www.thunderpoint.co.uk

For Seonaid

PAKISTAN

Chitral · Gilgit

Muzaffarabad

Peshawar · Mardan

Islamabad

Rawalpindi · Jhelum

Mianwali · Gujrat · Sialkot

Dera Ismail Khan · Sargodha · Chiniot · Gujranwala

Faisalabad · Lahore

Jhang Sadar · Okara · Kasur

Sahiwal

Quetta · Dera Ghazi Khan · Multan

Bahawalpur

Nok Kundi

Surab · Rahimyar Khan

Shikarpur · Sukkur

Khuzdar · Larkana

Panjgur · Dadu

Bela · Nawabshah

Gwadar · Mirpur Khas · Hyderabad

Karachi

| 0 | 100 | 200 mi |
| 0 | 100 | 200 km |

Prologue

Raseem Hasni roughly stabbed the needle of the well-used syringe into the grubby arm of the stupid Englishman lying on the mud floor of the hut. He pumped the solution of pure, clean heroin into the vein and the man relaxed gratefully as his body accepted the poison it now craved. Raseem counted the profit this latest fool would make him, until the smell of shit and urine almost made him gag. This mule would need a wash before he could be sent on his way with a kilo of heroin stuffed in his bags.

Using clean smack it didn't take Raseem long to get the pot-heads and naïve young backpackers hooked and pliant once he had them in his village hideaway. Though the process could be messy it was usually easy getting the youngsters he found at the Islamabad campsite hooked on the heroin. The hardest to control were the pretty young women like the one in the room next door, that he wanted for his own amusement as well, before he made some money from them. The women were, however, well worth the trouble. The harder they fought the more he liked them.

Every year he lost a few mules along the way. In the early days he'd overdosed a few accidentally, now they were more likely to go off the wall and be unusable, and once he'd drowned a boy in the river when he threw him in to clean the shit off him before he was sent home with a delivery. He'd enjoyed watching the boy struggle and drown, but hadn't slept for a week afterwards from worry that the police would come and arrest him.

He thought of them as collateral damage, minor losses along the way that hadn't cost him much. It was the occasional few who disappeared after he left them at the airport, along with his merchandise, that made him really angry. Raseem

1

thought of all the money he'd lost over the years and kicked the prone figure lying in front of him viciously in the balls.

Rubbing his own crotch fervidly, Raseem turned away and headed for the room next door.

*****

Matt Peterson spent a lot of time lying on his bed these days. It was six months since Jo's death and he'd lost the will to do much at all. Except read the book that Jo had hardly stopped talking about in the months before she died.

He'd read it three times in the last six months. Now he'd read *A Short Walk in the Hindu Kush* he could understand why Jo had wanted him to read it. The idea of two eccentric Englishmen walking into the mountains of Afghanistan was as ridiculous as much as it was so very British. Matt had looked up Nuristan on the internet and found that once again the *Land of Light* was off limits to foreigners.

Sometimes he even dreamed of the mountains he'd never visited. As massive as they were the mountains protected the narrow valleys below, their life giving rivers feeding the people who lived in their shadow with the ice cold run-off from their living, breathing glaciers.

From a table across the bedroom, Jo's passionate eyes watched Matt from the photo taken two weeks before she died, on the day they got engaged. Right from the start he'd known she was special and today would have been their second anniversary, the start of their honeymoon. They should have been flying out to Pakistan for a trekking holiday in the Hindu Kush.

As a student Jo had gone on a field trip to the glaciers of the North West Frontier Province and fallen in love with the majestic beauty of the high mountains at the western end of the Himalayas. She had wanted to go back to those mountains ever since, and spent months persuading Matt to go. Her old photos and exuberant enthusiasm for the trip had finally worn down Matt's objections over safety and the dangers from whatever armed group was currently trying to take over the

2

area. He'd also been in love and wanted to give her the honeymoon she wanted.

The photo album lay open on the bed. One photo covered each of the pages. A head and shoulders shot of Jo with the mountains behind her faced the massive peak of *Tirich Mir* at the top of the Chitral valley. It was a mini mountain range of its own with eleven peaks stretching along a ridge. Like many mountains in the area it had its own mythology, reputedly being home to faeries, and was impossible to climb. Jo had always been sad that foreign mountaineers had broken the taboo and climbed the beautiful peak.

Jo had been on her way to the travel agent to buy the plane tickets and arrange their Pakistani visas when a teenage joyrider, high on drugs, had ploughed into her as she crossed the road. His partially packed rucksack still stood in the corner of the room where he'd left it untouched ever since; the empty space next to it where Jo usually put hers the night before they went off together hill-walking mocked him, as if Jo had gone somewhere without him.

Tirich Mir and Jo stared at Matt from the photo album, her trusty rucksack propped against a rock beside her. They were pulling him to them.

Matt's own rucksack caught his eye again. I should go after them, he thought. It wasn't such a daft idea now he thought about it. Her trip to Pakistan had always been something that made her different from the other girls he'd known, and if he went there too it would make him feel closer to her.

He reached for his laptop to look for flights to Pakistan. He had a lot to do if he was going to get out there any time soon. And maybe, somewhere in the *Land of Light*, he'd find something to fill the vacuum he now had in his life.

*****

Annie MacDonald was feeling happy: all her hard work might finally be about to pay off. She'd sometimes regretted being the first member of her family to go to university instead of getting a job. The cost of being at university and living away from home had been very stressful. But she had worked hard to get her degree during the three years at Manchester University, with a full time job and hardly any partying, so she wouldn't start her working life with lots of debt. And now Oliver was leaving and she reckoned she must stand a good chance of being promoted into his job.

Oliver was surrounded by a group of adoring fans at the far end of the bar. He'd been to a minor public school, then on to Brasenose College at Oxford University. That had been followed by an internship with an MP, then straight into his assistant editors job at the TV production company where they worked. He was only a year older than Annie, but he was well on his way up the ladder and had the expectation that he was going a lot higher.

Charles was at Oliver's elbow laughing with the rest of them at something the golden boy had said. Then he glanced up at Annie and eyed her, far too lecherously for her liking. Usually he treated her with cool disdain, but tonight he was drunk and paying her far too much attention.

'Diet Coke,' said Annie to the barman. She never liked drinking too much on a night out in London, it was nerve racking enough getting home sober with all the muggings, robberies and murders, let alone when your senses were dulled by alcohol. Manchester was different; she'd never really felt threatened there despite it's reputation.

'I'll get that,' slurred Charles as he leant against Annie and held a twenty pound note out to the barman, who raised a questioning eyebrow at Annie.

'If you can stand up straight I'll accept,' said Annie more sharply than she'd intended.

'Just being friendly,' leered Charles as he wobbled upright and leant heavily on the bar, still too close for comfort.

'I'll have another whisky. A large one,' Charles added as the barman place Annie's coke on the bar.

'Don't you think you've had enough? Sir,' responded the barman coldly.

'Just pour it, barman. And do your job.' Charles glared across the bar, then smiled arrogantly as the student barman emptied the optic into a glass, twice.

'You're looking very happy tonight, Annie. Every time I catch your eye you're smiling at me.'

'Don't take it personally, Charles. I'm just pleased for Oliver.'

Charles stared at her for a moment, then laughed. 'No you're not. You really think you're going to get promoted in his place, don't you?'

Annie returned his gaze levelly. 'Well, I've done half his job for the past year so it would be the right thing for you to do. Especially since I've done it so well.'

'You don't get it, do you? Oliver got that job because of who he is, not because he was likely to be any good.'

'So now he's leaving you can replace him with me and you'll get someone who can do the job.' Annie could sense her voice rising and struggled to keep her tone even so that she didn't annoy Charles.

Her outburst only made Charles laugh again. 'Don't be so naïve. We recruit people like you to do the work cheaply and people like Oliver because it's good for the business.'

'Give me the job and I'll be better for the business than he ever was, the pompous toff that he is.'

'No danger of that deary. One of the reasons women never get to the top in this business is because they want to take time out and enjoy themselves. No one in their right mind would ever promote a woman so she could go off and have babies on a bigger salary. All they're good for is being assistants.' Then Charles actually patted Annie on the back of her hand as it lay on the bar by her glass.

Annie was too stunned to think of a reply. Charles threw his large whisky down his throat in one go and banged the glass down slightly too hard on the bar as he looked back at Annie, laughing. 'We've already appointed someone else. He'll be joining next month once he's finished his internship in the Foreign Secretary's office.'

5

Chapter One

The smell was so thick Matt could feel it. The rancid, stale, hot, sweaty, spicy air wrapped itself around him as he stepped from the aircraft; he had to be in Karachi. Europe never smelt like this.

The scent of herbs and spices mixed with the stench of sewers and heat. Matt had never known that heat could have a smell and air could be so thick it felt like a blanket. London was sweating through a heat wave, but the heat of Karachi was beyond comparison.

*****

Matt's old life was dumped with his meagre belongings in his mother's garage. He was already regretting his rash decision to resign his job and buy a one-way ticket to Pakistan, and he wasn't even inside the airport terminal yet.

Nervous tension about his first visit to Asia had fuelled his fertile imagination on the long flight. The dark night hours on the plane, with *kameez* clad tribesmen and veiled Muslim women all around him, had only helped remind him of all the dodgy stereotypes of Pakistanis picked up from God knew where. He would not have been surprised to walk into a *Blade Runner-Midnight Express* cocktail of dereliction, violence and open drug dealing.

The oppressive evening heat and humidity of Karachi soaked into the denim jacket he was wearing to reduce the check-in weight of his overstuffed rucksack. At the doors of the terminal building his clammy, sweat-soaked face chilled in fear as a machine-gun toting security guard glared at him suspiciously. He fully expected the guard to swing the gun at him and start shooting, just like in *Call of Duty* that he'd been playing a few days earlier.

A chaotic horde of slouching officials, nagging touts and impatient travellers met the new arrivals inside the building. Though red and green customs signs, baggage carousels and flight schedules tried to give the impression of airport normality, Matt was not convinced. It was just a façade, he thought to himself, as the noisy traders, touts and customs officials all competed anarchically for business. They would probably lose his luggage for a week.

None of the security arrangements that had been in place in London eighteen hours before made themselves apparent now. There did not seem to be anyone even attempting to control the flow of men wandering back and forth past the customs desks of the arrivals hall. They behaved like they had every right to be there and the officials in uniform mostly ignored them completely.

Whining offers of 'You want cheap, best price hotel?' quickly rose above the competing cacophony of indecipherable Urdu. The endlessly repeated question came from mouths and faces that instantly made Matt nervous. He looked around with fear-tinged expectancy, but he could not find any faces he thought were more trustworthy.

Back in London Matt had been confident and phased by very little of the big city attitude many people found intimidating. He quite happily used to wander London at night, jump into taxis and visit places he'd never been before. But culture shock was hitting Matt hard and he clutched his carry-on bag tightly to his chest to protect himself from the oppression of the claustrophobic crowd.

Finally through the tediously inefficient passport control, Matt tried hard to look relaxed as he waited interminably at the squeaking, rattling, empty baggage carousel. It was not hard for him to imagine his bag disappearing into the black hole of Calcutta, or landing in Caracas instead of Karachi, as he crouched anxiously against a rough concrete pillar and the carousel stayed empty.

When the suitcases eventually appeared through the blank hole in the wall, Matt stamped on a surge of hope that he would see his backpack in the untidy jumble of bags. Then, when his solitary rucksack did appear among the suitcases on the carousel, he idly watched its slow progress towards him, loathe to move too soon, in case it disappeared, or someone else grabbed it and ran. Only when there was no doubt it was his bag, and it was going to go past back into the bowels of the building if he didn't pick it up, did Matt move quickly to the carousel and heave it onto his back.

With the green and blue rucksack slung casually off one shoulder, Matt walked slowly through the officious scowls of the customs officers. He tried hard to look as if he knew where he was going, and was not as scared as he felt about what he would find outside the dust-covered swing doors. His heart thumped, his eardrums pounded. The noise around him faded as the fear drowned him.

The opaque glass doors spat him out into a mêlée worse than the bedlam inside. Evening had flipped to black night since Matt had entered the terminal. The number of touts multiplied and honking taxis, buses and the occasional donkey all competed in a symphony of noise.

A line of yellow taxis offered the tenuous safety of officially sanctioned transport. Taxi licences dangled from most of the rear-view mirrors and added to the image of familiarity, legitimacy and security. Ensconced inside the metal protection of a taxi, his rucksack on the seat next to him, Matt tensely watched the outside world, fearfully curious as the car left the airport terminal and broke another tenuous link to home.

Away from the airport the streets were relatively empty of people and the headlights of few cars pierced the darkness. The Pakistani night was darker than an English night. The few working street-lights glowed dimly, only serving to thicken the darkness between them.

The driver chain-smoked a foul-smelling tobacco and said nothing. He hardly even seemed to be aware of anything around him.

Matt could not see much of anything clearly and what he could see reinforced his doubts about the wisdom of having chosen Karachi as a destination. The level of noise from the ancient taxi washed out all sound that could have come from the streets. Matt closed his eyes to shut out the nightmare of Karachi and met the loving eyes of Jo smiling at him from the mountains to the north.

A blaring air-horn dragged a reluctant Matt back to the streets of Karachi just in time to see the weak headlights of a 1960's vintage car barely swerve away before the taxi hit them. Matt's heart pounded and his mind tried to equate the volume of the air horn to the decrepit car it belonged to. The taxi barely changed its line, the driver as calm as he was before.

The lights of Matt's taxi hardly made a difference to the darkness ahead of them, though he hoped they at least announced their presence to the oncoming cars, but if the other drivers were as vacant as his own he doubted they would even notice them.

Glassless windows stared down blindly from derelict looking buildings as they progressed into the city, while increasing numbers of malnourished people shuffled lethargically along the dark streets. Beggars materialised from the darkness at traffic lights, to tap beseechingly on his window, the yellowy-whites of their eyes glowing in the dark as they asked for money and food.

One legless cripple, his eyes barely reaching the window, clung to the door handle as the taxi drove away, the wheels of his trolley rattling along the road as his pathetic tapping fingers and bulging, harrowing eyes begged for food. Matt, frightened by the proximity of such grotesque desperation, wanted to beat the cloying, gnarled knuckles and chase the horror away. Only the glass of the window saved them both from his revulsion.

The constant tapping on his prized car awoke the driver who waved the cripple away and broke his silence to swear profusely in a melange of Urdu and English. The driver's horribly pockmarked face distracted Matt from the cripple

9

for a moment, before the tapping knuckles dragged his eyes back to the window where the beggar was not so easily got rid of.

Wild swerving by the driver finally forced the weakened cripple to loosen his handhold. The driver gunned his engine further and drowned a swarm of curses pouring after them as the cracked and suppurating lips fell away.

Unable, or unwilling, to find the guidebook recommended hotel Matt requested, the driver drove to another. It cost more than Matt wanted to spend, but it looked safe, clean and advertised air-conditioning in English in what Matt guessed was an effort to attract foreigners. Urgently needing to get on the right side of a locked door, alone, to shut out the shadowy city and its ugly, frightening faces, Matt took a room and prayed he had made the right decision.

*****

Matt's room was windowless and could have been a prison cell. It lacked the promised air-conditioning. Matt sat disconsolately on the metal-framed bed surveying his surroundings. Cracked and flaking lino pretended to cover the floor, the bed leant against one wall, a Formica table rested against another and a rusty chair wobbled awkwardly on its mis-matched legs. A dusty, wooden fan sagged limply from the ceiling as it circled ponderously.

The dirty flaking mirror on the wall opposite reflected a deflated looking figure back at Matt. He hardly recognised himself. He was no longer the confident, athletic figure he had been when Jo was alive. His face was drawn, his shoulders slumped, he had put on some weight and his muscles were no longer defined, while his brown hair was a little too long to be tidy and too short to be cool.

Drops of water shimmered on his naked body as Matt lay back on the bed under the listless fan. He finally felt cool and clean for the first time since stepping off the plane. The tepid water of the shower in the gloomy, unlit bathroom had cleaned away the dirt and for a moment he'd escaped to pleasant memories of Jo. But lying limply on the bed his fear returned.

Finally, as the cool wetness of the shower began to change into the warm dampness of the Karachi heat, exhaustion from twenty-four hours on the move overtook his tension and Matt drifted slowly off to troubled sleep.

*****

A furtive knocking disturbed Matt's doze; panic raised a chill sweat as he struggled to remember where he was. He almost fell as he scrabbled on his jeans, still uncomfortably damp and sweaty from earlier, and a fresh T-shirt spilling from his rucksack. Then Matt fearfully eased opened the flimsy plywood door of his room.

'You want whisky, woman, women? You like virgin? Young girls. Guaranteed virgin. You like hash? All foreigner I know want hash. I like you. You my friend. Best price. Cheap price.' A grinning, weedy, spiv of a man, wearing a shiny nylon suit and dripping fake glittery gold from his neck and wrists rocked from foot to foot in the corridor.

The practised sales pitch, half offer, half statement, left Matt unable to think of a verbal reply. Reflexively, he tried to close the door back. The thin wood bent around the pimp's outstretched foot. Matt kicked his bare foot at the outstretched shin and rammed the door back into its ill-fitting frame.

'You change you mind next time. You see. I'll be back.' The door was so thin the man sounded like he was in the room.

With his backpack piled against the door for added security, Matt returned to the bed, but the interruption had spoiled the exhaustion induced calmness and he could only toss and turn as he vainly sought to recapture the escape of sleep.

Expecting the pimp to return and fearful of being robbed, or worse, if he fell asleep, Matt kept an ear tuned towards the door. Filtered through the thin wooden door protecting him from the world outside, the endless patter of undoubtedly young and virgin feet on their way to and from the other cells allowed Matt no more peace that night.

Silence finally arrived sometime just before dawn, when Matt at last fell into an exhausted sleep.

Startled from distorted images of Jo and Karachi, Matt woke to the smell of heat and sewage, the sound of a rattling fan and white noise from far away. As his eyes opened they found the yellowing whitewashed walls and the cell of his room, cheaply and sparsely furnished to meet the needs of guests who normally only stayed an hour. Matt absorbed the unfamiliar surroundings, his heart pounding.

'Shit, Karachi. Still Karachi,' muttered Matt. The door rattled, almost as if someone had been listening for the first signs of movement from the sleeping occupant. Matt's heart pounded as someone tried to force the door. Falling from the bed in his haste to get his boots on, Matt stubbed his toe as he reached for the still new Gelert walking boots. By the time he was prepared, moved his bag and opened the door, the corridor was empty.

Matt glumly contemplated the empty grubbiness of the staircase and landing outside. Why the hell hadn't he gone to Bali instead, he thought, stepping back into his room.

The click of metal-soled shoes announced the reappearance of the grinning pimp before he descended from the floor above, too quickly for Matt to escape. 'You need a guide. Best-price English speak guide,' said the man as he appeared.

'Don't you ever sleep?' asked Matt.

'Oh no, sir. I have two wives, four children and two daughters to feed. I work all day and all night. Otherwise they die. You take guide, please. My children have no breakfast if you not pay for guide.'

Guilt almost made Matt say yes, then the fear of having to leave the safety of the hotel and trust a Pakistani who claimed poverty and glittered in gold took control. 'No. I don't want a guide.'

'You must have guide. People try to rob you if you walk on your own. My guide will protect you. Twenty dollar one day, very cheap price. Best price.'

With great difficulty Matt tried to persuade the pimp turned tour operator that he really did not want a guide. The persistent pimp grew angry as Matt resisted the offer. As the man turned away, his face in a sulk, he muttered loud enough for Matt to hear, 'My children will starve and have nowhere to live. All your fault. Foreigner like you are rich, you pay for guide and not care about money.'

Matt showered again, with none of the pleasant dreams of the night before, then dressed properly and carefully as he worked hard to talk himself into leaving his room. He read and re-read the Karachi section of his guidebook, attempting to memorise the city plan and make sure he did not miss anything important. An hour after the pimp's offer of a guide, Matt stepped from his room and descended slowly, like a man to his execution, to the front lobby.

*****

David stared up at Ricky. A bunch of keys dangled from one hand and the syringe that brought relief and suffering rested tantalisingly in the other.

A month ago David had come to Pakistan looking for cheap hash and the adventure of a lifetime. Now he was hooked on heroin and alternated between being scared for his life and wanting to die to escape this living hell.

Ricky had been charming at the campsite in Islamabad, with his educated British accent, fashionable clothes and stories about a harsh father sending him away from the England he had loved to experience traditional Pakistani life in the family's ancestral village. The offer of a chance to stay in a mountain village with a local family, with some free hash thrown in, had seemed a safe offer to accept from a fellow Brit.

The village was beautiful, not that David had seen much of it. High snow-capped mountains with wooded flanks had glistened in the sun above them as they drove to the house he was now locked in. Ricky had pointed out paths leading to the mountain passes and encouraged David to plan a trek for the following day. But his first meal had been drugged and since then he had been imprisoned in this room. He was not totally alone though, there seemed to be at least one other prisoner nearby; he had heard a woman fighting with Ricky and screaming at him in what was definitely a southern English accent.

'You can go home soon. If you behave yourself.' Ricky sneered now. The friendly smile had not surfaced since David had woken up feeling lousy from the drugged meal.

David stared at the syringe. For three days now Ricky had teased him with the syringe until the first symptoms of withdrawal made themselves felt. David lived in fear of the sweats, the cramps, the uncontrollable diarrhoea and the desperate need to feel the sick-sweet release of the strong, clean heroin in his veins. The panic he felt as he waited for the onset of withdrawal was almost as bad as the real thing when it finally arrived.

He had begged for the syringe the first time, when Ricky had made him wait too long to bear. But that didn't work. Ricky enjoyed watching the pain and fear and only injected him when he wanted to, not when David wanted it. The first time Ricky had just laughed, made him lick his boots, and still refused. David had ended up crying and screaming for hours until Ricky finally stabbed the syringe roughly in his arm as he lay whimpering and shaking on the floor.

The syringe floated forward. 'You want this? I don't know if I should waste it on you. I don't think you'll do what I ask.'

'I will. I promise. Please give it to me. Please.' David couldn't stop himself whining; the fear of withdrawal overrode everything else. He believed completely that Ricky would never let him go home if he didn't do what was wanted of him. Sweat ran off him, his stomach twisted fiercely and he shivered uncontrollably in the stuffy air.

'I just want you to take a present to my cousin in London. You think you can do that?'

'Yes. Anything, just give me the syringe and let me go home.'

'I'm not sure I can trust you.'

'Yes, you can. Believe me, I'll do anything, I promise. Please.'

David cried and squirmed in the dust as his body bucked and screamed for the poison it needed. Ricky grinned at him, then finally, when David really thought he was going to die, wanted to die even, the syringe and needle landed on the floor next to him. For the first time in his life he injected himself.

'I think you're ready now,' said Ricky happily as he left the room. As am I, he added to himself as he stepped towards the next room where he would take his daily pleasure.

Chapter Two

Annie sat at her desk, once again wondering why she bothered working at all. There was the money of course, but there had to be easier ways of earning the pittance that she did.

Four years since leaving college and she could see her life becoming one long session at the office, with the odd punctuation of exhausted sleep in a flat that would be claustrophobic if she actually spent any free time there to notice.

It was supposed to be glamorous working in television, but the glamour rarely surfaced and Annie had increasingly been thinking about Pete, her ex-boyfriend who had left her and gone to Goa. One of the last things he had said to her was, 'Don't kid yourself, girl. Your job's going nowhere. Your life's going nowhere. You're boring. You always talk about doing things, but you'll never have the balls to take any real risks and do something exciting with your life.'

But at the time the secure safety of having a job and a career had won out over the exciting fear of going with him, so he had left her behind and gone off to Goa on his own.

It was a week since the leaving party when Charles had drunkenly and so effectively crushed her illusion of a career at the company with his laughing comments.

The words were burned indelibly on her mind. 'One of the reasons women never get to the top in this business is because they want to take time out and enjoy themselves. No one in their right mind would ever promote a woman so she could go off and have babies on a bigger salary. All they're good for is being assistants.'

She had thought about suing him for gender discrimination, or constructive dismissal, but the thought of appearing in court and across the front pages of the newspapers was worse than doing nothing.

Annie had almost thumped him when he first said what he did, and still wished she'd had the courage to do so. But now she was almost grateful he'd actually said it. Pete was right, it was no fun working for a bitter, overweight chain-smoker, living off the success of a film he had made when he was twenty-six and his wife still lived with him. For the first couple of days after Annie had realised that she was never going to get promoted and be the boss like she had always wanted to be, she had been bereft. She'd gone through the motions at work, leaving earlier than usual, and suffering the condescending smirk from her misogynist boss.

However, leaving the office earlier when she was less tired had given Annie more time to think about her life than she'd had in a long time. She'd determined to take control of her life. Do what she wanted to do and not let Charles, or any bloke for that matter, stop her from making a success of herself. But the hard part was deciding what to actually do though. TV was all she had wanted to do for as long as she could remember and without that particular career path she was at a loss as to know what on earth to do next.

The colour supplement from a Sunday paper lay on her desk. She had to read them every week to scout for stories. The cover blared, 'Glamour at the Paris Ritz.' Annie flicked the pages to the main story, a photo spread on the rich and famous clientèle of the fashion world.

The photos sparked a sudden memory of her sitting at her beloved Grandad's feet listening to his stories. He had travelled the world as a soldier and at some point ended up in Paris after the war, dancing the night away at the Ritz. He had kept Annie enthralled with his stories of the glamour and luxury of what at the time had seemed, to her ten year old self, a distant, unattainably exotic destination.

Impulsively, Annie typed in the web address listed in the supplement. The pictures on the website looked even better and Annie had a sudden urge to be sitting at the same cocktail bar her Grandad had once leant against with his mates.

A few clicks later and Annie's heart sank when she saw the price of a short stay. She couldn't possibly afford it. As she sat staring at the impossible to justify figure Annie heard the whisper of her Grandad's voice as he had written his will: 'I leave a small sum for Annie, to spend wisely and make the most of.'

The small sum was actually £10,000, now invested wisely in a savings account against the day when she had enough to put down a deposit on a tiny flat somewhere in London, that everyone assured her was what she really ought to do as soon as she could. I am not making the most of the money though, thought Annie. I bet Grandad would have wanted me to be happy, not do what everyone expects of me. After all, he never owned his own house. A few more clicks and Annie was booked in for a short break to Paris the following weekend.

As she flipped through the rest of the magazines Annie pondered the thought of coming back to this job after a weekend in Paris. Her dull life stretched out ahead of her. The dream of staying away for longer than a weekend was appealing, exciting even.

Annie looked around the office at her overworked, stressed out colleagues. The older ones divorced, or on their second marriages. She looked at Charles sitting flaccidly in his office. Giving in to the second impulsive thought of the day, Annie marched into Charles's office.

Leaning across the messily cluttered desk Annie said, 'Charles, I'm resigning.' Then she blew the drooping, two-inch tube of ash from the end of his cigarette. With sadistic pleasure she watched most of the grey confetti fall in his coffee and the rest flutter over the scattered remnants of a script he was pointlessly trying to make into the next great blockbuster. 'You shouldn't smoke in here anyway. It's against the law.'

'For fuck's sake! What did you do that for?' His jowls wobbled as he blew the ash from his paperwork into the dirty snowdrift piled against his pen tray. 'You can't resign. I won't let you. I need you.'

'Of course you do. Someone has to do all the work around here, so you can sit on your fat arse pretending you're working on the next great prize winner.'

Charles huffed with shock, but no words came from his drooping mouth.

Annie carried on before he could find his voice. 'I have loads of holiday carried over from last year and I haven't taken any this year yet. So I'll be finishing on Friday, that's two days away. I'm only your assistant, so it won't take me long to hand over. Will it?'

*****

Almost as if he had been expecting Matt to appear at that precise moment, the spiv stood waiting on the landing of the floor below. Matt tried ignoring him, but the spiv fell in beside him. 'How long you stay in Pakistan? Where you go?'

'Don't know and north, to Chitral.' Matt tried his best to escape. The spiv hovered an inch from his elbow.

Dropping his voice to a whisper the spiv stopped Matt mid-staircase. 'I have hashish, best Afghani. Gift for you, you my friend.' He tried to put a black, almond sized lump into Matt's hand.

'No!' snapped Matt. 'I don't smoke!' He never should have watched *Midnight Express* before he came on this trip. The fear of being set-up and being sent to some Pakistani hell-hole of a prison sent him running down the stairs, the spiv cackling from the stairwell above him.

*****

On the Shandur Pass that separated Chitral from Gilgit, high in the Hindu Kush mountains of Northern Pakistan, Ishmael sipped his chai. The turquoise lake shimmered in front of him, reflecting the great white peaks above him. On the brown mud around him snow lay in patches, though within a week the brown would be tinted green as the grass grew quickly, providing summer pasture for the yaks. Ishmael wore the uniform of the Frontier Police, but in reality he was part of an elite anti-drugs unit that few people even knew existed.

Thirty-two years ago he had been born in a village even further north, near the Wakhan corridor. He loved the mountains, he spoke the languages of the people, he prayed five times a day and waited and watched for the men that spread poison around the world against the strictures of Islam. The same men who had killed his father, who really had been in the frontier police and tried in vain to stem the tide of opium and heroin that crossed their valleys.

A few days before a jeep had left him on the pass for his three-month stay in the mountains, while his wife and children were down in Gilgit. Leaving them behind was the worst part of this job; he missed seeing them every day.

He'd stay at the remote outpost for a few days, then trek to the hidden routes through the high passes searching for the camel trains carrying contraband both ways across the border. Opiates out, alcohol, cattle and household goods in.

*****

Stepping from the plane at Paris Orly, Annie imagined she could smell the flowers, the fresh air and the romance of the city of lovers. It was too late in the year to be Paris in springtime, but its reputation carried weight.

'Have a pleasant stay,' said the BA first class steward at the cabin door. Annie was looking forward to a few days of pampered luxury before she set off to find adventure and take some risks. The added pleasure of an upgrade to first class had convinced her she was doing the right thing and she'd relaxed happily on the flight with her glass of champagne.

Pete might have gone on the hippy trail to Goa, but she was going to do something really exciting. She wasn't sure what yet, but she'd think of something.

Leaving the customs hall behind her Annie saw a starched and uniformed chauffeur holding a placard with her name on it. He seemed rather put out when Annie walked up to him and smiled. He looked over her shoulder crossly then flicked his eyes back to her and the fancy rucksack she dropped at his feet as she introduced herself. The poor man had obviously been expecting a stylish, elegant lady, not the pretty, denim clad twenty-five year old brunette, giggly drunk on excitement and free champagne, that presented herself.

'I can show you my booking confirmation if you want,' offered Annie.

'There is no need, *mademoiselle*. Please follow me.' After his initial lapse of protocol the chauffeur quickly recovered his poise, placed Annie's rucksack on a luggage trolley, and majestically led her to a waiting Rolls Royce.

As he held open the wood panelled door the chauffeur said, 'The champagne is compliments of the hotel. Welcome to Paris.'

Sipping chilled champagne and watching the city glide by the tinted windows, Annie laughed aloud. Up yours, Pete! she thought. She was having more fun than she'd ever had with him, the arrogant bastard. She was going to take risks he'd never even dreamt of.

Her recently finished job might not have paid well, but as she had never lost the university habit of only spending money she really had to. Then as well, she had spent the last few years working such long hours much of the money she had earned remained unspent and been added to Grandad's bequest in pursuit of the ever increasing figure required for a deposit to buy some poky flat she wouldn't even like. Now she was going to have fun planning how to make the most of spending that money in a way her Grandad would approve of. She raised the glass of champagne in a silent toast to his memory.

The Rolls passed all the major Paris landmarks which the chauffeur dutifully and redundantly identified; La Tour Eiffel, L'Arc de Triomphe, La Defense, Le Louvre. When the car finally glided to a standstill at the foot of the famous stairs that lead down from the front doors of the Paris Ritz, a liveried footman instantly opened the door. 'Welcome to the Ritz, *mademoiselle*. I hope you enjoy your stay.'

Elegance and luxury abounded and attentive staff hovered discreetly nearby. It was all Annie could have imagined. Presenting more confidence than she really felt, Annie approached the reception desk.

There was no need for her to say who she was. The chauffeur must have already told them she had arrived. '*Mademoiselle*, we have upgraded you to a suite. I hope that will be acceptable to you. Your bags will be waiting for you and Louis will show you to your room.'

Upstairs, 'opulent' was not quite the best way to describe her room. Luxurious didn't quite fit either. 'It's gorgeous,' said Annie as she tried and failed to keep the grin off her face while surveying the delights of a hotel suite bigger than her old apartment. Thick, soft carpet absorbed her footsteps. The huge and decadent bed oozed comfort. An oak dining table, strategically positioned by the window, supported another bottle of chilled, vintage champagne and a sparkling crystal glass.

Having shown Annie the various gadgets, controls and how to call the concierge Louis hovered expectantly, though he seemed to be enjoying the pleasure of Annie's excitement more than he wanted his tip. 'Is this your first time, *mademoiselle*?'

'Yes,' said Annie laughing and blushing. 'Can you tell?'

'A lucky guess, *mademoiselle*. If there is anything you need you must ask. It is what we are here for.' He was still smiling as he left Annie to explore her suite some more.

Ten minutes later Annie sank into a steaming double bath. The champagne filled crystal flute sat on the carved table within reach of her hand. 'I could get used to this,' she said aloud.

*****

Raseem dressed slowly not taking his eyes off the naked girl in front of him. Her defiant gaze threatened to arouse him again. 'You enjoyed it really, didn't you?' he mocked. He didn't care if she enjoyed it or not, though he enjoyed it more if she didn't. More importantly, however, it helped satisfy his desire for revenge.

Isabelle Jones said nothing, but hatred flared in her eyes. Raseem ran his eyes over the teenager's naked body once more. She was almost as good looking as the bitch he had lusted after at university back home in England. That one had mocked him and flaunted her rich boyfriend at him. Now this girl, the others he had already fucked and the ones he would take in the future would pay for her sins. He was in charge now, and he took what he wanted.

'Don't worry, I'll be back later,' grinned Raseem. His plan was going well. He was getting rich sending drugs to England, he usually had women to play with and in a few years he'd be able to go back to England and be someone people looked up to.

Outside, the snow-capped peaks guarded the mountain village. He was close enough to Afghanistan to make it easy for him to organise his shipments and escape if anything ever went wrong. Compared to the big traders though he was just moving small amounts of heroin and no-one really cared what he was doing. But just to make sure, he paid the local policeman to turn a blind eye to the monthly visit of Afghan tribesmen and he did not expect any problems from petty officialdom.

*****

Annie passed her first Parisian morning in the Bois de Boulogne, admiring swan-dappled lakes, riotous flowerbeds and ancient trees.

In the afternoon she followed paths that led her to the Parc de Bagatelle, while she dreamt of being a lady in the Napoleonic court, with full skirts, sparkling jewels and dashing aristocratic admirers.

The meandering paths lazed through shrubs, bushes and flowerbeds offering vistas of fading irises, fresh blooming roses and luscious lawns. In the sixteenth century Château de Bagatelle, a café provided Annie with the perfect setting to finish her afternoon in a style to match her current residence at the Ritz. The setting was beautiful, but Annie was not finding it particularly adventurous. Boredom was beginning to set in already.

On her second day Annie set out on a cultural tour of the city, but the size of the entrance queues quickly changed her mind; half the tourists in Paris stood in queues while the other half stood in front of all the best sites and pointed their camera phones at whichever monument or work of art they had reached. In between they never stopped texting, tweeting and facebooking, hardly ever seeming to speak with whoever they were travelling with.

Annie wanted adventure and the attractions of romantic Paris were rapidly fading for the single traveller. Wandering away from the noisy tourist mayhem in a mood of increasing restlessness, Annie found the more graceful and quiet charms of the Latin Quarter. Idly perusing a flea market squeezed in against an old iron fence, Annie found a bookstall boasting a few English-language titles. In need of a book she bought a battered travelogue, gave up trying to find excitement and settled herself to enjoy fresh pastries and espresso in a nearby café.

Four hours later Annie finally stopped reading because the light was so bad she could hardly see the pages any more. Her mind buzzed excitedly. Eric Newby's amiable account of his *Short Walk in the Hindu Kush* had sparked Annie's imagination. The book was set near to where Grandad had been posted on one of his foreign tours and it sounded as exotic as he had described it and she had imagined.

Grandad had loved Peshawar and when Annie sat listening to him he had always talked about the fortress, the fierce but friendly people, the great food and the desolate beauty of the country, painting a very different picture to what Annie saw on the TV news. He had only once mentioned, regretfully, that he had seen action in the mountains. He preferred to talk about the expeditions they had made to the far north on patrols along the Afghan border where there were ancient forts and majestic snow-capped mountains. One story she had always loved was when he talked about riding the spectacular narrow gauge railway that snaked up the Khyber Pass towards Afghanistan.

From the café Annie returned to the Ritz for another soak in the glorious bath, then she curled up in her luxurious double bed, with a room-service dinner and a fine red wine. She read until the book was finished and fell asleep to dreams of the snow-capped mountains, glacial rivers, swarthy tribesmen and picturesque villages in hidden valleys. She saw herself wandering free in the mountains of Nuristan, following Grandad's footsteps, with nobody telling her what to do and where to go.

She woke early and lay wrapped in the soft comfort of the bed. She knew exactly where she wanted to go, but sometime during the night the realisation had sunk in that as enticing as it was, Afghanistan would be no picnic for a single female traveller like her.

Only when the automatic percolator had filled the room with the smell of fresh coffee at the pre-set time did Annie stir from her malaise. Wrapped in the Ritz-branded fluffy white dressing-gown Annie reclined on her bed and hit the internet through the hotel TV.

There had to be some way a resourceful girl like her could get to do what she wanted. It didn't take her long to find what she needed, though she left her coffee go cold while she surfed the internet. Eric Newby's Afghanistan was out of the question and currently far too dangerous for any traveller. India was old hat, everyone went there, and she might meet Pete too. However, Pakistan, challenging though it would be, was a distinct possibility. It would certainly be adventurous, there were the mountains her Grandad had enjoyed, the romance of the Great Game, and enough danger to make Pete eat his words.

Chapter Three

His heart was thumping so loud he almost expected the people in front of him to hear it and turn to look at him. Blood pounded in his ears, dulling the noises around him. As he emerged into the chilly, air-conditioned lobby at the bottom of the stairs, a sign promoting air-conditioning and the sound of a high-volume television drew him into the hotel restaurant in search of breakfast.

In the daylight Matt noticed what he'd not even considered on his arrival the night before. Grubby red velvet wallpaper covered the walls of the reception area and the gloomy restaurant. A DJ's console nestled in the corner of what looked more like a nightclub lounge than hotel dining area, and a glitter ball hung idly from the ceiling as if to confirm it. Though tables and chairs were laid out on the dance floor, set against the walls were curtained alcoves, with deep comfy sofas offering privacy and somewhere more intimate to lounge. The smell of stale beer and cigarettes seeped from the carpet and seats. Matt noted the first major error in his guidebook, the warning about having to get a permit from the police to drink alcohol and needing to go to the big hotels for entertainment.

Had he landed in the only brothel in the Islamic Republic of Pakistan? Matt was not sure whether to be shocked, amused or concerned.

The hotel delivered a passable breakfast of chapati and greasy omelette, though.

Impossible though it was, considering he was the only foreigner in the place, Matt tried to be inconspicuous while he ate his first meal in Asia.

As the few other diners watched him, Matt studied everyone entering the room and he was relieved not to see the spiv during breakfast. Thank God for small mercies, thought Matt. He hoped the little shite kept away from him in future.

Having surprisingly enjoyed his meal and survived the restaurant with no unexpected traumas, Matt felt secure enough to think about leaving the hotel and heading for the local sites. In his small, well-secured day-pack he carried everything he considered irreplaceable, or essential: his passport, camera, guidebook and money. Taking a deep breath before walking briskly from the lobby Matt turned right, and continued the pretence of looking as if he knew exactly where he was going.

Taking care not to look anyone in the eye, Matt picked his way purposefully, though fearfully, through the jostling crowds. Huge potholes gaped in the road and the traffic swerved recklessly to avoid them. Massive old lorries, brightly painted with traditional isometric patterns and images of daily life ruled the roads. Everything deferred to them. Beneath them in the pecking order came cars, then horse-drawn carts. At the bottom of the heap came tuktuks and rickshaws; pedestrians were a nuisance that drivers paid little, if any, attention to. The noise was deafening: standard car horns seemed redundant, the lorries favoured airhorns and no one noticed anything else.

The crumbling pavement threatened to trip and cripple Matt; random holes in the concrete and open manhole covers waited for the unwary walker. Alongside the pavement what could either have been a storm drain or an open sewer overflowed with rubbish, that barely hid the bloated body of a dead dog.

Horrifyingly unimaginable deformities on pathetically thin children inexorably drew Matt's eyes, though he tried not to stare. The children, squatting in the decay stretched their malformed hands upwards seeking a beggar's pay.

With his senses overwhelmed by the swirling poverty-stricken city of fifteen million people, Matt made it less than three hundred metres before his confidence crumbled and he retraced his steps to make sure he could get back to the hotel.

With his confidence restored by the time he reached the hotel entrance, Matt kept walking past the doorway, in case the street was any less traumatic that way. A similarly nerve-racking four hundred metres stroll beyond the hotel convinced him the whole city was going to be the same riot of noise and sensory overload. Mounting nausea, conspiring with the stench of open sewers, rotting waste and the bathhouse heat, forced Matt back to the cool safety of the hotel's air-conditioned bordello restaurant and a welcome glass of ice-cold Coke.

Matt had spent barely half an hour outside, but that time had shown him enough to increase his doubts about the sense of having bought a one way ticket. The beggars, the cripples and their deformities that had haunted the dark journey from the airport also littered the daytime streets. He had seen news reports, which he'd never really believed, of families on the sub-continent mutilating their children to make them better beggars, but his sickening half-hour on the streets of Karachi had convinced him they were likely true.

The images of the poverty and hunger, the dirt on the streets, the smells emanating from the drains, the disease oozing from scab-crusted children and the deformities of the beggars trailed him as he sat and sipped another Coke.

Inside the safe sanity of the cool hotel, Matt turned to the copies of the local English newspaper and the *International Herald Tribune* he had found in the hotel lobby. They would help him extend the length of time he could take sipping his restorative Coke, and allow him more time to regain his courage.

Except the papers didn't help restore his courage. 'Monsoon late. Karachi 45°C,' read the local paper. 'Riots and kidnapping in Pakistan. Foreigners Evacuated,' blared the headlines of the *International Herald Tribune*. For the first time in Karachi Matt actually felt cold.

More gloom followed the headlines. 'The Minister of Health has advised Karachi residents to stay inside between midday and three o'clock and to drink as much water as possible,' warned the local paper. A subheading recounted, 'Twenty people dead from heat exhaustion in one day.'

The lead story in the *International Herald Tribune* continued in a similarly alarming vein and Matt could mostly only absorb sentence fragments as the blood again began pounding in his ears. 'Major riots in Karachi. Two hundred people dead. Police open fire on rioters.'

Then a paragraph caught his eye and held his attention. 'Foreign businessmen and non-essential diplomats are being advised to leave Karachi and the southern Sindh province. This follows reported attacks and kidnappings involving foreigners on the Karachi-Lahore express train. The US State Department has evacuated all American citizens from the region and strongly advises that no one travels to the area without armed protection.'

As he recovered slowly from the shocking new knowledge that he was in the middle of bandit country Matt noticed another gut wrenching story stuck in the bottom corner of the page. '150 Americans Missing.' Matt scanned the text. 'The US Embassy in Islamabad reports that in the last few years almost one hundred and fifty American citizens have disappeared in Pakistan and Afghanistan. Most were young backpackers thought to have become mixed up in the region's violent drug trade.'

Matt snorted disparagingly. He had always thought that people who got involved in smuggling drugs had to be stupid, especially those young girls who, when they were caught, claimed they did not know what was in the suitcase they were carrying for a boyfriend. He did relax somewhat, though. If the problems foreigners in Pakistan were facing were because of drugs he ought to be okay; he never went near them and couldn't understand why anyone would poison themselves with drugs, let alone try and smuggle them. That was asking for trouble.

Lowering the paper Matt gazed at the glitter-ball swinging gently on its hanging as he contemplated his future in this violent country. It served him right for being so impatient to leave England. But he could not imagine going home so soon. England without Jo would be unbearable. In England Matt imagined he saw Jo on every street corner and even in Karachi Matt had already felt his chest constrict once when he thought he saw Jo's favourite sweater in the crowds on the street.

Gritting his teeth Matt worked hard to regain his composure and tamp down the tears he felt rising. He had came to Pakistan to get closer to Jo. He wanted to go north to the Himalayas, like he and Jo had planned. He wasn't going to let a bunch of bandits frighten him off.

Anyway, what did he have to lose if they did kidnap him, he thought. It might be a relief to be kidnapped and taken off to some mountain hideaway and held captive. He had nothing left to live for anyway.

A Muezzin's lyrical call to prayer reached Matt faintly. 'Allahu Akbar,' God is great, reminding the faithful of their midday prayers. The divergence between the Islam of the Muezzin and the hidden but available bordello entertainment of the hotel unsettled Matt. As he glanced discreetly around the nearby faces, to observe the reactions of his co-diners, it looked to Matt that they were overly intent on ignoring the Imam's reminder.

Observing the studiously concentrated faces ignoring the call of the muezzin Matt felt suddenly alone. The anger and pain he had hoped to leave behind in England overwhelmed any lingering thoughts he had about giving up the trip and going back there. He half hoped the bandits would kidnap him, to put him out of his misery; it would serve him right for letting Jo go and get the tickets without him while he played some stupid video game.

*****

30

Raseem sat happily on the veranda of his bungalow. The cool clear air let him feel he could touch the mountains high above him, which, though the valley was lush and green with the first crops of summer growing in the fields, were still well covered with snow. A local Kalash girl stood in the fields nearby, her colourful necklaces and the red embroidery on her black clothing adding more colour to the scene.

The latest delivery of heroin from over the border had just arrived; deliveries were much more reliable again now that the recent bout of fighting had stopped. The price was coming down too, even though the Afghans were processing the stuff before he got it. This all brought him more profit as the street price in England was still going up.

He did need to find another mule though. David was ready to send now, but he wanted to keep Isabelle a bit longer. She was the best fuck he'd had in a long while, so young and tender. The way she fought back and made him hit her before he was able to subdue her was a real turn-on too. He was glad people let their naïve kids travel on their own; it made it much easier for him to get laid.

He'd have some more fun with her tomorrow morning, thought Raseem. Then take David to Islamabad and put him on a flight home and see if he could find another sucker to come up here with him and enjoy the pleasures of the mountains too. Maybe another girl . . . two at a time would be really good.

*****

The old colonial gothic building that was Karachi's main railway station had no charms whatsoever. It was just big, hot, dusty and crowded. Humanity spilled from the platforms, through the arches and down the cathedral-like steps akin to a non-stop army of ants on the march. Nothing could have resisted the swarms of sweating bodies engulfing everything in their path. Matt expected to see dead bodies in the wake of the swarms, as occasional breaks in the crowds began to open up. But a new surge of humanity always spewed from

31

another arch to merge with the tail end and stop any clear space actually appearing.

When Matt found the ticket office it was closed, or at least the clerk behind the counter behaved like it was closed. In spite of this the pushing, shoving crowd of desperate potential travellers shouted, screamed and cursed at the averted head as if the office was actually open. The louder the crowd abused the man, the more intently he read his paper.

The stench of sweat united with the heat and the noise to overwhelm Matt's senses; he squeezed from the office to find a cooler and quieter spot to recover his composure. In the midday heat, looking for a cool quiet spot proved to be a futile exercise. Everywhere Matt found some shade, a litter of sweating bodies already covered the floor.

With much reluctance and his temper rising inexorably towards boiling point, Matt returned to the ticket office fully intending to attack and conquer the idiotic inefficiency of the train company staff, who made the long privatised British Rail look like the epitome of efficiency. After all, he only wanted to buy himself an onward ticket for the next departing train.

The country should have stayed part of the British Empire, then there would have been a special counter for people like him, Matt muttered crossly to himself as he pushed back into the screaming crowd. As he competed with the best of the mob, a rather smart official appeared behind the counter and caught Matt's eye.

'If you want a first class ticket sir, you can come into my office.' The prospect of getting a ticket without having to queue, albeit a more expensive one than he had intended, proved too much of a temptation to resist. Matt kicked and shoved his way through the crowd to a newly opened gap in the counter and escaped to the safety of a fan-cooled office.

'Tea, sir?' asked the polite and obsequious official as he waved Matt to a chair.

Matt sank into an old overstuffed armchair that was probably first put there when the British still ruled the place.

'Air-conditioned, or non-air-conditioned, sir?' Matt knew he could get used to treatment like this.

'Air-conditioned, I think. I am finding it rather hot at the moment.' He smiled condescendingly at the clerk, who nodded a response and began making out the ticket.

'The train is overnight and there are only air-conditioned sleeping berths. I hope that meets with your satisfaction. It leaves in two hours.'

Matt smiled and nodded, feeling rather pleased with himself. Buying the ticket was so easy he began to doubt the newspaper stories of bandits hijacking the trains. The timing was perfect too, and he would even have enough time to have a final cold drink at the hotel before returning to take up his luxury compartment.

The clerk completed the ticket and held it out, then dropped his bombshell. 'The army will of course be providing an armed escort, sir. We do not want any more esteemed tourists kidnapped from our railway.' Matt's new-found confidence fell away as quickly as it had arrived.

*****

For the last few years there had been reports of foreigners going missing in these mountains, but no one really took them seriously for a long time. Foreigners never did what they were supposed to do and it was commonly believed that most of them had crossed into Afghanistan, or travelled north to Kazakhstan. Ishmael supposed they thought their Western superiority would protect them. Needless to say, the authorities had never done much to investigate the reports. Not even the embassies pushed it too hard.

The rumours had persisted though, and eventually one particular family had made enough noise and convinced some politician to look into it when their child had failed to come home from a gap year adventure. As a consequence somebody had finally collated the lists of foreigners reported missing to the embassies in Islamabad, and checked that long catalogue of names against the lists of foreigners that registered at the various checkpoints around the country. The number that just seemed to vanish was high enough that the government wasn't able to suppress it, especially given the number of young women on the list, all of whom had been travelling alone.

Occasionally an over-confident fool of a foreigner was caught smuggling drugs at Islamabad airport, or they got caught somewhere in Europe, and though few talked about where they bought their drugs many had spent time in the North West Frontier Province.

Every foreigner who travelled north had to register with the police department. Ishmael was looking down into the district of Chitral, and in this remote and sparsely populated district the foreigners had to regularly enter their name and passport number in the record books kept at the various checkpoints spread around the area. Weeks of checking had shown that many names on the embassy missing persons lists showed up in the NWFP police books too. A worrying number had signed in at Chitral, then failed to appear in the books at the Lowari or Shandur Passes over which they should have left. None had ever bought a plane ticket either.

It was true that many foreigners disliked registering with the police and entered false names when they could get away with it, but even counting up all the weird and wonderful names that appeared in the lists, and discounting these, there were a worrying number of people that simply seemed to disappear.

Once the decision had been made to investigate these potential disappearances, Ishmael had been the obvious person to put on the task. He had been a soldier in the Chitral Scouts, patrolling the border areas and keeping an eye on the Afghan smugglers for many years. He had risen through the ranks of the Scouts and then been seconded to the specialist unit he now worked for. Ishmael knew these mountains better than just about anyone else.

A real Frontier Policeman had earlier in the day assured Ishmael that no foreigners had crossed the Shandur Pass out of Chitral in the past week, and before that the snow would not have receded far enough to let any of the jeeps through. The policeman, a local man from the village of Teru who normally manned the Shandur barrier, also assured him that he personally checked every passport of each foreigner that did pass through. But, having read some of the names in the register, Ishmael severely doubted the man's devotion to duty. Even so, there were a couple of names that were listed in the register at the Lowari Pass check-point, at the south end of the Chitral Valley, a month ago, that had not appeared on any list of travellers going out again, nor in any of the registers elsewhere in the valley. Ishmael was intent on solving the riddle of where they were.

Ishmael returned to his tent to check his kit again. His meticulous routines were infamous in the Scouts, but he never let his standards slip. He carefully dismantled his gun, and as he sat outside his tent in the sun he cleaned each component, placing them all in order, before assembling the much cared for weapon once more, with his eyes closed.

The Shandur barrier was half a mile behind him on the Gilgit side of the Pass. The lip of the pass that led down to the Chitral Valley was a hundred metres in front of him. His orders were to sit and wait for orders. It was just like the army, being sent out on a job not knowing exactly what was expected. 'Watch and observe,' his Colonel had said. At the Shandur there was usually nothing much to watch and observe, except the scenery and wildlife. Ishmael was happy though; the mountains were a second home to him. He would be happy to wait here for weeks.

*****

Raseem dropped Isabelle's pot of food and bucket of water on the floor. The stew was the same every day, just a few old potatoes stewed up with tomatoes and okra. It was often cold and never enough.

'Don't eat it all at once, it's got to last you tomorrow as well. I've some business to attend to and I won't have time to visit. You better just hope I don't forget about you.' His mouth twisted into what he probably intended to be a mocking face of concern, but came out a perverted leer instead.

'Drop the blanket, I want to see you naked.' Raseem was specific as always when he wanted some fun.

Isabelle breathed deeply and let her blanket fall. She had decided early it was better to fight only when she stood the chance of doing some real damage. It was weird how he got really angry when she disobeyed on the small things, but the more she fought against the rape, the more excited he became. Too excited on one occasion. But she was never going to let him do what he wanted without some sort of fight. One day she'd got a good kick in, perfectly aimed. That had reduced his ardour initially, but as he beat her mercilessly it had soon come back.

'I'm in a hurry today so don't mess around. Spread your legs, I want a fuck.' With that he grabbed her arm, threw her violently to the floor and let his baggy trousers drop to his ankles. Isabelle clenched her fists and waited for the right moment to cause him pain. Then he stunned her with a thump to the temple and was finished before she'd recovered enough to even think of fighting.

*****

Glowing pink in the late afternoon sun, Cantt railway station could have fallen right out of Rudyard Kipling's *Kim*. Street vendors battled to keep urchins from stealing fruit, immobile beggars prostrated themselves as they implored passers-by for alms, while the more mobile beggars clawed at clothes as they pressed their claims. Barbers shaved, shoe-shines polished and porters hauled mountains of luggage on rickety trolleys, while massed ranks of passengers sat and squatted patiently in the heat and dust, waiting for their trains to arrive.

Fearful excitement quickened Matt's pulse; images of himself in the heat of a gun battle between bandits and the army had distracted him enough as he enjoyed his drink that he'd almost been late for his train.

His anger and depression fostered through the last few months of guilty sorrow had found an outlet. Matt was almost looking forward to a violent encounter with bandits, where he could play out a fantasy video game gun-battle.

As he weaved his way through the crowds a dirt ingrained waif stretched up to tap Matt's elbow. 'I take you first class waiting room. Which train you want?'

'Lahore,' answered Matt warily.

'Come. I show you,' ordered the boy.

With nothing to lose and the prospect of some escape from the heat and the crowds pressing in on him, Matt followed the tiny guide. The little figure jinked quickly through the crowd, hopped from the platform onto two successive sets of rails and then proudly presented Matt with a heavy wooden door labelled with a shining brass plaque announcing, 'First Class Passengers Only.'

Matt handed over a fifty *paisa* tip. The waif stared at it in disgust and quickly lost his charm. 'One dollar. One dollar. Give me one dollar,' he demanded.

Matt tried to escape into the waiting room, but the demanding screech changed to an iron grip on his bag. A tug-of-war developed between the six-year-old and Matt, who was about to lose his cool and start screaming at the child when a railway official arrived. A sharp slap connected with the back of the boy's head and sent the waif tumbling in the dust.

'For Lahore, *sahib*?' The honorific embarrassed Matt to silence, though he managed to mutter the name of his intended destination half way up the mainline to Lahore in response.

'Wait in here. I will fetch you when the train arrives.' The guard held the door as Matt stepped into the haven of cleanliness and quiet. Three well-dressed Pakistani men smiled a welcome as the door closed out the turmoil of the platform.

'Chai-wallah,' bellowed one man as another waved Matt to a vacant seat at their table. 'Welcome, young sir. Please join us.'

Matt settled himself nervously while fresh tea and chapati were placed in front of him. Then a friendly barrage of introductions and questions began. Of the three names offered to him, Matt caught only one, Mohammed.

'Are you on your own?' asked Mohammed affably.

'Yes.'

'How long are you staying in Pakistan?' asked his plump companion.

'A few months.'

'Why are you here?' enquired the first, rather seriously.

'I'm on holiday,' said Matt, wondering what he had let himself in for sitting down with his fellow travellers.

'Are you married?'

He stared blankly for a moment, unsure what to say. 'Almost,' he managed, 'but she died.' He mutely accepted the condolences and sympathy that followed, while images of Jo flickered fiercely in his mind and his other senses came to a standstill. He failed to notice the renewal of the questioning, until a hand tapped his arm.

'Sir, are you all right?' Matt nodded absently as he looked around the three concerned faces. He tried and failed to remember what the last question had been.

'Where are you going?' tried one of the men again.

'Sukkur,' he answered desultorily. The excitement and anticipation he had been enjoying was gone, replaced by subdued disinterest. He barely listened to his hosts shocked warnings.

'You must not go there,' declared the plump man,

'We three all live there. It is too dangerous for you to go there. You will be killed,' stated the youngest of the men melodramatically.

'Only last week three Japanese tourists disappeared on their way to the train station from the Sukkur Hotel. It is said they were trying to escape being caught up in a drug deal,' said Mohammed as he held Matt's gaze.

'That's okay then,' said Matt. 'I don't do drugs, I'll be fine.'

Chapter Four

Annie searched through Google for a cheap flights website and clicked on the first with an airline she vaguely recognised. Her excitement was tempered by nervousness, but she was determined to face her fears and prove to herself as much as to Pete that she could live life to the full.

'Paris,' she entered in the first search box. 'Islamabad' went into the second. She wondered if she could get a flight by the weekend.

The unfamiliar set-up of typing on her lap, then refocusing on the distant TV slowed her down and Annie almost searched for one month's time. As the icon swirled on-screen Annie held her breath. Then the results popped up and Annie watched a stream of Middle Eastern Airlines dominate the screen. It made no difference to her which badge was on the plane, all she cared about was the destination.

A flight for just under £400 was available in three days time. Annie checked the box next to the Etihad Airways logo and clicked through the booking process, deftly typing information as she adjusted to working on her bed.

Only as she nudged the pointer towards the Confirm icon did Annie think of the need for a visa. Her finger hovered over the select button as she pondered what to do. Did she need one, or didn't she? She didn't really have a clue, but she thought she probably did need a visa. Who could she ask?

Louis would know.

The bedside phone was to hand and it took only a moment before the steward was purring into her ear. 'How can I help, *mademoiselle*?'

'I was wondering, do I need a visa to go to Pakistan?'

'Pakistan? Are you sure that's where you want to go?' he asked in surprise.

'Yes, yes. I've just read a book about the mountains in the north, and my Grandad was there years ago. It sounds wonderful. There's a flight in a few days time and I wanted to check if I needed a visa. Do I?'

'*Mademoiselle*, it is your choice, but may I suggest that the book might be somewhat out of date? Pakistan, it's not the calmest of places at the moment.'

'It's not as bad as Afghanistan. And they play cricket there. I'm sure it'll be fine if I'm careful.'

Annie could hear the keys of a computer clicking on the other end of the phone. Then Louis said, 'A visa is necessary, but if you have a valid airline booking we can obtain your visa for you by tomorrow.'

'Great,' replied Annie excitedly. She was anxious to be on her way. 'One more thing. Is there an English language bookshop near here?'

Five minutes later Annie stepped onto the Paris streets, intent on finding some more information about Pakistan. She was not even sure what language they spoke there.

Confused by a choice of five, Annie pondered indecisively over guidebooks. 'Can I help you?' asked the shop assistant.

'Yeah. I'm going to Pakistan at the weekend and I need a guidebook.' Annie tried hard not to sound as impetuous and naïve as she felt.

'If you're backpacking, most people prefer the *Lonely Planet*, though if you're on a tour or going for business you may prefer something with more photos.'

Annie picked *Pakistan and The Karakoram Highway*, from *Lonely Planet*, wondering while she did what was so special about this Highway that it was included in the title. Unasked, the assistant handed her a map too.

'Can I go to China from Pakistan?' said Annie as she perused the Michelin map.

'Of course. The Karakoram Highway goes up to the Khunjerab Pass, which crosses to Xinjiang Province and the city of Kashgar.'

'In that case, I'll have a book and map for China too,' said Annie looking back at the shelves.

The assistant offered an alternative. 'Have you thought about buying an electronic reader? You can get any number of guidebooks and maps that way and not have to carry all the weight around.'

An hour later, sitting in a nearby café with her newly bought electronic device, loaded with electronic books and electronic maps, to compliment the old fashioned paper version of the Pakistan guidebook, Annie found out how unprepared she was. It was going to be hot and humid, but a Muslim country was not the place to wear the short skirts, dresses and sandals she carried in her rucksack. Trekking in the mountains could be cold and dangerous, unless she bought good boots, warm clothes, sleeping bag, ground mat, water bottle, emergency food and mosquito repellent. Vaccinations would also be essential to protect her from the hotbed of disease the region seemed to be.

There was also the political situation that seemed to be much worse than she'd really considered. But Annie reckoned the news reports were sensationalised to sell more papers; ever since Tony Blair's 'sexed up' 45 minute claim she'd been sceptical of news reports from the Islamic world.

Sobered though she was, when Annie left the café she was on a mission to re-stock her rucksack with suitable clothes and fill her arm with the necessary vaccinations.

*****

David's last meal of badly cooked rice with a few scraps of mushy tomato and a single square of potato had been drugged, and he'd woken up in a different, cleaner, room.

Ricky had come in to see him and was being politer than he usually was. 'Tomorrow you'll be going home. I'll give you a ticket, your passport and some money. Just get on the plane and don't say anything silly to anybody. There's your bag. It's already packed and everything's there, including the present for my cousin.'

'What have I got to do?' David was suspicious of Ricky's renewed civility.

'Just what I told you. My cousin will find you in London. Just do what he says,' said Ricky seriously.

'It's hours to London, I'll need some stuff to see me through.' David could feel the future prospect of the withdrawal pains, and it frightened him.

'You'll get some pills before you get on the plane. They'll sort you out until you get to London, then you're on your own. Shouldn't be too hard to find some heroin in London, I send enough over with people like you.' Then almost as if it had just come to him he added with a smile, 'You could buy some off my cousin once you've delivered it.'

'What if I dump the stuff and just go home without it?'

'Someone did that once. My cousin followed him. That foolish mule went cold turkey with a few broken bones before he got to the hospital. He's still in the wheelchair.'

David stared at Ricky in horror, but in his drug addled state he couldn't see any other options for getting out of Pakistan. His hands started to shake at the prospect of going through customs with a bag full of heroin, getting caught and ending up in a Pakistani jail.

Ricky unnecessarily pressed his point one more time, but with more menace than David thought possible. 'You can't beat me. You cut and run, we'll find you. You confess at the airport here, you get executed for drug smuggling. You do it in London and they'll lock you up for life. You do what you're told, you can have your life back. Easy.'

*****

'Vaccinations for Pakistan? Most of my patients only go as far as Monte Carlo, or the Caribbean and the worst they suffer from is too much sun, food and champagne.' The doctor seemed positively amused that his patient was going to such a place. It was not often he administered vaccines for typhoid, hepatitis and meningitis.

The vaccinations hurt physically, even though the doctor was gentle. One went in her backside and one each in both arms. 'You should have had them over a few weeks. But it is better to have them like this than not at all,' grinned the doctor. Annie winced as she rolled her shoulders and sat gingerly back on her chair.

The next visit was the camping shop, which hurt financially. Annie was sure it must have been the most expensive in Paris, the one that outfitted fashion-conscious, *de rigeur* Parisians, who never actually climbed in Chamonix, just posed in a fancy mountain bar.

An hour of visits to the changing room and self-conscious strolls in chic designer hiking books preceded a frighteningly large amount of Euros being added to the increasingly well used credit card.

*****

The luxurious comfort of the glorious bed was little compensation for the aching arms and sore backside the following morning. The competing serums of typhoid, hepatitis and meningitis made her hot, feverish and vaguely sick. Annie was glad she was mostly prepared. A day in bed reading and an evening in the bar honouring her Grandad with a fine bottle of wine would not be wasted.

*****

A hangover had replaced the vaccine-related nausea when departure day dawned. With an over-stuffed rucksack on her back and a couple of carrier-bags for posting back to England by Louis banging against her knees, Annie took an archetypal deep breath then left her room for the start of her big adventure.

A familiar face smiled in recognition as Annie's luggage disappeared into the cavernous boot of the Rolls. 'I hope you enjoyed your stay, *mademoiselle*?'

A courtesy chocolate selection and a half bottle of the 1979 Bordeaux she had drunk in the bar the previous night sat on the courtesy table in the back of the car. As Annie wondered whether to drink it or keep it, the driver spoke to her through the intercom. 'The staff at the hotel enjoyed your stay. We hope you will come back sometime, or at least send us a postcard.'

'I'd love to. It's a beautiful hotel and I've had such a lovely time,' grinned Annie.

The chauffeur wheeled the luggage trolley to the Etihad Airways check-in desk for Annie. He seemed almost reluctant to say good-bye. '*Au revoir, mademoiselle.*'

As Annie dug in her pocket for a tip the chauffeur shook his head. 'No, there is no need for a tip. I am pleased to have met you. If you were my daughter I would be proud of you. Take care.'

The chauffeur turned to the check-in steward behind the desk and spoke quickly in French, then he kissed Annie Gallic style on each cheek and returned to his car.

Annie laid her passport and booking number on the check-in desk and prepared herself for returning to cattle class on the plane. Moments later the steward smile at her as he held out the boarding card. '*Mademoiselle*, you have been upgraded to business class. You may use the Executive Lounge in the departure hall if you wish. *Bon voyage.*'

*****

Annie felt out of place in the Executive Lounge. She was both under-dressed and the only woman in a crowd of tailored businessmen. Eyes scanned her appraisingly, calculating whether she was a young modern business woman, or how much she cost her sugar-daddy.

It was a relief to hear the heavily accented announcement. 'Flight 241 to Islamabad is boarding at gate 14.' Glad to be on her way, Annie quickly left the anti-social business travellers and went to find her plane.

To the rear, Economy Class strained under the pressure of a full load, but Business Class carried only three other passengers. No complimentary champagne this time; instead it was deliciously hand-pressed fresh orange juice to settle her queasy stomach. Annie settled herself and experimented with the wide, soft, lie-flat seat, planning to pass the flight reading her guidebook and formulating an itinerary for a cheap and adventurous stay in Pakistan.

Night one would be the first test of her resolve. She had decided where to stay, and it would be spent sleeping on the concrete floor of a dormitory at the Tourist Camp, Islamabad. A huge change from the Ritz in Paris. She'd had some luxury, now she wanted to prove she was a proper traveller experiencing the country as it really was, not just some tourist passing through taking photos on her smartphone.

Taking a break from reading up on her destination, Annie discreetly scanned the cabin to assess her fellow passengers. Two of them were nondescript middle-aged businessmen, but across the aisle, to Annie's left, reclined an archetypal Frenchman with a smooth tan, stylishly cut wavy dark hair and perfectly tailored clothes. After a lingering look Annie dropped her eyes back to the book. Then surprised herself as she snatched admiring glances at the handsome traveller while attempting to concentrate on her book. It was not like her to check out the talent.

Half way into the flight to Abu Dhabi Annie became aware that the man's gaze was fixed upon her from his rear facing sofa seat. He'd noticed she was looking at him and was trying to catch her eye. She let him. 'You wish to join me?' he said. 'I would be glad of the company on such a long flight.'

Overdosed on information and feeling safe in the restricted environs of the plane, Annie nodded an acceptance. As she settled herself across the low coffee table on the forward-facing sofa, the Frenchman ordered vintage Champagne and canapés from the stewardess.

'My name is Dominic Renard, I am a diplomat for the French government. I live in Pakistan. I noticed you reading the travel guide and wonder if I may I be of any assistance to such a beautiful young lady?'

Annie allowed herself to be flattered by his Gallic charm. The compliments and attention continued through the journey and the later hours of the flight passed by much quicker than the earlier ones.

Dominic waxed lyrical about the sights and sounds of Pakistan, commenting frequently on how he would enjoy escorting her around the country. Annie basked in the attention and slipped easily into the comfort zone offered by a confident protector, discussing travel options and listening to Dominic's opinions on where to visit. Then Dominic spoilt the illusion and invited her to stay with his family at their apartment in the diplomatic quarter in Islamabad. 'It would be much more pleasant and safer for you than the mosquito ridden campsite. It would also be too pleasant for me to have such a wonderful young lady at my home,' he said gallantly.

'Why do you say safer?' queried Annie, more sharply than she intended.

'Pakistan is not Paris. The government is not always the law of the land. Not everything around you that you take for granted is what it seems. People like you disappear all the time.'

'Disappear! People don't just disappear!' Annie was annoyed he thought she would be so easily frightened into changing her plans.

Dominic shrugged, with Gallic insouciance. 'As I say, Pakistan is not Paris. According to the estimates of the European Consulates and the Americans, over two hundred of their nationals are missing in the North West Frontier Province and the Northern Territories.'

'What exactly do you mean by 'missing'? Surely I would have read in the paper about so many people disappearing,' responded Annie dubiously.

Dominic waved his champagne glass expansively. 'Officially, it means that their last known whereabouts was

Pakistan. Unofficially we guess that many of them were involved with drugs and crossed the borders to Afghanistan and Kazakhstan where they became caught up in the wars and were killed, disappeared north into Central Asia, or ended up in Pakistani jails for drug smuggling. Of course, the families all deny any known involvement with drugs, but the lure of quick money and too much dirty Hashish does strange things to young people a long way from home.'

'So if I don't do drugs you reckon I'll be okay?'

'You will certainly be safer, but not everyone and everything in this country is what it seems. You must be very careful. And I would be happier if you would stay in my home,' said Dominic as he focused his large, soft eyes on Annie.

'No. Thanks anyway, but I want to do this on my own,' said Annie. She was annoyed with herself, as much as with Dominic. She had obviously under-estimated the dangers, but Annie was still confident that if she was sensible, kept her wits about her and stayed clear of drugs she would be safe enough and didn't need to hide away behind the walls of an embassy. There was also the rather disconcerting thought of having to look a wife in the eye after the compliments she had enjoyed from the husband.

'If you change your mind, please call me,' said the diplomat as he passed over a card, bearing an office number only. 'By the way, the French Embassy club opens to guests on Thursday evenings. Please come along.'

'I might, if I'm still in town,' Annie allowed.

*****

Ishmael watched the driver of the jeep talk to the policeman at the barrier. He had waved when the policeman pointed at him, but that was almost an hour ago and the two men had smoked a few cigarettes and enjoyed some chai since then.

Only when the jeep headed towards him did Ishmael walk down to the road from the hillock where he had pitched his tent.

'Ishmael Khan?' said the driver as he studied Ishmael with open interest.

'Yes, that's me.' Ishmael took the sealed package held out to him by the man who by the pattern embroidered on his waistcoat was a farmer from a village not far below the pass, on the Gilgit side. Ishmael signed the chitty with his service number and surname. It was common practice to use trusted locals to deliver his orders and a few even worked for him sometimes, though they risked much to help expose the smugglers he looked for.

With the jeep continuing on its journey and a fresh pot of tea prepared, Ishmael opened and read his concise orders: *'Investigate the trekking route from Mastuj to Phander. Determine how many foreigners avoid the Shandur Pass by crossing the Chumarkhan Pass.'*

What a waste of time, thought Ishmael. The Pass was over 5000 metres high; few foreigners would ever cross it and certainly not enough to account for all those missing. Despite that, he would enjoy a few days trekking through the mountains. Ishmael finished his chai, before slowly and carefully packing his kit.

*****

David was feeling paranoid, unsure who was there to trap him and who in the airport lounge was there to keep an eye on him. Sitting on a plastic seat in an unobtrusive corner David was trying hard not to be noticed.

Ricky had given him a small shot of heroin this morning, just enough to take the edge off his withdrawal, but not enough to space him out. He was now in Islamabad airport and feeling like shit. He had waited two days in the last room until Ricky had finally come up with the tickets. The wait had intensified David's tension almost to breaking point. He hadn't even known where he was and only when they left for the airport was it clear they were in Islamabad.

'I had to wait until my friend in customs was working,' was Ricky's only explanation for the delay.

At the airport drop-off Ricky had repeated his instructions again, 'You will act normally in the airport and on the plane. And you will give your rucksack to the man who asks you for it when you get to London. If you do not do exactly what you are told you will have big trouble, either from the police, my cousin, or me. If you want to go home, do exactly what you're told.'

*****

Diplomatic assistance speeded Annie and her escort through the immigration queues at Islamabad airport and their passage only slowed long enough for Annie to receive her requisite entry stamp from an obsequious customs officer.

There was no standing around in the baggage hall for Dominic and Annie. A locally employed staffer was waiting at the immigration desk and escorted them to an air-conditioned office where they waited while their luggage was collected and loaded into the embassy car.

Through the windows of the office looking out over the airport concourse Annie watched the disordered and chaotic mayhem with a sense of detachment, struggling to comprehend the transition from the comparative calm of Paris.

It was only a short wait until the embassy employee returned to lead them to the air-conditioned and blacked-out car. As they moved through the pressing crowds Annie was caught between the desire to fend for herself and the urge to unashamedly change her mind and ask to stay with Dominic.

From air-conditioning to tropical heat, then back to the isolating air-conditioned embassy car, Annie was partly shielded from the reality of a Pakistani afternoon on the journey into the city. The darkened windows enhanced the separateness, though the dirt, barrenness and disrepair outside the diplomatic cocoon still managed to unsettle Annie further.

At the Tourist Camp Dominic kissed her on both cheeks. 'I hope to see you again very shortly. And *mademoiselle*, please take care.'

Annie felt terribly alone as the car disappeared and she turned towards the campsite gate.

*****

Raseem didn't trust anyone, least of all his mules. The security men at Islamabad were mostly all right, they'd do anything for money, and all he asked them to do was nothing. They were just supposed to ignore the occasional passenger he pointed out. Even so, he liked to be at the airport when a shipment went out, just to make sure it really did leave.

The latest fool was doing his best to look normal, but it was obvious he was scared. If only the mules realised they could dump the stuff in the airport toilet and there was nothing he could really do to them in Pakistan, let alone England, he wouldn't be able to make such easy money.

As David disappeared into the departure area, Raseem turned towards the arrivals hall. It was always better to catch a new mule within the first few days after their arrival, before they had the chance to link up with someone else who'd been in Pakistan for a while and get enough confidence not to be so easily taken in by him. It was amazing how gullible a newly arrived backpacker could be, particularly if they were fresh from home and inexperienced

It made his job much easier if they were lonely, nervous and young. He usually targeted the campsite in town to watch for single travellers, but when he was at the airport he always made a point of checking out the arrivals hall.

Raseem had watched an Etihad Airways Airbus coming in from Paris land as he waited for David to do what he'd been told. Male French travellers liked to smoke a lot of dope, but they were noisy and attracted attention. The women on the other hand were a catch to be savoured, and he was sure they secretly enjoyed his attentions even if they wouldn't actually come with him to the mountains.

Two businessmen emerged from the front of the plane as business class enjoyed their privileges and disembarked first. In a few years he'd have enough money to join them in the luxury of the business class seats, where the stewardesses pampered and simpered to the whims of the rich.

Then a mistress stepped onto the steps at the door of the plane. She had to be a mistress, women never came to Pakistan on business and this one was far too young to be the wife of the older guy just behind her; unless she was a second wife.

Definitely her first time to Pakistan though. She was both nervous and excited. Raseem checked her body as if he was buying a horse; legs, ass, hips, waist, tits, neck, face. He dropped his cigarette and nausea kicked bile to his throat. 'The fucking tart,' he said aloud. A few faces around him turned to check what he was looking at.

Raseem lit another cigarette to calm his stomach. It was either her or her twin. As she approached the terminal building and moved closer to him Raseem grew certain it was her. It was that bitch from university. She was just as sexy now as she had been then. And as usual she had some fancy boyfriend in tow.

As the bitch disappeared inside the terminal building Raseem headed down to the arrival hall to wait for her reappearance, so he could follow her into the city.

The wait was short and given that she got into an official embassy car, with a flag flying on the bonnet, it would be easy to follow them from the airport. Deciding to leave his jeep in the car park until later, Raseem took an anonymous taxi to hide in the congested traffic, while the diplomatic car stood out. Raseem seethed with lust-filled jealousy in the back seat of his comparatively diminutive yellow car as he watched the black embassy limo. How could that bitch turn up in his country and still be out of reach, under French diplomatic protection?

Then his jealousy turned to glee; he couldn't believe his luck. The diplomatic car stopped at the campsite and she got out alone. As Annie walked slowly up the drive of the campsite Raseem smiled. This time he knew he was going to have her.

Officer Christopher Sinclair sat at his desk in Heathrow Airport, a messy pile of reports scattered over his desk. Most of his work involved reading other people's paperwork. He had two main jobs at the moment.

Number one was trying to catch some baggage handlers stealing individual items from passenger's luggage.

Number two was trying to work out the sense in the reports filed by frontline officers last month who had discovered another bloody idiot with a kilo of heroin in his bag, who also claimed he was forced to carry it but would provide no details about who was doing the forcing. There probably was some truth in the story given that the myriad of fingerprints all over the drug pack didn't match those of the idiot carrying the bag, but they did match the fingerprints on the drug packs carried by the previous two backpackers they'd caught.

Chris was bored. Every report on the thefts had been read five times and nothing matched. No single baggage handler was on duty every time something went missing and not every robbed passenger came through the same terminal anyway. There must be a bunch of people working together, or individually, which made catching them even more difficult.

As for the drug mules, it would take someone with balls to admit how and why they had ended up at Heathrow with a kilo of heroin in their bag and no previous history of drug dealing. It was a pity that so far all the mules seemed more scared of the people they carried the stuff for than they did of going to prison.

All Chris needed was one decent lead and he could get away from his desk and do something more interesting. Tossing the report back to his desk, he gave up on reading and went for another coffee.

*****

An overweight guard watched sullenly as Annie passed the gate and walked up the drive to the campsite office. She was pleasantly surprised to find a number of other young travellers already sitting in the shade of a tree. Given the news report she'd read on the internet in Paris she had half expected to be on her own, never dreaming so many people visited Pakistan on holiday.

'Welcome.'

'G'day.'

'*Bonjour.*'

The disparate group welcomed Annie like a long lost sister; Annie noted wryly that she was the only single girl in sight, though her jet lag and the energy sapping heat refused to let her worry about it too much.

The evening light faded fast as Annie registered and was pointed vaguely towards the various concrete huts. The heat dipped less slowly as the sun disappeared, but the mosquitoes came out to feed in force, and they did so ferociously.

Having been shown to an empty room in one of the five concrete sheds arced around the campsite, Annie dumped her bag and for the first time in her life proceeded to enjoy a cold shower.

Emerging nervously from the hut Annie found a man lazing on the steps, smoking. '*Bonsoir,*' he said laconically as he sat up. What must have been a local style cap sat rakishly on his head, spiky hair poking randomly out from underneath it.

'Hello,' responded Annie automatically and cautiously.

'You arrive from London today?'

'No. Paris.'

'Ah. How I love Paris. Let me show you around and you can tell me how is Paris.'

'My pleasure,' smiled Annie, entranced once more by the languid French accent.

'I am Pierre,' smiled the man with a gentle dip of his head.

Despite herself Annie relaxed and smilingly returned the introduction as they strolled around the campsite where a number of groups of travellers were cooking and eating around open fires. Annie noted that it was the second time that day a Frenchman had taken it upon himself to look after her.

Tour over, they joined a group circling a camp-fire where a joint passed hand to hand. Annie observed the group of individuals, but her eyes kept reverting to the rake-thin Pierre. She loved his accent, and smiled to herself as she remembered how his eyes had jumped so animatedly as he talked non-stop on their little tour. He obviously loved Pakistan, as he had said about ten times in the five minutes that he had monopolised her. He obviously wasn't smoking dope either, he was too wide awake.

Though she'd been cooler, cleaner and smeared in mosquito repellent when she emerged from the hut after her shower, she had quickly grown clammy again in the humid heat. Smoke curled gently and aromatically from a glowing campfire and mixed with steam rising from a cast iron pot slung above it, which combined with the smoke from the joints and a pipe helped keep the mosquitoes at bay.

'We are all agreed that you should join us for dinner,' said Pierre.

'Take a pew,' added an Australian.

Annie accepted with a smile, relieved that she would not have to explore Islamabad for the first time alone, at night, looking for food. Or worse, go hungry if she was too scared to go out since Dominic's warning was still bouncing round her head.

A stereo played the Doors and Pink Floyd, the smoke of the fire mixing with the sweet aroma of hashish. They could have been in *The Beach*, if they'd been anywhere near the sea. Annie was surprised to see so many smoking dope; hardly any of her friends at university had smoked it at all and she'd always felt vaguely uncomfortable with the idea of taking drugs, despite the coke snorted so regularly by people in the media world at the parties she had never gone too. She was glad, therefore, to see Pierre pass over the hash pipe as it made its rounds.

While the hashish and dinner slowed everyone else to a stupor, Annie and Pierre chatted easily in the dark. Pierre ate hardly anything, but he made sure Annie ate well, refilling her small plate twice before she insisted he stop.

For the most part Pierre regaled Annie with tales of the mountain valleys and villages he obviously knew well. Annie listened enthralled; this was the romantic excitement she had left Paris to find.

'I have been here for years, it is my second home. I'll be going back to my adopted village soon, you should come with me. I have a piece of land where I live the simple life, growing a few crops and raising chickens.'

'Yeah, maybe. Where is it?'

'Up near the Afghani border. It's called Shawal. It's very small and very secluded, hardly on any maps.'

'I'll think about it,' smiled Annie. 'But now I think I need to sleep. See you tomorrow.'

'We all sleep outside.' Pierre waved his hand around the campsite, where bodies lay stretched out wrapped in sleeping bags and blankets. 'You'll be safe. There are plenty of people around.'

The lawn was cooler, airier and softer than the bare concrete floors of the huts and Annie felt surprisingly relaxed lying out under the stars. Almost everyone laid their sleeping bags outside, with many identified by little red dots at the end of joints as people had a final smoke before sleeping.

From a plot near the middle of the alfresco sleepers, Annie lay on her back enjoying her first spectacular sight of the star splashed Pakistani sky that was hardly polluted by the orange glow of streetlights.

Mellowed by the exotic atmosphere and the stray fumes of hashish, Annie pondered Pierre's invite. A bit of mountain air sounded perfect, and she might even get into Afghanistan while she was there. The stars blurred as Annie drifted off to sleep, happy and content that adventure had been found.

Chapter Five

An hour after its scheduled departure, the train had still not even arrived at the platform. Only to be expected, thought Matt. He pondered on the disorganisation that surrounded him and began to doubt that the train would turn up at all. He had moved to a low sofa directly under a gently turning fan, ostensibly to rest, but mainly to escape the endless friendly questioning. The fan signally failed to move the stagnant air of the waiting room and his shirt was relentlessly moving from clammy to wet.

When the train eventually slid alongside the platform passengers were already overflowing from the press of people inside; even the buffers and roofs of the carriages carried bodies. Before the train had squealed and juddered to a lumbering halt the passengers on the platform began throwing luggage to those already on the train.

Matt watched incredulously through the grubby window of the waiting room as his concern grew at the thought of trying to board the packed train. From the table Mohammed was watching him and chuckled as he explained. 'Many tickets are sold 'Without seat,' so people go to the siding and claim their seats early. Those that can afford it pay someone poor to go and claim it for them.'

'What about our seats? Shouldn't we go and make sure we get them, before someone else does?' asked Matt worriedly.

The men laughed at Matt's concern. 'First class is different. The carriages are guarded to keep the riff-raff out. The guard will escort us to our seats when the train is ready for us.'

Matt relaxed at the reassuring explanation, more relieved than ever that he had splashed out the extra money on the luxury of a numbered ticket. Then he hastily checked his wallet to make sure the valuable ticket was still there.

Soon after, the guard arrived to escort the four men to their seats. A porter readied their luggage on a wooden handcart and a policeman cleared a path through the crowds with his bamboo lathi, so the privileged elite could reach their seats unsoiled. Whilst Matt trod nervously through the crowd, his travelling companions stepped lightly through the clamouring mass of people as if they were untouchable royalty.

The guard ushered the four men into the same compartment, disappointing Matt; if he had been able to choose he would have taken a cabin to himself, so he could lock himself safely away in protective isolation.

Fresh sheets and blankets lay ready for four bunks. The carriage was impressively clean, even the windows, so noticeably different to the state of the rest of the train they had passed on the way from the waiting room. Sweetmeats and chapatis arrived through the window as the men took their seats, though Matt could not decide whether the refreshments were courtesy of Pakistan Railways, or whether his new acquaintances had ordered them without him noticing.

More than happy to have the company of a stranger, especially a foreigner, the three sociable Pakistanis renewed their good-natured interrogation as they pressed the biscuits and sweetmeats on Matt.

Two hours behind schedule the train slowly and jerkily left Karachi station. Only Matt had been impatiently checking his watch; his hosts hardly seemed to have noticed the delay at all as they chatted away without a care in the world.

It was dark by the time the train left the sprawling suburbs of Karachi and the landscape of Sindh province was hidden by the night, frustrating Matt's attempts to see the province that was reportedly so dangerous.

It was close to midnight before tiredness overtook the three men and their questions and conversation began to fade. When the bunks were allocated they just about ordered Matt to take the best bunk and he was given no choice but to accept an extra blanket to counter the uncontrollable icy blast of the over-active air-conditioning.

Snugly wrapped against the cold air, Matt pondered the reception from his new found friends. He was more used to public transport in England, where nobody made eye contact, let alone spoke to another passenger. In Karachi, he had been too suspicious to even acknowledge most people who had tried to speak to him, and he began to consider the idea that his preconception that every Pakistani was untrustworthy and out to rob him had been wrong.

Sleep eventually overtook his musings, but not for long. Matt started to itch. As the itch grew more persistent and his scratching stronger, he slowly woke from his slumber. His feet itched the worst; it felt like somebody was sticking them with hot pins. As he floated closer to consciousness the itch consumed him till he grasped for the nearest light-switch.

Red-black bed-bugs were crawling over his skin and bed. As he swung his feet to the floor he saw the whole carriage was crawling with them. Red spots of blood spoiled his clean white sheets and red welts on his chest marked the lines of attack. Matt beat maniacally at the bugs with his shoe, but the armour-plated bloodsuckers ignored his hammering. Three dopey faces watched him with amusement as he flailed futilely.

'Do it like this,' said Mohammed as he struck a match and shrivelled bugs one by one. 'It's the only way to kill them.'

Matt took to the burning with an obsessive vengeance. His welted skin still itched, even though it was bug free. He had a sneaking suspicion the carriage was flea ridden too.

Forty minutes of burning saw his bed cleared of bugs. Matt felt calmer for the revenge he had wreaked, but he continued to itch. His fellow passengers only half-heartedly killed bugs, as if to humour Matt, not solve the problem.

Completely disturbed by Matt and the smell of singed bed-bug, no one wanted to sleep any more. They spent the rest of the night chatting and playing cards, though Matt totally failed to understand the Pakistani card game. Occasionally, through the long dark hours, all four of them unconsciously scratched. If a bug showed its head for long enough, Matt abandoned his cards to flare a match and exact more revenge, to raucous cheers from his companions.

Eventually, when the conversation moved on to the dacoits who attacked the trains on the Lahore-Karachi line they were travelling on, even Matt forgot his war on the bugs.

'You know of these dacoits, Matt? The bandits?'

'I've heard of them. Do they really stop the trains?'

'Yes, truly. These dacoits they stop the trains by riding alongside the engine in jeeps and threatening the driver with machine guns.' Mohammed related his story with studied calmness.

The other men laughed with concern at Matt's grimace. Mohammed continued. 'The dacoits go straight to the First Class carriages and rob only the rich passengers, like your Robin Hood. If they find foreigners aboard, they take them away, in the vain hope of raising a ransom.'

After a moment's thought, Matt asked, 'Why a vain hope?'

'Oh, the government will not let anyone pay a ransom for a foreigner. They think it will encourage more bandits to join in. No foreign hostage has ever been recovered alive,' said Mohammed, smiling apologetically at Matt

'Bloody hell, that's not good,' said Matt whilst thinking that the real possibility of being kidnapped was nowhere near as appealing as when he was feeling sorry for himself in Karachi. 'Have any of the dacoits been caught?' Matt looked questioningly around the carriage hoping that the potential for kidnapping was not that high.

'No. Some people say the police are in league with the bandits. The government says they come across the border from India to cause trouble for Pakistan.' Mohammed shrugged, almost as if he were apologising for not having a proper answer.

'Don't worry,' countered a more optimistic voice. 'The army has guards with machine guns riding with the driver now. They will shoot the dacoits if they attack us. And anyway,

Mohammed won't let anyone take you away, you are our friend.'

Matt looked at Mohammed for an explanation, but Mohammed only smiled and wobbled his head from side to side in the fashion of the Indian sub-continent that meant 'Don't ask.'

The fat man said, 'His father is Governor of Sukkur, no one would dare rob him.'

Mohammed scowled at the speaker, who fell silent and began intently examining his cards.

The benefits of first class travel had paled significantly with this new piece of information. Matt now thought he knew why there were so few passengers in this part of the train. The wild thoughts he had imagined earlier, of being captured by bandits, seemed closer to reality than Matt had actually thought possible. And the reality was a lot more scary than his romantic ideas had been back in Karachi. With Mohammed in the same compartment, he also wondered if the danger was increased or reduced. Would the son of the Governor be a valuable hostage, or more trouble than he was worth? And what about his foreign travelling companion, would they think he was someone important and worth keeping, or a nuisance to be disposed of before he got in the way?

The hours before dawn dragged, with the worry of marauding dacoits obviously playing on everyone's mind. The card game was abandoned, the conversation died, but nobody settled down to sleep properly. In unspoken agreement they took it in turns to doze sitting up, leaving one of them awake to listen for trouble. As the western sky began to lighten, all four men began to relax and they abandoned the pretence of sleep and sat glued to the windows, greeting the sunrise with relief.

As the great Indus River slipped past them heading south to the coast they had left behind them hours before, their companionable silence was finally broken. 'The dacoits never attack in daylight,' murmured a tired voice.

'And we will be in Rohri soon,' said another.

Soon was longer than Matt expected. And it was another hour before the train screeched and clattered into the town of Rohri, which sat on the opposite side of the Indus River to Sukkur.

'I will take you to Sukkur in my car,' announced Mohammed. 'The train will stay here for an hour before it crosses the river. And anyway, Sukkur is too dangerous for you to arrive on your own.'

Matt shook his head. Accepting a lift from someone he did not really know would have gone against his natural instincts in England, let alone a foreign country. 'No, I'll be fine. I'm sure.'

Three serious and concerned faces concentrated on him. Then the youngest man said, 'You must go in the car. You cannot go on your own. You are our friend and we cannot let you be exposed to so much danger.'

'I thought you said the dacoits would not attack in daylight?'

'It is not the dacoits you need to worry about in Sukkur. It is just there are too many outsiders here now.'

Matt considered the intense seriousness of Mohammed's concerned face as he silently pressed the offer of the lift. The other men nodded encouragement. The fear of accepting a lift from a stranger competed with the fear of facing the ill-defined threat of *too many outsiders*. He wished he could stay securely in the relative security of the train carriage.

The train screeched to a halt in the station and the mass of other passengers began leaving the carriages along the platform. Matt made a decision. 'OK, I'll come with you,' he said.

The evident relief on the faces looking at him lifted his confidence, but there was still a mixture of excitement and tension knotting his stomach as he stepped from the compartment into the damp heat of the morning.

A modern road bridge crossed the wide Indus River adjacent to the older railway bridge, and brought them to

Sukkur in Mohammed's chauffeur driven Mercedes that had been waiting at the station entrance. Despite his initial fears provoked by the dire warnings on the train, there was no evident signs of the dangers he had been warned of. The greatest threat of injury came from the ruts and potholes in the baked mud of Sukkur's main street, which bounced Mohammed's car as dust and rubbish swirled in the eddies. Mohammed's chauffeur drove slowly as he picked his way along the broken down road, searching for a hotel that was open.

'I must choose a place where you will be safe. Some of these people will sell you to the highest bidder,' said Mohammed casually.

Matt looked at him incredulously, but Mohammed was concentrating on the line of buildings along the road.

A bearded, Kalashnikov toting tribesman guarded the doorway of the first hotel Mohammed had chosen. The car slowed to a halt and Mohammed spoke to the guard through the car window, but he was aggressively waved away. The next few hotels were obviously locked and barred.

'We will try what used to be the best hotel in town,' announced Mohammed finally. 'It is the government guesthouse. They always used to take tourists in the old days, but it is so long since I've seen one here I do not know if they still do.'

Money was becoming insignificant to Matt by now. The only thing he was interested in was having somewhere clean and bug-free to rest his exhausted itching body. He was also beginning to wonder if Mohammed was part of the problem with him getting a hotel and staying safe. With Mohammed's father being Governor he might have enemies that would use Matt to get at him.

Matt expected something grand from the best hotel in town, but the simple flaking sign said only 'Hotel.' Yellowing paint peeled from the walls.

The snoozing receptionist jumped to attention at the sight of a prospective guest, but it took a while for the man to admit the hotel was actually open. Mohammed argued with the man, then shouted at him. Turning back to Matt he said, 'I have made sure you will be allowed to stay and that they will take good care of you. Anyway, they have nothing else to do. You are the only guest, which is why this man did not want you to stay because he is lazy and does not want to work.'

*****

Raseem lay frustrated on his bed in Islamabad, angrily watching porn movies from Europe. His temper was foul as he cursed the woman who had been his fantasy for years. She had been the woman on the screen in every porn film and the woman who floated before his eyes every time he had fucked some tart since leaving college. But now she was close his hatred overwhelmed his lust and left him impotent. Even the expensive Russian whore he had bought with US dollars at the American Hotel had proved incapable of provoking a reaction.

*****

The Gulf Air Airbus touched down at Heathrow airport. God, it was good to be home. David had sweated through Islamabad airport and the stopover in Abu Dhabi. He'd caught a few people looking at him strangely, but no one had come near him. He wasn't surprised really; he smelled of stale sweat, his clothes were grubby and he was nervous as hell.

An hour before they landed he had sat in the tiny toilet cubicle and written a brief note. It had taken him hours to pluck up the courage to do it, and just as long to decide what to write.

In the end he had taken the last few pills Ricky had given him in one go and their steadying effect had allowed him to think more clearly and settle on what he thought was a smarter attitude to his problems. He'd decided that it would be better to try and explain all the drugs in his bag to a customs officer and ask them for help than be caught by a customs officer trying to walk through the green channel at Heathrow. He also reckoned the customs officers would know what to do about Ricky's so-called cousin.

Purposely last off the plane, David dawdled up the ramp into the terminal. At the doorway a security man of Indian extraction smiled a welcome. Panic-induced sweat ran down David's back as he worried if he was one of Ricky's men. The terror of indecision clouded David's thoughts. Only with great effort did he reassure himself that Ricky's cousin was hardly going to be inside the terminal building if he was going to collect the drugs. He was going to let David do the risky part and go through customs.

Only a few groups of passengers from his flight were left in the corridor of the terminal building, all families struggling with kids, though the first passengers from other flights were beginning to appear from a gate further along the building.

David shuffled forwards, trying to hold his nerve and stick to the plan. An information desk appeared. A lone woman sat at her desk. David's courage failed him and he held back from approaching the desk. Then a middle-aged security man, who looked like a former soldier, appeared from a doorway ten metres away and stared suspiciously at him. Clipped to the guard's shirt was a small radio, with an earpiece snaking to his left ear.

The words came out in a tumbling hurry before he thought too much about them. 'Hi. I'm lost, can you tell me where to go please?' Then David held out his hand as if he wanted to shake hands with the security man. After a slight hesitation the man took it. He looked down in surprise as he felt the note. David looked at him helplessly, then said, 'Thank you,' before slowly walking away, looking miserably at the floor as he shuffled to his fate.

A few moments later, just as he stepped onto the escalator and began moving slowly down to the immigration hall David looked back to the guard. The man's head was bent to the radio as he spoke urgently into it. In his hand was the small scrap of paper David had given him.

Slowly returning to his desk with a plastic cup of metallic coffee, Chris heard his telephone start ringing. He reached it on the fourth ring. 'Yeah, Chris Sinclair.'

'Sir, one of our security men just reported meeting a doped out passenger in the arrivals area. The man was sweating profusely and very nervous. He gave the security man a note that reads, *Help. Please arrest me.*'

Chris's eyebrows rose. 'What's he look like? Where is he now?' He stood again only seconds after sitting down, his coffee forgotten.

'He's in the immigration queue. Our man is keeping an eye on him. The passenger is wearing dirty jeans and a filthy T-shirt. Hair's a bit long and unkempt. You can't miss him.'

'Thanks. I'll be waiting for him in the customs corridor.'

Chris almost knocked his coffee cup over as he rounded his desk and began to run for the arrivals area. His day was looking up. Something more interesting to do had just arrived and he could put his frustrating cases to one side for a while.

*****

The EU passport holders line inched slowly past the solitary immigration official.

'Where have you come from, sir?' David held out his pink booklet.

'Pakistan.'

'Business or pleasure, sir?'

'It certainly wasn't pleasure.' David tried to smile, but his face pulled to a grimace.

'Thank you, sir,' said the official neutrally.

David felt his heart falter as it occurred to him that no-one was going to apprehend him. At least he'd tried, he thought, as he headed for the baggage reclaim.

He trudged towards the rows of carousels to collect his backpack and its incriminating contents. A single thought repeated itself in his head. I tried. I tried.

The milling crowds waited impatiently for their luggage, and all looked relieved as one by one they hauled their heavy bags onto trolleys and headed away to the customs hall.

With his own rucksack slung casually over one shoulder, David followed the straggle of passengers. The green '*Nothing to Declare*' sign mocked him as he stepped into the wide corridor that was always empty of customs men. David scanned the two-way mirrors lining the corridor, trying to see if anyone was watching him. He was wishing now that he'd not written that note. All he wanted to do was leave the building and get rid of his cargo so he could forget this whole nightmare and get on with his life again.

As he approached the last empty desk a door opened and a solitary figure, looking rather flushed in the face, stepped towards him. 'Excuse me, sir, could you step over here? Is this all your luggage?'

*****

Annie woke early, sweating profusely inside the four-season sleeping-bag that was designed more for cold icy mountains than hot humid plains.

When she re-emerged from the hut after taking another cold shower and dressing for the heat in cotton cargo pants and a long sleeved t-shirt, Pierre was lounging on the steps again. He smiled at her appreciatively. 'I'll come with you if you're going into town. I'd like to show you round, I know the place quite well.'

Relieved from the prospect of exploring on her own, Annie accepted the offer. She liked the attention of such a charming man, felt assured by his presence and confident his company would allow her to relax more than if she went alone.

The campsite hung on the south side of the city. Islamabad itself sat north of the old city of Rawalpindi and the Rawal Lake. Having crossed the broad, tree-lined boulevard that separated the campsite from the city, Annie and Pierre wandered through square grids of dilapidated roads, overgrown pavements and peeling whitewashed blockhouses lacking the soul, aromas and colour that Annie had expected of Asia.

Predominantly a harsh, dirty-white, concrete conurbation built in the 1960s, Islamabad was a capital built for the new country of Pakistan and it had many of the worst architectural aspects of any pre-fabricated 1960s urban sprawl. It had served its purpose, though, manufacturing a neutral seat of government and bureaucracy, safely away from the regional power-bases of Lahore and Karachi and the ever-present threats from India.

Occasional new shiny glass and steel structures seemed oddly out of place and Pierre avoided them dismissively. 'They're not the real beating heart of the city,' he said when Annie suggested going inside a shopping mall whose windows were hung with brightly coloured saris.

Pierre instead headed for the darker side streets and narrow alleys, which were pleasantly cooler, though more intimidating for Annie as the real Pakistan pressed closer in on her. As if by accident they arrived at a tiny café, though by the welcome granted Pierre it was obvious he had been there before.

In surprisingly good Urdu, Pierre ordered food and chai, though he ate almost nothing of the strongly spiced omelette put in front of them. Surprising herself, Annie ate the majority of the generous plate of eggs, chilli and tomatoes even though they were dripping in oil. She was so hungry Annie forgot the qualms she'd felt back in Paris about eating at the local restaurants when reading the dire warnings of food poisoning, dysentery and worse in her guidebooks. The omelette was delicious too, which helped.

Pierre spoke to the owner more than to Annie during the hour they spent in the café. After she devoured the omelette her chai glass was endlessly refilled as the men chatted animatedly in Urdu. Pierre and the other men continually kept looking at her and smiling, though not so much at her as to each other. At first Annie had smiled too, but then she began to feel somewhat nervous. In the end Annie had felt so uncomfortable she stood up and announced it was time to leave.

'I want to find the diplomatic quarter. I've been invited to drinks at the embassy on Thursday evening and I want to go there now so I can see where I'm going when it's daylight.'

All laughter in the restaurant stopped and both Pierre and the owner looked at her worriedly. It was suddenly obvious that the owner spoke better English than he'd let on.

'Which embassy?' said Pierre slowly.

'The French one. I met this guy on the plane, a diplomat. He's invited me to the Embassy Club and I think I want to go look for it now.'

Pierre and the café owner looked at each other. Pierre shrugged, then looked at Annie. 'OK,' he said, 'let's go.'

Back on the streets Pierre led the way and Annie followed along assuming Pierre was heading in the right direction, but not really knowing where they were, let alone if they were heading towards the embassy.

The four towering minarets of the Shah Faisal Mosque grew closer as they strolled through the narrow alleyways linking the wider streets and boulevards. At each intersection the starkly modern towers became increasingly dominant, imposing their power on the streets below them.

Glaringly bright open spaces of parks, cricket pitches and channelled streams broke up the harsh concrete of the new build city and the cooler, shadowy streets sheltered by the canopies of corrugated steel and tarpaulins.

Pierre's meandering route disrupted Annie's sense of direction so much she gave up trying to keep track of their path and the way back to the campsite.

Markets, street stalls and open-fronted shops sat amongst modern concrete villas and walled compounds. Annie was disappointed at the lack of Asianess in the architecture and ambience.

Then, suddenly, they were standing on the bank of a flowing river of traffic. The Margalla Road. The noise and heat and dust made their presence felt in a story book intensity. Annie would not have believed the sensation could be so intense that the pressure on her temples would make her head hurt and press her body into a slump.

'Oh look,' said Pierre disingenuously. 'There's the zoo. We'll go look around.'

Annie looked at him and said unusually bluntly, 'You were heading for this all the time weren't you? You had no intention of taking me to the embassy, did you?'

Pierre shrugged and pouted, with typical Gallic charm. 'There are much more interesting things to see in Pakistan than an embassy.' Then he stepped into the flow of traffic to cross the road, effectively cutting off further discussion.

Despite her misgivings, based entirely on the premonition that the zoo would be an upsetting experience, Annie nervously followed Pierre into the traffic and across the road after him. Annie had always taken her time making friends in England, but she had instantly been drawn to Pierre, seeing in him the perfect travelling companion. Despite her current annoyance at him not taking her to the embassy, it never crossed her mind to walk away from him and go find it herself.

The zoo was busy, and much as Annie had anticipated. The compounds were dry and dusty, with hardly a blade of grass to be seen for the grazing animals. There were none of the wide open spaces of the wildlife parks she had visited as a child in England and the caged animals looked miserable in their concrete cells, though they were clean enough and didn't look too underfed.

Pierre talked more volubly than he had previously, like an excited child on a day-trip. But despite his best efforts, Annie spent most of the tour wishing she could escape the oppressive atmosphere of the zoo.

The human visitors were much better cared for and Pierre found Annie a cool spot to relax in while he wandered off to find some mango ice-creams he assured her were both delicious and safe to eat. Left alone for the first time since her arrival, Annie soaked up the sounds of families at play in the profoundly different country she had picked almost at random to visit. Her nervousness gone, Annie lay unconcernedly on the dusty ground people-watching, listening to the occasional screech of a peacock mixing with the sounds of middle class Islamabad children playing much as children anywhere in the world would do on a day out with their parents.

A returning Pierre broke Annie's reverie. 'A *paisa* for your thoughts,' he smiled while placing trays of food on the ground in front of her. 'The smell of hot food was too good to resist,' was all he said by way of explanation for the change from mango ice cream.

It was true. The exotic aroma of the spicy food was immediately enticing and Annie found she was surprisingly hungry again. The fiery local take away was unlike anything she had eaten in a curry house in England. Despite the heat of the chillies the underlying flavour was exquisite. Annie laughed as she learnt how to eat her meal the traditional way, with chapati not cutlery.

'Best place to learn this, outdoors. Doesn't matter if I make so much mess here,' said Annie between and around scoops of food she only mostly managed to get to her mouth with the fresh flat bread. Pierre lay on his elbow smiling as he enjoyed the spectacle, picking only at a small piece of chapati and sipping at his mango lassi. 'Don't you ever eat? This is good, you should have some,' said Annie through a mouthful.

Pierre looked into the distance for a moment, then said, 'I ate rice early this morning. I'm purging my body of toxins. I do it once a year for the benefit of my health.'

'Oh, sorry,' mumbled Annie, embarrassed.

'Don't worry, I don't mind if you eat.' smiled Pierre.

It was late afternoon when they emerged from the zoo, leaving behind the cooler gardens to sweat back through the streets of the raucous city.

'We might as well head back to the campsite now. Seeing as it's so late in the day.' Pierre stood and stared at the four finger-like minarets topped with what looked like pointy hats reaching skywards a mile away along the road.

'What about going to the mosque, or the embassy? I really wanted to find it during daylight today.' Annie mentally scolded herself for sounding like a demanding child. She searched Pierre's face for any sign of annoyance, but it showed only vague puzzlement.

'But it will be closed by now. And anyway, it is so far from here we would need to take a tuk-tuk.'

'What about the Faisal mosque, then. Surely that doesn't close?'

'No, but evening prayers will start soon and they don't like foreign women being around when they're praying.' Then he closed the conversation by darting into the traffic and crossing the road back towards where they had come from earlier in the day.

Once again Annie found herself following quickly behind him, not wanting him to think she wasn't interested in going with him. Getting left on her own was not an appealing prospect either.

'No problem, I can go tomorrow,' apologised Annie as she re-joined Pierre on the far pavement, as a cacophony of car horns protested behind her, which she thought may well be aimed at her, though she wasn't going to check.

Pierre stood motionless on the pavement and did not respond as he gazed towards the hills behind the mosque. Annie stood nervously next to him, wanting to say something and regain his attention, but loathe to interrupt his thoughts and risk annoying him.

'Near where I live in the mountains are the Kalash valleys, where the Kafirs live. They're the last non-Muslims in the region. They worship faeries and believe a Toad-God lives on the mountain.'

Annie wasn't sure if a response was expected, but took a deep breath anyway and said, 'I want to go north to Chitral. My Grandad was there when he was in the Indian Army in the 1930's. He used to tell me stories about how beautiful it is up there.'

'That's close to my place. I go there all the time. It's a wonderfully beautiful valley, the mountains are so imposing there. You should come and visit with me, I can take you there.'

'Oh can I?' gushed Annie excitedly. Then blushed like a schoolgirl for being too eager.

A coy smile played around Pierre's mouth. 'Of course you can. The pleasure would be all mine.'

*****

Isabelle huddled in the corner of her cell. Ricky was late. He usually arrived ready for his fun soon after he woke up, but not today. Her loathing of his attentions fought with a rising need to know she was not forgotten.

She almost wanted him to appear. The fear of being abandoned and dying alone and so far from home in this room far outweighed the horror of his abusive attentions.

There was always the hope too, that the charming friendly Ricky would reappear and she'd awake from the nightmare.

*****

'Sit down, please. My name is Chris. Would you like tea, coffee, something cold?'

'No. I mean yes. A Coke, please. If that's all right?'

The customs officer signalled to his colleague who left the room. 'Now, sir. Please could you explain the meaning of this note you handed one of my officers?'

'The note?'

'Yes. This note. The one that says, *Help. Please arrest me.*' Chris laid the scrap of paper on the table between them. David stared at it.

'Oh. Yes. That one.' David sat in silence for a moment as he fought a last battle between his fear of Ricky and the thought of prison. 'It's a long story, but the stuff in the bag's not mine.' Chris sighed to himself. It never was, he thought cynically.

'I see. Did you pack the bag yourself?'

'No. I don't even know what's in it.'

'Is it yours?'

'Yes. I mean the bag is. But I don't know what's inside it. Please believe me.' David became aware that he was babbling. He clenched his fists then clasped his hands together in an attempt to stop shaking.

The second man returned with a plastic cup of Coke.

'Well. Let's see what we have in the bag first. Then you can tell me your story.' Chris indicated to his colleague that he should unpack the bag. Chris and David stood attentively watching his every move, suspicion, mistrust and tension thick in the air.

*****

The trekking route over the Chumarkhan Pass from Mastuj to Teru lay to the north of the Shandur Pass. Ishmael should really have started from Teru if he was to check it properly, but if he crossed the mountains from where he was he could join the route mid-point. There were a few people living in the valleys to the north of him; he'd known them for years and he could ask them how many foreigners they saw every year.

As he climbed steadily higher, the Shandur Pass spread out below him. The two half-frozen lakes, one much bigger than the other, spread among the snow and grass. The lakes would grow over the next few weeks, as the melting snow filled them for another year. Between the lakes stood the polo ground, where Chitral and Gilgit now competed annually and violently with mallets and balls, instead of the more lethal weapons they used to compete with in the not so distant past.

When Ishmael had been young, the men of Gilgit and Chitral had regularly fought each other over blood feuds no one could remember the cause of, but the army had worked hard to stem the bloodshed. Now, instead of killing each other in battle, the people of each valley approached the polo tournament as a proxy war rather than a game, as the pride of each valley depended on the outcome. The polo field was almost clear of snow and a hint of green showed the spring grass was starting to grow even at this altitude. In a few weeks hundreds of people would be gathered on the shores of the two lakes for the three day tournament; the Pass would not be so quiet then. Despite the presence of hundreds of soldiers, fights and shootings still happened every year however, and sometimes full-scale battles occurred as the long-held rivalries boiled over.

Leaving the Pass behind him, Ishmael crossed the spur of a mountain peak and crossed into the next valley where he hoped to find a herdsman before dark. He would be sleeping higher tonight than he had been recently, and it would be much colder too, with snow still covering much of the ground. A warming fire and hospitable company would make the night much more comfortable, and help the time pass more pleasurably too.

*****

A final bag of shrink-wrapped white powder emerged from his bag. David was shaking now, the effects of withdrawal hitting him hard. 'It's not mine,' he snivelled. 'Honestly.'

The two customs men stared impassively at the haul of drugs lying on the table. Chris raised his eyes to the obviously agitated man in front of him.

'Tell me, sir,' he said. 'If it's not yours, can you explain to me how it comes to be in your bag?'

'Yes. Yes. I'll tell you anything you want to know. But can I have some? I need some, I feel like shit.'

'Not just yet, sir. When you've told me everything I think you have to tell me, I'll see what I can do. I'll help you if you help me.' The two customs officers stared expectantly at David.

*****

Revived by a cold shower, Matt went in search of breakfast. Doubting that the hotel would be serving food, he prepared to go out and find some. He was starving.

With no signs of life in the dark, unlit lobby, Matt headed for the door and the sunlit street outside. The thick chain and heavy padlock on the lobby door brought his planned excursion to an abrupt and alarming end. Matt grabbed the padlock and ineffectually shook it . The door rattled but it wasn't going to open.

'Can I help you?' said a quiet voice behind him. Matt jumped, spun on his heel and banged into the wall.

'Let me out?' Matt's voice was higher than normal, his panic translating into a demand for escape. The receptionist wobbled his head and shrugged in response. Matt asked again. He asked politely. He begged. He shouted. The only response was a shake of the head or a mumbled, 'No.'

Then an old patriarch coughed unexpectedly from nearby in the lobby, where he had quietly arrived. 'I work for the Governor of Sukkur. For your own safety you cannot go out on your own.'

'I'll be fine,' said Matt. 'I've just come from Karachi, I won't get lost in Sukkur.'

'You must have men with guns with you, so other men with guns don't kill you,' came the simple reply.

Matt gaped at the man, lost for words. He'd also lost the will to argue further and press the point that he wanted to go out.

'Would you like some breakfast?' Without waiting for a response the hotel manager clapped his hands and shouted at the more junior staff member who bowed and hurriedly left for the kitchen.

Matt allowed himself to be led to the empty hotel restaurant, where he was placed at a central table and promised breakfast, before he was left alone to ponder his situation.

*****

The escort arrived as Matt finished up his small and simple breakfast of curried omelette, that was surprisingly delicious. Two fresh-faced Kalashnikov toting youngsters, parading as soldiers, seated themselves outside the restaurant door to wait for him. One was almost as tall as Matt and sported the first fluff of manhood on his chin. The other was just about a foot shorter and lacked even the fluff.

Matt soon discovered the soldiers would be taking their job seriously. As they walked from the hotel Matt signalled that he wanted to get some bottled water from a shop. One gun directed him to stand against the shop wall, then turned to cover the street. The second gun entered the shop and cleared it of customers. Only when the shop was empty was Matt allowed to enter and buy his water. The first gun continued to sweep the street while he shopped. Matt found the whole experience surreal, like some video-game come alive.

Wandering through the fading oasis town, Matt got his first taste of rural subcontinent life. Tuk-tuks, three wheeled Vespa scooters, buzzed the streets. Passengers clung onto the bench seats behind the driver, who wrapped himself intimately around the handlebars. Farmers and traders used mostly donkey carts, but the richer few had camels. Cars were a rarity, as were women.

Once, a horse drawn gig trotted past and Matt caught a glimpse of beautiful, high-born Pakistani women as they peeped through the enclosing curtains. From the looks on their faces they obviously enjoyed the illicit pleasure of showing their normally veiled faces to a foreign man. The body-guards glowered at him, but carefully averted their own gaze from the buggy.

With his bodyguards no more than a pace away, Matt felt safe enough to wander into narrow streets and alleys he would otherwise have avoided if he were alone. With his watchful guards to keep him out of trouble, Matt relaxed enough to notice the subtleties of his surroundings, which fear in Karachi had blotted out.

The few women he saw on the street hid themselves behind all enveloping black chadors; the country was much more conservative than the image portrayed by the late Benazir Bhutto on TV, the only Pakistani woman he had ever really heard of. They all walked with bowed heads as they tried to look insignificant, not even daring to lift their hidden faces. The black robed figures looked inhuman, like a sub-species of the Stepford Wives.

Men dominated life, ruling the businesses, tea shops and the streets.

Matt was examining the bloody mess of a butcher's shop when his escorts started tugging at his sleeves. He resisted their attentions as the unhygienic display held him fascinated. Then he sensed their urgency and suddenly realised the street around them had emptied. Matt was not sure where everyone had gone, but his group of three was very much alone and conspicuous. The soldiers were nervous and pale. Then the noise of roaring engines echoed from a junction along the road. The soldiers pulled Matt against a wall and cocked their guns. Three heavy trucks churned into the junction, but they were blue not green and sported the logo 'Police' on their engine covers.

The soldiers held their guns ready as the lorries rumbled closer. Armed police stared fiercely from behind their own guns at the three men pressed back against the wall. The soldiers pointed their guns at the lorries till they disappeared back into a side road a hundred metres along the street. When the street was once again quiet, the soldiers un-cocked their guns and pulled out cigarettes. Matt looked from one nervous soldier to the other and took a cigarette too. His hands shook as he sucked on his first cigarette in years. He'd given up shortly after meeting Jo, as she hadn't liked it.

The fun gone from the walk, the soldiers seemed anxious to move quickly back to the hotel through narrow streets they had not used before. Though the route was unfamiliar, Matt could tell they were moving in the right general direction. The three men smoked their cigarettes as they walked, almost at marching speed, a group of comrades now, not a man and his unwanted guards.

In a cool shady street a pasty-faced man appeared abruptly from a low doorway in front of Matt. Five heavily armed men in baggy nylon suits quickly followed him out. The leader motioned Matt to enter the doorway.

Matt shook his head and looked to his bodyguards for instructions, but the the nylon suited men stepped forward and roughly disarmed and spread-eagled the white-faced bodyguards against a wall. A gun pressed harshly into Matt's elbow, so he ducked his head to enter the doorway with as much grace as he could muster.

A chicken and a tiny, dung-smelling courtyard awaited Matt inside the doorway. The gun pressed him quickly through another door to a narrow, low, dark corridor. Matt moved warily into the gloom. Pasty-face caught Matt's elbow and pointed through a grated opening to the left. Matt almost vomited. Five men cringed on the floor of a filthy, straw carpeted room. Manacles held them to the wall. Over his shoulder Matt heard Pasty-face chuckle and say, 'If you bad boy, you go in there too.'

Cold sweat chilled Matt as he entered a room three metres past the cage on the opposite side of the corridor. A fat, ugly man sat behind a desk to the rear of the twelve foot square room. Ranged around the gloomy corners of the office an entourage of faceless acolytes leered sycophantically. A fancy leather jacket, embossed with an American eagle, hung from a hook on a second door behind the fat man.

The multi-chinned fat man nodded at a lonely seat in front of his desk. Matt sat, with great reluctance, the space around him feeling bigger than it should have done. Every rattle of the five guns in the room echoed loudly round his head. His rising panic made logical thought impossible.

*****

'You want a cigarette?' A half empty packet and a lighter slid across the table. David reached for them greedily; he needed something in his blood stream, and he didn't care what.

As David lit his cigarette he heard a voice repeating the words he had heard so often on television. 'Anything you say will be recorded and may be used as evidence in a court of law.'

David sniffed his runny nose and rubbed the goosebumps on his arms. His stomach cramped and his joints twitched. David inhaled the nicotine deeply and tried to tell his story. The two customs men sat opposite him impassively. David sucked hard and repetitively on his cigarette. Disjointedly and ramblingly fast he began to recount what had happened to him over the past few weeks.

'I've been travelling in Pakistan. I was in Islamabad and there was all this dope there, it grew wild in the streets. Man, you wouldn't believe it.' His eyes grew vague at the memory. The two customs officials glanced at each other and rolled their eyes, they saw junkies like this all the time. 'I wanted to get away from the city and go to the mountains, everyone was going north up to China. I wanted to go somewhere different, somewhere real, not your usual backpacker hangout. There was this guy, he was Pakistani, but had grown up in England. He said his name was Ricky. He said he had a place in the mountains, up in the north, where they played polo like in the old days. He said he'd take me there. He had this great dope, it was really strong, came from Afghanistan so he said. We left Islamabad in his jeep and we smoked some dope. It must have had something else in it. I was so doped I don't really know where we ended up. We drove over a pass in the mountains, there was lots of snow, the road was really bad. I don't remember much else.'

The two customs officers were looking less impassive now, interest sparking in their eyes. 'Where was this pass?'

'I don't know. Honestly.' David tried so hard to sound convincing he knew he probably did not.

'Come on. You must know. You must have asked where he was taking you before you got in the jeep.' The customs officer smiled as if he thought David was joking.

'No. I was really spaced out from all the dope. It didn't seem to matter.' David couldn't hold their gaze and dropped his to the floor, sucking hard on his cigarette again.

'What happened next?'

'I think he must have drugged my first meal. I woke up in a room. He was slapping me around the face. When I woke up he stuck a needle in my arm and injected me with this dirty brown stuff. Then he laughed. He told me later it was heroin. I had all these wild dreams.' He stubbed out his cigarette compulsively, scratched the needle marks on his arm and reached for the cigarette packet again with trembling hands.

'Had you used heroin before?'

'No. Never.' David started to cry. He felt sick. He needed another shot. 'Can I have some stuff? I need it. Please.'

'Tell us the rest of your story first.'

David squirmed and rocked on his chair and thought about begging and promising like he did with Ricky, then decided it probably wouldn't work now. The man wanted to hear a story, not hear him promise to smuggle some drugs.

'He kept me there for ages. I don't know how long. He kept giving me more heroin. When he had me hooked he took me back to Islamabad and put me on a plane. He said the customs officers worked for him. He said he'd hurt my mother if I didn't deliver the stuff.' Chris nodded encouragingly at him, he looked genuinely interested. 'Where were you going to take the heroin?'

'Nowhere. Ricky said his cousin would find me. He said they knew where I lived and they would come get it.'

'So why did you hand yourself in?'

David rubbed at his face with the back of his hand, wiped his nose on his jacket sleeve. His left leg bounced up and down on his toes. 'I don't want to be a junkie. I don't want to die. I don't want to go to prison. Give me some stuff, please. I need it.'

'Five more minutes,' said Chris, soothingly. 'Was there anyone else at this house in the mountains? Did you see anyone?'

David shook his head. 'No. I only ever saw him.'

'Are you sure?'

'Yeah.' David twitched and jerked on his seat. His hands shook and Coke spilt as he tried to drink. He tried and failed to light yet another cigarette. The two officers sat and watched him quietly for a while, then the un-named colleague leant forward and lit the cigarette for him

'What did he look like? This Ricky,' Chris asked as he leant forward in his chair.

'Pakistani. I don't know. I can't remember. I don't want to remember. I was drugged most of the time. I can't remember,' said David, his voice rising hysterically.

'Think about it for a while. See if you can remember anything.'

The three men sat quietly, while David sucked heavily on his cigarette.

Halfway through the cigarette David sat up straight. 'There was this girl. I never saw her. I just heard her screaming and shouting. She had this English accent, southern I guess. I never saw her though.'

'She was English?' The two men glanced at each other, concern creasing their faces.

'Yes. Definitely.'

'Is she still there?' Chris leant forward and stared hard into David's eyes. He looked positively sick.

He shrugged. 'Probably. How the hell would I know?' Sweat was rolling down his face. His shirt was soaking wet. He shook uncontrollably. He didn't even know what day it was.

The door of the interview room opened suddenly and a third man entered. 'Excuse me, this interview must finish now. This young man must come with me.'

'Can you wait five minutes, doctor?' Chris stood, annoyance clear on his face, and tried to usher the doctor from the room.

'Please. Can I have something? I'm gonna die if you don't give me something soon.' David stood and shuffled towards his saviour.

Chris looked at David and snapped, 'Just wait a while. I'm sure my colleague can wait a few minutes?' Then he looked back at the doctor and appealed to him for more time.

David was crying again. 'I wish I'd never gone there. I wish I'd never talked to you guys. I could have got some stuff by now. That bastard's gonna kill me if he finds out what I've done.'

The third man stepped forward and took David firmly by the arm. 'I'm a doctor. Please come with me. I'm here to help you.' The doctor stared coldly at Chris. 'He's had enough from you, I should been called straight away. This man is clearly not fit to be questioned.'

Chris gave up his attempts to keep David longer with a dramatic shrug of his arms, then added, 'Before you go I have one last thing to say. Later today you will be formally arrested upon suspicion of smuggling a Class A drug.'

David's shoulders slumped and the doctor helped him from the room, a broken man.

Chapter Six

Having disappeared without explanation shortly after they had returned to the campsite the night before, Pierre reappeared the next morning and behaved as if he'd never been away.

As Annie drank fresh chai and ate chapati, delivered to her on the grass by the chowkidar, Pierre enthused about the pleasures of a picnic by the lake and the Faisal mosque and was all for taking her on another tour of the city tourist sights.

He made no mention of going to find the French Embassy in any of his plans, though. But Annie let it pass, excusing him in his excitement at showing her around and feeling flattered that he wanted to impress her so much.

As the other tourists sleeping outside on the grass and inside in the huts awoke, they joined Annie and Pierre and took their breakfast as they planned their days. Pierre seemed anxious to be away, but Annie was enjoying the companionship of the motley collection of international travellers and lingered over her chai.

'We're leaving for Gilgit today. Aiming to be in China by the end of the week now we've got our visas.'

Annie turned towards the smiling well-spoken English boy who looked too young to have been let out on his own. He was earnestly chatting to a beautiful Swedish girl who was not really listening to him, and was travelling with her girlfriend in any case, though by the way the lad was behaving it hadn't sunk in on him that he was never going to be her type.

'Did it take long to get the visa? I thought I'd be able to get it on the spot when I went to the Chinese Embassy,' interjected Annie, to the relief of the Swedish girl who instantly started talking to someone else.

The boy laughed with genuine amusement. 'You must be joking. You have to be there before 8am, when they open, and fight your way to the counter within an hour, when they close up again whether or not there's anyone still waiting. You'll need the exact money, two photos, a perfectly completed form and a lot of patience. Most people have to go to the embassy three days in a row to get their visa. Once to get the form. Once to submit the application. And a final visit to collect their stamped passport back again.' The teenager smiled at Annie, who laughed with pleasure at the boyish smile on the over-confident face of the public school boy sitting across from her.

Pierre snorted. 'Who wants to go to China anyway? It's an oppressive communist dictatorship.'

Annie was surprised at Pierre's sudden antipathy, then enjoyed the sensation of realising that the two boys both fancied her. She smiled at the English boy and chewed her thumb as she thought out loud. 'I was planning to cross the Khujerab Pass into China after travelling north from here. I'll need to find the Chinese Embassy and apply for my visa today then. I wasn't planning to stay here very long and I certainly don't want to come back to Islamabad again to do it later.'

The youth nodded in agreement. 'It's not far from here.' With someone more interested in what he had to say, the Swedish girl was forgotten. 'You go up to the main road and go right along. . .'

'I'll take you there. We better leave now if you want to get your form today.' Pierre spoke over the English lad, who faltered and looked away as Pierre glared at him.

'Thank you, both,' said Annie, smiling at both Pierre and her new admirer, who she felt slightly sorry for given Pierre's reaction. 'I don't know what I'd do without you guys to help me.'

'Come on. We'd better get going.' Pierre was already on his feet and obviously pleased to have found an excuse to leave.

True to his word, Pierre helped Annie with her visa application, helping to clear a path to the counter and keep the press of bodies back for her as she dealt with the less than enthusiastic embassy officials. She was pleased to have found a friend to help her with the bureaucracy, and benefit from the famous travellers' camaraderie the guidebooks talked about. They even managed to get the form filled in and submitted just before the counter closed again.

Following the early morning visit to the Chinese Embassy, Pierre showed Annie the few sites of the city, bought her meals and escorted her on a romantic picnic near the lake. Though he only nibbled at the food again. After some reminding, he even showed her the French Embassy.

His attentiveness was enjoyable, but Annie did wonder why he never seemed to be interested in doing more than accompanying her. Not once did he really get close enough to suggest he was interested in more than a platonic relationship. She was almost insulted he didn't make a pass at her. It would be nice to have an exotic, Urdu speaking, Frenchman interested I her.

On the evening of the second day though, he disappeared again when he knew she was planning to go to the French Embassy party. Almost all the campers were going, excited at the rare chance to drink some alcohol and eat some western food.

Elliot, the English lad, took his opportunity with Pierre's absence and kept close to Annie as the group of tourists hailed tuk-tuks and made their way to the French Embassy club.

Having exhibited passports to the Pakistani policeman at the gate and then handed them over to the French official inside, the scruffy group of travellers crowded round the bar at a safe distance from the better presented diplomats and businessmen already there. Elliot ordered Annie a glass of French red wine and was still in the process of handing it to her when Dominic appeared at her elbow and whisked her away from the increasingly frustrated lad.

'*Bonsoir mademoiselle*, may I present my wife Elise and my daughter, François?' He was polite, but not half so attentive as he had been on the plane.

About Annie's age and having just finished university in London, Françoise was staying with her parents for a holiday. The two girls hit it off immediately and spent the evening dancing and flirting with the few eligible expatriate men that dotted the party, some of whom they were sure had wives elsewhere. Annie was amused to see Dominic watching her and Françoise nervously as they laughed and gossiped together like old friends.

Diego, a young, aristocratic Spanish diplomat, monopolised the girls attention though. He paid for most of their drinks, at a price for each of them that would have covered one night's accommodation at Annie's campsite.

The party faded to its conclusion in the early hours of the morning and Diego invited Annie and Françoise to join him for a drive to Rawal Lake. Only as Annie looked around the room did she guiltily realise that Elliot had disappeared and she had not even noticed. Despite his attentions early in the evening she had forgotten all about him, enjoying herself with Diego and Françoise.

'Do you think we'll be safe?' whispered Annie to Françoise as they left the party.

'*Bien sûr*! Papa is an ambassador. If anything happens, Diego's ambassdor will make sure he'll be out of his job.'

Excited by the prospect of seeing the sun rise over an Asian lake, and high on a cocktail of flirting and fine wine, Annie grinned like a schoolgirl as she climbed into the shiny Japanese jeep.

The lake appeared among the trees at the end of a secluded dirt road just before dawn. They swam in their underwear as the sun rose over mountains and burned the water from black, through the colours of autumn, to the dull grey of the filmy smog that hung over the city.

Françoise and Diego dropped Annie back at the campsite after they'd eaten breakfast at the plush Marriott Hotel, where Diego had greeted what seemed like half the other guests as if they were old friends.

Tired from her long and exciting night, Annie dozed away the morning in the shade of a tree, dreaming flamenco, caballeros and exciting swims in fiery lakes.

The erotic Spanish fantasy merged into a French one, then stopped dead as Annie realised Pierre was trying to wake her. 'It is time to collect your Chinese visa. Then we can go to buy the plane tickets to Chitral.'

'Are you coming to the embassy with me?' asked Annie as she packed her bag.

'No, I have to go to the bank. I'll see you back here.'

Pierre waved and said, 'A bientôt,' as they parted at the campsite gate. Annie walked slowly to a rough parking lot where a line of jeeps waited for passengers. Each jeep served a specific part of Islamabad and some went as far as Rawalpindi, ten miles away; they left when a driver thought he had enough passengers to make the journey worthwhile.

Halfway to the jeeps a young, clean shaven Pakistani man stepped up to her. His eyes twinkled as he smiled reassuringly and asked, 'Hi. You speak English?'

'Yes.' His London accent surprised her.

'Thank God for that. Can I talk to you for a while? I find it so difficult talking Urdu all the time. I was brought up in England, but my Dad sent me back here to run his business. I hate the place, but I don't have a choice. Pakistani fathers are very strict.' He looked momentarily sad as his eyes dropped to the ground, then he smiled again as he looked back at Annie.

'Yeah, so I've heard.' Annie studied the young man suspiciously. She wasn't used to people approaching her in the street without reason.

'I find this place so confusing. It's an Islamic country, so there's no alcohol. But you can buy drugs off half the policemen and then the other half will arrest you for possessing them.' The young man looked genuinely nonplussed.

'I don't even smoke, so I've nothing to worry about.' Annie was torn between feeling sorry for the guy, and wanting to run away from a situation she found uncomfortable. He was as English as her, but said he was forced to live and work here against his will.

'You have to be careful though. The police sometimes use foreigners they've caught with drugs to inform on other foreigners. A month ago that French guy you were with supposedly planted some heroin on a young girl he'd met at the campsite, then shopped her to the police. He was caught smuggling a kilo of Hashish a few years ago at the airport and he's probably working for the police now to get a few years off his sentence. Plus they've also let him out to play while he does it, which is bound to be better than sitting in prison.'

'You're joking,' said Annie warily. It was hard to tell if he was serious, or part of some scam to get her trusting him.

'Nah. Everyone was talking about it and part of the story was in the paper,' responded the young man earnestly. 'You'd be as well to get out the city as soon as possible. The mountains are safer and the people are honourable Muslims, unless they're pagan Kafirs. I always like going up to the villages to find carpets and other stuff to export to England. That way I can make some money my father doesn't know about. He's really mean with money.'

'Yeah, I'm heading up that way. Chitral I think the place is called.' Though now she'd heard the story about Pierre allegedly being a jail-bird Frenchman she wasn't sure if she wanted to go with him any more. Even if the story wasn't true she wouldn't be as relaxed with Pierre now.

The young man helpfully checked she had the right jeep and waved goodbye as it pulled away, heading for the Chinese Embassy. She soon forgot the face of the young Pakistani, but not the story he had told her.

As the jeep passed the French Embassy, Annie decided to visit Dominic after collecting her Chinese visa, to check on the story she had just heard.

*****

'*Oui*, I am afraid to say it is true,' said Dominic, handing her a china cup fragrant with fresh ground coffee. It made a pleasant change to all the chai she'd been drinking recently. 'The man you have described sounds like the poor fool. He was caught a few years ago smuggling hashish. The police let him out to inform on other foreigners; for everyone he informs on he gets a few months off his sentence. Sometimes it seems he gets over zealous and sets people up. But after being inside a Pakistani jail for five years I'm sure we'd all be like that too.'

He rummaged through a filing cabinet for a moment, before triumphantly pulling out a photocopy from a file.

'Ah-ha! Here's a photo of him.'

'That's him,' said Annie as she stared at the photo. 'I'd better be more careful in future. I assumed that since he was French he had to be OK.'

Dominic nodded and sighed, spreading his hands out in a resigned gesture. 'Unfortunately, there are Frenchmen who are disreputable and wicked, just like people from other countries. Who told you about him?'

'I met a guy from London who works here exporting stuff to his father. If you spoke to him on the phone you would never guess he was Pakistani.'

*****

A twisted grin split Raseem's face as he watched Annie leave the French Embassy compound in a chauffeur driven diplomatic jeep. He had followed her to the Chinese Embassy, then on to the French one. As he'd expected, she had gone to check on Pierre with her friend at the embassy.

He let the jeep drive away for a moment then eased his own into gear and followed them along the road to the campsite. The diplomatic jeep waited with its engine running, so Raseem did the same. Ten minutes later the two jeeps were on the road to Rawalpindi.

*****

The bus from Rawalpindi, or 'Pindi, as Dominic referred to it, was labelled 'luxury', but Annie took an instant dislike to it. Dripping, icy air-conditioners made the seats wet and carried on their own version of Chinese water torture. The reclining seats had a habit of moving on their own accord. Non-stop Hindi-pop videos ran on the two TVs bolted to the roof, with the speaker system turned up so high all sound distorted to a screeching, indecipherable noise that quickly turned her irritable and bad-tempered.

Annie was still tired from her late night outing and tried to sleep, but the noise of the video and the smog of cigarettes made it impossible. The memory of the small sack of heroin she and Dominic had found in her backpack also made her nauseous.

Dominic had driven her to the campsite where they had retrieved her bag from the concrete hut she had rented. Insisting she should check it to make sure there was nothing planted in it, Dominic had made her empty the backpack and unroll every item so carefully folded. Inside her small toiletry bag she had found the bag of heroin. Dominic had taken it, assuring her his diplomatic immunity would protect him if the police turned up, and made her search through everything again, just to make sure it was the only bag.

Staring at the bag of heroin, sweat trickling down her back, Annie had decided that it would be best if she left Islamabad immediately and headed for the mountains. Not only had Pierre wasted a small fortune in smack, but his intended prey was about to escape, taking his chances of further parole with her. He was not going to be very happy.

Dominic didn't think that Pierre would follow her outside of Islamabad without permission, and he was unlikely to get that, given his past record. So Dominic had suggested it would be best if he drove Annie across the river to Rawalpindi, from where she could safely catch a bus to Peshawar.

Now, as the bus bounced along the rutted road Annie twisted and turned, raising and lowering her seat, but nothing could make the bus comfortable, or erase the terrifying memory of that bag of heroin in her toiletry bag. The one good thought she had was that the unknown British Pakistani had saved her from ending up in jail. She would thank him greatly if she ever had the chance. After all, she owed him her life, or her freedom at the very least.

After ninety minutes that would have made even the hardiest traveller ear-sore and saddle-sore, the bus weaved to an emergency stop. The passengers spilled out on the roadside and Annie smiled as she saw the blown tyre; a forced repair stop would allow her to regain her hearing, lose the pain in her bum and sip a long cool Coke from the nearby stall.

Sitting under a tree to try and enjoy an almost cold Coke in peace and quiet, Annie got neither. The local children circled her staring, pointing and whispering excitedly, their wide eyes betraying the novelty of a single, white, unveiled woman, sitting in their sun-baked, dusty village.

'Come here,' smiled Annie. She beckoned with her hand as she tried to get the children closer. She held up her guidebook and showed them the pictures, but the children kept their distance. When she brought out the camera a wave of screams rent the village as the children ran.

Half an hour of relief from the damp chill of the noisy bus was tempered by the drying heat of the village and the relentless flies. The noise wasn't much less either. Buses, lorries and cars roared past in clouds of dust, or stopped with horns blaring, touting for business or ordering drinks from the stall without wanting to leave the air-conditioned comfort of their vehicles. The wary kids grew in confidence too, until their non-stop attentions became wearisome.

It was a relief for Annie to finally climb back on the bus, where relative silence now reigned. The video had finished during the stop and no one had bothered to replace it with a

92

new one; though a few passengers snored gently in their seats, they hardly disturbed Annie.

As the bus travelled along the Grand Trunk road Annie was able to get her first glimpse of harsh, rural Pakistani life, that ran dry, dusty, run-down and apparently derelict alongside the road. Only scrub vegetation and a few wispy, leafless trees broke the monotony. A heavy, dusty heat haze cut the visibility to a few miles and obscured any view of the Himalayan foothills running parallel to the north. Despite its drabness, or even because of it, Annie was enthralled by the novelty of the strange, almost desert land she had never seen the like of before.

It was easy for Annie to imagine that the view had not changed much since her Grandad had travelled this way over eighty years before.

*****

In the air-conditioned comfort of his Cherokee jeep, Raseem kept close to the bus. He guessed Annie would not notice she was being followed. Why would she even expect to be? She had not recognised him earlier when he had spoken to her, which had pissed him off incredibly, but at least it made his plan easier to put into practice.

The wicked grin had hardly left his face for the last few hours, as he exulted in the luck that had placed her unexpectedly within his grasp after all these years.

*****

The speeding bus slowed again, but less frighteningly than before. A huge traffic jam blocked the road ahead. In the distance Annie could just make out the mangled wreckage of two buses, burst open and twisted from the trauma of their head on impact.

Impatient drivers soon began turning their cars to retrace their route and find an alternate way forward. The scale of the wreckage and lack of activity in clearing it also convinced the bus driver he was going nowhere soon too. Despite the narrowness of the road and the drainage ditches each side,

93

the driver began a complicated multi-point turn that forced all the returning traffic to wait in a traffic jam for the second time as they tried to reach Peshawar.

As the bus headed back towards 'Pindi in search of an alternative route, Annie was surprised to notice that a jeep, turning to retrace its route, waited for the bus to pull in front of it before joining the flow of traffic. Considering how everyone else was fighting to get ahead of the bus it had made her turn and look behind to see what the jeep was doing. Nothing, was the answer, so Annie promptly forgot it and returned to scanning the passing world outside her window.

The bus turned into a narrow, single-track dried mud lane, heavily rutted from use during the wet season. The detour was not going to be smooth going. It was definitely going to be longer and slower than a clear Grand Trunk Road too, but the scenic route immediately demonstrated advantages to thrill Annie.

The farms and villages Annie now saw were something she would never have seen if the Grand Trunk road had not been blocked. It was the Pakistani equivalent of turning off the M4 and driving through rural England.

Anticipating the coming monsoon, farmers guided huge water-buffalo dragging heavy wooden ploughs through the rock-hard earth, flicking their canes through the rising clouds of dust to keep the buffalo in line.

The track skirted the farms and ran in the lee of a high embankment for miles, then climbed to reveal a huge canal, where splashing, swimming, carousing children stopped their games to wave at the passing bus. Near the children, water-buffalo stood motionless in the flat water, only their heads and horns reflecting off the brassy surface.

Crossing the canal over a massive lock gate the bus rejoined the main road, disappointing Annie who'd had an unexpected but eye-opening view of rural Pakistan. The scenery and life bordering the Grand Trunk road was not half so interesting.

Unnoticed by Annie, the solitary jeep bumped after them back onto the tarmac.

The smoother tarmac lulled Annie to sleep and the suburbs of a dark-oppressed Peshawar had replaced the fields by the time she awoke. The weak streetlights hardly cast a glow on the ground, let alone upwards to the sky. The bus came alongside and followed the old walls of the glowering Bala Hisar fort, before abruptly stopping outside the main gate of the fort, all the passengers sighing with relief that their journey was at an end.

This was the India Annie remembered from her Grandad's stories, from the time before partition had made this part Pakistan.

As Annie stepped off the bus with eyes agog at the sights around her, a tuk-tuk instantly pulled up at her side. 'Where you go?'

'The Khyber Hotel,' replied Annie. Prepared and confident, as advised by Dominic.

'One hundred *rupee*. Special price for pretty lady.'

Annie tried to haggle, but the driver refused to budge on his price. So, once again following Dominic's crash survival course during the short ride to Pindi bus station, Annie walked five metres to the next tuk-tuk. 'Fifty *rupee*,' said the driver when Annie asked how much to go to the Khyber Hotel.

Point made and too tired to argue further, Annie hopped in the back. The journey took longer than Annie expected and she was just beginning to get nervous that she was going to be in trouble again when the tuk-tuk finally pulled up at the kerb. 'Khyber Hotel,' shouted the driver as he pointed down an alley to where a weak bulb barely lit a battered sign with the hotel name on it.

Annie smiled with relief and pride as she climbed the staircase to the hotel; she had travelled from city to city and found a hotel without any help. It might have been an unexpected and sudden trip, but she'd done it and was enjoying the sense of self satisfaction it gave her.

A yak-dung fire crackled and hissed in the darkness. The old herdsman poured chai into Ishmael's mug first, then filled his own with the steaming liquid. They both held the hot mugs tight and sipped slowly at the warming drink, as they stared at the fire in companionable silence. A small hemp bag lay open on the grass, the creamy yak cheese it held glistening in the firelight.

Mountain herders saw so few people they grew reticent and hardly spoke when they did have company. Ishmael waited patiently for the man to talk first.

The tea was almost cold before the man hawked phlegm into the fire. 'What brings you up here?'

Ishmael sipped his chai and answered carefully. 'I'm on patrol. Just routine.'

The herder made no acknowledgement to Ishmael's answer. Frost grew on the ground around them as the temperature dropped steadily. Ishmael waited.

'It's not your usual route. Something wrong?'

'No. Nothing wrong. Just checking the pass to make sure it's safe for foreign trekkers. They're not as used to the ground as you.'

A gentle nod this time signified the herdsman had heard. The man refilled the mugs with chai. 'Don't get many up here these days. They all go to watch the polo at Shandur.'

'It's good polo.'

'Not like the old days, though. When I was young we settled our differences with guns, not a game of polo.'

'I want my sons to live a long time, not die young because of some ancient feud that no one can remember the cause of. Do you have any sons to look after you in your old age?'

'Two. One lives in London working for some fancy bank, the other lives in Chapali, north of Mastuj. He guides tourists over the pass sometimes.' Ishmael could hear the pride in the old man's voice.

'They pay well, the foreigners?' he asked, pleased with the way the conversation was going.

'Yes. But there are so few. Only two trekking groups last year. Both small. The tourists stay on the main routes now. They've all heard about the ones who disappear.' The old man wrapped himself in his blanket and lay down to sleep. 'Is that who you've come to look for?' said the herder as he dropped off to sleep.

Ishmael watched the stars and thought of the parents whose children had disappeared far from their homes in his mountains. He prayed his children never suffered the same fate in someone else's mountains.

*****

Raseem sat unnoticed in his jeep a few metres behind the tuk-tuk. He tossed a few coins to an urchin who miraculously claimed to work the Hotel where she was staying, and ordered him to watch the girl. Raseem wanted to know how long she was staying in the hotel and what her plans were, and this dirty little boy was going to help him make sure she didn't escape him.

Then he drove a few metres down the street to a separate hotel, where he knew from a previous visit that he could get some extra special room service.

*****

A narrow twisting staircase led from the alley to the Khyber Hotel. The staircase let out on to a courtyard set with tables and chairs; doors around the walls of the courtyard led directly into bedrooms. On top of the courtyard rooms, balcony-fronted rooms sheltered under a canvas canopy spread from roof to roof.

A blast of air billowed out from the top floor room when the small boy sent to show her the way opened the door to her room. It was small and hot, but at least it had a relatively soft and clean bed. She'd enjoyed sleeping outside in Islamabad, but Annie was grateful she had this room to herself, with a real bed.

Half an hour later, showered and changed, Annie wandered back down to the courtyard and took the last available seat at a table full of girls her own age. They smiled a welcome and adjusted their seats as she sat, then carried on talking as if she'd been there all night. Some were eating and others sipping drinks; they were obviously a disparate table of individuals rather than a group.

Annie had eaten relatively lightly in Islamabad's heat, despite enjoying the food, but the evening air of Peshawar cooled quickly and she ravenously ate two spicy omelettes and drank the green tea called *kawa* that the waiter brought her unasked.

Annie enjoyed listening to everyone talking about their travels as she ate, though she kept quiet for fear of seeming too much the novice. Everyone else in the loose group of travellers seemed to have been travelling for years.

With the dinner dishes cleared away, the girls around Annie's table began discussing the destination for an outing the next day. One of the girls had arranged a visit to an Afghan refugee camp and was offering the others a chance to go too.

'Would you like to join us?' she said to Annie unexpectedly. 'We leave at eight, Michel's collecting us in his jeep.'

'I'm not sure, I haven't decided what I'm doing yet. I only arrived here an hour or so ago,' Annie responded, determined not to get caught again by her naïveté.

'Well, it's up to you. But if you do decide to come, you can meet us here at seven in the morning for a bite of breakfast first,' said one of the girls as they all rose to leave. 'Good night.'

Chapter Seven

A teenaged boy draped himself across one puffy shoulder as the fat man eyed Matt lasciviously across his desk.

Requests from the fat man's slack mouth subliminally entered Matt's mind. He responded automatically. Fear and tension slowed Matt's actions as he passed his passport and money-belt over the desk.

The decorative boy began to talk, in Urdu, as Matt's passport and belongings were pushed around the table by podgy fingers. The acolytes laughed a frightening, high-pitched screech of sadism as the boy tipped his head like a cheap, B-movie whore.

The boy switched to broken English. 'You like tea? We drink tea. We go to back. Have fun.' He rubbed his crotch suggestively. The men roared with laughter.

Matt shook his head. His voice had drowned with anxiety

'I keep your pen. Gift for me, your friend,' smiled the man behind the desk. Sweaty fingers placed the pen among a rack of others before Matt could reply.

Then the nameless man turned to business. 'You smoke hashish? Heroin? I sell you cheap price.'

Matt found his voice at that. 'No, thank you. Why am I here?' He tried to sound reasonable, but the words came out as a whine.

'You are here because I say so,' came the sharp response. 'Of course you want to buy drugs. Why else would a foreigner come somewhere like this?'

Matt shook his head again as he wondered if this was how young tourists became involved in the drug trade and one hundred and fifty foreigners went missing.

The teenage boy leant forward and smiled his most alluring smile. His blood red mouth held scarlet needle-like teeth, slowly chewing betel. A foul stench of bad breath carried the boys words and the smile twisted into an order-question. 'You. Me. Fuckee fuckee. I like white men.'

Cackles filled the room from the men surrounding him.

Offended horror replied for Matt. 'No! No way!'

'Why not?' The boy looked angry and hurt. The acolytes lost their smiles.

Matt felt his already weak position growing more tenuous by the second. His disgust and fear overtook caution. 'Because you're ugly,' he snapped.

Deathly silence chilled the room. Everybody tensed for an explosion of anger. Then the fat man bellowed with laughter as he pushed the boy away and the acolytes quickly joined in the cruel laughter now aimed at the teenager. Slinging a look of pure hate at Matt, the boy slunk sulkily out the room.

The grinning fat man handed back Matt's passport and money-belt, but not the pen. A Parker pen seemed a small price to pay for the freedom Matt hoped would follow soon.

'Goodbye. Enjoy Pakistan.' The fat man dismissed Matt with a wave of his podgy hand. Matt needed no second bidding and headed for the door.

The prison cell horrors reached out to Matt as he scurried along the corridor to freedom in the welcome sunlight of the courtyard. Footsteps followed Matt into the sun and his waiting bodyguards gratefully received back their guns as rough hands pushed all three of them back out into the narrow alley.

With shaking hands Matt eagerly grasped an offered cigarette from an equally relieved looking bodyguard, and gratefully sucked in the harsh Pakistani tobacco.

'Hotel,' said the bodyguards in unison. Matt nodded his head in ready agreement and the group headed hurriedly to relative safety. All Matt wanted to do was lock himself in his room and hide behind the imaginary safety of the flimsy door for a while, but other plans had already been made.

The hotel receptionist ordered Matt to a seat in the lobby. Tea arrived almost immediately. The patriarchal official arrived soon after.

Matt and the patriarch sat opposite each other, exchanging pleasantries over their tea as they partook in a polite English conversation about Sukkur and the weather. Despite the relaxed nature of the conversation Matt felt there was an undercurrent of tension in the room and he waited pensively for the next disaster to arrive.

Slowly the patriarch drew the conversation round to its point. 'Sukkur is not too pleasant at this time of the year is it? Too hot.'

'I don't know. I was enjoying myself this morning and this is Pakistan. The weather is as you'd expect.'

The man nodded in agreement. 'It is not the weather I was really meaning. You had some excitement this morning.'

Matt looked across at his bodyguards who were staring glumly at the floor.

'No. They did not tell me. You were followed and we knew exactly where you were at all times. Those two *bay-wagoof* should never have taken you down that alley.' The patriarch waved a dismissive hand at the guards and launched into a stream of Urdu directed at them, which Matt could not understand but could guess was not complimentary. Then he reverted to English. 'You were lucky to get away so soon. They like to play with their guests in that place.'

Matt shuddered at the memory of the leering boy propositioning him.

'You must leave,' said the patriarch bluntly, looking Matt in the eye, and putting his tea glass down firmly on the table for added emphasis. 'You are attracting too much attention here.'

'So soon?' Matt protested. 'I've only just arrived.'

Holding up his hand in a conciliatory manner the patriarch said, 'We have heard rumours that you are to be arrested, as a drug smuggler.' The man smiled apologetically as if he were reporting that it might rain in the afternoon. Matt stared at him in horror.

'Who were those men? Police?' demanded Matt.

'No,' smiled the man. 'They are smugglers and any foreigner they speak to is arrested.'

'Oh. In that case, when do I leave?' Matt asked, gracefully conceding defeat.

'The train to Lahore leaves in one hour. You leave here in twenty minutes.'

Matt went to pack. He did not even take time for a shower. Anyway, he would have felt too exposed taking all his clothes off for a shower with the threat of arrest hanging in the air.

*****

Matt was back outside the hotel in just ten minutes with his two soldiers unsuccessfully trying to hail a tuk-tuk. The tuk-tuk drivers expertly avoided looking their way, almost as if there was an unwritten rule about not picking up soldiers.

Finally one soldier lost his temper. Pointing his gun at the head of the next driver he shouted abuse at the top of his voice. The tuk-tuk stopped.

Three passengers, plus luggage, was more than the tuk-tuk could really manage on the five kilometre trip back over the Indus to Rohri train station. The guards had their orders though and insisted on accompanying Matt to the station. The two gun-toting soldiers rode shotgun, Matt sat on his rucksack and the driver wrapped himself closely around the handlebars. Matt almost found the ride fun, though the thought of being arrested killed any real enjoyment.

At the ticket-office both Matt and the soldiers argued and shouted, but the only forthcoming ticket was labelled, 'Third class, No seat.' Matt asked for a later train, but the soldiers refused that option point blank.

The ticket clerk translated their forceful statement. 'You must go now. On this train. That is their orders.'

The bodyguards' open friendliness had disappeared soon after crossing the bridge. They were increasingly uncomfortable and once they were on the platform they kept their distance from Matt as well, sitting twenty metres away along the bustling platform, though they never stopped watching him and scanning the milling crowds of people.

The young men were soldiers again, holding their guns at the ready with their fingers on the trigger guards. Six more soldiers, with bigger guns and bandoleers, watched from another platform. Expectant tension hung over the busy station, subduing the noise such a large crowd should have made.

Matt was glad to see the train haul slowly into view, even though it overflowed with humanity. Along the platform the policemen waved their guns at him, in obvious insistence he board the train as soon as it stopped.

People spilled from the train under pressure from the masses inside. As the flow ebbed Matt climbed a ladder from the low-level platform to the carriage door. He squeezed inside the press of people, the heavy door slammed into his rucksack, knocking him forward into the crush of passengers, who bounced him back into the sealed door.

Amused at the presence of a foreigner squashed in with them, Matt's 'Third Class, No Seat' travelling companions cheerily shuffled around to generate extra space for him. Soon there was enough room for Matt to sit wedged on his rucksack and lean against the carriage wall. He could barely move more than his head and shoulders, but at least he could take the weight off his feet.

Twisting out the window for a last farewell to his bodyguards, Matt saw them running across the tracks to rejoin their agitated colleagues. The main group of soldiers was shouting and pointing towards the main road.

Gun-toting policemen spewed from three dust-shrouded lorries at the station entrance. Landing on the run they charged the station. Matt's stomach clenched violently. Acid burned his throat.

The train jerked violently. Then stopped.

The platform cleared of passengers as if a giant broom were sweeping the dusty concrete. Eerie silence replaced the previous hubbub. Guns clattered as the soldiers dropped to their knees. The first row of policemen stopped as they saw the kneeling soldiers behind the gates.

A second wave of blue pushed the first rank of startled men further towards the waiting soldiers. Rifle bolts snapped home. The soldiers settled over their gun-sights.

Silence. Seconds passed as two sets of uniforms eyed each other.

Slowly, gently, as if it were trying to sneak away unnoticed, the train inched forward.

A blue arm waved a pistol, but quickly dropped as an army rifle swung towards it.

Gaining speed the train eased round a bend and the guns disappeared.

The passengers recovered their composure remarkably quickly. Volubly and generously, Matt's new travelling companions welcomed him to their cramped accommodation with mango juice and chapati. Sunflower seeds and betel nuts cracked a staccato around him as the Urdu conversation effortlessly included Matt, though he could not understand a single word they said to him.

An hour into the six hour trip, a voice forced its way through the hubbub and woke Matt from a doze. 'Why are you here? Esteemed visitors should not have to stand.'

'I only have a 'Third Class, No Seat' ticket,' Matt replied sleepily as he blearily focused on the man who had woken him.

The ticket collector examined the rough cardboard voucher, then squeezed silently away through the crush. Matt never expected to see him again, but twenty minutes later the man returned, spouting repeated and gratuitous apologies. 'Sorry, no seat in First Class. Whole train full.'

'No problem,' shrugged Matt.

'Big problem. Esteemed guest of Pakistan must have seat.'

Shoving his way through the press of people, the collector imperiously waved Matt to follow. Inside the nearest third class compartment the collector began shouting and waving his arms at a row of passengers who dutifully shuffled along the bench seat.

Miraculously, a person sized space appeared and Matt floated over the litter of luggage and bodies, on a cushion of helping hands, to a real, if uncomfortable, wooden seat. A few moments later his rucksack landed on a nearby neighbour, who promptly pulled up his knees and filled the vacated space with the bag.

To complete Matt's embarrassment the coiled up neighbour produced a bag of biscuits from inside his jacket and offered them to Matt.

As the train travelled slowly north, Matt's mistrust of the Pakistanis slipped further away. His fellow passengers seemed genuinely interested in him. They exchanged names, he explained where he was from and they reeled off a list of their home villages, that he had never heard of and was as unlikely to ever see as they were to see his home. One man spoke limited English and translated for everyone else; he had been a school teacher and was proud of his language skills.

Matt ate well too, as everyone wanted him to sample their home cooked picnic food. An endless variety of vegetable and meat samosas appeared, as did pakoras, mini kebabs and spiced chapatis.

Within three hours he was laughing and chatting as if he was one of the family. After four hours a baby sat on his knee.

But as the passengers grew tired and quieter on their long journey, Matt's happiness began to slip away with the daylight as the train approached Lahore. He'd been happy on this journey through Sindh and didn't want to lose the feeling,

The conversations around him ceased altogether as the passengers prepared to disembark in their family groups. Matt suddenly felt lonely; the absence of Jo hit him hard. If only he hadn't let her go on her own, he thought, remembering the fateful day Jo had gone out on her own to book the tickets for their joint trip to Pakistan. He should never have come here. This was her place, not his.

Once the train stopped in Lahore Matt's rucksack went out the window with a little boy who promptly sat on it, raising one final moment of hilarity with his new found friends as Matt drifted along the train aisle with the cloying scrum of passengers, that eventually spat him out a doorway near the grinning boy and his bag.

Alone again on the concourse of the grand colonial station, having waved his friends goodbye, Matt looked at his map again and reckoned he could walk to the Salvation Army hostel. The air was hot and dirty, but the thought of cool trees and a green garden at the end of the walk spurred him along the cracked concrete pavement his guidebook said he should follow.

After forty minutes of walking Matt's water-bottle was empty, his twenty kilo rucksack was chaffing his shoulders, his legs burned from fatigue and his head was swimming from the heat. He was also lost and admitting to himself he really needed a ride.

The highway reeled under him as he searched for a tuk-tuk, a rickshaw, or even a taxi.

Taxi after taxi sped past him, none stopping when he hailed them. Then, as another empty taxi sped past, a car stopped at his side. The passenger window slid down with electric smoothness and cool conditioned air stroked Matt's face.

'You want a lift?'

With grateful carelessness Matt slipped his bag from his back and sank into the car's cool interior, never even considering the consequences of entering a stranger's car. He hardly even glanced at the driver, let alone registered what he looked like. The cool seat soothed him as he clasped his rucksack between his knees.

'I like to trek in the Himalayas. I saw your rucksack. I hate walking in the city, I'm sure you hate it too.' The driver talked volubly to his sweat-soaked passenger.

All Matt could do was nod and grunt in return. He was wondering when he should tell the driver where he was going, not that he was worrying too much about it. All sense of responsibility for his own welfare had melted in the heat and now the orgasmic pleasure of the cool air kept all concerns at bay.

As the car slowed in heavy traffic Matt listened to the voice beside him. 'You are going to the Salvation Army, right? You should have taken a taxi. It's miles from the station.'

Matt clawed his way back to reality. 'How did you know where I was going?' Belated concern about his safety hit him. 'How did you know I arrived by train?'

'The Salvation Army is famous. All foreigners stay there if they can. And the only way to arrive in Lahore is by train or bus, and they arrive at the same place.' The driver smiled reassuringly.

Matt relaxed again. The driver fell silent, concentrating on driving. Minutes passed as the car moved slowly forward in the evening rush hour. Suddenly the traffic cleared and the car surged forward.

'Look over there,' said the driver loudly as the car picked up speed. Matt's head swung to the right, but as it did so he saw a huge sign proclaiming 'SALVATION ARMY CLINIC' in big bold capitals to his left. Matt spun his head back in time to see a smaller sign tied to the fence, 'Salvation Army Hostel.'

'I think you missed my stop,' said Matt.

The car kept moving and the driver relapsed into silence.

'Please stop,' said Matt more forcefully.

The car picked up speed on the cleared road. 'Stop! Where are you taking me?' Matt was frightened now.

Two hundred metres past the hostel the car slowed so it would not have to stop at the approaching traffic lights. 'I know a much better place for you to stay,' said the driver suddenly. 'My brother has a hotel, it's not far from here.'

'No. I want to stay at the Salvation Army.'

'It will be closed at this time of night. And anyway, it's always full.'

The traffic lights stayed on red, forcing the car to stop. Matt wrenched open the door and fell into the road. 'Where are you going?' wailed the driver through the open door as Matt scrambled away through the noisy traffic.

*****

Chris read through his notes one more time as the steward cleared away his dinner tray. Debriefing David had been tough; the guy had been so strung out it was hard to tell what was fact and what was fantasy. He would have liked to have spent more time interviewing the guy, but the doctors always pushed to sedate people like him as soon as possible. They claimed it was immoral and dangerous to make people suffer withdrawal. Despite the frustration of not having as much time as he wanted to interview people, Chris could see the logic, especially for someone like David who was probably the victim and not on heroin by choice.

But the girl worried Chris. He had a teenaged daughter planning a gap year in India and his worst nightmare revolved around her getting caught up with the sort of people he tried to put in jail. He would have liked to press David for more details, but the doctors had said he would not be fit for another interview for at least another two days.

He liked travelling and was fed up spending so much time in the office, so it hadn't taken Chris long to convince himself his best plan of action to solve this case was to go to Pakistan and try to find the girl himself. He'd left someone else to extract more information from David, if possible. If they got anything useful they would email him.

David seemed to have forgotten much of what had happened since Ricky had befriended him in Islamabad and supplied him with the finest Afghani black hashish he had ever smoked. 'Short-term memory loss and paranoia are the main symptoms of too much hashish,' went the standard drugs lecture Chris delivered occasionally to schools and colleges. If only the students could see David now, they would never smoke the stuff.

As senior special investigator with the Customs Service Chris had an open brief to act as he saw fit. He liaised with undercover agencies around the world in the losing battle against international crime. His anti-drugs contact in Pakistan was so secret only three people in London were supposed to know who he was. Not even the First Secretary, Cultural, in Karachi, who would meet him off the plane and was the British Government's sole anti-drugs agent in the country that exported hundreds of tonnes of heroin a year, knew about the contact. The overworked young officer spent more time interviewing and helping young Britons arrested for possession and smuggling than he ever did investigating the major drug syndicates.

Soon, though, the young diplomat would be earning his money. Chris thought about reading his notes again, but tiredness won out and he dozed lightly as the plane flew over Turkey and approached Iran.

*****

Twenty minutes after exiting the car in dramatic style, a chastened Matt waited patiently as the Sally Army clerk checked him in. He desperately needed a cigarette and his hands were shaking again. His hip was sore and he wondered how big the bruise would be from when he hit the road.

In the cooling night air of the hostel's garden, a lively crowd of foreigners lounged on the grass, variously recovering from strenuous sightseeing trips, the fatiguing daytime heat or the general rigours of travelling the subcontinent. The whiff of dope also explained some of the more relaxed attitudes of those on the grass.

Finally checked in and with his bag dumped on an empty bunk in the dormitory, Matt lay flat on his back amongst the other travellers as he sucked greedily on a cadged cigarette, ignoring the nausea and enjoying the buzz of the strong Pakistani tobacco.

Happy though he was to be back in the company of Britons and Australians, Matt found it difficult to talk to most of them. Listening to the boasting arrogance of the voices around him, Matt wondered why they were in the region at all. When they weren't trying to impress each other the conversation mostly revolved around the ignorance of the locals and the best places to get cheap drugs, which offered a likely reason as to why they were really there.

Matt found himself comparing his last few days with real Pakistanis to the stories he was hearing from the foreigners around him. He felt a smug satisfaction that he was seeing the real Pakistan, not some faux hippie-tinged version of the guidebook trail.

After two cigarettes and some chai Matt felt better and more benevolent to the people around him. When Scott, the archetypal, darkly tanned, blonde Australian he had got the cigarettes from offered to show him where to buy some of his own, he gratefully accepted the offer.

As they walked along the pavement Scott chatted amiably. 'Bloody awful bunch of people. Ought to be sent back where they came from. Bet they never even realise the locals hate 'em most of the time.'

'Couldn't agree more,' said Matt. 'They're just following the hippy trail. I've come up from Karachi, via Sukkur, saw a very different Pakistan that most of them will never see. The locals are really friendly if you treat them properly.'

Scott switched to Urdu when they entered the shop and chatted away to the shopkeeper as if he were a local.

'Where did you learn to speak the lingo so well?' asked Matt, somewhat embarrassed at his earlier disparaging thoughts about his fellow travellers.

'At uni. Did Asian studies and concentrated on India. Hindi and Urdu are almost the same. Love the place myself, it's a bit screwed up, but so's most places I've ever been.'

'What do you mean, screwed up?' Matt was not sure if the Australian use of the word was the same as his own understanding of it.

'Too many foreigners interfering and too much TV. They get told what to do by the West, while thinking Americans all live like Dallas and all foreigners smoke dope like the assholes in the hostel. Not surprising really if your only view of a country is through the TV.'

Back out on the street Matt almost brought up his experience in the car, but he knew he had been stupid and did not want Scott to think he was too naïve. He asked a roundabout question instead. 'Are there many kidnappings in Pakistan?'

'Not so much kidnappings as disappearances. Mostly dumb stupid people smoking too many drugs and not having the cash to pay the bills. They get hauled off by the dealers and robbed. If they don't have anything worth robbing they sometimes reappear at the airport with a kilo of H strapped to their stomach.'

'How do people get caught up in things like that?'

'Well, there's a Frenchman in Islamabad who got caught at the airport a few years ago with hashish, he befriends people, plants drugs in their bag, then shops them to the police for a reduction in his sentence. The police pretend to catch them at the airport as a result of good detective work and the whole world reports with outrage that another innocent young backpacker is being set up for drug smuggling. Which of course they are, actually.'

'Wow,' gasped Matt. 'So you don't actually need to do drugs to get into trouble?'

'No,' laughed Scott as he stopped to buy two cokes from a vendor. 'Just naïve, or gullible. There's another guy who appears in Islamabad now and again too, he's British-Pakistani and real charming, so people trust him. He sometimes sells dope at the campsite and offers to take people to his village in the mountains. He's always after the women though. I've never seen a guy so desperate to get laid. He must make his money from dope, and I reckon he tries to find mules at the campsite to take his stuff to England. He certainly dresses too well and drives too fancy a jeep to be doing anything legal.'

'How's he get away with it?' Matt was beginning to realise he was far more naïve than he imagined. His mother might have been right when she said he had a lot to learn about the world, he thought wryly. He offered Scott a cigarette and took one himself too.

'He's small time. Nobody's going to worry about him when there's people shipping it out by the tonne. If they catch some foreigner at the airport with a kilo of hash in their luggage they make a big fuss, but one Pakistani guy in Islamabad with a single kilo and nobody's interested.'

'So if I don't do drugs and I'm not a pretty chick, I'll be all right?' said Matt, surprising himself by trying to sound cool.

Scott laughed loudly, 'Yeah, probably. Where you headed anyways?'

'North. Chitral, then China. Probably.'

'Just got back from Afghanistan myself. Great place, if you can avoid being killed. I was up in Nuristan.'

'I thought it was closed to foreigners. There's always fighting there, isn't there?'

'They're always fighting someone, either each other or anyone daft enough to invade the country. But it's mostly quiet at the moment mate, especially up north. If you're up in Chitral you should go over the pass into Afghanistan while it stays quiet, it's fucking beautiful.'

'Is it safe?' asked Matt.

'Course it is. Just be careful. I had no problems. You're more likely to have problems in the North West Frontier Province, and that's in Pakistan. That's one place they say people do go to and never come back out of again.'

'How did you get in to Afghanistan then? Don't you have to go through the North West Frontier Province to get there?'

'Yes, but some parts are much less safe than others. You can go over to Afghanistan from Peshawar, via the Khyber Pass, sticking to the safe main roads, and then travel north from Kabul, but I went over a pass from Chitral. It's the southern parts of the North West Frontier Province that are really unsafe. Chitral is up north and mostly safe enough. There's a few routes you can use up there, though it's a hard walk at high altitude that way.'

Chapter Eight

None of the girls Annie had talked to the night before were at the tables of the Khyber Hotel. She'd stayed in her room until after eight, to make sure she'd miss the trip to the refugee camp. It was easier than making excuses early in the morning. She'd had enough, for a while, of hooking up with people she didn't know.

It was still early and she had a choice of empty tables to choose from, while the chai-wallah prepared the tea and two omelettes she ordered for breakfast. The same small boy who'd shown her to the room the night before delivered the food, which was identical to what had been presented to her then too, and as she looked around it was clear this was the only dish the chef prepared.

At the tables around her travellers compared notes about their plans and gossiped about departed friends and the strange travellers who had passed through the hotel recently.

'Most people have gone north to Gilgit and Hunza. It's cooler up there,' said one.

'Yeah, I think the best way is through the Swat valley, it's supposed to be beautiful.'

'It's quicker going straight up the Karakoram Highway from Pindi, and it's been a bit dodgy in Swat for the past few years. That's where the girl who wanted to go to school got shot in the head.'

'It was, but it's calmed down a lot recently, ever since the Pakistani army sent more troops in.'

'That's enough to make me want to go there, people like that need support,' said one girl.

'You hear about the two guys going to Afghanistan? Bet we never see them again.'

Annie listened to the hubbub of overlapping conversations around her, wondering where to go next and whether or not it was wise to go north to Chitral on her own.

Two gorgeous blonde guys walked into the courtyard and, after glancing around, sat at the table with her. 'You here alone?' said one.

'Yeah,' said Annie warily, almost overawed by their stunning good looks. She wondered if she was ever going to trust people again, whilst pondering how there were so many good-looking guys in this country.

'Mind if we join you?' said the second belatedly in a lightly accented voice Annie couldn't quite place. 'I'm Stig, that's Nils,' he added easily.

'I'm Annie,' she responded non-committally.

'This is an unusual place for a single girl,' Stig continued without waiting for a reply, 'Where you heading?'

'I don't know. I haven't decided yet,' said Annie, cautiously hedging her options until she knew them better.

'You were in Islamabad yesterday, weren't you? Hanging around with Pierre. He was livid when he found out you were gone. You're better off away from him, never seen anyone smoke so much heroin and keep walking,' said Nils with a big grin.

'I heard some stories about him, that's why I left,' said Annie, warily. 'Were you staying at the campsite? I don't remember seeing you.'

'Yeah, we were. We were camping under the trees off by ourselves. We like a bit of privacy.'

The guys talked animatedly, passing small talk and anecdotes that made Annie laugh.

She resolved, though, that she was definitely going to have to be more careful in future; she had never even considered that Pierre was doing drugs, she'd just thought he was thin. She wondered how she could have been so unsuspecting.

Stig and Nils looked all right, though. They were an obvious couple and not at all interested in her as Elliot had been. It was kind of nice not to have any of that boy-girl thing floating around. Nor any of that girl-girl competition thing she often found when she hung out with girls and there were guys around. These two were non-smokers, clean, neat and funny, which helped as well.

As they talked about what they'd done so far in Pakistan, Annie pondered what she would do next. She'd left Islamabad in a hurry and not really made plans for Peshawar. 'What've you guys got planned?' she asked with the vague notion of getting some ideas.

'We're going to Darra today and Landi Kotal tomorrow.'

'What's there?' Annie had never heard of either.

'You've not been reading your *Lonely Planet* have you?' said Stig in mock school teacher tones. Nils laughed good humouredly and Annie joined in, the ice now well and truly broken.

'They're in the middle of the tribal area. One's a gun factory and Landi Kotal is at the top of the Khyber Pass, looking down onto Afghanistan.' Stig tried to keep his stern tone in place but ended up grinning himself as Annie and Nils laughed out loud.

'Can I come?' asked Annie, forgetting her earlier resolve not to attach herself to anyone else as easily as she'd done in Islamabad.

'Yeah. No problem. We'll be off as soon as we've eaten one of these famous all-day breakfasts,' said Stig as he made an elaborate pantomime with his hands to order breakfast from the small boy now sweeping the floor around them.

*****

Sitting in the dark shadow of a teashop, Raseem watched Annie leave the Khyber Hotel. She wasn't carrying her rucksack so he reckoned she probably wasn't going on anything more than a day-trip today. Just like her though to pick up two guys. Raseem fantasised about storming across

116

the road and shooting them in the head as he pulled hard on one of the cigarettes he'd started smoking again. Business was out of the question; even Isabelle locked in her room with her limited supplies back in the village was forgotten. Annie consumed him.

*****

First Secretary Ian Davies sat on the wrong side of his desk in Karachi. Chris Sinclair sat behind it and listened to the junior officer.

'Most of the backpackers travel up the Karakoram Highway from Islamabad to China. There's a town called Gilgit way up north where they all stay. From Gilgit, one road goes north to the Khunjerab Pass and China. Another road goes up to the Shandur Pass, where they play a polo tournament once a year. It's the highest polo tournament in the world. I want to go there before I leave here. I'd fly to Gilgit though; eighteen hours on a bus from Islamabad sounds no fun to me.'

'David talked about crossing a high pass with lots of snow. He talked about polo too. Never knew they played it out here. Did they learn it from the British Army?'

'No. They taught it to our guys. It's a Persian game originally.'

'So you reckon David was up in the mountains near Gilgit?'

'Probably. That's where most of the foreigners go. It'd be easy pickings for someone handing out free dope to travellers with no money.'

Chris sat and stared at a painting of a wooden hut high in Alpine mountains that hung on the opposite wall. He came to a decision, and pushed himself up from the chair. 'Right. I'm off. I'll be back in an hour. Book me a flight to Gilgit,' he said, his mind already moving on to other things.

Ian leapt to his feet, too. 'It'll be two flights. You'll have to change in Islamabad and probably stay overnight. There's not that many flights to Gilgit and they're popular.'

'You better come as far as Islamabad too. I might well need you there while I'm up north.'

Chris left the Office of the Deputy High Commission and took a taxi across the city through the mayhem of traffic that strangled this burgeoning port of eleven million people. Leaving the taxi a hundred metres from the building he was heading for, Chris walked the long way round to make sure he was not being followed. Chris hated the clandestine stuff, it made him feel like some Cold War spy, but over the years more than one of his overseas agents had got themselves killed by drug barons from being careless.

When he had been to Pakistan before, he had always been in Karachi trying to trace a major shipment that had been found on a cargo plane, or in a container at Dover. The world of backpackers in Pakistan had never entered his thinking: he was surprised any came here. Pakistan had never struck him as the sort of place people went travelling in search of some fun while they were young. He'd always presumed they went to smoke dope in Goa, trek in Nepal, or lie on a beach in Thailand.

Paint peeled off the concrete walls of the run down office block housing the Pakistani anti-narcotics bureau he was on his way to visit.

Two floors up a painted glass door he knew was bullet proof bore the label 'Punjabi Trading'. Chris pressed the buzzer. A voice came back at him in Urdu and Chris gave the pre-set codename he had checked and memorised before leaving London. The door lock clicked and he stepped into the room.

Behind the door three plain-clothes Pakistani customs officers sat shuffling paper like clerks in any office, but these were struggling to make sense of all the various leads and information on international drug-smuggling that came their way. An armed guard stood with his gun at the ready behind the CCTV screen he had just been watching Chris on.

The men looked at him expectantly without saying a word. Though he had met at least one of them before they waited tensely for him speak, surprised at his sudden and unannounced appearance.

'I want to see the boss.' Chris knew no names in this office. They were never used. Conversations only took place face to face and non-urgent information went through the High Commission. Occasionally they used a secure email system, but only when there was technical information to share.

'Come in,' called a voice through the open door of an inner office.

Chris recognised the man he had met four times in the past three years. They usually swapped information and then left the other to do business on their own turf, but this time Chris wanted to change the rules. All the information Chris had received from this man had proven perfect, unusual in this game. Much against his better judgement, Chris trusted him. He rarely believed much anyone told him these days, a disconcerting side effect of the job. However, there was something in the man's demeanour that just about demanded trust.

'Good to see you again.' The tall elegant Pakistani gentleman smiled a welcome and leant over to shake Chris's hand, then switched from his perfect cultured English to Urdu when he bellowed for chai.

Without any more preamble he turned to business. 'What brings you here? It must be important.'

'It is. I have information that leads me to believe that a British Pakistani is holding a British citizen, a young woman, prisoner here. I want your help in finding her.'

'Of course, of course. Where is she? What do you want us to do?'

Chris ran through the story as best he could, based on David's ramblings and the input of Ian, stopping only when the chai-wallah arrived.

'Sounds a good lead, but there's a lot of ground in the North West and Azad Kashmir. It'll take us a while to get people on the ground and a lot of luck to find her.' He refilled the two tea-glasses and waited for Chris to be more specific on the help he was seeking.

But Chris just announced his plans. 'I know, that's why I'm off to Gilgit as soon as I can get a flight. I'll ask around the backpackers up there to see if any have run across this Ricky guy. I'll pretend I'm a relative of hers, or something. I think I'll be more likely to get some decent information quickly than if your guys start asking questions.'

'But since you do not know her name, that will be difficult,' pointed out his contact.

'I'll think of something. But I don't know what else I can do,' responded Chris with some embarrassment.

The two men held each others gaze across the desk. Chris knew that he could be turfed out of the country for what he was proposing, but hoped his counterpart would have some empathy for the situation. Maybe he had a daughter of his own.

'Officially, you'll be on your own. Off the record, we're already looking into these stories and our men will now be put on higher alert. We know that foreigners have disappeared in the region, but our information is rather vague. Maybe we can solve the problem with this new info.'

'Thank you. You are generous with your support as always.'

The two men rose and shook hands. As Chris turned to leave the Pakistani man said, 'I have a daughter, too.'

*****

No one had bothered changing the warning labels inside the rickety old German bus left over from the days of the hippy trail across central Asia to India. Now it was a service bus heading for Kohat, but it would pass through Darra on the way. A little after ten o'clock it rattled out of the Peshawar suburbs with Annie and her two new travelling companions. By quarter past, the bus, twisting and turning on all three of its axes, was winding through the foothills of a western spur of the Himalayas. A billow of dust marked their progress.

The local commuters did not seem overly concerned, or surprised, that three foreigners sat amongst them. Annie noticed there was an almost studied indifference to the presence of foreigners in their midst, a marked difference to the reaction she had experienced in the village where the bus had stopped on the journey from Pindi.

It was not long before the bus slowed at a checkpoint. Police stood around, with guns slung over their shoulders. Annie held her breath to see what they would do. A scruffy policeman climbed to the first step, had a quick and cursory look into the bus, then flopped back to the shade of his canvas tarpaulin outside the concrete building beside the checkpoint.

At subsequent checkpoints, Annie and her two companions ignored the policemen who climbed on the bottom step; instead they watched the lazing policemen reclining at the roadside. None of the inspecting policemen gave any indication they noticed the foreigners on the bus; their heads hardly came inside to look properly anyway.

'What's the point of them stopping the bus when they don't really check it?' said Annie.

'The area is supposedly closed to foreigners, but the government only controls the roads and the rest is controlled by the local Pashtun tribes. No policeman is going to risk upsetting the locals by being too intrusive unless he really needs to be.'

Forty minutes from Peshawar the bus stopped and the driver shouted, 'Darra! Darra! Darra!' If it hadn't been for the announcement, neither Annie, Stig nor Nils would have known of their arrival.

'It doesn't look like a place that produces death, violence and destruction,' said Annie, looking around.

'Neither does the Pentagon,' said Stig caustically.

Darra was small, dusty and poor. One unmade road led into town, that was really nothing more than a village, and continued out the other side. The town sat in a hollow among the mountains, sharp peaks rising steeply behind it, defending its manufacture of deadly equipment.

The streets and houses oozed frontier-land lawlessness. Covered, wooden terraces graced some houses. Most shops openly displayed weapons of war: pistols, rifles, small machine-guns, big machine-guns, artillery, even anti-tank rockets. All on sale for hard cash.

Pen guns were sold like souvenirs, with 'Darra' neatly engraved in the burnished metal.

'Hundred fifty *rupee*. Special price. Real working gun, real working pen,' shouted the salesmen as the three foreigners meandered along the street.

'One pound, in real money. Not bad for a gun. Wonder if it's safe?' pondered Annie aloud.

'Guess we're just about to find out.' Nils pointed to a salesman loading a small bullet in place of the biro insert.

'Ten *rupee*, one bullet. You shoot gun?' offered the salesman.

Nils handed over his money and received the toy-town weapon in return.

'Point it at sky,' said the salesman gesturing urgently upwards.

Nils pulled back the top popper that doubled as a hammer. Annie and Stig shrank bank as Nils averted his face. When the gun fired it was almost a disappointment. The .22 calibre round popped, Nils' hand shook and everyone relaxed, laughing.

'Bet it would have difficulty making a hole in a tin can, let alone doing some real damage,' said Nils as he handed the gun back.

Annie declined to buy a pen gun, but was tempted into buying a full magazine of bullets to test-fire a Kalashnikov AK47, as were Stig and Nils.

With the bullets paid for, the arms dealer led the group to the back of his shop on the edge of the village, the mountains rising up directly in front of them. The magazine clicked home into the breech. Annie accepted the hard, slick metal of the gun and weighed it in both hands.

A young boy scampered over the litter of stones and scrub to set a watermelon on a rock fifty metres from where Annie stood.

Adrenalin surged through Annie as she fired the infamous weapon. The experience was exhilarating, there was no other word for it. On her fifth attempt Annie hit the melon. Watery-red innards exploded skywards.

A hand reached out and switched the gun to its automatic setting. As the final twenty bullets sprayed noisily from the muzzle, the barrel of the gun rose uncontrollably and dangerously skywards. Puffs of dust from up the hillside showed how wildly the bullets were spraying across the area.

'Wow!' A sense of power surged through Annie as the echoing noise of gun and ricochets ebbed slowly in the hollow. 'God. Now I know why people say some things are as good as sex.'

Stig reached out for the gun. 'You look all flushed in the face, dear,' he said, laughing saucily.

'It felt good, but I never want to do it again.' Annie quickly handed the gun to Stig and walked away towards the main street. Stig, then Nils, fired off their magazines too. The sound of gunfire echoed around the village, and Annie's exhilaration turned to perplexity as she considered the almost erotic pleasure derived from using the murderous weapon.

As Annie mused over the shocking surge of adrenaline and pleasure that had consumed her when she fired the gun, more automatic gunfire crackled deafeningly close to her. She ducked to the wooden floor of the gun shop terrace, cowering in a reflex of fear. 'Shit!'

Nearby tribesmen laughed uproariously. Looking to where the noise originated, Annie saw a bearded Pashtun tribesman trying out a new gun before buying it; all the bullets had been fired in the air not ten metres from her, hopefully over the roofs and away from the village. 'Huh, bet you did it on purpose,' she grumbled quietly, glowering back at the laughing men.

'Wonder where they all come down again,' said Nils, as he and Stig rejoined Annie on the terrace.

'Don't leave me again. You're supposed to be my chaperones,' said Annie somewhat tetchily.

'If I remember rightly, you abandoned us,' said Stig, putting his arm around Annie and giving her a hug.

'It's hot. Would you like a drink, ma'am?' Nils grinned cheekily and stood to attention.

'Where?' Annie hadn't seen anything but a gun shop since they arrived.

Nils quickly ascertained the whereabouts of a shop selling refreshments from a local who pointed them further along the street to the village limits where a terraced, wooden hotel served the only cold refreshment available. Louvred half-doors to the interior rattled in the breeze.

'Looks like John Wayne's gonna walk out that door in a minute,' drawled Stig.

Nils swaggered towards the hotel, then acted out a shoot out with both hands in the universal children's imitation of pistols, giving a passable impersonation of John Wayne. Annie hooked her arm through Stig's as they followed him, laughing.

Barely cool Coke bottles came from a broken fridge stuffed with ice, but only sticky boiled rice and dry chapati came from the kitchen. They picked at the food, but the three trigger-happy foreigners emptied their Cokes and ordered more, twice.

A fat man wandered out from the hotel's dark interior onto the balcony. 'You no stay here. Police trouble. Last bus to Peshawar leave soon.'

'Excuse me?' said Stig.

'You leave now. Bus not wait.' The man pointed a finger back to the nearby main road by-passing the town and started shooing them off the premises.

'You wait in my brother shop. That him there, on corner.' The innkeeper waved and an answering wave came from an open-fronted shop a hundred metres away. Annie drained her bottle of Coke as Nils stuffed his guidebook back in his bag.

Wearily Annie trailed through the heat and dust to the shade of the shop. Hashish lined the walls in A4 sized brown slices, sandwiched by greaseproof paper.

'Better grade at top, badder grade at bottom. Darra hash here, other village here,' the shopkeeper lectured, like a vintner.

Annie tried to guess how much the inventory would be worth back home.

'I bet there's no trouble with the police. They just wanted to try and sell us some of this stuff.' said Stig as he and Nils perused the shelves like connoisseurs.

'First cigarette free,' said the shopkeeper to Annie. A heavy match lit a thick joint.

'I don't smoke,' said Annie, stepping backwards away from the glowing joint.

'I do,' grinned Stig, reaching for the cigar-sized tote.

'Me too,' said Nils.

'I thought you didn't smoke,' said Annie disapprovingly.

'Only the best,' laughed Stig as he enjoyed the hit of the joint.

'This stuff has the same effect on us as shooting that gun did on you.' Stig and Nils laughed outrageously as they passed the joint to each other.

Heavy pulls on the joint produced clouds of sweet smelling smoke. Stig and Nils giggled. Annie watched the eyes of her chaperones cloud over and the pupils shrink to pinpoints. By the time the bus arrived, Nils lay smiling on the floor of the shop. Stig and Annie carried the somnolent figure to the last bus of the day.

'Hope the police don't cause any trouble on the way back,' said Stig as Nils stumbled and tripped towards the bus. 'Imagine trying to explain this away to a policeman.'

*****

The first two checkpoints passed as uneventfully and casually as on the way out. The guards were as subdued by the heat as the dozing passengers on the bus. With only one more checkpoint to go, Annie relaxed into the thought that the warning at the hotel in Darra was as spurious as they'd thought back at the dope shop.

Then the bus rounded a corner and slowed at the final checkpoint. Around her, passengers stirred and the volume of conversation increased.

'Looks like your trouble's arrived.' Annie tapped the dozing Stig on the shoulder and nodded to a red and white pole across the road. One lorry, two cars and a horse and cart waited in line. A policeman actively nosed in both the first two vehicles.

'Guess the police are more concerned with what comes out, than what goes in.' Nils grinned inanely, the effects of the hashish blatantly obvious.

The police checked each vehicle thoroughly. The bus received special treatment, two uniformed men climbing on board. The owner of every package on the bus had to claim it and open it as the police moved slowly towards the rear.

There was no hiding behind a seat this time.

'I guess they're looking for someone,' giggled Nils. Stig just looked worried.

'Shhh,' said Annie. 'Not so loud.'

When the first policeman saw Annie and her companions he shouted to his friend. Turning back to the foreigners he waved his arms and shouted at them to move. '*Chelo, chelo*!' His waving arms left no room for doubt about what he wanted.

A sergeant, sitting regally in the shade of a roadside tree, demanded their passports. The searchers had given up looking through the bus and now stood behind them.

'Why you here? Foreigners no allowed here. This Tribal Area. You smuggle drugs? You American spy?' demanded the sergeant.

All questions went to Stig and the swaying Nils. Annie might as well not have existed.

'We're only tourists. Not even journalists. Don't even smoke.' Stig did his best to be serious and not look concerned, with as much success as a Friday night drunk trying to look sober.

Nils grinned inanely.

'It is foolishness to visiting such a dangerous area. The tribal men will kill you and rob you. We police carry guns to protect ourselves.' The sergeant shook his head in sad admonishment. The burst of activity tired him in the burning heat. He waved a hand in dismissal.

Stig held out his hand for the three passports. The sergeant stared covetously at the pink covers of their European passports, then regretfully handed the booklets over.

The three foreigners climbed back on the bus and re-took their seats. The policemen didn't follow them to continue their interrupted search, instead waving the bus through the barrier and on its way.

Out of sight in the dust-cloud behind them, the checkpoint lost its danger. Smiles, handshakes and backslaps showered Stig and Nils.

'*Shukria! Shukria!*' shouted the passengers to the bemused foreigners.

A bearded tribesman leant across the aisle, winked and placed an apricot-sized lump of hashish in Stig's hand. '*Shukria*, thank you. You save us much baksheesh.'

The leathery tanned face of another tribesman creased into a heart-warming smile as he said, 'Thanks be to Allah, the police didn't find my whisky.'

Floor panels, roof panels and cushions opened to allow the removal of bootleg packages. Bottles of whisky, tennis balls of hashish and handguns appeared from the recesses of the bus. From between the pages of newspapers came sheets of hashish, like those in the Darra drug store.

Expertly rolled joints soon circulated and the Pashtuns relaxed happily as the bus drove through the suburbs of Peshawar.

Stig enjoyed a joint to himself, while Nils slept.

'Guess we made their day. Wonder how much profit we made them?' Annie asked, glancing around the bus at the smiling faces. She was also wondering how much she was going to be affected by the thick cloud of hashish smoke filling the bus.

'I don't care. The amount of hash they've given me I can save myself a fortune,' said Stig. 'And we'll try for the Khyber Railway tomorrow. If we can get a ticket it'll be a much nicer trip that going by bus to the top of the pass.'

Annie relaxed into her seat and grinned to herself. This life was more exciting and fun than work any day, and she was beginning to feel like a real traveller.

Chapter Nine

Nuristan, Afghanistan. Matt lay awake for hours that night, replaying his conversation with Scott. When he did finally sleep he was transported to the mountains of Nuristan. Jo was there too. He never quite saw her, but he knew she was there just out the picture. When he woke early, unrested and uncomfortable, he was struck numb with the fear that he could not remember what Jo looked like. He concentrated hard till the vision of her smile came back to him.

While he waited for the other travellers in his dormitory to wake Matt pondered what to do. China, or Nuristan? By the time the first of his room-mates stirred Matt had extracted his guidebook and made a decision.

He packed and left the Lahore Salvation Army Hostel while there were still people in their bunks. Out on the road a tuk-tuk stopped alongside him as he began his walk back to the bus station.

'Yes, sir. I take you to the station. Too far walk with that big bag.' Impatient to be on his way now he'd made up his mind where to go, Matt hopped in the tuk-tuk without even thinking of agreeing a price first.

Leaving the smiling tuk-tuk driver with the price he asked, having not bothered to haggle, Matt strode into the bus station to find himself a bus to Pindi. He picked the luxury bus with an advertised non-stop run through to the city from amongst his various options. It surprised him by leaving on time.

Settled into a much more comfortable seat than the one he'd had on the way from Sukkur to Lahore, Matt checked out his fellow passengers. They were a lot different to the travellers he had shared the carriage with on the train the day before. Smart western clothes dominated, and the passengers were all male. They were mostly plugged into iPhones and other electronic devices, separated from their fellow passengers by thin strings of electrical wire and ear-plugs.

Matt sank back into his comfy seat and pulled out a few books from his backpack. He was looking forward to the four hour trip through the Punjab, anticipating new sights and images passing his window as he read up on his intended destination.

The bus moved slowly through the traffic of Lahore, while Matt read his guidebook. It picked up speed as it moved clear of the city and onto the new road to Pindi. A combination of the tiring train journey the day before and the lack of sleep last night conspired to weigh heavy on his eyelids and Matt soon drifted off to sleep.

He woke with a start when the engine of the bus cut in the terminal at Rawalpindi. It took him a few moments to realise he was at his first destination. He was scrambling quickly for the books that he had dropped on the floor, when he saw his backpack landing heavily on the ground outside his window as all the luggage was unloaded.

Matt spotted some other foreign travellers and wandered over to ask advice on where to find his next bus. They pointed him across the rows of concrete shelters to a where a man sat behind a table selling tickets. 'That's your best option. The new buses go slower, but they crash less.'

His luck was in, the bus he approached was leaving within the hour. He was excited to be getting on to Peshawar, and closer to his goal of Nuristan. He'd forgotten about his vague plans to head for China and all thought of getting a Chinese visa from Islamabad on his way north had gone from his head.

Three more impatient hours on his second bus of the day, cruising along a dull featureless road, brought Matt to Peshawar. He was stiff and tired and increasingly hungry. His only food of the day had been a packet of biscuits bought at the bus-station in Lahore, washed down with bottles of Coke bought from a street-seller along in Rawalpindi.

Flopping into the back of a tuk-tuk, Matt began the final leg of his day's journey, from the walls of Peshawar fort to the Khyber Hotel in Saddar Bazaar. Almost nine hours after leaving the Sally Army Hostel Matt had crossed from the east of the country near the Indian border, to the far west, and Afghanistan was almost in touching distance.

There were noticeably more guns on the streets of Peshawar, though like in Sukkur, the army and the police kept to their own areas. Bearded Pashtuns strode confidently along the pavements and across the roads; men with full beards, that before now Matt had only seen on the TV, dominated the landscape.

The faces and atmosphere on the streets of Peshawar were different from those in Sindh and the Punjab. These men were more rugged and their clothes coarser for a tougher way of life, but the late afternoon sun softened the passing images and the air was cooler than it had been since Matt arrived in Pakistan.

It was a relief for Matt when the tuk-tuk stopped outside the Khyber Hotel. He was looking forward to completing his day's impetuous journey from one side of the country to another. With his backpack slung casually off one shoulder and his day-pack dangling from the opposite hand, Matt walked the few steps from the roadside into the narrow alleyway leading to the staircase up to the hotel's courtyard.

Guests lounged around the courtyard and a few were eating what looked like bread and omelettes, and drinking tea; they mostly ignored Matt as he registered for the cheapest dormitory bed available, though a few idly watched him as he dutifully filled in the mandatory form with his name and passport details.

Travellers lay dozing on their simple wood-framed, rope strung charpoys across his designated dormitory, but Matt identified what he hoped was a vacant bed in the far corner away from the doorway, where he dumped his backpack before heading back to the courtyard for some much-needed food.

At a shady corner table, in the lee of the staircase, Matt sat alone. He wanted to think about his trip and observe the other travellers, not in the mood for company at the end of his tiring day. He had tried to persuade Scott to return to Afghanistan, but Scott was broke and heading for home. Now he had made the decision to head this way on his own, he hoped to meet someone else who would be interested in going with him. Matt surveyed the other travellers, wondering which of them he would want to travel with and who would even want to go with him.

Ten minutes after ordering it, green tea and an omelette arrived at his table. The small boy who acted as skivvy, manager's assistant and waiter smiled cheekily as he placed the food in front of Matt. The eggs were freshly prepared, piping hot and dripping in oil, the unusual tasting green tea refreshing and the perfect accompaniment to the deliciously spicy omelette.

*****

Annie, Stig and Nils tumbled off the tuk-tuk and into the hotel alley. Exhilaration and dope-induced lethargy made the boys stumble as they started climbing the stairs. Annie encouraged and guided them gently up the stairs towards the courtyard and left them to order tea from the ever-present small boy, while she went to shower then stand wet and naked under the fan in her room to cool herself down after a long day in the heat and dust.

*****

Matt watched two stoned men stumble into the courtyard and across to a table, ordering chai and omelettes as they did so. They were asking for trouble, he thought to himself. Prime candidates for getting ripped off, or caught up in something they couldn't handle.

He ordered a coke and sipped it while he thought some more about his intended trip to Afghanistan.

A clatter of boots on the stairway above him caught his attention and pulled Matt back from his reverie. A girl jumped down the last few steps into his line of sight. The light t-shirt she wore emphasised her shapely curves. Her wet hair flicked up as she turned towards the two stoned men.

Matt stared after her as she swayed through the tables, her figure hypnotising him.

Sloe eyes caught his as the brunette sat. She held his gaze for a moment before turning to her friends.

Matt dragged his eyes from the girl, his heart pounding as he tried not stare. He meticulously placed his coke back on the table in front of him, desperate not to spill it while the girl hovered in his peripheral vision.

With the glass back on the table Matt casually glanced around the courtyard so he could take a second proper look at the girl without appearing to do so. But she caught him looking at her as his eyes lingered for a fraction of a second. He smiled, but it was only absent-mindedly returned.

*****

Raseem sipped his chai as the small boy recounted what he had overheard while working in the Khyber Hotel. Raseem was enjoying his luck and finding this boy who even spoke English capped it all. This morning he had heard that Annie was going to Darra that day and Landi Kotal tomorrow. The boy confirmed she had been to and returned from Darra, laughing as he recounted his news. 'They are talking non-stop about the guns, the police and Darra. The two boys she's with, they're really stoned. She doesn't smoke, but she laughs at them.'

'Where's she going next? When she leaves Peshawar. You tell me that.' Raseem glared at the boy while he lounged arrogantly in his seat and sipped some more at his chai.

'She says Chitral. She wants to see the mountains.' The boy smiled at Raseem, all the while thinking he'd tell this corrupted bastard anything, while he threw his dirty money around trying to impress people. The boy wasn't impressed by the likes of Raseem, but money was money when you had two younger siblings to help feed.

Raseem tossed some coins on the floor for the boy and waved him away dismissively. 'You find out anything else about that whore, you come tell me. You hear?'

'Oh yes, *sahib*,' agreed the boy, picking up the money and mentally giving him the finger.

It was all coming together for Raseem, who relaxed back in his seat. Chitral was where he had his mountain hideaway. Absent-mindedly he stroked his crotch again, then cursed when it dawned on him there was still nothing happening. It was all that bitch's fault. He growled angrily after the boy, who was already running back to his work.

*****

Eight hours of walking, interspersed with a long midday break and a few chai stops saw Ishmael reach the outskirts of Mastuj. There was no snow down here and the vegetation was past the first flush of spring and moving into its summer colours. It was hot during the day, but the temperature would drop as the sun went behind the mountains, though at this lower altitude it wouldn't drop as far as it had the night before when a frost had covered him as he slept in the open with the herdsman.

Soon Ishmael would reach the combined army and frontier police base where he would be able to enjoy good food and get his mail. Life was more relaxed here in the mountains where the army and police actually worked together, unlike in the big cities where everything was more political and complicated.

An old twin-bladed Huey had arrived and then left the base as he approached. When he saw it approaching Ishmael had sat and observed the helicopter through his binoculars, always suspicious of flying visits in remote outposts. Snap inspections, or Generals on a jolly, were often trouble, usually generated questions, and always demanded formality.

When a two-star General had dismounted on the landing pad next to the base, followed by an aide and a flunky, but no luggage, Ishmael had settled himself to await their departure and avoid attracting attention to himself.

Ishmael smiled as he saw a steward flick a cloth across a table on the verandah of a bungalow that was obviously the officers' quarters. A set of tea-cups arrived along with the tea and the table was ready by the time the General was ushered across the mini parade-ground while the entire compliment of men lined up at attention for him.

The nervousness of the soldiers on the base floated up the slopes to Ishmael. He could feel their discomfort at the unexpected visit from the top brass who hardly ever ventured somewhere as humble as this. His sensitivity to the mood of a place and the people around him was something he had only ever talked to his wife about. She'd laughed and said it was just one more special thing about him she loved. It had saved his life on occasion, though it unsettled him sometimes when he knew a situation was just about to explode in violence before anyone else was even aware there was something wrong.

The General inspected the parade from the verandah, his aide standing next to him. The indistinct bark of a sergeant rose up to Ishmael a second after the men shuffled and straightened in their ranks for a salute.

The parade dismissed and the General sat for his tea with the aide and the flunky hovering behind him, while the local commander presented himself at the foot of the verandah steps. Within seconds the aide, the flunky and local commander quickly stepped across to the admin building leaving the General to enjoy his tea alone.

A chai-wallah slipped from the barracks to refresh the helicopter crew and Ishmael took a few sips from his water bottle as he waited for the General to leave.

Ishmael enjoyed the warmth of the sun as he watched an eagle soar overhead and the General sip his tea down below for thirty minutes until the three men returned from the admin building to report.

As abruptly as they arrived, the visitors left again. Swooping low over the village, billowing dust in the clear air as it did so, the helicopter charged for the pass Ishmael had left the day before.

With the valley returned to its more tranquil setting, Ishmael bypassed the village and approached the main gates of the base across the fields and the recently vacated helipad. It was more an outpost than a base, but it was a pleasant place to stop over and more relaxed than most military locations, despite the tall, dominating radio mast pointing skywards from the rocky outcrop sprouting in the centre of the compound. His identification papers listed him as a frontier policeman, under special command from Islamabad, and quickly gained him entry. He headed for the admin block to check-in and collect any messages.

'Sergeant Ishmael Khan, Frontier Police. I'm on patrol and need a bed for a few days.' The corporal behind the desk smiled and rifled through a sheaf of papers.

'This package arrived for you an hour ago with the mail; a General in a helicopter brought it in. You just missed him, he left in that helicopter you will have seen. Said he was checking arrangements for the polo tournament in two weeks time. They're expecting trouble this year.'

The Corporal waited expectantly, hoping Ishmael would open the package in front of him. 'I'll read it later. Thanks. Where can I put my stuff?'

Disappointed, the Corporal shuffled his papers again. 'There's a space in the sergeant's mess you can have. You're just in time for dinner.'

Ishmael dumped his pack and joined the duty-sergeant for a quiet dinner of potato, tomato and okra stew, where he was softly questioned on his orders and equally as gently deflected the questions. He left the package until he could retire for the night. It was too late for him do anything about it now if it was orders, and if it was a letter from his wife he wanted to enjoy it at leisure and in privacy.

Later, while relaxing with chai and a cigarette in his room, Ishmael opened the package as he lay on his charpoy. With disappointment, Ishmael pulled out new orders, then smiled as a thin white envelope bearing his wife's distinctive hand-writing fell from the official military envelope. He'd read the orders first, saving the news from home till after.

'A British tourist has reported that a British citizen of Pakistani origin held him prisoner, injected him with drugs and compelled him to smuggle heroin to England. The tourist also reported that a second tourist, female, was being held at the same time. Our best information leads us to believe that the prisoners are being held in the region of the Shandur Pass, in a small village away from major tourist routes. You are to return to the Shandur Pass immediately, via Harchin and Laspur, and make extensive enquiries as to the location of any Pakistani men who have spent time in England. The name of the man is believed to be Ricky, though this may be an alias. If you locate the man in question, use your discretion as to the best course of action. We would, however, prefer to arrest this man. Further orders and information will follow in due course.'

Ishmael was saddened at the thought someone could be so horrible to others, all to make money killing people with drugs from the beautiful flower that was the poppy. Then he turned to the letter from his wife and news from home, wanting reassurance his own family were safe and well.

*****

'You've got an admirer,' pouted Stig. 'The hunk in the corner. Can't take his eyes off you. You lucky thing.'

'You're just jealous. Anyway, he probably hasn't seen a woman in weeks if he's been here a while.' Annie glanced at Matt and gave him a quick smile as she caught him looking at her, again. Embarrassed at being caught staring, he returned her smile quickly, then looked away.

'You're welcome to him Stig, he doesn't look like my type,' grinned Annie as she turned her gaze back to her friends. He was quite good looking though, thought Annie to herself as she considered the smart haircut that was just growing out and the shy smile he had given her.

'So. Landi Kotal tomorrow then.' Nils stirred from his hash induced lethargy.

'Yeah, if you wake up in time,' laughed Stig.

*****

Raseem sat in his jeep waiting for the boy to report. The tuk-tuk, with Annie and only one of the guys from the day before, was trying to enter the flow of traffic.

The boy shouted, 'Khyber Railway, for Landi Kotal,' as he held out his hand for another coin.

Raseem flipped a coin to the dirt again and pushed the jeep quickly into the traffic. He was concentrating so hard on Annie's tuk-tuk that he missed the obscene gesture expertly, but incongruously, executed with both arms by the small boy standing in the middle of road behind him.

*****

'Foreigner Forbidden To Purchase Ticket.'

'Foiled before we start,' said Annie as she disappointedly read the sign above the kiosk.

'Bugger,' said Stig. 'What do we do now?'

'Don't worry, I'll buy you the tickets. You're not allowed to buy them yourself here. Only official Pakistan tourist guides are supposed to be able to buy tickets from this office, but no package tour foreigners would dare travel on this line at the moment, they're all too scared of the Taliban. I know the manager here though, so I'll sort them out for you.'

Annie looked up and saw the smiling face of the English Pakistani who had told her about Pierre in Islamabad. 'Hi. What are you doing here?' she asked in surprise.

'I'm collecting some Afghani carpets someone's supposed to be bringing down on the train. What about you?'

'We're going to Landi Kotal for the day,' said Annie smiling broadly at him. 'I need to thank you for the tip about Pierre. I found some heroin he put in my bag. I owe you one. Thanks'

Stig looked questioningly at Annie. 'You know this guy?'

'Yeah. He warned me about Pierre in Islamabad. He's okay.'

138

She turned back to the young Pakistani offering his help. 'Sorry, I don't know your name,' said Annie accepting his excuse for being at the train station without question. 'I'm Annie, by the way. And this is Stig.'

'They call me Ricky in London. I'll be back in a sec with your tickets.'

'Thanks again,' said Annie. 'I really do owe you one now.'

Ricky smiled depreciatingly. 'No worries. Always happy to help a fellow Brit when I can. You'll enjoy the trip.'

Five minutes later the two foreigners were sitting on a hard wooden seat and a chai-wallah was serving them *kawa* through the window. Around them sat an eclectic mix of families with children and fierce looking bearded tribesmen.

The women with small children fussed and did their best to settle them for the trip, as mothers anywhere in the world would do. The bearded tribesmen, however, made themselves totally at home without a thought, carefully separate from the women travellers.

Ricky stood outside and waved as the train pulled away from him. 'Good luck, see you around,' he shouted after them.

'He seems really nice,' said Annie. 'Specially as he wouldn't even let us pay him for the tickets.'

'Yeah, but there was something about him I didn't like,' said Stig dubiously.

*****

Raseem watched the train leave from among the crowd on the platform. His stomach twisted in sick excitement as he imagined ripping Annie's clothes off and fucking her hard on the floor of his mountain hut. I'll give you more than one when I get hold of you, he thought, as Annie gave him one last friendly smile as the train pulled away.

It had taken all his self-control not to grab Annie instead of giving her the tickets, but that would have ruined everything and caused him lots of trouble. He had never got used to how overly-protective Patan tribesmen could be with women, even foreign ones, and he just knew one of them would have jumped to defend the bitch's honour.

As far as he was concerned women were for pleasure, especially ones like her. He was certain she'd enjoy it, just like all the ones he'd taken to his hideout before.

*****

Matt had spent the last two hours riding tuk-tuks around Peshawar and ducking through the low picket gates of old military forts. It should have been an enjoyable way to spend a morning, visiting historic forts and exploring the cantonment of Peshawar. But finding exactly the right man to sign a form, to allow another man to stamp it, to authorise another man to issue a number to validate a permit would ruin even the most happy-go-lucky person's day. And given that Matt was impatient to continue his journey to Afghanistan as soon as possible, he was beginning to get seriously frustrated with the process.

It was only a sense of duty to Jo that kept Matt going long after he really wanted to give up the quest and go back to the hotel, where the gorgeous brunette had smiled at him again this morning as she came down the steps from her floor and he was heading out for the day. He also felt guilty that he had come here because of Jo, but some other girl was grabbing his attention.

The brunette looked even better in daylight, and her smile this morning had seemed genuinely warm, quickening his heart, and other places, like a hormonal teenager's.

Matt had been meticulous in his plans. His bed was paid four days in advance, and slung over his shoulder was a small backpack with only the essentials to see him through a few days of hard quick travel to Kabul and back. His main backpack was chained to the underside of the bed frame, with nothing in it he could not afford to lose.

He told anyone who asked and listened long enough that he was planning a tour up the Khyber Pass, to visit the abandoned roadside forts of the British army. Matt had even gone as far as memorising a few names to make himself sound more plausible when he applied to the Khyber Agency, the Frontier Police and the Peshawar Regional Government Office who, in theory, could issue passes authorising him to make the trip.

His plan, however, was to head straight up to Landi Kotal at the top of the Khyber Pass, from where he planned to try and get down to Torkham and over the border into Afghanistan, where he could head for Kabul.

In practice, Scott had also told him back in Lahore, the Frontier Police who controlled the road exercised randomly applied discretion to limit visitor access and even with the correct authorisations it would be unpredictable as to whether he would get as far as Landi Kotal.

A few moments after the final permit received its last stamp a gangly boy of a soldier paraded into the office and saluted.

'I am your official bodyguard, *sahib*.'

Behind his desk the official smiled proudly at Matt. 'You will be safe with this bodyguard.'

Matt eyed the boy suspiciously. Having someone keeping an eye on him was going to make it harder, if not impossible, to slip down to Torkham and across the border.

'I don't need a bodyguard. There will be plenty of soldiers on the road already who will protect me.'

'You will be much safer with a bodyguard. No one will try to rob you or shoot you.' The proud official pressed his point hard and long. Matt argued firmly in return.

Eventually the official got bored and surprisingly relented. 'Okay. No bodyguard, but do not come and complain to me if somebody kills you.' Matt had trouble controlling his smile as the man waved him away.

Back out on the street outside the fort Matt spotted a tailor selling ready made tribal-style clothes. Amid great hilarity, from the owner and other customers, Matt tried on long baggy trousers, with a huge waist-band tightened with a drawstring, then added the upper component of dress-length shirt. At least his clothes would not stand out now, which he hoped would make it easier to look inconspicuous, though his lengthening brown hair and pale skin still made him look too much like an out of place urban European.

The fifth tuk-tuk of the day trundled him to the main gates of an Afghan refugee camp. To his relief a bunch of rickety old German tour buses, left over from the days of the hippy trail, were loading passengers in the dusty parking lot.

Convincing the driver of an almost full bus that he really did want to go to all the way to Kabul, that he was neither a journalist, a Russian, nor a drug dealer looking for a ton of hashish, took Matt's finest negotiating skills. The task was made easier by the helpful input of a small boy who took it upon himself to help Matt overcome his lack of a common language with the driver. Other passengers helped too, seeming to find the thought of smuggling a foreigner across the border a great game to be involved in.

For ten minutes, Matt didn't believe he was going to persuade the driver to let him on, then the man shrugged theatrically, snorted resignedly and said something Matt couldn't understand, but which made the passengers all laugh. As Matt looked around the laughing faces, not sure what was happening, the small boy grabbed his sleeve and dragged him on board the packed out Mercedes bus.

The aisle, luggage space and leg-room overflowed with sacks of tomatoes, rubber shoes and rice, suitcases sat precariously on the piles of sacks and the youngest passengers perched on the top of these uncomfortable looking mounds as Matt took his seat a few rows behind the driver.

'*Chelo! Chelo! Chelo!*' shouted the children. '*Chelo!*' echoed the driver as he pulled away.

'Too late to stop now,' muttered Matt as the other passengers murmured ritual prayers.

*****

'Listen to this.' Stig re-arranged his paper as the train steamed away from Peshawar.

'An Afghani refugee girl recently eloped with her Pakistani paramour. The girl's parents, after pleas for her return gathered a posse and went to retrieve her from the man's village in the tribal region outside Peshawar. After an assault of several hours, using mortars, rockets, automatic weapons and similar weaponry, the girl, her lover, the lover's grandmother, sister and two others were killed. Forty houses in the village were also destroyed.'

Stig lowered the paper. 'Still want to go?'

Annie pulled a face in horror. 'Too late now. We're on our way. But perhaps Nils is better off in bed today. You reckon he's going to be all right?' The narrow-gauge steam engine whistled again as it broke free from the last of the city slums.

'Of course. Once he's slept all that dope off, he'll be fine.'

'What about this though,' said Annie. 'My guidebook says the local tribesmen ride the train for free because their fiercely independent forebears negotiated free travel in return for granting permission for the British engineers to build the railway through their land. Smart guys, huh!'

The train moved slowly through the crowded slums of Peshawar, with Annie glued to the window not wanting to miss a thing. As the buildings receded from the trackside and the line moved out onto the arid fields around the city the engine picked up speed, though it was never going to be classed as an express train.

'My Grandad used to tell me stories about riding on this train in the 1930's. I can't believe I am actually on it now.' Annie's excited smile faded as she felt the sudden pain of missing her Grandad like she hadn't done in years. 'I feel so close to him, but right now I miss him more than I have since I was a little girl.'

'Your Grandad was here? What was he doing?'

'He was in the Indian Army before independence. He loved it here, it was his favourite posting of all the places he went in the world. He hated the fact he had to fight the locals in a military campaign to the north of here.'

'Wow. That is so cool. My Grandad never left the village he was born in.'

Villages and farms passed by, some close to the tracks, some far away. The two travellers fell into a companionable silence as the mountains moved closer until the train started to rise and the air began to cool. When they were well out from Peshawar and into the Khyber tribal area a guard appeared. His job was quite simple really, given the locals didn't actually need tickets.

When he reached Annie and Stig the guard looked for their guide. 'Who you with? What your guide?'

'No guide. We're on our own,' said Stig with a smile.

The guard shook his head and smiled broadly with worry. 'No foreigners allowed, no foreigners allowed.'

The guard's high-pitched voice would have been comical if he had not been so obviously worried. Stig and Annie sat speechless, unsure what to do. An old man with a long hennaed beard and fine turban sitting on the bench seat next to Stig harangued the guard loudly, waving him away. The stunned guard frowned at Annie and Stig again, then shrugged his shoulders and moved on to the next compartment without another word.

'Wonder what that was all about?' said Annie.

'Can't have been anything serious,' muttered Stig as he accepted a biscuit from his new friend.

Once in the approaches to the Pass the railway ran parallel to the road for the most part. Heavily laden lorries, stuffed buses and wobbling donkey carts struggled up the hills towards the top of the Pass. At checkpoints random searches frustrated drivers and passengers, and waving arms signified vociferous arguments with armed policemen.

No police checks bothered the railway travellers though; they relaxed and enjoyed the scenery.

As they rose higher the Pass narrowed tightly and at the narrowest part the gorge shrank to a width of only sixteen metres, as Annie read in her guidebook. River, road and railway squeezed together, stacking in layers above each other.

As the route grew steeper, the wheezing of the twin-engined train grew louder. The line moved in and out of tunnels and balanced over high bridges across gorges as the noise of the train hissed and bounced from the walls.

At the steepest part of the pass the train shuttled back and forth on a series of saw toothed spurs, where the technical skills of the 1920's British engineers had reached their peak, and the train climbed what should have been an impassable ridge.

Fortified Patan houses capped the lesser hills alongside the railway; they looked more like forts than homes. Annie thought of the women cloistered inside, ostensibly for their own safety. According to her guidebook, in the bazaars of Peshawar the men came down from the hills with a piece of string measured against the feet of their women, to buy them shoes. In the mountain areas either side of the railway line it was not considered safe for the women to go out at all, let alone on their own, because of the simmering blood feuds that often seemed to descend into battles and bloodshed.

On the precipitous flanks of the surrounding hills, stick figures edged their way along narrow tracks. Long lines of camels strung along the thin lines of the tracks.

'Who are they?' Annie asked the carriage in general, hoping someone would understand her.

'It's the smuggling road. The tracks are in the Tribal Area. The Government cannot go there. The tribesmen carry whatever goods they want with those camel trains.' The elderly man who had chased away the guard surprised her with eloquent English, then relapsed back to sleepy silence.

'I read in the newspaper yesterday that three hundred and twenty tonnes of opium would be smuggled out of Afghanistan over the Khyber Pass this year. I guess that's the

Opium Road.' Stig clicked his camera at the precarious smuggler's road.

Annie was keeping a special look out for the British war graves at Ali Masjid, from the second Afghan war and massacre of retreating British troops in the nineteenth century, but couldn't spot them. She did see two imposing forts though, which were strikingly unmissable in their dominant presence.

The Shagai Fort faced the Ali Masjid Fort, and the two dominated every building on the Pass. The Ali Masjid stood guard at the narrowest point of the pass where the retreating British army had fought a rearguard action against the Afghans and it overlooked almost the entire passage. 'No wonder the Brits had so much trouble up here, the locals had a much better stronghold.' Stig never took his eye from the viewfinder as his camera clicked on.

Almost six hours after they had left Peshawar, and having travelled slowly through some of the most breathtaking scenery Annie had ever seen, Landi Kotal appeared huddled at the end of the line, sitting on the crest of the infamous Khyber Pass. Afghanistan lay on one side, Pakistan on the other.

'We made it,' said Annie hugging Stig. 'We made it.'

The elderly saviour stirred from his sleepy silence again and leant across to Stig conspirationally. 'You better get off quickly, just in case the guard comes back. The Frontier Police can cause big problems and may even keep you at the station then send you back to Peshawar before you see what you've come to see.'

*****

Chris sipped a glass of fine French wine as he enjoyed lunch with Dominic during his stopover on the way north. He and Dominic had met each other at an embassy party a few years back and been great friends ever since, even meeting up in Paris on one occasion.

'So, Chris. Why are you here so suddenly? It's not the sort of place a man like you comes for pleasure.'

'It seems that one of our nationals is being held prisoner somewhere in the mountains by a drug smuggler. What makes it worse is that the smuggler also seems to be one of ours. I got a tip-off two days ago about the poor girl, so I thought I'd pop over.'

Dominic nodded without showing any surprise. 'How old is the girl?'

'I don't know. I don't even know her name. She's probably a backpacker, so I guess she's somewhere around her mid-twenties.'

'Françoise is twenty-one.' Dominic swirled his wine and stared through the windows at his meticulously maintained gardens, where the girl in question lay stretched on a sun lounger reading a book. 'A few days ago I met a young British woman on the plane. She came to the party here two days ago; she and Françoise got along well. I hope it's not her.'

'I doubt it. The girl we're looking for has been there at least ten days. When they go to the mountains, where do most of these young backpackers go?'

'Gilgit. It's the one place they all go. Don't ask me why, the place is a tourist trap on the way to China. Give me beautiful Chitral any day.'

Chris smiled. 'What's so special about Chitral?'

'It's isolated deep in the Hindu Kush in the north west of the country. It's easier to get to Afghanistan from there than it is to reach the rest of Pakistan. It's not really on the tourist trail, either.'

'So where do you reckon I should start looking for this girl? If anyone knows where pretty young tourists can be found it'd be you.'

'Probably,' smiled Dominic. 'Gilgit would be high on the list for you though, because it is easier to get to than Chitral and more likely to attract the sort of people you're looking for. It's also easier to reach the Shandur Pass for the annual

147

polo tournament from there too. Then of course, it's also on the way to China. It's where Nick Danzinger got his bus to China from on that journey of his that's gained something of a cult status among the thrill-seeking sort of traveller.'

Chris had no idea who Nick Danzinger was, but wasn't going to admit it. 'My source talked about polo and crossing a high pass in the mountains, do you reckon he meant Gilgit and this Shandur Pass?'

'Most likely, it's where the lazier sort of backpacker goes. Chitral is for the more discerning traveller and the passes round there are much harder work to get over.'

Coffee arrived and the conversation lapsed as their large lunch settled. Dominic was the first to speak again.

'This British national who's holding the girl. What's his name?'

'We think it's Ricky, but that could well be an alias. He's ethnically Pakistani, but probably born and brought up in England.'

Dominic steepled his fingers together and gazed thoughtfully at the ceiling for a moment. 'Annie MacDonald, the young woman I met on the plane, said she met a man who sounded English, but was Pakistani. He told her about one of our nationals who sets up foreigners to get himself out of jail. It's a long shot and I'm probably grasping at straws, but maybe he's the same man and he was trying to ingratiate himself with Annie as his next target.'

'Did she mention his name?' Chris suppressed his hope that someone would know where to find him.

'*Non.* I don't think she knew it.'

*****

The ramshackle suburbs of Peshawar dropped away to dusty plains that separated the city from the mountains. The driver ignored the potholes and Mercedes would have been proud of the strength of their ancient bus.

Within an hour they entered the Khyber gorge and soon the road moved off its floor to cling to the steep walls on a ledge cut into the rock.

Directly above the bus the rock face rose to the glaring white sky; across the way steep valley walls marked the edge of the visible world as they too reached upwards.

An eclectic collection of vehicles filled the road. Not all the contraptions were motorised, and even those that did have engines were not always as fast as the bus. Stuck behind a plodding donkey cart, or a straining, decoratively painted heavy lorry, the faster traffic impatiently crawled through the dust with their horns blaring till they found a way past.

The road criss-crossed the railway line as they competed for a route to the top. An old-fashioned steam train pumped smoke and steam into the dusty air as it crawled slowly along its traffic free path towards the top of the Pass.

Along the opposite side of the valley, a narrow track wound its even more precarious way to the top of the pass. Caravans of camels and donkeys plodded the alternative route with slow, resolute steps. The caravans coming from Afghanistan sagged under the weight of huge sacks hanging down each side of the animals' backs; those going the other way seemed piled high with boxes.

The metal Mercedes bus radiated heat and Matt sweated continuously. The claustrophobic hills dampened any movement of air. The passengers sank into indolent quiet.

Two checkpoints passed by with only cursory checks of the passing vehicles. Scruffy policemen just popped their heads through the windows of cars and the door of the bus. With only quick looks at the passengers, they waved each vehicle forwards. Matt kept his head down and his woollen hat pulled low in his efforts to avoid attention and minimise the risk of being sent back to Peshawar.

Four hours into the journey an impatient, tooting queue of vehicles announced the presence of a more serious checkpoint. A fifteen minute wait punctuated by short, sharp five metre jumps brought the bus to the red and white pole blocking the road.

Two policemen hauled themselves into the doorway. One stood guard with his gun at the ready, while the other laboriously checked the ID of every passenger. Ducking his head would serve no purpose so Matt feigned sleep, but to no avail.

The policeman kicked Matt and demanded his papers. The man stared as he quickly realised Matt was a foreigner, then he shouted loudly in Urdu as he hustled Matt off the bus, all thought of checking the rear third of the bus forgotten.

Standing under a roadside tarpaulin, Matt listened to the obvious demands of the sergeant sitting behind a desk and handed over his passport, with the booklet open at the page with his Pakistani visa.

Ignoring the proffered page, the sergeant scoured the rest of the passport. Comparing passport to owner, the sergeant checked Matt's visual identity.

A rough, grubby finger stabbed at Matt. 'You going to Afghanistan. Many guns in Afghanistan, you go there, you get killed.'

'I'm only going up the Khyber Pass, to look at the forts.' Matt pointed at the flimsy permits.

Impatient stabs on a horn behind Matt indicated the bus driver's irritation at the delay. Matt thought about offering money to the sergeant, but the man suddenly lost interest and handed back the permits and passport.

'If you go to Afghanistan you will not be allowed back to Pakistan,' warned the sergeant as he waved Matt away.

Cheers greeted Matt as he climbed back on the bus. It was clear the Afghanis did not like the Pakistani police and were glad to be helping Matt across the border, despite knowing it was illegal.

Climbing further up the pass, great walled forts and fortified villages slipped past: the places Matt was supposed to be visiting. Sightseeing was out of the question. Everyone was too keen to be over the border, not least Matt.

At the highest point of the Khyber Pass they passed Landi Kotal. A steam train stood smoking at the station. The road snapped to the right and dipped sharply towards the border village of Torkham.

Hairpin bends threatened to tip the bus down in to the valley below, where scavengers picked a precarious living from the broken remains of a lorry, the driver lying dead at its side.

'Aafhgaaneestaan, Aafhgaaneestaan, Aafhgaaneestaan!' shouted the Afghans as they pointed excitedly into the dusty, hazy distance. Leaning on Matt's shoulder, a small hand supported a young boy getting a glimpse of his homeland.

Matt grew tense at the realisation that he was soon going to be illegally crossing an international frontier.

Dreary and dusty, the crumbling, brown mud buildings of Torkham were the same colour as the surrounding landscape. Over the low rooftops, twin spurs of the circling hills reached out to seal in the featureless dust bowl that stood as the gateway to another country.

Huge numbers of lorries stacked up in a lorry park alongside the village, all heading across the border to supply the military powers liberating, or occupying, the country, depending on your point of view, as part of the US-led war on terror.

Suddenly the buildings dropped away. Fifty metres ahead a stand of trees lay down black shadows. Two sentry boxes hid in the shade. Barbed wire stretched away from the road on one side and a customs building stood on the other. Gates stood open and a white line across the road marked the border. Traffic moved slowly through the gateway as the bus approached.

A policeman began waving his hands at the bus to slow down as it came to the head of the queue. From his exertions and the way he pointed at the vehicle it looked as though the policeman had been waiting for the bus. He wanted it to stop. Matt sank low in his seat.

The bus driver blasted his air-horn. The policeman waved more frantically. To the enthusiastic cheers of the Afghans, the bus started to speed up. Matt's heart hammered in his chest with excitement. The policeman unslung his gun and pointed it straight at the driver. Another policeman stepped from the shade and aimed his gun at the bus too. The driver capitulated and the bus slowed to a halt.

Chapter Ten

Landi Kotal was less a village and more a bazaar.

Merchandise was crammed into single-storey wattle and daub buildings and spilled into the dusty road. Haggling and deal-making were the predominant activities of the tribesmen in their flowing *kameez* and fine beards, and the western-styled businessmen in designer jeans and Gucci sunglasses.

'Definitely a trading post,' observed Annie.

Electrical goods, whisky, beer and guns stood blatantly on display, though other products were surprisingly hidden away. A youth approached them. 'My cousin have shop here. We drink tea. You see hashish.'

Stig grinned at Annie, then happily accepted the invitation. A few moments later they were sitting on a fine silk Afghan carpet, inside an almost derelict plywood shack. Annie leant on a well-stuffed sack as she drank the tea which had appeared as soon as they took their seats.

The room was unlike that in the drug shop at Darra. There were no shelves displaying the sheets of hashish, only jute flour sacks. Annie only casually wondered where the promised drugs were, though Stig was obviously anxious to see them. Then the serious-faced shopkeeper leant forward and offered Stig a dinner-plate-sized brick of the finest Afghani-black hashish.

Stig's jaw dropped as he accepted it with both hands. The brick must have weighed at least five kilos. He frowned slightly as he concentrated on it. 'It would be worth a fortune if I could get this back home,' he muttered to himself.

'You must be joking.' Annie gasped, worried that he was serious.

Stig continued to stare at the hashish in his hands. 'I'd never do it, but think of the money,' he said at last.

'Do you have opium?' Annie asked the shopkeeper. She'd always wanted to see what it looked like, but had only ever read about it in books.

The man laughed. Tapping the stuffed sack at Annie's back he said one word, 'Opium.' Annie felt her jaw drop.

'I can't even guess how much that would be worth,' muttered Stig.

Tea finished, Annie wanted to get away from so much illicit produce. She was getting uncomfortable with so much opium and hashish around, and she could see the temptation of all that profit rising in Stig. Standing up, she placed her hand firmly on his shoulder. 'Come on,' she said, 'I want to go and look at Afghanistan.'

Walking away from their host's shop they reached the main road running past the village and headed for a wall running alongside it to get a better view of Afghanistan in the distance, the youth who had showed them to his cousins shop following them closely.

As they looked down the hillside to the Afghani border they saw a series of hair-pin bends carrying the road dangerously around the crumbling hills to the valley floor below. Far below them, ant-people picked over a truck that had only recently fallen to its death from the treacherous road.

Torkham lay in the hollow of the flat-bottomed bowl; the border lay just beyond it. A break in the hills let out to the war-scarred country beyond. Concrete tank-traps, barbed wire and a spindly red and white pole set between telephone box guard huts marked the man-made division of the Patan territory.

Scores of lorries sat in a massive parking lot alongside the village waiting their turn to head along the road to Kabul and the NATO bases around the country. On the Afghani side of the border a long snake of lorries waited to come back in.

At the border crossing itself sat a bus, surrounded by policemen and crowds of people. A path led down from a circle of trees around a few colonial style buildings, protected by a ragged Pakistani flag drooping from a flagpole. The nose of a green jeep poked out from under the trees.

Pointing down to Torkham, the youth said, 'See the ruins there? The Russians bombed them then the Afghani communists did too. The mujihadeen lived there then. Now the Taliban bomb them because the Americans use them.'

Annie and Stig stared wonderingly at the ruins and the unapproachable and infamous country of Afghanistan beyond, until a voice disturbed their reverie. 'You want food? You come my cousin's restaurant.' It was their friendly youth, recruiting them again to the business of another of his relatives.

*****

Matt stood in the centre of a shouting mob of Pakistani border police and Afghan tribesmen. He had no idea what was happening. Nobody really seemed interested in him. They were too busy arguing among themselves.

It was twenty minutes since the bus had been stopped. The police had been waiting for him; the earlier check-post must have radioed ahead.

Matt was seriously worried and just hoped they would send him back to Peshawar now. The waiting had made him change his mind about crossing the border and he wished he had never set out on this particular adventure.

Then a single gunshot silenced the crowd. A pistol waving officer had obviously decided enough was enough. The man waved his gun around carelessly, to indicate that Matt was to get in the jeep standing under the trees nearby. Matt climbed in; he had no choice.

A soldier jumped in the driver's seat and two more climbed in the back. The driver wheel-spun the jeep away from the bus, the checkpoint and the border, heading back into Pakistan. The Afghans waved goodbye, their broad smiles displaying yellowing broken teeth, then they turned back to harangue the border guards some more.

Matt held his breath as he hung on for dear life and the jeep sped back up the road to Landi Kotal. He wasn't really sure that he was safe just yet.

*****

The policemen in Mastuj denied all knowledge of anyone who could talk English like a foreigner. One man had been to England and a few others could speak English too, but when Ishmael spoke to them he found their English was worse than his.

Ishmael was proud of his English. He had spent hours listening to the BBC on his radio and he took every opportunity he found to speak with tourists. His father had always impressed on him the benefit of education, especially English. Ishmael could still remember the lecture: 'If you want to be more than a farmer or junior soldier, you must learn English. Without English you will never impress anybody.'

By lunchtime Ishmael had exhausted the possibilities of Mastuj. In such a small place there was little the policemen did not know about local villagers and who was passing through. The village headman was also a man he had known a long time, and was a cousin of his wife too. Over lunch, Rashid Khan confirmed there was no one like the person Ishmael was looking for, either in the village or any of the hamlets nearby.

'Why do you want to find him?' asked the headman as they sipped tea at the end of their meal.

'I'm trying to check the quality of the guides that take people over the Chumarkhan Pass. There've been some complaints from foreigners about a man that speaks perfect English. I doubt there's anything in it, but you never know.'

'I know you and the job you do. There must be more to it than that.'

Ishmael considered Rashid to be an honourable and trustworthy man, and decided to to trust him now. 'There is.

This man who speaks English like a foreigner is not an honourable man like you, he brings shame to this country. If you find him, send me word as soon as you can.'

Mindful that the walk to his next destination at Harchin would take four hours, Ishmael made his excuses soon after and left the village just past one o'clock.

Feeling fit and happy, his legs went straight back into the swing of the slow mountain pace the hill men learnt from childhood and Ishmael followed the gently rising herdsman's track to Harchin. Along the way he chatted casually with two shepherds, and heard the same report twice. The guides who took foreigners over the Chumarkhan Pass lived on the other side of Mastuj and they were all local men, some of whom hardly spoke English at all.

It was almost teatime when he reached Harchin; Ishmael had timed his walk perfectly. Local hospitality being what it was he knew he would be offered some food and a floor to sleep on.

At the first building of the widely spread village he shouted hello. It was the one place that had the room to take guests and all the foreigners stayed here before they crossed the Shandur Pass, if they did not stay in Mastuj. Unless of course they were camping, which was becoming more common these days much to the dissatisfaction of the locals who were able to make more money from the tourists who stayed with them.

His use of the local dialect and the fact that he had married a girl from a village three miles north of Mastuj produced the offer of hospitality he was expecting. He would have been welcomed wherever he was from, except if he was from Gilgit, when he would have been treated with suspicion. Though the old feuds were fading, there was still too much history for everyone to forgive and forget completely.

The family ate a watery stew of tomatoes, onions and a grey potato, with bread and chai, as they sat on carpets in the guest room. There were no other guests and none were really expected until shortly before the upcoming polo tournament. Ishmael let the conversation flow of its own accord; it naturally revolved around tourists and the income it brought without him having to nudge it in the direction he wanted it to go.

He learnt nothing new though. He heard only what was common knowledge, that the tourists usually arrived here in jeeps they had picked up in Chitral. Very rarely, one or two tourists would stop off in Mastuj for a day with their jeep before continuing with their journey. More rarely still, a lone tourist would hitch to Mastuj and hope to find another jeep to take them over the pass with some other tourists or a local travelling on business. Only rarely did they come the other way, from Gilgit.

But the favoured foreign visitors were the research students, climbers and film crews. They spent money like water, paid well over the odds and stayed for weeks. They were of little interest to Ishmael though, they were far too well monitored to be linked with his investigation.

Ishmael retired for the night vaguely frustrated. It had taken him three days to learn there was nothing much to learn. If foreigners were disappearing, they were unlikely to be doing it around here.

*****

As Annie and Stig left the restaurant, stuffed on a surprisingly spicy chicken dish accompanied by a mound of steaming rice, and headed for the road, a green jeep roared up from Torkham and slid to a halt in the dust. Two policemen jumped from the back of the jeep, rifles held casually in one hand while they half helped, half dragged, a foreigner out after them. The man stumbled to the ground and held up his hands placatingly to the policemen.

One of the policemen noticed Annie and Stig. 'Why are you here? What are you doing?'

Annie and Stig stood in lonely isolation, unsure what to say. The strolling tribesmen melted away from them to watch from a safe distance.

Without waiting for a reply the policeman shouted, 'You must go back to Peshawar! Now!'

Casually swinging their Kalashnikovs over their shoulders, the two policemen pulled the nervous foreigner to his feet and waved Stig and Annie to a nearby checkpoint.

'You wait here. You go next bus Peshawar,' shouted the policemen and left all three of them in the charge of the men at the police post.

Annie recognised the new arrival from the Khyber Hotel. 'What are you doing here?' she asked with a smile. He was covered in dust and looking rather shaken.

'Got caught going into Afghanistan. Fortunately they brought me back here. Looks like they're not going to arrest me. Thank God.'

'Good job for you they're not going to. I wouldn't fancy being in a Pakistani jail.'

'God, no. I saw one of them last week and don't want to go near one again.' Matt shuddered at the memory.

Annie and Stig exchanged glances. 'Anyway, I'm Annie and this is Stig.' She gave him an encouraging smile.

'Hi. I'm Matt.' Then it dawned on Matt who she was. 'You're staying at the Khyber Hotel too, aren't you? I saw you there yesterday.' Then he blushed and started slapping dust from his dirty clothes.

Stig raised an eyebrow at Annie and smiled mischievously. 'Yes, we noticed you'd noticed us. You must join our little group. An adventurous fellow like you is always good to have around. If we ever get out of this place alive you must have dinner with us tonight.'

'Thanks,' muttered Matt as he smeared dirt across his sweat-stained face instead of cleaning it away, while Annie and Stig smiled in amusement at the mess he was nervously making of himself.

A pick-up truck laboured up the hill from Torkham, to be stopped at the checkpoint. Without asking the driver for permission, the policeman waved the three foreigners onto the open back. Annie and Stig climbed in unhindered, but the policeman made Matt wait, then hurried him in last with the barrel of his gun whilst shouting instructions to the driver. Matt fell clumsily to floor as the truck pulled away quickly, before he'd had the chance to find a seat and sit down.

Matt clung to the hot metal side of the truck, trying to stop himself being thrown around as the vehicle raced down the pass, away from Afghanistan. He stared silently at Landi Kotal as it faded into the dust, cursing his failure and the embarrassment of meeting Annie in the manner he had. All those guns had scared him more than he'd thought possible and he needed to calm his nerves before he'd be able to have a sensible conversation with Annie and Stig.

Annie and Stig watched him with interest as he stared at the passing landscape, grim-faced and tense. They left him to his reverie, wondering what he had actually done to incur the wrath of the police.

*****

Back at the Khyber Hotel Matt strode to his dormitory with little more than a grunt to Annie and Stig. He was annoyed now. He'd failed to get to Afghanistan and to make it worse Annie and Stig had witnessed his humiliation.

Sitting on his charpoy, Matt pulled a map from his bag and scoured it for possible crossing points into Afghanistan further north in the country. He found what he wanted. The road through the Chitral valley to the Shandur Pass weaved along the border, and a few valleys cut to and across the border from the main Chitral valley. That was where Scott had said you could get across the border too, and Matt resolved that tomorrow he was going north to try his luck again. It would also get him away from Annie and save him further embarrassment.

Stuffing the map back in his bag he slipped out into a darkened Peshawar in search of dinner. He didn't want company tonight, especially Annie, since he must have looked such a fool to her earlier when he was lying cowering in the dirt, all covered in dust.

In a narrow alley, not far from the hotel, Matt climbed three wooden steps to an open fronted restaurant. The smiling waiter waved him to a seat on the terrace and asked what he wanted. Matt pointed at the plate of a nearby diner. 'Same, same,' he said in imitation of a phrase he'd heard used often by other travellers the last few days. 'And Coca Cola,' he added glumly. He might not want company, but he still felt lonely.

The waiter scurried from the restaurant and shouted orders from the middle of the street. A kebab seller began cooking shish on his charcoal grill, while a baker slapped chapati on the side of his beehive oven and another chef began tossing onions, tomatoes and other local delicacies in a great iron wok over an open fire. A few minutes later the shish slid off their skewers into the wok, the bread hit a plate to be chopped with a razor sharp knife, then the wok-seared mixture splashed over it.

As the plate arrived in front of Matt a small boy ran up with a dripping bottle of Coke and popped the lid as he set it on the table.

Matt sat admiring his compilation dinner as he sipped the ice-cold Coke, until a voice startled him from his contemplation. 'Can we join you?'

'Yeah. Why not?' said Matt, trying to sound enthusiastic.

There was not enough room for Matt and the four newly arrived backpackers to all fit on the veranda, so they moved inside. Matt ended up with his back to the open window, the alley behind him.

'Where have you been all day?' asked one of the group.

'I tried to get into Afghanistan.' Matt smiled nervously at the group, unsure how they'd react.

'I thought there was a war on,' said one of the group.

'Nah. It's stopped for a while. I met this guy in Lahore, he just got back, said it was a great place.'

After four more meals were ordered the conversation came back to matt.

'Guess you never made it to Kabul, then. What happened?'

Matt took a deep breath and launched into the story of his day. He began at the start and quickly fell into the pattern he had derided in Lahore. As he ate and the other meals arrived, Matt embellished the story of his hunt for permits and the trip up the Khyber Pass. Eventually he got to the point where the bus was driving at the border guard.

'This border guard had his gun out. He was firing in the air. The passengers were all shouting at the driver to keep going. I was screaming at him as well. Then the border guard brought his gun down and pointed it at the bus. Everyone ducked, including the driver. When the bus stopped the police came on and dragged me off it.'

'Weren't you scared?' asked one of the intently listening group.

'Nah. I demanded to be let through. Said I could go to Afghanistan if I wanted. I argued for ages, but they wouldn't let me carry on. Eventually they just threw me in a police jeep and took me back up to Landi Kotal. I was so angry with them I gave them abuse all the way back up the Khyber Pass.'

'Looked like you were scared shitless to me when I saw you.'

Matt spun round to see Annie staring at him, with Stig laughing behind her.

Tension silenced the restaurant. Then Matt's audience started laughing.

Matt threw some money on the table and stormed out into the street, his humiliation complete.

*****

Mountains spread across the vista below him, all the way to the horizon. K2 glistened in the distance. The view was spectacular and it was not often that Chris got the chance to experience such beauty in his job. Ian had pulled diplomatic

162

strings and secured Chris one of the VIP tickets held in reserve for every flight from Rawalpindi to Gilgit. Even from the air the road looked terrible and he was glad to be seeing it from above. Scars on the road marked where frequent landslides had slid down the mountains and slashed across the infamous Karakoram Highway.

Most of the other passengers were visiting mountaineers, heading towards K2, Rakaposhi or one of the other major mountains of the Western Himalayas. Climbing gear filled the hold and lay strewn in the aisles. Chris listened with bemusement to the climbers trying to outdo each other with stories of the climbs they had completed, or disasters they had survived. He wondered why they did it; the more dangerous the climb the more pleasure they seemed to gain from the experience, or at least the re-telling of it.

The descent to Gilgit was best described as exciting. The plane rocked and bucked frighteningly as the competing airflows from the mountains and the valleys battled for supremacy and carelessly tossed the twin-engined Fokker about as it fought to reach the runway.

First off the plane and travelling with hand-luggage only, Chris left the Foreigners Registration Office before any of the climbers reached it. With the name of a travellers' hostel picked at random from the notice board, Chris headed straight for the simply named 'Tourist Hotel and Campsite' to start his enquiries.

*****

Annie, Stig and Nils sat at the table Matt had just vacated. Raucous laughs had filled the restaurant as Stig carelessly recounted how they had met with Matt earlier in the day, embellishing his own story in turn, and trampled Matt's credibility further into the dirt.

Annie had joined the laughter to start with, but her discomfort had grown as she remembered the tension that had etched Matt's face as he lay in the dirt then crouched on the floor of the truck as they returned to Peshawar.

She now felt guilty at having made his day even worse and couldn't stop thinking of him after the conversation had moved on to others subjects.

As they'd arrive much later, Annie, Stig and Nils were soon left to themselves and Annie returned the conversation to Matt. 'He was not happy when they dragged him out the truck and he looked awfully tense in the truck on the way back to Peshawar. I wonder what really happened to him today?'

Stig looked at Annie with bemusement. 'Does it really matter? You can't go telling tall stories like that and expect to get away with it.'

'I'm sure you've told a few tall stories in your time, too,' said Annie seriously. 'He was probably trying to rebuild his confidence after the shite day he'd had.'

'Who knows? Anyway, he won't be talking to you again any time soon after you showed him up like that,' laughed Nils.

'It doesn't seem so funny now,' said Annie forlornly.

Nils scowled. 'Let's forget about him. This is our last night of travelling, we're off home tomorrow.' Then he winked at them, 'I need to get my own tall stories ready to impress all the guys back in Stockholm.' He raised his bottle of Coke and laughed. 'Chin chin! We're having a wild night on the town, Pakistani style.'

Annie allowed herself a smile and clinked bottles with Stig and Nils.

'What about you?' Stig asked Annie. 'Where're you off to next?'

'I'm going north. I want to visit the Kalash valleys near Chitral. I might not be able to get to Nuristan, but at least I'll get to visit the next best thing. I'll head off tomorrow morning, since you guys are leaving anyway.'

*****

Outside on the restaurant's veranda, Raseem sat uncomfortably in the unfamiliar clothes of a northern tribesman. He had never liked wearing them, preferring Levis and T-shirts, but he wanted to look like a local so he could follow Annie without attracting attention.

He'd chosen a seat where he could overhear everything that had been said and carefully used Urdu as he ordered his own food. Having heard enough of Annie's plans Raseem slipped away to make his own preparations for heading north. She was heading into his trap; he would have her soon.

*****

Matt scurried down the stairs of the hotel and out onto the street. Only the chef and small boy saw him leave, as they prepared the first brew of chai for the day and swept the dusty floor.

The street was relatively empty and peaceful, with little of the dust that would be stirred up as soon as the city started work. A sleepy tuk-tuk driver happily accepted the offered fare and pulled away past an empty jeep.

At the Bala Hisar fort Matt found a large collection of partly filled buses waiting in the lee of the walls. The drivers shouted their destinations at him as he stepped from the tuk-tuk and weaved through the milling throng of passengers.

'Chitral? Chitral?' he asked. In reply he received shaken heads but the men pointed him onwards through the crowds. He kept moving along the rank of buses.

Matt was near the end of the row when a driver eventually got more specific and pointed along the road past the last bus and said, 'Chitral bus from Broadway Station.' Half a mile along the road another collection of buses sat on the opposite side of the highway.

Broadway Station boasted an eclectic collection of dilapidated, rickety looking mid-size buses that had seen better days. 'Chitral?' Matt asked the first driver he met, but another man grabbed Matt's arm and ushered him to a bus.

Matt watched as his rucksack was heaved onto the roof-rack, to join suitcases and sacks, and be secured with rope.

Helping hands pulled him aboard the bus and showed him to a seat right at the back.

Though the previous day had been exhausting, Matt hadn't slept well. He'd been too wound up by the stressful failure of his border crossing and escape back up the pass from Torkham. He'd also fretted over the embarrassment of the scene at the restaurant, particularly the fact it was Annie who had shown him up. He was tired now though, and once he was settled in his seat Matt closed his eyes and quickly began to doze.

*****

Annie waved goodbye to Nils and Stig as the tuk-tuk spluttered away from the hotel, barely noticing the same jeep Matt had passed ten minutes earlier.

The traffic was building up quickly and though the tuk-tuk went straight to Broadway station it took longer for Annie to complete the journey than it had for Matt not so long before.

As soon as the tuk-tuk stopped touts started shouting the destinations of their buses. Annie nodded acceptance to the one shouting Dir, the name of the village where she would stay the night part way to Chitral. Within moments her bag was lashed to the roof of his bus and covered with netting. The driver was already starting his engine as Annie climbed aboard to find a seat.

She was pointed towards the back where one seat remained empty, next to a sleeping foreigner who she immediately recognised with a pang of consternation.

*****

Raseem stepped from the teashop when the tuk-tuk was only metres from the hotel. Annie was going alone; life was getting better by the minute.

At Broadway station he hid between two buses and leered as Annie watched her bag loaded on the roof of a nearby vehicle, then climbed on board herself.

As the bus roared to life he scurried back to his own jeep and prepared to follow it. She might have said she was heading to Chitral, but he wasn't going to let her slip away by being careless and presuming she was going straight there.

*****

Matt woke as the bus jerked forward and a body bumped him as it sat next to him on his bench seat.

The bus bounced across the rutted parking lot and lurched onto the road as Matt cleared his head and turned to look at his neighbour.

'What the fuck?'

'Hi.' Annie smiled nervously at him.

'What are you doing here? Come to make a fool of me again, huh? Once wasn't enough?' Matt glared angrily at Annie.

'It was your own fault. You shouldn't have lied so much,' said Annie more defensively than she'd intended.

'What's it to you anyway? I was just telling a story like every other traveller in the country,' retorted Matt.

'I can't stand people who lie, especially when I know they're lying,' said Annie somewhat pompously.

'Fine. Well fuck off and sit somewhere else then if you don't like me so much.' Matt's face was flushed, but Annie couldn't tell if he was angry, or embarrassed.

'Sorry, can't. This was the last seat. We'll have to put up with each other for a while,' she snapped back.

'What are you on this bus for anyway?' said Matt as he edged sideways to give her more space. 'I don't believe it was just an accident.'

'Don't worry. I wouldn't have got on this bus if I'd known you were on it. Just go back to sleep and pretend I'm not here.'

'I will,' said Matt, closing his eyes and pretending to sleep again. Instead of sleeping, though, he found himself increasingly conscious of Annie's hip pressing against his on the narrow seat. And he found it surprisingly comforting to

167

have another foreigner travelling with him, even if he was still bloody angry with her.

With great difficulty, Matt feigned sleep. He tried not to move in case Annie moved away from him. Then Annie saved him from further pretence by jabbing him harshly in the ribs with her elbow.

'What did you do that for? I was sleeping,' he protested grumpily.

'No you weren't, you're too tense to be asleep. Anyway, the driver wants his fare.'

Money was passing forward to the driver, who counted it, worked out the change and sent it back, all the while steering with the back of his wrist. Matt and Annie exchanged nervous glances as the driver suddenly grabbed the wheel to steady the bus when it hit a pot-hole. They watched the flow of money and soon worked out the fare, chatting stiffly despite their initial harsh words. The fare-paying process took its time; nobody seemed in a hurry and any way, as Matt opined to Annie, the journey was going to be a few hours long and no-one was going anywhere.

By the time Matt thought to look out of the window again, to see if they had left Peshawar, the bus was climbing the foothills of the Hindu Kush and he was feeling less angry with Annie.

*****

Enjoying the luxury of his air-conditioned jeep, Raseem listened to Bollywood Gangsta rap and fantasised. He had almost crashed twice as his dreaming distracted him from the road. Cigarette ash dusted the carpet and upholstery as he chain-smoked to calm the lust, frustration and anticipation of what was to come. Another whore had failed to work her stuff the night before, and suffered the consequences; he could still hear the pathetic whimpers she'd emitted as he repeatedly slapped her.

Her failure had even cost him, twice. He had tried to claim she was no good to get out of paying, but the bastard pimp had charged him damages for the black eye he'd given her, on top of the fee he refused to waive. Raseem thumped the steering wheel again and the jeep lurched dangerously.

*****

Rising steeply, the road wound around deep cuts in the barren hills, where the run-off from many monsoons had taken soil down to the muddy waters of the Indus, which eventually flowed south past Sukkur to the sea east of Karachi.

The climbing took its toll on the bus. They stopped frequently at the many hairpin bends, where sparkling streams offered refreshment for the bus and the well-practised driver carefully let off the pressure in the overheating and leaking radiator, before adding ice-cold water from the stream to cool the still running engine.

The passengers grabbed any opportunity to escape from the cramped interior, stretch their legs and cool themselves. Many struggling buses stopped at the streams, and enterprising locals sold Coke, water, mangoes and melons, all chilled to a thirst quenching cold in the glacial streams.

It took an hour or two until Matt was sure, it being a new experience for him in Pakistan, but the temperature was definitely dropping as they headed north into the hills. By lunchtime Matt was beginning to wish he had a jumper, and the cooling breeze they'd enjoyed at the refreshment stops, had become a chilling wind that almost made him shiver. But his bag and the jumper were secured out of reach on the roof of the bus. Annie seemed better prepared, and pulled a fleecy from her bag once the temperature began to drop.

Though they were still wary of each other, at the stops Matt and Annie stuck together from an unspoken need for companionship. On the bus Matt was relaxed enough again to doze properly and catch up on his sleep.

Suddenly, or so it seemed to Matt, the bus was in a parade-ground sized mud patch in the middle of a village. When the bus stopped, everyone disembarked, quickly collected their luggage and disappeared into narrow alleys. Then the bus drove away too.

With his rucksack at his feet, Matt was at a loss to know what was happening. Annie was standing close by, though they hadn't spoken to each other during the disembarkation. When the parade ground was empty, apart from a few kids playing on the far side, Matt broke the silence. 'What happens now?'

'How the fuck should I know?' Annie sounded tense and Matt eyed her carefully. He smiled to himself as he thought how little she would like it if he said how attractive she looked when she was angry.

'What are you laughing at? It's not funny.' She was almost shouting at him now.

'I know, but I only asked a question.'

Annie laughed nervously. 'It was more an accusation than a question.'

He rolled his eyes. 'For God's sake. Give me a break.'

Annie stared at him for a moment then said, 'You didn't know the bus stops here and we have to swap to another for the next part of the journey?'

'No. I just presumed it went all the way. Where are we anyway?'

Annie snorted dismissively and walked over to a stall, where a vendor dozed in the shade, to buy a Coke. After a moment's indecision Matt followed her.

'Are you following me now?' snapped Annie.

'Can't a guy buy a drink when he wants one?'

Neither of them noticed a jeep pull into the square and park casually in the shade of a willow on the far side of the square.

Annie leant her rucksack against a wall and propped herself against it to wait patiently. Matt deposited himself nearby and pulled out his guidebook, feeling an urgent need to better acquaint himself with the details of the journey he was undertaking.

An hour later, and another bus pulled into the parade ground from a different corner. Passengers disembarked quickly while the driver and the stall-holder began unloading luggage from the roof.

'Guess this is for us,' said Matt, having found no mention in the guidebook of a break in the journey.

'Clever boy. Whatever gave you that idea?' snapped Annie.

A crowd miraculously emerged from the lanes leading off the courtyard to mill around the bus and start loading their luggage. Matt and Annie pushed determinedly towards the bus and Matt shouted 'Chitral?' to the driver standing atop the bus. When the man nodded and smiled, Matt unconsciously took Annie's bag from her to hand it up to the children now clambering over the roof, before handing his up after it.

'Was that a peace offering, or some male chauvinist crap?' said Annie neutrally.

'Whatever you want. Makes no difference to me,' responded Matt as carefully as he could.

Annie looked at him closely for a moment, then seemed to make a decision. 'I'll assume it was a peace offering then, because if I have to travel in such close proximity to someone, I'd rather do it with them talking to me. I never did like confrontation, despite what I might have said the past two days.'

The vague guilt at the way she had treated Matt in the restaurant the night before had been nagging at Annie all day, making her more grumpy with him than she should have been. She felt better already for being a bit nicer to him.

The driver impatiently honked his air horn to summon any latecomers, a couple of whom came scurrying from the alleys as Annie and Matt climbed aboard, then he revved his engine to drag the overloaded bus northwards.

Older and noisier than the conveyance of the first leg of the journey, progress was slowed to jogging pace. The scenery though, began to change and trees appeared, sparse and thin, but increasingly green.

The Panchkora River, fed by melting snow and hidden glaciers far upstream, tumbled over the boulder strewn valley floor alongside the road. River spray cooled the air further and pines competed with sweat soaked bodies to scent the bus.

Slowly and painfully Annie and Matt exchanged desultory conversation, trying hard to find common ground between them. They fell back onto safe travellers subjects, pointing out anything remotely interesting that passed the bus and comparing where they had previously been since leaving the UK. Unnoticed by either of them, the jeep followed a hundred metres behind.

Dusk hit suddenly and when the sun had dipped below the surrounding peaks the temperature plummeted equally quickly. The pale blue sky high above them contrasted sharply to the creeping shadows around the bus.

A thick copse of trees lined the road. The river gurgled ten metres away. There was no sign of habitation or human activity when the bus stopped.

'What's happening?' Matt had no idea why the bus would stop where they were. The men all disembarked quietly, leaving the few women on board. A jeep moved past them on the road, but Matt and Annie didn't pay it any attention as they worried about why they had stopped. Matt momentarily feared another change of bus, but with the women staying on board and there being no move to unload the luggage he quickly discounted that option.

Following the men off the bus Matt and Annie found them lining up for prayer time. An open-air mosque nestled under willow trees on the banks of the river. Not wanting to intrude, the two foreigners moved away to sit on a river-cooled boulder. They were close enough to discreetly watch and hear the devotions of the faithful, whilst far enough away not to feel as if they were prying.

Chilled air rose from the river. Goosebumps rose on Matt's arms. In the peace and serenity of the forest only the murmur of prayer and the babble of the water could be heard.

'This is so romantic,' Annie murmured to herself.

Matt watched her out the corner of his eye, suddenly overwhelmed with the desire to lean forward and kiss her.

*****

Two hundred metres upriver Raseem abandoned the jeep and crept back through the trees to spy on the bus. He was paranoid Annie would slip through his fingers if he let her out of his sight for a moment. When he was close enough to get a clear view of Annie sitting on a rock, the sight of some unknown foreigner sitting so close to her sparked a vicious flash of jealousy that overtook his lust and he gave free rein to a fantasy of smashing the man's head open with a rock.

The prayer time had caught him unawares and he had been forced to drive past the bus, desperately hoping Annie wouldn't notice him, to find somewhere inconspicuous to stop. He himself never prayed unless his father was around and forcibly made him go through the ritual.

*****

An angry blast of the air horn dragged Matt back to the hard reality of his lonely boulder. His daydream had developed and the worshippers had got back on the bus unnoticed. He was the last passenger to board again and he had not even taken his seat when the driver lurched the bus forward to begin what Matt expected to be the final stage of the journey to Chitral.

'Penny for your thoughts. You were in a world of your own out there,' Annie teased him gently.

'It was nothing,' muttered Matt as he felt himself blush and he turned away from Annie to look out the window.

Matt had no idea where they were, or how far it was to Chitral. In his haste to leave Peshawar he had not checked the length of the journey in his guidebook, only the departure point. And when he had checked the guidebook during their unexpected stop he could not find any information on how long it took to reach Chitral from Peshawar. The section on Chitral was quite brief really and it only listed a few minor villages along the way. Now, as they headed north and he managed to relax a bit, he found it rather liberating not to be bound by time and to take the trip as it came.

Outside the windows of the bus it was so dark Matt could have believed he was in a tunnel. He had not seen much more than a few metres of the rough dirt road ahead of them in the weak beam of the headlights for more than an hour, though if he stared hard he could just make out what might have been an occasional blurred tree alongside the bus.

When the bus cautiously entered a darkened village Matt breathed a sigh of relief. His shoulders and neck were knotted and sore from the violent jolting of the bus during the journey.

From what Matt could not see in the darkness, he assumed the village had no electricity. It was definitely a small village, consisting of little more than one street squeezed between steep valley walls.

Stopping against a dry stone wall the bus driver killed the engine. By the time Matt was off the bus passengers had already begun unloading their luggage and were disappearing into the darkness.

'Thank God we're in Chitral at last. I'm knackered'

'You really have no idea, do you?' Annie's voice had more than a hint of surprise and Matt found himself feeling somewhat inadequate compared to her, though he wasn't too sure why.

'About what?' he responded somewhat tartly.

'Are you being ironic, or are you really that uninformed?'

'What? You've lost me.' Matt really was confused now.

'This is probably Dir. The bus usually stays here overnight and crosses the Lowari Pass in the morning. There are

174

insurgents from across the border in the hills around here, so it's too dangerous to cross the pass at night.'

'Ah,' said Matt as it sank in that he was well and truly lost. 'I didn't know about any of that,' he said, trying to make light of his mistake. 'It's a good job you're here, or I'd really be in trouble. My guidebook mentioned Dir, but I thought that was the last place we stopped.'

'I'm amazed you've got this far in one piece. How did you manage it?' Annie looked at Matt in open surprise.

'Luck, I guess,' muttered Matt, appalled at how he had once again got himself in a situation for which he was totally unprepared.

Annie took pity on him and decided to let him know where he was. 'We're just over halfway to Chitral, as the crow flies. It's a long trip.'

Matt looked around disconsolately, unable to see more that the outline of a few houses. 'Is there a hotel around here? It's going to be cold tonight and I'm not sure I want to be sleeping outside if there are insurgents around.'

*****

Fifty American dollars lay on the rough counter. The receptionist watched the money in anticipation of securing such a welcome boost to his meagre income, for doing nothing.

'Make sure you lock the door and hide all lights. If you screw up I'll be back for my money and you'll be paying me to leave too. Got it?'

The receptionist nodded eagerly. The money was a good enough incentive to do what was asked; the threats were superfluous, even if they'd carried any weight. This city boy who everybody knew smoked too much dope and chased Western women wouldn't leave the mountains if the headman decreed it. And it was the headman the receptionist was afraid of, not this boy.

As the hotel door closed behind him, Raseem listened for the bolts to click home. Happy that his instructions were being followed he sat casually on the hotel steps and lit a cigarette.

He enjoyed being flash with his cash and getting the simple-minded villagers to do what he wanted. The power cut was also playing into his hands, the darkness would make Annie more amenable to his suggestion.

Annie's bus was disgorging its passengers fifty metres away and Raseem watched for a glimpse of his prey. There was only one hotel in the village and he was reasonably confident they would try and stay there since it was where most of the few foreigners stayed on their way through and it was listed in the *Lonely Planet*. He'd stayed here a few times before on his way north with girls he'd picked up in Islamabad. It was a crap place and he doubted they'd remember who he was.

Figures faded away into the night until only three were left. The woman had to be her; only a foreign whore would go unveiled around here. The unknown foreign man was still with her. Raseem knew he was going to have to deal with him. 'Fucking bastard, where did you come from?' Raseem hissed his anger at the man talking to the last of the locals as Annie heaved her rucksack onto her back.

*****

Pale white light weakly illuminated the scene as a new moon rose above a mountain.

'Hotel?' Matt asked the last of the departing passengers.

Pointing only with his chin, the man indicated a dark, lopsided, wooden, two-storey building fifty metres away along the road. A cigarette glowed briefly on the front steps. A parked jeep sat quietly on the road at their base.

'Looks like there's somebody there anyway.' Annie stepped forward. Matt trailed along behind her thinking he would leave the arrangements to her and see what transpired.

A lounging man blocked the steps, puffing away on his cigarette.

'Excuse me,' said Annie wanting the man to move so she could get up the steps without having to climb over him.

'No point. It's closed.' The man peered at her more closely through the darkness. 'Hey, aren't you that girl I met in Islamabad and Peshawar? What's your name again?'

Annie peered back at him and smiled with recognition. 'Yeah, hi. It's Annie, you're Ricky aren't you? What are you doing here? Anyone would think you were following me or something.'

'I'm on my way up to the mountains. I've got some stuff coming over from northern Afghanistan to send back to my Dad in England.'

'Why's the hotel shut?' demanded Matt nervously. The last thing he wanted to do was spend the night sleeping outdoors.

'No idea, mate. It was open last time I came through.'

'Is there anywhere else to stay in this place?' Matt looked over his shoulder at the darkened village behind him, worried they really would have to sleep outside. He eyed up the hotel verandah as a possible campsite

'No. I'm just having a break before I keep on driving up to Chitral.'

'I thought there were insurgents on the road.' Annie glanced nervously around the dark street as well.

'There are. But an army lorry just left a few minutes before the bus arrived. I'll catch it up and stick with them. It'll be safe enough.'

'Are you sure there's nowhere else to stay?' said Annie apprehensively. The idea of having to rely on the army to get to Chitral safely was a lot to accept.

'No. This is it. I'm not looking forward to driving all night by myself, but at least it'll be warmer.'

Annie and Matt looked at each other, partners now in an adventure they hadn't planned, or wanted, and unsure what to do next.

'I know. Why don't you come with me?' Ricky was sitting expectantly upright, a pleased grin on his face. Matt stiffened.

'How do you know this guy?' he asked Annie.

'He's all right. I met him Islamabad and he warned me off some druggie French guy. He also bought my train ticket for the Khyber Railway.'

'Exactly where are you going?' demanded Matt of Ricky.

'Are you always so rude?' Annie looked slightly embarrassed and smiled apologetically at Ricky. 'This guy has helped me a few times already.'

'I bet he's going to buy drugs. What else comes out of Afghanistan these days?'

'Matt!' said Annie, horrified.

'It's all right. I don't blame him.' Ricky turned a humble face to Annie. 'I wouldn't trust people I'd only just met around here either.' Ricky turned on his best smile. 'I'm going to see if I can buy some carpets from an old friend of my father's and I also plan to look in on my old family home in a valley among the hills above Chitral.'

'Is it a Kalash valley?' said Annie with interest.

'No. But they're just over the pass above my house and it's almost at the Afghan border. So,' chuckled Ricky, 'seeing as I'm not a drug dealer, just a dodgy carpet salesman, do you guys want to come with me tonight?'

Annie looked at the dark hotel, the hard boards on the verandah and the silent village behind her. Then she made a decision for her and Matt. 'Yes, we'll come with you, won't we Matt!' she said, more as a statement than a question.

Matt stared at Ricky, weighing up his options. It seemed he could stay here on his own, or go with Annie and Ricky. 'I guess it'll be okay. We don't really have a choice anyway,' he said grudgingly.

Chapter Eleven

'All aboard! Luggage and the lady in the back, men in the front.' Ricky was trying to be the life and soul of the party. Then as an afterthought he said, 'It's not me being sexist, it's just that it looks better for the locals. They're not so sophisticated as us Brits.'

The road curved through the village and was climbing steeply even before it left the last of the buildings behind it. The glare of the jeep's powerful headlights tunnelled the view forward along the unmade road, highlighting huge black potholes. Ricky weaved around them going far too fast for Matt's liking.

'Gotta go fast to make sure we catch the army before they're too far up the mountain.' Ricky seemed to sense Matt's unease. 'The road only opened again last week after the winter. The last snowfall was late this year and delayed the thaw for a couple of weeks,' he added.

Blurred shapes gave the only hint that pine trees still lined the road. But the landscape seemed inconsequential as everyone stared at the road to watch for the potholes that threatened to swallow the jeep.

'The government spent billions of *rupees* building a tunnel through this mountain, you know?'

Matt and Annie exchanged glances. 'So, uh, why aren't we using it?' asked Annie, uncertainly.

Ricky laughed, 'Because they never quite finished it. The lights rarely work. It floods. The road breaks up all the time. Typical Pakistan.'

'Not much different to England, they can't build a road properly there either.' In spite of himself, Matt was softening towards Ricky as he relaxed in the safe cocoon of the jeep.

Time lost its value in the dark warmth of the jeep. The heaving, bouncing, jarring ride soon prevented all but desultory conversation. Ricky politely asked a few questions and made occasional observations about the road, but driving mostly absorbed his concentration.

*****

Though Raseem had pretended to worry about the insurgents, he wasn't that bothered. It had been quiet here for a while and they rarely struck at night. It was a pity the tunnel was closed at night as he hated going over the pass, the isolation on the mountain frightened him when he was on is own. He didn't have much choice though if he was going to get Annie in his jeep tonight.

The presence of Matt, however, was a real problem. Raseem fumed to himself about what the fuck he was going do with this guy sitting alongside him. Matt had not figured in his plans. He'd planned to charm Annie to his house, or failing that, take her there anyway. But now there was a complication. All the way from Peshawar until they'd stopped at the outdoor mosque he'd been dreaming of having Annie to himself. He'd fantasised about having her in the jeep with him, where he could run his fingers up the inside of her thigh and feast his eyes on her body as they drove leisurely through the mountains.

But now Matt was here in the jeep with them he was worried Annie would remember him from university and start to laugh at him again. The mere thought of it fired an urge in him to hit someone, particularly Matt. Once he'd tamped his anger down again he reassured himself with the thought that in the dark, with Annie safely in the back of the jeep, there was little possibility she would recognise who he was. It was funny how foreigners believed any rubbish he told them about the local sensibilities towards women.

Annie was frustratingly out of reach and out of sight though. He had to get rid of Matt somehow.

*****

Isabelle's throat was sore and dry, her lips cracked from dehydration. She had screamed for hours until her voice gave out. It was now getting dark and her anxiety was turning to desperation.

It had been five days since Ricky last visited her, and though she had gone easy on the water it had given out yesterday. The food had all gone on day three.

Returning to the door she continued picking at the frame around the bottom hinge. She had kicked until her feet were bruised and bleeding, but the wood was cracked and slowly the splinters were coming away to reveal the rusted screws holding her prisoner.

Fear of being left to die had given way to a burning desire to escape. She was not just going to give up without a fight.

*****

Less than an hours slow drive from Dir, a police checkpoint loomed out of the darkness. A barrier blocked the road and a small table stood in front of a simple wooden hut.

Ricky and a Frontier Force policeman shouted incomprehensibly at each other through the window of the jeep.

'Can I have your passports, please?' asked Ricky quietly. He looked apprehensive and perspiration stood out on his forehead, despite the cold.

The policeman examined the two passports by the light of his torch and spoke forcefully to Ricky again in Urdu.

'The policeman advises us not to cross the Lowari Pass tonight. He says it is dangerous because there have been Patan bandits from across the border robbing travellers on this road recently.'

'I thought you said they were insurgents, and what about the Army lorry you said was up ahead?' asked Matt sharply.

'It's ten minutes ahead of us. If I drive fast we'll probably catch it and be OK.' Ricky pointed upwards through the windscreen.

Matt looked through the glass and saw headlights floating upwards in the darkness ahead of them as the policemen copied their names and passport numbers into a book in his hut. 'How far are we from the border here?'

The passports came back through the window. 'Not far. A few miles.' Then Ricky asked, 'Do you want to go on, or go back to Dir?'

Annie went to speak, but Matt spoke over her. His desire to impress her was surprisingly strong. 'We're not scared to go on, but it's up to you, it's your jeep.'

'*Chelo*,' said Ricky firmly.

With a casual shrug of, 'I've warned you,' from the policeman, Ricky revved the engine and continued upwards in an attempt to catch the army truck.

Matt and Annie searched the night for signs of gun-wielding bandits, but instead of bandits they soon saw frozen snow glowing in the beam of the headlights as they swung around the hairpin bends on the steeply climbing road.

Ricky pushed the jeep as fast as he could, splashing it through icy run-off and slipping it sideways on the greasy corners. He was increasingly agitated and tense. Matt clung to the door handle of the jeep and began to wish he'd stayed in Dir.

'Whoa,' shouted Annie from the back seat. 'I'd rather take my chances with bandits than die in a car crash.'

'Sorry,' answered Ricky contritely as he slowed the jeep.

The lights of the army lorry crept slowly closer.

Then Ricky slammed on the brakes and snaked the jeep to a halt. Matt and Annie lurched forward in their seats. The bonnet hung over a trench slicing across the road. To their right the sheer walls of a fluorescent glacier rose fifteen feet above them, to their left another wall showed where the ice carried on its journey below the road.

Black emptiness loomed ahead. The ground in front dropped away and the headlights picked out nothing beyond the dip.

'What the hell is it?' asked Matt after a few moments silence.

'A glacier,' answered Ricky. 'Let's take a look.' He jumped down to the road. 'At least the water flow drops at night,' he said.

Annie and Matt followed Ricky and stood either side of him as they stared at the great gouge the glacier had scraped from the road. Water raced from the foot of the glacier on the right and poured back into an ebony cave on the left.

'Have they cut a path through the glacier?' whispered Annie, awestruck at the sight.

'Yes, they have to slice a bit more off every few days as the glacier creeps across the road. You two will have to walk through ahead of me and stand either side of the road to guide me over. Make sure there are no big holes under the water. Occasionally it washes the road right away.' Ricky smiled encouragingly at them and directed Annie towards the high side of the road, away from the chasm under the ice falling away down the mountain on their left that he nudged Matt towards.

Annie and Matt carefully waded through the icy, ankle deep water that soaked into their boots and numbed their feet.

*****

Caressing the gear stick Raseem engaged four wheel drive while staring at Annie, who was highlighted nicely in his headlights. Slamming the gearbox into first he aimed the headlights of the jeep directly between Annie and Matt on the far side of the channel. Edging slowly over the lip of the glacial river Raseem inched forward through the water towards them.

Creeping forwards, Raseem was distracted by the vision of Annie highlighted ahead of him and he watched her anxious face as much as he did the road. It was clear from the smooth face of the glacier and the fresh cut ice piled up each side of the flowing water that the road builders had been working there that day. They would have smoothed the river bed, plus the army lorry had been through only a few minutes earlier and it had hardly slowed down. So he knew there was no real danger, it was just a good chance to drink in the sight of Annie up close with nobody watching him leer.

Accelerating towards the far bank, Raseem floored the accelerator and charged the jeep at the upward slope. Bucking and rolling the vehicle dragged itself over the far-side lip. Annie reached the jeep door first as Matt slipped and fell back to the bottom of the slope.

Only with massive self-restraint did Raseem wait for Matt to scramble back up to the road and climb in too. He was still too far from his hideout to risk alerting Annie that he was not who he pretended he was.

*****

The tail-lights of the army lorry appeared ahead of them again as they rounded a shoulder of the mountain.

'Thank God for that.' Matt relaxed in his seat as his eyes watched the twin red glows in the blackness above. 'How far ahead are they now?'

'Not far. It looks further than it is. We've nothing to worry about, now,' said Ricky reassuringly.

They never did catch up with the lorry in the hour before they reached the crest of the pass, but the view alone would have been worth the risks and exhaustion. The mountain peaks that had previously placed the road in pitch black moon shadow now framed the saddle-backed pass and clear blue-white moonlight bathed everything in crisp cold clarity. Hundreds of metres below them, on the north side of the pass, a sharp line marked the limit of the trees, but the pine scent rose upwards and wafted over the pass.

Majestic snow-capped peaks stretched away to the horizon, powerfully and immovably serene. In the distance *Tirich Mir* stood proud, its massive peak shrouded in its own weather system.

Ricky stopped his jeep to take in the view and they all climbed out to stare in wonder at the mountain-scape around them.

'Looks like the mountains of Mordor in the *Lord of the Rings*,' muttered Annie to no one in particular.

'It's stunning, isn't it?' answered Matt. 'I loved that film.' But Jo hated it, he thought. Then added, 'But it doesn't look evil enough to be Mordor, though.'

Ricky looked from one to the other. 'I don't that movie and *Tirich Mir* always gave him the creeps,' he mumbled.

The two travellers, seeing it for the first time, stood awestruck by the incredible panorama stretching away from them, and the stunning arc of the Milky Way above them.

After a few minutes Ricky was shivering miserably. 'It's too cold to hang around here, no matter how good the view is,' he implored. Then herded them back to the jeep, taking the opportunity to put his hand on Annie's back as he did so. Safely back inside the warm jeep Ricky relaxed as they began the descent to Chitral down the breathtakingly snake-like road that clung spectacularly to the side of the mountain.

The road on the Chitral side of the Lowari Pass was in a better state of repair and Ricky let the jeep coast down the mountainside in a roller coaster of twists, turns and switchbacks.

'Got to use the gears to slow us down, otherwise we'll burn the brakes out and we won't have them when we really need them,' he explained.

'Thank God we got over there safely,' announced Annie from the back. It seemed much safer now they could see more in the moonlight. 'Do people really get attacked on the pass?'

'Oh yes, sometimes. We were safe though. I know the guys they call bandits. I have lots of friends around here,' Ricky boasted vainly.

Matt scowled and thought he must be lying, wondering as well what sort of guy would think a boast like that would impress anyone.

After an hour's drop and a continuous popping of eardrums Ricky stopped the jeep at a flimsy wooden chalet.

A few trucks and another jeep lay abandoned at the roadside. A few small rickety huts stood nearby.

'I'm knackered.' Ricky killed the engine. 'Let's get some food and a rest.'

The warm glow of a welcoming fire beckoned from inside the hut and a samovar of hot tea helped make stale chapati a passable snack. Despite the other vehicles parked outside, there was only the rest-stop worker in evidence.

'Where's everyone else?' queried Annie as she chewed the dry bread.

'Sleeping,' yawned Ricky. 'They have one empty room. I've booked it already. I need to sleep, soon.'

Tiredness soon overwhelmed the pleasure of the hot chai and they moved across the road to a one-roomed bunkhouse graced with only two rope-strung charpoys.

*****

Ricky had only a small holdall, lightweight compared to the rucksacks Annie and Matt carried with them.

Wonder if she'll get undressed, thought Raseem as they considered the charpoys. He undressed her mentally anyway.

His lust was threatening to overwhelm him. It was a good job Matt was there thought Raseem, otherwise he might not have been able to control himself. He really wanted to take her slowly, not in a rush in some dirty shed by the side of the road.

As Matt and Annie rifled through their rucksacks without saying anything, Raseem continued his musings, wondering if she'd share one of the beds with him.

*****

Annie was also wondering what to do about the sleeping arrangements. She didn't want to share a bed with Ricky, nor make Matt do so either. The other option of sharing a charpoy with Matt was also not very appealing. She glanced across at Matt, but he was obviously struggling to know what to do, too.

Ricky saved them further embarrassment. 'You two will sleep on that bed.' Ricky smiled as pleasantly as he could. 'It wouldn't do for a foreigner to share a bunk with me. The locals wouldn't like it. They might turn nasty'

'It's too small for two. I'll be much more comfortable on the floor.' Matt jumped in before Annie could embarrass him with what he knew would be a forceful rejection.

'No,' Ricky insisted, 'you must sleep on the bed.'

'I'll be fine. No problem.' Matt would have loved to lie next to Annie, but he was not going to give her the chance to reject him.

Ricky laughed, 'You don't have a choice, you must sleep on the bed. Otherwise the rats will try to eat you.'

'What do you mean?' demanded Matt, wondering if Ricky was taking the piss.

'There's lots of rats here. And they're hungry. See those pots the charpoy is standing in,' Ricky pointed at the charpoy nearest him. 'They have water in, with some petrol poured on top. That helps stop the rats climbing up to you during the night.'

After a moment's silence as Annie and Matt stared at the charpoys, then back at Ricky, Annie grinned slightly and said, 'I can't have that on my conscience, can I?' She looked at Matt, 'I'll try and behave myself, but I can't promise.' Then she laughed, like she was really enjoying the adventure.

Annie and Matt climbed inside their separate sleeping bags and struggled onto the shaky charpoy, head to tail. Ricky wrapped himself in a blanket he'd pulled from the jeep and fell asleep almost instantly.

The charpoy was so small it was impossible for Annie and Matt not to lie in contact with each other, their bodies resting warmly against each other. The room was icy cold, a damp draft wafting up from the river and working its way in through the openings of their sleeping bags. Matt lay on his side, back towards Annie. Through the padding of the two bags he could feel the pressure of Annie's legs stretching from his shoulders to his hips.

Sleep was impossible. Desire and cold competed forcefully.

*****

Annie dozed intermittently. She wished Matt would relax, she could feel the tension radiating from him.

It was almost funny how scared he had been about sharing a charpoy with her. As she dropped into another doze she thought that if he wasn't so uptight he'd be really gorgeous. She adjusted her position slightly to ease the pressure on her shoulder. Matt's body settled along hers and she relaxed into its warmth as she fell properly asleep.

*****

Raseem lay and stewed. He'd desperately wanted to suggest that Annie share a charpoy with him, but lacked the courage to suggest it. She leapt at the chance to sleep with Matt though, just like she always did with any good-looking guy that came along. Bloody whore that she was.

Chapter Twelve

Relief filled Matt when daylight arrived and movement from Ricky gave him the excuse to sit over the side of the bed and stretch his stiffened limbs. Despite the initial pleasure of lying alongside Annie, the pain and discomfort caused by the charpoy had quickly overwhelmed him.

Annie stayed where she was, enjoying the relative comfort of a charpoy to herself. She'd slept much better than she'd expected and wanted to extend the pleasure by dozing in her warm sleeping bag for a bit longer. Only the arrival of hot chai and fresh chapati dragged her upright to face the cold and begin a new day.

Morning ablutions took place in the ice-cold glacial river beneath the bunkhouse. Matt headed for the point of easiest access, though Annie wandered further upstream to take advantage of some huge boulders and gain some privacy.

As Matt clambered back up to the road a movement among the rocks caught his eye. Twenty metres upstream Ricky was crouched by a boulder with his hand inside his trousers, peering down towards the water, just where Annie would have been after disappearing around a rock.

Matt stared disbelievingly at Ricky for a moment, amazed that he cared so little about being seen. Then Matt clattered on up the bank, making as much noise as possible and swearing loudly to himself, while his mind roared. What a fucking dirty bastard. The sooner they got away from him the better. He didn't want to look at Ricky again, the urge to charge down the slope and punch him would be over whelming, but given the noise he was making Ricky would definitely see him and with any luck realise he'd been spotted perving behind his rock.

Despite the tenseness of his relationship with Annie he surprised himself by thinking of the two of them as travelling companions. The thought of leaving her alone to travel with Ricky never crossed his mind.

Five minutes later Annie arrived back at the jeep looking for Ricky. 'Where's he gone, did you see?'

Not wanting to upset Annie by telling her what he had seen, Matt dissembled. 'No. Didn't you see him down by the river?'

'I was busy. Thank God for those boulders, I was desperate for the loo.'

Though the morning was fresh and restful in the subdued light of the dawn atmosphere, with pine trees dotting the rugged scree slopes, Matt found no enjoyment in it. His rage against Ricky ruined it all.

Staring down at the hypnotic river Matt watched it rolling around and over the rocks in eddies and whirlpools to rest a while in pools of clear serenity, before pouring ever downwards to the hidden valley below. He just knew Annie would not listen to him even if he did try to tell her what he had seen Ricky doing.

'Hi. Let's go.' Ricky stomped towards the jeep and started the engine as he violently slammed the door.

Annie climbed in the back oblivious to the glares exchanged by Matt and Ricky as they settled themselves in the front.

*****

The bitch. The bitch. Raseem silently cursed the woman in the back seat of his jeep. She had happily spent the night with that bastard. She'd probably recognised him by now and knew who he was. Raseem was certain she was taunting him again, just like she had at college with that arrogant bugger of a boyfriend she'd had then.

It was all her fault he could not get it up any more. He'd make her suffer for that.

The descending gorge soon opened out into the valley proper. Annie fell in love with the fairytale view. High mountains sheltered the long, narrow, flat-bottomed valley as it stretched away northwards, sealed in remoteness, the intrusions of the outside world locked away behind the Lowari Pass. Nothing in sight destroyed the vision of isolation. The dispersed pattern of smallholdings, farm workers and houses only added to the aura of regal, untainted history.

Ricky slowly relaxed in his seat, though Matt sat fuming in his. Annie day-dreamed romantic fantasies of the isolated, peaceful valley around her, and wondered if her grandfather had enjoyed the same views.

On the valley floor the road had improved beyond compare and was improved further by daylight. Ricky picked up speed and let the warmer air rush in through the open window and snatch at their hair.

Annie pulled her guidebook from her bag and turned to the section on Chitral. 'It says here that the Mirdom of Chitral fought off invaders so successfully that it survived till 1972, before finally being abolished and incorporated into Pakistan.'

'They're a macho bunch of guys up here.' Ricky grinned as he watched the road ahead.

'They don't all hide behind rocks then, do they?' snapped Matt.

The jeep swerved as Ricky's head jerked round towards Matt. Hate sparkled in his eyes.

'Whoa, let's stay on the road,' said Annie as she clung to the grab handle in the back.

'I wish I could have been here last century. It would have been fun trying to civilise the locals.' Matt stared malevolently at Ricky, who did his best to ignore him, though his hands tightened on the steering wheel.

'That's a bit arrogant, isn't it Matt?' said Annie angrily. 'I bet they've got it sussed up here, no pollution, few cars, living off the land. It's paradise. Look at Ricky, he's almost a local and he's as civilised, as you'd put it, as you.'

'He's nothing like me,' snapped Matt.

'The British tried to conquer us, but they never succeeded. We didn't want them here, so we killed hundreds of them. I don't think they enjoyed their visits here.' Ricky almost snarled as he spoke. Annie sat back in her seat, bewildered at the sudden anger from both men.

'Okay, you two. Calm down. What's the problem with everyone this morning?'

Neither Matt nor Ricky answered. All three of them returned to staring out the window, two in anger and Annie in confusion, her romantic day-dream ruined.

Agriculture flourished in the flat-bottomed valley. The pale early green of new grass in the fields looked soft compared to the hard arid land of the south. Apricot and mulberry trees randomly dotted the panorama, laden down under the weight of unripe fruit. Shady arbours under trees provided welcome coolness for playing children and sleepy old men. Stonewalled fields protected the first crop of the year in tiny fields.

'Why all the walls and the tiny fields?' Annie said, wanting to break the tension.

At last Ricky answered. 'The stone walls come from the stones and rocks that the farmers pick from their fields. It's taken centuries to clear the valley floor, but the land is so fertile the farmers collect two harvests each summer. Seems too much like hard work to me, though. And the winters are freezing and snow bound.'

'So what is it you do, exactly?' asked Matt.

'As I said before, I export carpets and stuff for my father. I come up here to buy carpets brought in from Afghanistan and rubies collected in the mountains by the local tribesmen.

'No hash then?'

'No. Wouldn't touch the stuff. Too risky and not much profit anyway.'

'Matt. Give it a rest, will you? Ricky's being nice to us. The least you can do is be polite.'

'I'll be as polite as him,' muttered Matt, sounding childish even to himself.

*****

Feeling distinctly out of place and totally overdressed, Chris sat on the veranda outside his room. A few tents sheltered under the willow trees and backpackers lounged on the grass reading, smoking dope and chatting. His chair wobbled, but he wanted to observe his surroundings before he tried to talk to people.

Though they tried not to be too obvious, the backpackers were eyeing him warily. His chinos and polo shirt looked too smart and new and he was twenty years older than anyone in sight.

'Hi. Can I join you?'

Chris looked at the man who had just climbed onto the veranda. In a patterned silk shirt, orange Indian-silk trousers and leather sandals, with hair down past his shoulders, the man should have been on a beach in Goa. He was also old, compared to all the other guests in sight. He was just about the same age as Chris, but looked well worn.

'Sure. Make yourself at home.'

The visitor eyed him from head to foot with bloodshot eyes. He shook his head. 'You sure are dressed strange, man. Want some dope?'

'Uh. No. Thanks anyway.' Chris stuttered in surprise at being told by this man that he was dressed strangely.

'Suit yourself. It's some of the best in the world around here.' He eased himself into the chair next to Chris's.

'So I've heard.' The quality of the local hash was something Chris knew a lot about.

'What brings some fancy dude like you to a place like this? You've caused quite a stir. The current betting is you're a copper. That right?'

'I'm not a policeman, sorry.' Chris was sure he could feel a blush rising on his cheeks.

'Shit. I've lost my money then. So what are you?' The man extracted a leather pouch from his shirt and began preparing a joint.

'I'm looking for someone. My niece has disappeared, so I thought I would come out here to try and find her.'

'She run away from home? Lots of them kids out there done that. Did it myself twenty years ago and never stopped running. If she don't wanna be found, you ain't gonna do it. What's her name anyway?'

'Annie. Annie MacDonald. She's twenty four years old.' Chris wanted to find Françoise's friend, the one Dominic had met on the plane. If he could find her she might know something, she might even have met Ricky. In the meantime, using her name was as good a way as any to get people talking to him.

'I don't know the name, but I'll ask around. They trust me. I have the best dope around here. You keep quiet and go get some better clothes, man. You look so strange no one's going to talk to you if you stay dressed like that.' The man lit his joint and strolled away from the balcony back towards the lounging backpackers who were now watching openly.

*****

Isabelle kicked the door again. The wood around the hinge cracked and more splinters fell to the floor. Blood dripped from her split toes, damaged before she'd thought to use the soles of her feet.

Dropping to her knees Isabelle dug her ragged fingers in the gap between the door and the frame. Her fingertips caught. Sharp wood pierced her skin. Isabelle pulled. The corner of the door creaked, then folded and sent her sprawling to the floor.

Lying naked in the dirt and filth of her cell, Isabelle waited for someone to come and beat her.

Chapter Thirteen

As they drove up the gorge-like valley, black thunderclouds materialised around nearby peaks. The Lowari Pass disappeared in the swirling storm developing around them.

'Thank God we aren't up there now,' said Annie.

'It would have been fun.' Ricky glowered at Matt from under lowered brows as his two passengers watched the storm develop.

'But I'm not sure we're actually going to be much better off down here,' said Matt as he caught sight of Ricky's none too friendly gaze.

The horizon slid rapidly down the mountain slopes towards the valley floor, and a deafening thunderstorm broke over the jeep as torrential rain swept the road. Lightning speared indiscriminately into the mountains and valley floor, thunder crashed simultaneously, shaking the jeep as the ground seemed to heave. Rain lashed the jeep with monsoon intensity, drumming out all possibility of further conversation.

Within minutes, though, the thunder stopped abruptly and the storm clouds raced back up the hills to disappear into another valley. The returning sun worked hard to dry the ground and soft swirls of steam replaced the angry rain-formed mist around the trees.

'Wow,' breathed Annie. 'That was something else.'

'It was nothing. You should see it in winter when it does that with snow. We'd be stuck in a snowdrift now,' laughed Ricky as if he hadn't been angry at all.

Widening as it headed north, the slim valley opened up and the surrounding peaks lowered to a less threatening height. They passed the widely separated houses of peasant farmers, nestling under groves of trees, hardly impacting on the tranquillity of the peaceful haven.

Then a village came into view. It sat comfortably on the valley floor sheltered by trees beside the Kunar River.

'That's Drosh and the river runs down into Afghanistan,' said Ricky as if he was a tour guide.

'Afghanistan. Are we close to Afghanistan?' Annie leant up against the window to get a better view.

'Of course. Those mountains up there are are in Afghanistan.'

'The river must run down into Nuristan,' said Matt authoritatively.

Ricky ignored Matt and tried, unsuccessfully, to point out to Annie the remains of Drosh Fort on a hill across the river.

They lapsed back into exhausted silence for a few miles, with Annie and Matt dozing fitfully while Ricky drove.

Suddenly Ricky slowed the jeep and pointed across the river. 'The Kalash Kafirs live up there.' Ricky pointed over a rope and wood suspension bridge towards a narrow cleft in the valley's steeply sloping wall. The side road slipped through the cleft into deep shadow, closely flanked by crumbling rocky walls.

'Do they still call it Nuristan?' Annie strained to see past the narrow entrance to the land that she wanted to see.

'No. Only foreigners call it that.'

'Where's your house, Ricky?' asked Annie, keen to visit a traditional village home.

'It's up in the mountains, off a branch of the valley I just showed you.'

'So why did you say you were going to Chitral?' Matt did not even try to hide his suspicious tone of voice.

'Most people call the whole valley, from the Lowari Pass northwards, Chitral. Anyway, I've got some business in Chitral town itself, which is not far from here. It's on the other side of the Kunar River, further upstream and just over the bridge up ahead. Plus, Chitral is where you guys are going so it'd be rude to drop you off short of your destination.'

The jeep rocked and swayed as they crossed a bouncing suspension bridge, like the one they had recently passed. A single row of mud houses straggled along each side of the road as they swept onto the far bank. A gap in the houses gave them a view of a polo field and the bruising match in progress.

Fifty metres past the polo field Ricky stopped the jeep by a small doorway in a blank wall. An angry crowd of bearded tribesmen, dressed in brown robes and sporting turbans, milled noisily outside a building on the other side of the street. Tension filled the air and an atmosphere of suppressed violence dampened the activities of everyone else on the street as they went about their business with one eye on the crowd.

'Tadjik Afghans,' sneered Ricky. 'They're not so proud as the Patans. The Tadjiks are here to collect their resettlement money from the UN. Stay away from them, they're dangerous.' Pakistani police, who obviously thought the same, suddenly appeared from a side street and began cracking heads with their bamboo lathis to subdue the shouting, angry men.

Turning away from the Tadjiks, Ricky pointed through the low gateway in the wall beside the jeep. 'You can stay in this hotel, the owner is a friend of mine. I'll return later to see if you are all right.'

'If this place belongs to a friend of yours, why aren't you staying here too?' asked Matt suspiciously. Annie shook her head and rolled her eyes at Matt's continuing rudeness.

'I might, but the man I have business with will probably want me to stay with him, and I dare not refuse because it would upset him. He is an old friend of my father and he would be angry if I offended his friend. He also supplies us with good Afghani carpets and I don't want to have to find a new supplier.'

*****

197

Annie waved goodbye with a smile, then ducked through the gateway. Matt was glowering at him, but Raseem stared unashamedly at Annie's ass until it disappeared through the gate, then smiled maliciously at Matt.

Annie still thought he was okay, which was good. It was obvious, though, that Matt had mistrusted him from the start and clearly did not like him now. It could get awkward, especially if Matt told Annie what he had seen on the Lowari Pass.

Raseem was pretty certain, though, that Matt wouldn't say anything. He reckoned that Matt would not take the risk of Annie disbelieving him and thinking he was becoming possessive. It was something he had learnt about those free and easy English girls, they hated guys who got jealous and tried to control them. Raseem was more confident now that if Matt had been going to say something about what he had seen on the Lowari Pass, he would have done it already. He was quite pathetic really, thought Raseem arrogantly. If he had seen someone leering over his girlfriend like that, he would have killed him.

Now that he had Annie in the mountains Raseem knew he had to work out just how to get her to come with him, without Matt, to his hideaway. The thought of Annie, naked and tied to his bed, made him grate the gears as he drove off to another hotel, where he could try again to release some of his pent-up frustrations.

*****

Isabelle stuffed the blanket through the hole in the door, then crawled after it. There was no one in sight as she quickly covered her nakedness.

Silence surrounded her. Slowly and carefully Isabelle crept along the grubby windows of the building, peering inside. Nothing moved. Clutter filled the end room, a cross between living room and kitchen. The door stood open on its wooden hinges.

Gulping so quickly the water dribbled down her chin, Isabelle emptied the jug of warm stale water that sat on the table. As she dropped the finished jug she saw all her belongings discarded in an untidy pile on the floor in a corner of the room. Her empty rucksack lay nearby, along with two more that looked like they'd been there longer, given their covering of dust.

Sobbing with relief Isabelle dressed quickly in her crumpled clothes. She stuffed her sleeping bag and a few extra items of clothing in her bag, along with her map of Pakistan, though it was now crumpled and torn by Ricky. Then Isabelle grabbed a handful of dried apricots from a dirty plate and hobbled from the room.

Not wanting to risk meeting Ricky coming back as he'd promised, Isabelle ignored the dirt road they had arrived on, and crept slowly in the opposite direction. Battling the fear Ricky would return just as she was getting away, Isabelle forced her stiff and aching body to move towards safety.

*****

'We only have one room.' The hotel-keeper kicked open a rickety door and pointed at a bare mud-floored room with two charpoys resting against separate walls. 'Chitral is very busy now. You're lucky we have a room at all.'

'I suppose it will have to do.' Annie eyed the room balefully. It was not what she had expected in this mountain paradise.

'At least I won't have to sleep with you again.' Matt tried to make a joke, and failed.

'You didn't sleep with me last night, so don't get any ideas. You were so rude to Ricky today. What got into you? He gave us a ride, brought us up here and saved us having to sleep in the open last night.'

'I don't like him. I don't trust him. And I'd be happy if I never saw him again.' Matt headed for the charpoy furthest from the door and dropped his rucksack on the ground next to it.

'Why? He's been nothing but helpful since I met him. What's wrong with you?' demanded Annie as she slipped her own rucksack off her shoulder and let it fall to the floor.

'Nothing. But….'

'No buts. Just shut-up. I've had it with you and your condescending attitudes. I started to think you were maybe all right on the bus, but not any more. I'm going to get my own room as soon as I can and then I won't want to talk to you again and you won't have to talk to Ricky.' Annie took a book from her bag and left Matt alone in the room.

*****

In a seedy hotel on the outskirts of Chitral town, Raseem flicked through the collection of porn stored on his laptop. The pictures weren't doing what they used to do to him. He almost threw his computer away in frustration, but managed to stop himself just in time.

If she wouldn't come with him tomorrow, he'd make her. Alone again after being in such close proximity to Annie, frustration stretched Raseem to anger. His hands shook, his palms sweated and his neck was tense. Everything else, though, remained limp.

*****

Annie sipped *kawa* at a wooden table under a weeping willow, her book lying unread on the table. A thin stream trickled past the garden, under the wall of the toilet hut and down to the river below. The room was awful, but the garden made up for it. The smell of fresh bread and cooking omelettes mingled with the clean fresh scent of mountain air.

Why did she keep meeting up with idiots like Matt, mused Annie, contemplating why Matt would dislike Ricky so much. He was probably jealous, she thought. After all, Stig had seen Matt staring at her in the Khyber Hotel. So he fancied her, but the last thing she needed at the moment, she thought, was a boyfriend. Especially one like Matt.

*****

Matt could see Annie sitting at a table eating lunch as he headed for the gate, but he ignored her. If she was going to be stupid over Ricky, she could learn the hard way. She wasn't his girlfriend anyway. She was nothing like Jo and she wasn't even his type.

The Tadjiks had disappeared when Matt re-entered the street and turned left towards the main thoroughfare of Chitral. Strolling down the main street, Matt idly eyed the trinkets and rough uncut gemstones the local traders sold from their open fronted shacks. 'Town' was too generous a word to describe Chitral, thought Matt, with it's narrow, congested streets and single road of shops.

The mouthwatering smell of grilling meat and onions drew him to a restaurant in the last building of the street. A single room, bare of furniture, held cross-legged Afghan tribesmen eating their meals from the fine carpet that stretched from wall to wall. A doorman ushered him inside the entrance before he had time to consider the fact these men looked remarkably similar to the Tadjiks Ricky had warned him of.

Having left his shoes at the doorway, in the untidy arrangement of sandals preferred by the other diners, Matt sank to the soft floor and looked around the room nervously. But he was reassured by the welcoming looks on the men's faces, and the plate of spiced meat and onions and glass of mango lassi that soon landed on the carpet in front of him. Communal plates of hot chapati lay in the centre of the rough circle of men, who encouraged Matt to help himself.

The smiling Afghans chatted about him and to him, though Matt understood not a single word as he began scooping the food to his mouth, carefully using his right hand. He listened hard, but came to the conclusion these men were speaking a different language to the Urdu he had been hearing so far on his trip. Along one wall a wide unglazed window, covered in fine mesh, drew Matt's attention to a panoramic view of the old fort beside the tree-lined river below the village and up to the Mir's abandoned palace on a hilltop nearby.

Then a disturbance from the street drew his eyes away from the view. The doorman was hurling abuse into the street and throwing stones at a figure slinking past. Matt stared in amazement as Ricky skulked away down towards the river.

The Afghanis laughed, making rude gestures with their hands. 'Bad man. Bad Muslim,' explained a man from across the room in stilted English. Matt nodded his agreement while wondering what it was Ricky had done to upset these men.

*****

Isabelle struggled up the near vertical slope. Her map told her that another village must lie in a village over the pass above her, if Ricky had pointed to the correct valley on the map as they had driven up to the house when he was still being his charming wonderful self.

Exhaustion overtook her and she lay down to rest. It was only an hour since she had started out, but the deprivations of the last few days and the horrors of the previous weeks had taken their toll. She was feeling light headed, but her legs felt so heavy it was a struggle to lift them, let alone use them to haul herself up towards the crest of the pass.

*****

'Annie, the Afghans hate him. It's not just me. They were throwing stones at him in the street.' Matt rehearsed ways to tell Annie what he had seen on the way back to the hotel. He had to at least try to tell her and he just hoped she would listen to him.

When Matt got back the Garden Hotel, he scanned the garden and outdoor dining area for Annie. But she was nowhere to be seen and the whole place was surprisingly empty. Matt walked quickly up the stairs to the terrace and their room. The door swung open at his push and Matt stepped inside the gloomy room. For a moment he was unable to see anything, then his eyes adjusted to the light and it was clear Annie was not there either.

*****

Glowing red in the bright mountain sunshine, the ancient fort oozed history and dilapidation. 'The British held out here for weeks, but they gave up in the end. Only Alexander the Great successfully invaded Chitral.' The old caretaker slowly led the way into the dogleg gatehouse, the river swirling rapidly past twenty feet below.

Annie gazed around, awe-struck. Her Grandad had told her about this dog-leg gatehouse in one of his stories, but she'd never realised it was somewhere that would still exist, or thought she would ever see it for herself. The abandoned far-flung remains of the British Empire, from a time when her small country had subdued half the world, had a sad romanticism to them.

As they climbed up the stairs to the battlements a small boy arrived with a cup and a jug of tea. 'That is *Tirich Mir*, enjoy the view for as long as you want,' said the old man pointing northwards, as the boy poured some chai for Annie.

Left alone, Annie sat against the battlement of the fort sipping her chai, mesmerised by the mountains above her and the river running below her as she enjoyed the memory of her Grandad's stories and felt his presence beside her.

*****

In the dark shadow of a tree, not far from the gates of the fort, Raseem waited impatiently for Annie to reappear. He had come down to the river to clear his head and devise a plan to get her back to his hideaway, but the fucking Tadjiks and this bitch would not let him have any peace.

All he'd done while eating lunch in that restaurant one day was to pass comment on the size of the tits on some blonde backpacker he was trying to shag as she walked past. But those bloody mountain men had taken offence on her behalf, and then chucked him out halfway through his meal. As for Annie, 'she's only here to taunt me,' he muttered to himself.

Eventually, his wait was rewarded. Smiling happily to herself, Annie left the fort and strolled along the river. Raseem watched her intently, rubbing his unresponsive crotch as he used his imagination to undress and abuse the object of his frustrating lust as she explored, carefree and unaware that she was being stalked.

*****

Mist hung gently over the nearest lake when Ishmael reached the flat bowl of the Shandur Pass, hiding the barrier gate, polo ground and the farthest stretch of water. In the three days since he had left the snow had melted and receded. Though the snow reached down from the peaks, the pass itself was clear and a hint of fresh green washed the dank remains of last year's grass being grazed by the yaks of his herdsman friend.

Laspur had been as devoid of information as Harchin. So few tourists came this way that any going missing would have been too obvious, and cost the locals more than they would have gained through robbery by frightening away the rest.

In a hollow, fifty metres from the road, Ishmael Khan pitched his tent and built a fire. He had enjoyed his trek and talking with the villagers, but it was good to be back in the high pass where he could enjoy the mountains again in solitary isolation.

*****

It was dark by the time Annie returned to the hotel. Matt waved from his seat in the garden, but she ignored him and went straight to their room.

Ten minutes later Matt followed. Knocking gently he waited for her voice. 'Who is it?' she called, though who else it was going to be Matt couldn't think.

'Me. Matt.'

'You can come in.'

'We need to talk,' said Matt as he entered.

'No we don't. And don't talk to me like I was your girlfriend.' Annie was wrapped in her sleeping bag facing the wall.

'It's important. It's about Ricky.'

204

'I said no. Now shut up and let me sleep.'

Matt sighed and shrugged his arms in frustrated annoyance.

*****

An hour after dark Isabelle reached the crest of the pass. Her hands and legs oozed blood, scraped and torn by the grasping shrubs and sharp rocks. The darkness was intense and only her fear that Ricky might be coming up behind had driven her onwards into the frightening blackness.

Clouds of steam from her condensing breath hung around her in the still air. Her chest hurt, her lungs struggling to drag in oxygen at ten thousand feet above sea level.

Isabelle needed to rest. She found a grassy hollow among the rocks to shelter herself from unseen eyes and crawled into her sleeping bag. Mentally and physically exhausted she promptly fell asleep under the stars and the open sky.

*****

Matt lay awake for hours in the darkness, wondering if he should tell Annie what he wanted to say about Ricky, even though she didn't want to listen. The charpoy grew increasingly uncomfortable as he tossed and turned. Annie seemed to be sleeping the sleep of the innocent across the room.

It was daylight when Matt opened his eyes to a shaft of bright, late morning sunshine streaking across the room. He lay still for a moment wondering where he was, then sat up sharply making the charpoy creak worryingly.

The second charpoy was empty. Matt scanned the room, relaxing slightly when he saw Annie's rucksack partially hidden behind the bed, relieved she hadn't left.

Quickly slipping into his shoes Matt left the room to look for her.

From the terrace of the building Matt saw Annie sitting at the table he had been at the night before when she ignored him. Matt ordered tea and omelette on the way over, then sat opposite her. Annie ignored his morning greeting and avoided catching his eye as she ate her breakfast.

Taking a deep breath Matt spoke. 'I'm leaving this morning. I'm going up to one of the Kalash valleys. You won't have to find another room.'

'Good. Have fun.' Annie's curt reply cut off further conversation. Matt was now too annoyed to attempt telling his story even if she didn't want to listen, as he'd planned to do. It was her life and she'd made it quite clear she didn't want him interfering.

They finished their breakfast in silence. Matt left first, as soon as he'd finished gulping his down, and went to pack his bag. The omelette was not as hot and spicy as the ones he'd had further south; either that or he was getting used to all the chillies.

*****

With no great desire to see Matt again, Annie left him to pack his bag and went straight from breakfast out onto the street. She wanted to peruse the market, to see if she could find some of the rubies Ricky had mentioned.

Sloping gently down to the far side of Chitral, the main street Matt had followed the day before led past an array of tiny shops. Each one was little more than a cubicle, stacked with goods for sale. Most of the shops specialised in clothes, shoes, weapons or food. A few, however, looked more like curio shops. Their shelves and floor space were stacked with second-hand goods: knives, guns, tools and pictures. These she found much more interesting and almost entered one, but the urge to shop was tempered by her niggling annoyance with Matt and she continued meandering aimlessly along the road.

*****

When Matt stepped through the gate a crowd of Afghans were again milling outside the building along the street where they had been when he arrived. He stopped to watch them, no longer so nervous since he had enjoyed his lunch with a similarly clad group of men. Annie was gone from the hotel garden and he hoped he would not see her in the street, or he might give her a mouthful. He was annoyed with her now for treating him like an idiot.

The local destination public transport hub operated at the corner of the street fifty metres from the hotel. Drivers and their helpers shouted the destinations of their open-topped Suzuki jeeps that provided the bus service.

Taking the last cramped space in the back of an open jeep to Bumburet, Matt settled himself as securely as he could and prayed he would neither fall out nor get too sun-burned.

*****

Raseem sat in his jeep at the bottom of the hill. He was mostly hidden behind an overloaded lorry, waiting for Annie to wander down through the shops. Sweat stained his shirt, despite the air-conditioning. He was going to get her to his house, whether she wanted to come or not.

The bitch was taking her time. He could see her wandering along the road, looking in the shitty little shops, smiling and chatting with the stupid local traders, but not really doing any shopping.

His excitement rose as she reached the last shop. She was only thirty feet away now, but stopped and went in to it. 'Bitch.' He thumped the steering wheel so hard the jeep shook. Passers-by glanced his way and hurried past.

*****

The last shop caught her eye. Some beautifully patterned stitching on the woollen waistcoats drew her in. Wonderfully soft, the jackets looked striking on the men in the street and matched their round caps. Matt would look good in one of these, she thought idly. Then, too tense and unsettled to make a choice on which one to buy, Annie gave up looking and left the shop.

Seeing a path leading across the fields over open ground, immediately next to the shop, Annie stepped quickly past some grazing goats and headed back down to the river. She wanted to hide until she was sure Matt had left. Perhaps he was right about Ricky, though she doubted it. Anyway, she was not going to go anywhere with Ricky on her own. She had learnt her lesson in Islamabad and Matt had no right to think he could be so protective of her and tell who she could, or could not, hang out with. She was a grown woman, who knew how to take care of herself.

*****

Exhaustion had let Isabelle sleep well, though she had woken stiff and sore as the sun warmed her in the safety of the hollow.

When she sat up, Isabelle was stunned by the view. Snow-capped mountains stretched from horizon to horizon. It was what she had come to Pakistan for and momentarily the desperation of the situation she was in was pushed to one side as she revelled in the spectacular scene before her.

Then the raging thirst that was sticking her tongue to the roof of her mouth dragged her back to reality. It had not crossed her mind yesterday that there would be no water along the way and neither had she realised it would take her so long to cross the pass. If she didn't get to water soon she was going to be in a lot more trouble than she already was.

Vague nausea and a light head made her seriously think of leaving her belongings behind and coming back for them later as she awkwardly repacked her sleeping bag, but a nagging worry that she might really need them later kept her going.

Isabelle tarried a moment to enjoy the view, before beginning what she knew would be a struggle down the almost vertical descent on the far side of the pass. Awkward limbs slowed her movements and made her stumble frequently as she resumed her journey to safety.

Rock gave way to loose scree, then rough vegetation. Isabelle slipped and lurched her way downwards, desperate not to lose her footing and tumble down the precipitous slope. When she reached the uppermost trees cooler air refreshed her and took the edge off her thirst. Soon the trees surrounded her, blocking the view. She used the rough trunks to slow her downward descent. A hundred metres into the copse the trees began to thin. Twenty metres further they faded away almost completely, leaving a long slope of more dangerous looking loose scree in front of her.

To the left, Isabelle saw a sparkle of water dropping down the cliffs to a stream not far below her. Thirst had dried her tongue completely and it felt thick in her mouth, making it hard to breathe. Isabelle sat and stared at the loose ground between her and the water, picking a path that looked least likely to give way beneath her.

Smoke rose lazily from a house on the valley floor; a tiny figure moved around the grass in front of it.

The rock beneath her left foot slipped away and Isabelle lost her balance, slipping and sliding dangerously down the slope for a few meters before catching a hold once more. Her heart pounded fearfully and her stomach clenched in panic.

Taking a deep breath Isabelle began working her way across the slope to the stream and the life saving water. Fatigue and thirst slowed progress, but desperation kept her going. Time lost significance as Isabelle concentrated hard. When the hard work finally brought her to the edge of the stream, Isabelle eased the bag from her shoulders and lay flat to suck the clear liquid tricking down the mountain into her mouth.

*****

The violence of the bouncing jeep, as it made its way along the deeply rutted river road, prevented Matt from taking in much of the scenery. Occasionally, he took a glance down to the river, or up to mountains, but mostly he worked hard to stop himself being smashed against the jeep's metal sides.

After half an hour of torture he sighed in relief as they ground to a halt, in a cloud of dust, to wait their turn to cross a single-track suspension bridge to Ayun, similar to the one

Ricky had pointed out at the narrow entrance to the Kalash valley where his house was.

Taking the chance to admire his surroundings, Matt hoped Annie wasn't stupid enough to go anywhere on her own with Ricky.

*****

As Annie walked across the fields to the river, Raseem drove his jeep along a track to head her off. The object he coveted entered a copse of trees on the riverbank and Raseem moved his jeep close into the shadows of the same copse one hundred metres away. He stepped from the door and followed Annie on foot, a paper parcel of food in his hand.

*****

A sound behind her made Annie jump and spin round. 'Oh, it's you. Thank God. I thought it was Matt.'

'You expecting him?' smiled Ricky cheerfully.

'No. I'm avoiding him.'

'Oh, sorry to hear that. I quite like him.' Ricky smiled his warmest smile. 'I come down here quite a lot for the peace and quiet. It's so restful.'

'It's lovely, isn't it. I came down here yesterday too. Sit down, if you don't mind me spoiling your peace and quiet.' Annie waved her hand at a spot on the grass alongside her.

'You wouldn't do that. So thanks, I will join you if you don't mind.' Ricky sat a few feet from Annie, opened his parcel, and held out his hand. 'I've brought a picnic. You want some?'

*****

Carefully making sure the drugged piece of chapati was on top, Raseem offered Annie the unwrapped parcel.

'Thanks. The mountain air makes me ravenous. I only had breakfast an hour ago, too.'

Nibbling carefully at his own piece of bread, in case any of the drug had leaked from the other, Raseem lay casually against a tree and tried to contain his impatience.

Annie popped piece after piece of the still warm bread into her mouth, hardly chewing it before swallowing.

For ten minutes, shielded behind his mirror shades, Raseem raked Annie's body with his eyes. For the first time in days he felt his manhood stir. Relaxed and unaware of him staring, she watched the river, spotting fish rising in the lazy water.

Raseem wondered how long the drug would take to affect Annie. Though he'd done this a few times now, it was different every time.

Just when he was beginning to worry he hadn't used enough, Annie lay back against a tree holding her head. 'Ooh, I feel horrible. I think I'm going to pass out. Help me.'

Raseem leant over her, working hard to look concerned. 'Don't worry. I'll get you to the hospital. It must be something you ate. Come with me.'

Using the excuse of helping Annie to his jeep, Raseem ran his hands over as much of her body as he could without dropping her. She hardly noticed, but felt too ill to worry about it anyway.

By the time Raseem got her to the jeep, Annie was barely conscious. As he clipped her into the seatbelt and pulled it tight to keep her upright, Raseem loosened her shirt and slid his hand inside. His mouth watered as he broke into a sweat.

A shepherd appeared on the road nearby, walking towards the jeep. Raseem withdrew his hand and quickly climbed into the drivers seat and turned the jeep towards the road home.

Whenever the road let him, Raseem rested his hand on Annie's leg, stroking her thigh lovingly.

'She's mine. She's mine,' he chanted to himself. His excitement forced his foot harder on the accelerator.

*****

211

It took thirty minutes for the slow procession of vehicles to cross singly from the far side of the river, with no one seeming in too much of a hurry. When the oncoming queue had disappeared, Matt's jeep moved slowly forward onto the rocking and bouncing bridge. The vehicle edged carefully forward, the passengers sitting still as if anxious not to rock the bridge more than it already was. The slender steel cables hardly seemed strong enough to carry their weight, though it must have been, considering a lorry had come the other way as they waited.

On the far side of the bridge Matt let out the breath he had not realised he was holding. As his jeep pulled off the bridge it turned sharply to the left and Matt glanced back to where they had come from.

He sat up straight with surprise as he saw a familiar jeep race up to the far side and stop to wait while the jeep currently crossing the bridge completed its journey.

He was almost sure it was Ricky's before the bridge passed out of sight and they entered the street of houses that made up the village of Ayun.

As they passed slowly through Ayun, Matt kept glancing back along the road, waiting to catch a glimpse of the jeep and confirm it was Ricky's. The sick feeling in his stomach told him Annie would be in it if he ever got close enough to check.

Ricky's shiny jeep finally pulled into view in the distance and moved quickly to catch them up. Matt's own driver was going slowly, looking for one more passenger to fit into the already overcrowded jeep. As the last of the houses fell away on the far side of Ayun, Ricky's jeep pulled close, then swung out to overtake them. Matt saw Annie in the passenger seat, and ground his teeth in annoyance. Stupid bloody woman, he thought.

As the jeep changed its line, though, Annie's head thumped sickeningly into the window and Matt realised by the way she lolled in the seat that Annie was unconscious. Ricky was staring crazily at the narrowing road ahead as he accelerated past them to get in front before the road narrowed to a single track.

Terrified for Annie's safety, Matt stood to look over the cab of his jeep after Ricky as he pulled ahead of them. But a hand sharply pulled him back down just in time before a low slung telephone wire whipped over the top of the jeep, so low it would have caught him at neck level if he had been standing fully upright.

Sickened by his lucky escape and the horror of seeing Annie unconscious in Ricky's jeep, Matt retched over the side of his jeep. By the time Matt was recovered enough to look forwards again Ricky's jeep had passed from view into the narrow gorge ahead.

As Matt's jeep followed, the Bumburet River competed for space with the road, while the overhanging cliff face both threatened to drop massive lumps of crumbling rock into the restricted space and scrape the top of the jeep, or decapitate anyone mad enough to stand up. The narrow gorge hid the sun and the light faded to deep shadow below the high cliffs.

*****

A few minutes past Ayun Raseem aimed the jeep down a hidden track, leaving the Bumburet road and heading instead into the Birer valley.

His unconscious plaything flopped around beside him. Within the hour he would be able to enjoy the pleasures he had dreamed of for so long.

*****

Too slowly for Matt, his jeep followed the winding track after Ricky. Fear for Annie racked him with guilt that he had not stayed to keep an eye on her, or even tried to warn her about Ricky. The fact that he was on the same road as them and he could attempt to help her at some point barely consoled him as he had no idea where Ricky was taking her.

Matt constantly peered forwards hoping for a sight of Ricky's jeep, with the recurring thought that this was just like what had happened to Jo all over again. He should never have left Annie to go off on her own.

The narrow gorge suddenly opened out and a wooden bridge took them across the Bumburet River, to a T-junction and a police checkpoint blocking the road. One exit was blocked by a landslide, the other was clear.

Having made Matt stand in front of his roadside desk, like a naughty schoolboy, the policeman officiously and slowly checked Matt's passport and issued him a 400 *Rupee* visitor permit for the Kalash valley. 'Only seven days. Then back to Chitral,' said the man as he waved Matt back to the jeep.

'Have any other foreigners gone up here today?' asked Matt urgently.

The man waved him away. 'None of your business. Police business.'

Matt almost ran back to his jeep and leapt back aboard, his anxiety and impatience growing to nausea.

Chapter Fourteen

An acre of grass separated the solitary wooden building, and the possibility of safety, from the trees where Isabelle sat hidden. Fear that Ricky had friends in this valley stopped her stepping into the vast open space, though fragrant woodsmoke drifting from the chimney of the house offered a reassuring symbol of welcome and safety.

Hunger had replaced thirst as the biggest problem, with many streams providing ample water on the lower slopes of the pass as Isabelle descended. Pains gnawed at her stomach while her mouth salivated at the smell of fresh bread now carrying on the breeze with the wood smoke, but fear kept her paralysed and hidden in the trees.

Isabelle had sat hidden for two hours already. The longer she stayed where she was, the less she wanted to move. Her courage was weakening all the time.

One man had already appeared from the hut, then headed leisurely up the valley. Isabelle had sunk lower in her hiding place while he was in view, fear and indecision winding knots in her stomach, intensifying the hunger pains.

All the while one thought kept running through her head: What if Ricky had friends here? The prospect of being sent back to Ricky was too awful to contemplate, so she sat immobile and continued to wait.

*****

Raseem drove too fast, his tension weighing heavy on the accelerator pedal. In less than an hour he would have his dream toy secured away from interference. At the top of the valley, his secluded bungalow was far enough away from the ignorant villagers to let him have his fun undisturbed. He paid them enough rent to leave him alone with foreign friends, and the other, more dangerous, friends he kept across the border helped too.

The track wound alongside the river, under overhanging trees and rocks. With potholes bouncing him violently, Raseem was rarely able to reach out his hand to stroke the sleeping body next to him. Only once so far, as he drove up the narrow valley, had he managed to glance across and steal a look at the bare skin showing through the opening in her shirt. The tantalising view promised so much more. He would have ripped open the shirt but a small voice had warned him it would attract too much attention from the policeman at the checkpoint, or anyone else who happened to look though the windows of his jeep.

The lazy policeman had not bothered to rise from his desk when Raseem arrived, forcing him to leave the safety of his jeep and pay his bribe like some common villager. But at least it meant the man had not been able to look too closely at Annie. An unconscious foreigner slumped in his passenger seat would have attracted the attention of even the laziest official and would certainly have taken some explaining.

Now he was past the policeman the urge to rip the shirt was growing stronger. Ricky glanced across at Annie to check if he could see down her shirt and not have to rip it. A loud bang made him twitch and the jeep swerved harshly towards the river. Raseem dragged the wheel back to the right, the river sparkling below his window. The wheels lost their grip on the loose surface and slipped sideways. A wheel dipped into another pothole and threw the vehicle at the flaking rock to the right.

Metal screamed as the side panels dragged along the rock. Another bang sounded as the jeep hit debris at the bottom of the cliff and jerked away from the rock face.

Dust shrouded the jeep as it shuddered to a halt. Raseem gripped the steering wheel so hard his knuckles whitened and his nails dug into his palms. Annie snored lightly, oblivious to the danger she was in.

At a safely sedate pace, Matt's jeep headed leisurely up the Bumburet valley. A few kilometres past the police checkpoint the gorge widened enough to allow sunlight the chance to help a few fields grow food for the resident Kafirs.

Desolate mud huts hid dangerously under the crumbling cliffs and farmers sat in the shade of apricot trees admiring their fields while chatting with their friends. Women beat dirt from clothes in the river, their white shell necklaces glowing brightly in the sun.

Matt strained forward, looking for Ricky's jeep on the road ahead, but not a single vehicle was in sight, let alone Ricky's. Matt scoured the roadside, desperate to find any sign of Ricky and Annie.

As they moved ever more slowly up the valley passengers jumped from the jeep at ramshackle houses, or at the start of narrow paths that lead across fields to more distant huts.

*****

Raseem kicked his jeep repeatedly. Both front tyres were burst and he only had one spare. He hated physical work, it messed up his clothes. The first hut in Birer was almost a mile away. 'It's all your fault, bitch,' he screamed at Annie. He was so angry he could have slapped her and it took all his self-control to hit the jeep again instead of her. Despite his anger he had enough clarity of thought to realise slapping Annie now might wake her up, which just at this moment would cause him a problem. Later, he consoled himself. He could do anything he wanted to do to her later.

He turned away and stalked up the road looking for help, leaving Annie still asleep and strapped to her seat.

*****

An hour of slow travel later, with stops becoming more frequent, and Matt had still not seen Ricky's jeep. Most of the stops were to make deliveries of goods, not people. Matt had assumed the sacks and boxes he and the other passengers were sitting on belonged to his fellow travellers, but few of them did.

Every stop was leisurely and required an exchange of news, as well as a discussion about him. Most of the valley's residents would know about him by now.

The unhurried progress was excruciating. Tension was giving way to panic. Matt was thinking he must have missed the jeep. But how? The valley was so narrow there was hardly anywhere to hide. And he was sure there had been no turn-off along the way. Where the fuck was he, thought Matt increasingly frantically. As the driver stood next to the jeep chatting to a villager he had just delivered a sack of something to, Matt said aloud, 'I can't have missed them. It wasn't possible.'

At the sound of Matt's voice the driver turned to smile at him, shaking his head and responding with an explanation of something Matt couldn't understand.

Turning back to the road ahead the driver pointed up the the track and said, 'Hotel'.

A low hut made from mud and wood, but larger than most of the ones they had passed so far, stood to one side of the road a hundred metres away.

Matt pondered walking the short distance to the hotel, but the driver was showing signs of getting back in his seat, so Matt stayed where he was. Finally, the driver brought the jeep to a halt under a large weeping willow and turned off the engine.

'Hotel,' said the driver happily, looking very pleased with himself..

Matt was the last passenger left on the vehicle. As soon as the driver opened his door he started calling out to someone. Matt jumped down from the back of the vehicle, knowing for certain that Annie was not here either. He'd lost her and the sick, familiar feeling of losing someone he cared about settled in his stomach and brought a cold sweat to his forehead, despite the heat.

The road ended a few metres past the hut so she had to be somewhere behind him, but where?

A brightly dressed Kalash woman appeared from the dark interior of the kitchen, smoke billowing after her. She smiled coyly and called Matt along the balcony of the building to show him a tiny room half filled with a rickety charpoy. The driver dropped Matt's bag in the dirt by his jeep, shouted a cheery goodbye and drove away.

Silence descended. Matt had never felt so desolately alone.

'*Kawa*,' said his host shyly as she wandered back to the kitchen, leaving Matt standing on the terrace looking at the snow-capped mountains hemming them in, the river rushing past nearby, stony fields struggling to grow some crops and a copse of dark trees across the valley. High above him a pass between the peaks suggested there was a world somewhere outside of this hidden valley.

Matt strolled to the road and gazed around the valley. Cropped green grass stretched down to the river; the copse of trees looked cold and forbidding in an otherworldly way.

As he surveyed the surreal surroundings a sudden movement by the trees caught his eye. A figure broke from the shadows and started stumbling in his direction. He stared intently. It was definitely a foreign woman, he could tell by the way she was dressed. Matt watched her stagger, rooted to the spot in horror, then started running towards her. 'Annie!' he shouted. The figure slowed and stopped.

Matt sprinted as fast as he could. The figure turned to run away. 'Annie!' shouted Matt again. The woman tried to run, but fell clumsily to the ground.

As he reached the cringing figure Matt could hear the sobs that racked her. Congealed blood smeared her hands and face but it wasn't Annie.

'It's all right, I won't hurt you,' he said cautiously, crouching near her.

The woman flinched away from him and curled tighter into the foetal position, covering her face.

'What's wrong? I won't hurt you.' Keeping his distance, Matt moved round so he was facing her and crouched down a few feet away.

The girl watched him from hooded, wary eyes.

'It's okay. Do you speak English? What's your name?' encouraged Matt.

Still sobbing the girl peered between her fingers at him. 'You're not with him, are you?' she whispered.

'Who?' responded Matt, confused.

'Ricky.'

Matt felt his stomach clench and a sudden fear that Ricky was behind him made him glance quickly around the area. 'No. I'm looking for him. He's got my friend.'

Slowly, the girl uncoiled herself and sat up, looking nervously around. 'Where is he? He's not here is he?'

'No. I was following him, but now I can't find him. Where does he live? Where was he taking my friend?'

Pointing with her tear stained chin the girl looked at the pass. 'Over there. You're in the wrong valley.'

'Shit. Fuck.' Matt stood and cursed more than he had ever done in his life before. The pass loomed over them and he tried to work out how long it would take to climb it.

'Did you come over there?' asked Matt in disbelief, looking at the high pass then the frail figure before him. 'How long did it take?'

'You won't get over there tonight. It took me hours to climb it yesterday. I slept on the top and came down this morning.'

Matt kicked a rock in frustration and hurt his foot. The girl started sobbing again and Matt realised he would have to help her first before he could go and look for Annie.

'Let's get you to the hotel. You probably want to get cleaned up.'

'I want to get out of here as fast as possible.'

'The jeep that brought me has gone. We'll work something out as soon as we can, don't worry.' Matt watched her carefully, wondering what the hell Ricky had done to her to get her in this state.

*****

Two villagers sweated with the second wheel. The first was changed and now they were trying to patch the other.

Raseem sat on a nearby rock, smoking, a pile of butts at his feet. Annie was still comatose, though he was worrying how long she would stay that way. It was a good job she had been really hungry and eaten so much of the drugged chapati back in Chitral. The villagers had taken his explanation that she smoked too much hash without a second thought; they knew all foreigners smoked too much and selling cheap hash to the few foreigners that came to their village every year was how they made some extra money.

Two hours after the accident, Raseem threw a handful of *rupees* at the villagers and roared away. The thought of giving them a lift home never occurred to him. They stood and glared at him as he drove away, but in his eagerness to be back on the road he didn't notice. Not that he would have cared anyway.

Annie started to stir soon after they restarted their journey. Raseem was out of cigarettes and his head thumped viciously from the whole packet he had smoked in the last few hours.

As dusk fell the house he rented came into view. Annie sat dopily in the passenger seat, staring blankly through the windscreen with no idea of where she was. Raseem wanted to throw up his head hurt so much. Every lurch of the jeep made him feel worse.

With a four-wheel slide the jeep rocked to a halt in the few metres of dirt that was the parking space at the side of the house. Raseem fell out the door and threw up. Behind him he heard the door of the jeep open and from the corner of his eye saw Annie start staggering for the road as he retched again.

221

Ten metres from the jeep, just as she reached the road, Raseem tackled Annie and they hit the dirt. Annie lay still, her eyes glazed, fearful and confused. Raseem wretched again and sharp-scented vomit splashed their clothes.

Dragging himself to his feet, Raseem pulled the still groggy Annie by the collar of her shirt towards what would become her prison. Raseem hoped the material would rip and display her body for him. But the shirt disappointingly held firm as he climbed onto the balcony and threw her roughly into an empty room. Annie slumped to the floor, dazed, with terror in her eyes as she held his gaze before he closed the door on her.

Raseem felt heat in his groin as he returned the gaze of the frightened woman before him, until the stab of pain in his head killed his passion dead.

Raseem pulled the door to Annie's room closed, then bolted and padlocked it safely. A few moments later he fell onto his own bed, a dirty mattress on the floor of a nearby room. He didn't think of Isabelle once.

*****

Steaming *kawa* waited for them on the balcony. The Kalash woman brought a second cup and stared with concern at Isabelle, then returned silently to her kitchen.

Unsure what to say, Matt poured the tea and passed a cup over. The girl sniffed pathetically and sipped her drink.

They sat in silence for ten minutes, sipping their tea. The host reappeared, placed two loaves of hot flat bread on the table with some apricot jam, and left again. The girl ripped the bread and scooped up jam, stuffing it ravenously into her mouth. Matt picked idly at the other, uncomfortably trying not to stare.

When she finally showed signs of slowing down Matt asked, 'What's your name?'

The girl looked at him suspiciously while she finished her mouthful, then replied. 'Isabelle. I'm English too. What's your name?'

222

'Matt. What happened to you?'

'I don't want to talk about it. I want to leave. Will you take me back to Chitral? Today?' Isabelle looked Matt in the eye, daring him to say no.

Matt shook his head regretfully. 'I can't. I've got to find my friend.'

'You can't do it on your own. He's dangerous. Take me to Chitral and get some help there. Then you can come back for her. Just get me out of here. I want to go home.' Isabelle wiped her dirty face with the back of her hand, smearing the dirt and blood further, as she steeled herself not to cry.

'I have to try. There isn't time to go back to Chitral and get help. Who would I ask anyway? You can stay here tonight and go back in the jeep tomorrow, before I go over that pass to find Annie. You'll be safe tonight, I'll look after you.'

'No. You can't leave me. He'll come find me, and kill me.' Desperation burned in Isabelle's eyes as they pleaded with Matt.

'I'm not going anywhere tonight. Don't worry,' said Matt reassuringly. 'Let's sleep on it. We'll see how you feel in the morning.'

A pot of stew landed on the table between them soon after the bread had disappeared. A small child placed a bowl of hot water on the grass in front of the balcony and held out a clean towel towards Isabelle. Her mother nodded encouragingly to Isabelle, who smiled gratefully and moved to wash in the clear steaming water.

Her face and hands less disconcertingly covered in blood and dirt, Isabelle ate the steaming stew straight from the pot. She shovelled five spoonfuls into her mouth, then turned to throw up over the balcony of the terrace onto the ground below.

'Careful. Try slowing down a bit,' said Matt as she returned to the table. He poured another glass of chai for her as she took more spoonfuls of stew.

'I'm so hungry, I haven't eaten in three days. He left me to die,' said Isabelle in explanation. 'The fucking bastard.'

'Where did he leave you?'

'Over that pass. I told you. He locked me up and left me to die.'

'Where on the other side?'

'You can't miss it. Just go straight over the top and down the other side. Right at the bottom is his place. You can't miss it.' Crossing her arms over her chest, Isabelle sat back in her chair and stared at the pass above them.

'I'm going to go over the pass tomorrow to find my friend, before its too late. We can get you on the jeep to Chitral first thing in the morning, or you can stay here. I'm sure the woman who runs the place will look after you, all the Pakistanis I've met have been really hospitable. She seems kind, she brought you the water and towel.'

Isabelle looked at him forlornly, too tired to argue with him further.

Dusk settled quickly over Bumburet as Isabelle slowly ate the rest of the stew. Matt declined any; the thought of Annie and the sight of Isabelle eating like a refugee destroyed his appetite and made him nauseous. He desperately wanted a cigarette, but didn't have any with him.

With a padlock borrowed from Matt, Isabelle locked herself inside his room. He wrapped himself in his sleeping bag and lay on the wooden floor of the terrace outside it, gazing up at the silhouette of the pass leading to the next valley, and Annie.

*****

The bare room was dusty, but otherwise relatively clean. A dirty blood-stained blanket lay in one corner, looking so sickeningly filthy Annie would not touch it.

Though the drug was wearing off, she still felt muggy and distinctly nauseous. She was in shock. The last thing she remembered was talking to Ricky on the riverbank in Chitral.

Now she was locked in a room and the clean cut charming Ricky had mutated into a violent thug.

Bruises covered her arms and her shirt was was undone. She tried to remember why.

All her body wanted to do was sleep; all Annie wanted to do was stay awake. Despite the hardness of the floor, her body won and Annie dozed, upright against the wall.

*****

Mosquitoes plagued Matt, dive bombing his head and chewing on his face. Proper sleep was impossible, not just because of the mosquitoes, but from his nagging fear of what was happening to Annie across the mountains.

As he dozed and dreamed, confusing memories of Jo ran through his head, interspersed with images of Annie, Ricky and Isabelle. He had left Jo to travel alone and she was dead. He had abandoned Annie and she might be dead too, but there was a chance he could rescue her. Now there was Isabelle to think about too. All the time Ricky hovered malevolently on the edge of every image. Matt's mind struggled to cope.

His insomnia won out and he finally left his sleeping bag on the floor outside the room where Isabelle had locked herself in. Matt sat on the steps of the hotel, leaning against the handrail, and stared up at the moonlit pass. Annie was over there somewhere and as soon as it was light he knew he would have to start climbing it and rescue her. But he worried about Isabelle too; he didn't want to leave her and risk anything further happening to her.

Whimpers crept through the locked door; from the scuffling and thumping noises Isabelle's sleep was far from restful.

He'd left two people to travel on their own and look what had happened. He couldn't leave another one to do it. But he couldn't just abandon Annie to her fate, either. Matt gnawed at his thumb, racked with indecision.

As the moon traversed the sky Matt got no closer to an answer. The whimpers, moans and occasional screams of Isabelle only made him more confused and added to his anxiety.

A bucket banging on a doorpost woke Matt from his doze. Pain lanced though his stiff neck as he jerked upright in the early morning sun to see their host moving along the terrace.

'Matt? Are you there?' Isabelle's urgent voice sounded behind him from inside her room.

'Yeah. I'm here,' he responded, his voice thick with sleep.

Isabelle unlocked the door and peered warily out. Slowly she stepped forward and sat a few feet away from him.

'How're you feeling today? Did you sleep at all?' asked Matt as she settled herself.

'Badly. You? Was it too uncomfortable for you on the floor out here?

'I dozed a bit. It was quite nice outside under the stars,' he said, not wanting to worry her about taking over his room.

'You're going to go find your friend, aren't you?' said Isabelle looking directly at him.

'I have to. I can't leave her with him.' Matt could not bring himself to look at her as he admitted his decision.

'I know. You're doing the right thing.' Isabelle smiled at him.

'I'll make sure you get on the jeep for Chitral and then I'll go. You'll be safe once you get to Chitral.' Matt tried to sound more confident than he felt.

'No. I can't leave someone else in the same situation I was in. Anyway, you'll get lost if you try and cross the pass to find his house on your own.' Isabelle took a deep breath and stated firmly, 'I'm coming with you.'

'You're in no fit state to go back over that pass! At least stay here and wait for us to come back.' Genuinely concerned about the prospect of Isabelle trying to cross the pass again,

Matt protested he could find Ricky on his own, but Isabelle insisted.

'I've made up my mind. So don't argue.' Isabelle raised an eyebrow at him, daring him to try. 'I know where he is. You have to get your friend and it'll be better if there's two of us. I know what he's like and I can't leave someone else with him just to get myself home. I'd never forgive myself.'

'OK,' shrugged Matt, surprised at the strength of personality coming through in her statement.

*****

Soft early morning light seeped under the door and woke Annie. She listened carefully, but heard nothing. It was early, not long after dawn.

Her head ached gently and her arms were stiff and sore. Otherwise the effects of whatever drug Ricky had given her had worn off. She sat up slowly and tested her limbs, then stood carefully. She seemed all right physically, though she struggled to control the fear threatening to overwhelm her.

Having examined the room carefully, Annie crouched with her back against the wall opposite the door, and settled herself to think and wait.

*****

Cold air washed around the valley as Matt and Isabelle started climbing. Two sleeping bags, food, one water bottle, and a spare set of shoes and clothes that Isabelle had insisted on taking for Annie, was all that Matt carried in his rucksack. Everything else was locked in the room at the hotel.

Loose scree and the steep incline slowed their pace to almost nothing. Isabelle was still drawn and tired looking, but she stepped forward purposefully. Matt suggested they slow down, 'We have a long day ahead of us.'

'We do. And it will be longer for your friend Annie if we dawdle,' said Isabelle without changing pace.

Isabelle's comment concentrated Matt's mind on the task in hand. It was going to take a long time to climb over the pass and Matt prayed they would be in time.

Matt kept pace with Isabelle and he occasionally wondered if she was actually holding back for him to keep up. At every stream, though, Isabelle stopped to wash her face and neck and scrub her hands.

It was still less than an hour since sunrise and a peak to the east kept them in shadow; the air was cool and refreshing. A few trees struggled to survive among the rocks, though up above they grew more densely, hiding the heights where they would disappear altogether, leaving the rock and scree bare. Matt knew it was going to get very hot before they started going down the other side. It was a good job he hadn't tried to do this climb a few weeks before; he hadn't been half so fit back in England. All the walking and carrying his rucksack around Pakistan had been better for him than going to the gym.

'This is the last of the water until we get down the far side. You better fill the water bottle,' said Isabelle. Matt waited until Isabelle had drunk deeply from the stream, wondering at how she had taken charge, before filling the bottle to the brim and sealing it carefully.

Two hours of climbing put them among the thicker growth of the trees. The sun was over the mountains now, but the trees shaded them nicely. Isabelle looked pale. Her breathing was as laboured as Matt's from the steep climb. Once an hour she broke off a small piece of bread for each of them and nibbled on hers slowly, then drank a few small small sips from the water bottle. She didn't complain once.

Matt felt terrible. His chest hurt from the effort of the climb, his legs ached and his shoulders burnt from the weight of the rucksack. But Isabelle's silent perseverance kept him from saying so.

*****

Heavy footsteps outside the door prompted Annie to stand defensively. The padlock rattled, the bolt slammed back and the door swung open. Ricky stared at her.

'Hi,' he said expectantly.

Annie stared back silently.

'You don't recognise me, do you?' He looked ill, stubble darkening his face, his eyes bloodshot. She raised a quizzical eyebrow.

'I'm Raseem.'

'I thought your name was Ricky.'

'Depends. You knew me once before as Raseem. You were a right stuck up little bitch then. You used to ignore me.' She watched a muscle in his cheek twitch.

'I don't know what you're on about, I never met you before Islamabad.' This was not the conversation that Annie had expected and she was thrown off balance.

'Remember university, with all your fancy friends and that rich rugby playing boyfriend? You treated me like shit then, but now it's my turn to show you I'm as good in bed as anyone else.'

Raseem stepped forward and reached for Annie's shirt. She stepped back against the wall as he slapped her with his other hand. 'Come here, bitch.' She cried out with shock.

Pawing at her breasts with one hand, Raseem ripped at her shirt with the other. Annie fought back, launching herself at him with nails, fists, feet and head. Clothes ripped, hers and his, as they fell to the floor. A dull thud echoed around the room as Raseem hit his head on the boards.

'Fucking bitch!' Raseem slapped her again, hard, and Annie fell back into the corner, stunned. They lay staring at each other. His temples thumped viciously as the migraine ripped back through his head. Raseem's vision blurred, acid burned his throat and vomit rose in his stomach. He dragged himself to his feet to leave and go back to bed, his lust frustrated by this bitch once more. He was surprised by the sudden sound of her voice, cold and clipped.

'I remember you now. You used to buy porn mags in the union and leer at girls sunbathing on the grass.' Annie stared at him, her left eye starting to swell where he'd hit her. 'You used to grope girls in the bar when they'd had a few drinks and you thought you could get away with it. I slapped you once you bloody pervert.'

'I'm not a pervert. Don't call me that. It was you and your friends who were all tarts, out for anything you could get! I just didn't have enough money back then. I'm rich now and could afford you, but I don't have to pay any more.' Raseem held his head and kicked Annie hard, then he stumbled from the room as she lay winded in the corner. The padlock clicked back into place and he rolled to a shady spot on the grass and slumped on a charpoy to recover.

*****

It looked less than four hundred metres to reach the crest of the pass, but Matt could hardly move. The sun was hot now and burned his uncovered skin. The last stream was a long way below them and their water was low.

The air was thinner and hurt Matt's lungs as he desperately sucked for oxygen. He was amazed that the effects of altitude were as noticeable as they were. That morning he had never considered that the pass was so high the altitude would be affecting him by the time they reached the top.

Isabelle was struggling now too. He had tried to help her, but she just waved him away saying, 'I don't need any help. Leave me alone.'

They were going very slowly now. Matt just hoped they wouldn't be too late to find Annie in the valley on the far side.

Isabelle caught him up and Matt began climbing slowly beside her, three feet away. She had not spoken in two hours since they filled the water bottle and he had given up talking too, it hurt so much.

As they trudged slowly higher, Matt thought of Jo and Annie. Two so very different women, but one whose death he felt responsible for and the other's he knew would make him guilty for the rest of his life if he did not find her alive.

Then there was Isabelle, who despite the trauma she had obviously been through, was fighting back and wasn't going to let Ricky do the same to Annie as he had done to her. Matt tried not to think about what Ricky had done to her, but the way she had insisted on the spare set of clothes for Annie left him in little doubt as to what had happened and what could be happening to Annie right now.

The incline began to lessen, which eased the pain of climbing higher. Matt tried not to look upwards too much, it was disheartening never seeming to get any closer to the top. Instead he gazed behind them, as he paused to wait again for Isabelle, over the spreading peaks of the Hindu Kush. A rescue mission wasn't quite what he'd planned for his trip, he thought to himself as Isabelle inched past him.

Six hours after leaving the hotel, they reached the crest of the pass. Isabelle slumped to the ground and appeared to pass out. On wobbly legs Matt tottered to the far side, looked down and swore. An almost vertical descent, much deeper than what lay behind him, disappeared into a dark, shadow-filled gorge of a valley. There was no building in sight.

On a patch of grass, ten feet from where Isabelle lay immobile, Matt lay down and slept.

*****

Dented, battered, but unbroken, the door to her cell taunted Annie. Ricky had been quiet for two hours after he left the room, then the jeep had roared to life and raced away.

Annie had taken the opportunity to attempt an escape, without success. Inside her heavy boots her feet were sore and bruised. Her fingers were torn and bloody, her fingernails ripped to the quick.

*****

Raseem was in a tiny restaurant that catered to the few day-trippers who ventured this far from Chitral; it was two miles from his house. The restaurateur sold joints ready rolled to foreigners and Raseem usually teased him about the sky high prices, but today he paid for a medicinal joint because his trembling hands made it impossible to roll his own and he was desperate to ease the pain in his head.

Once he'd smoked his joint and the pain in his head subsided, he got the munchies. He ate the standard fare of fresh bread and a vegetable stew of tomatoes, okra and onions, then he suddenly remembered Isabelle and wondered if she was still alive. Not that he really cared, she would be a nuisance now he had Annie. He'd have to get rid of her somehow, but he'd worry about that later. Once he'd enjoyed Annie for a while.

Chapter Fifteen

'Matt? Matt!' Isabelle's strained voice dragged him awake. Her hand shook him.

'What? What's wrong?' he said groggily as he sat up looking around nervously, half expecting to see Ricky clambering towards them.

'Nothing. I couldn't stand it any more. The waiting. You haven't moved in a hour.' Isabelle sat back against a nearby rock and kicked at a stone with her boot.

Stretching his stiff and sore limbs Matt asked as casually as possible, trying not to sound too anxious himself, 'You all right?'

'Yeah. I want to get this over with, though. So we'd better get going.'

Going down from the pass was faster than climbing up had been, though dangerous and just as painful. The steep slope threatened to tumble them straight down to the bottom and Matt's knees ached as they absorbed the heavy impact of the precipitous descent.

They quickly found it was easier to almost run, bending their knees on impact and hoping they could find a tree to slow them down every ten metres. Isabelle seemed to have made a remarkable recovery while he slept. She led the way most of the time.

After two hours of downward travel through the narrow gully, it widened suddenly. Isabelle stopped abruptly. Matt joined her and stared at a building a few hundred metres below them.

'Is that it?'

Isabelle nodded slightly. She wrapped her arms tightly around herself and shuddered.

'I can't see his jeep. Where does he park?' Matt surveyed the area carefully.

A slight shrug of her shoulders was the only indication she had heard. Isabelle was scanning the area, looking for any movement and Ricky's jeep.

'You want to stay here, while I go on?' asked Matt in the mistaken belief she was having second thoughts.

'No!' snapped Isabelle. 'Two pairs of fists will be better than one.'

Matt raised his eyebrows and looked back at the building. They had come within sight of their destination, but now he was wondering what to do next. He would have preferred to leave Isabelle safely hidden in the trees and go reconnoitre on his own, which would have been by far the most sensible thing to do. He took a deep breath and began to rethink.

'All right, it looks like he isn't here at the moment. Let's go look and see if your friend Annie is in there.' Without looking to see if Matt was following, Isabelle went in search of Annie.

Surprised at her decisiveness, Matt followed.

*****

Mellow from the hash, Raseem slowly drove home. He was fantasising about Annie. In his drug-enhanced dreams she was compliant, willing, and passionate, just like the women in all the movies he watched. He rubbed his crotch, then swore as his mind registered the fact there was no reaction.

'Fucking bitch.' His foot pressed the pedal to the floor. The jeep slewed wildly as he drove recklessly along the dirt track. Ten minutes later he almost hit the building when he slid to a halt.

Leaving the jeep door hanging open he charged for Annie's room. He kicked the door as he fumbled with the padlock. The door banged against the wall as he threw it open, the padlock flying through the air and rolling in the grass ten feet away.

Annie met him head on, screaming manically. Her fists hit his face before he knew where she was. Raseem grabbed a handful of her shirt to hold her at bay; it ripped and the buttons flew off. She clawed at his eyes. Raseem grabbed her arms, fighting to save his face. It was not supposed to be like this, but at last he felt a physical stirring in his trousers.

The two brawling bodies fell to the floor. Raseem's elbow caught Annie in the stomach, knocking the wind from her.

Taking advantage of Annie's loss of breath, Raseem clawed at her bra.

*****

Sitting still waiting for something to happen was not what Ishmael wanted to do. He had been told to use his initiative, and while his boss might not agree with his current plan, Ishmael felt he had enough justification for doing it if anyone ever objected.

It would take him less than a day to walk around the largest lake. If he was asked why he had done it he would say he was looking to see if there was another track on the far side of the lake. Even though he already knew there was not.

He said it aloud again as he left his tent. It sounded good, no one could object. A note inside the tent explained where he was, just in case someone came looking for him. His pack contained a stove, a saucepan, food and a water bottle. His map was in its waterproof pouch around his neck and another water bottle weighted his webbing comfortingly.

As quietly as he could, Ishmael began his circular trip. He kept his gun loose in his hand; there was bound to be game around that would supplement his tasteless army rations.

*****

When they were twenty metres from the building and about to step onto open ground, the sound of a jeep startled them. By the sound of its engine it was going full speed. Matt dragged Isabelle behind a tree and pulled her arm to make her crouch out of sight. She pulled against him, eager to keep going. 'Wait, let's see if it's him. And if he's on his own,' hissed Matt.

Dust billowed into the air as the jeep slid to a halt. Ricky tumbled from his seat and sprinted for the balcony along the front of the building. He was on his own and there was no sign of Annie.

Matt watched uncertainly and slipped the rucksack slowly from his back in preparation for he knew not what. Isabelle glared at Ricky and tensed to run.

'What shall we do?' Matt spoke aloud, but he asked the question more of himself than Isabelle.

'Let him get inside, then we can get closer without him seeing us,' whispered Isabelle.

A muffled scream reached them. Isabelle stood, steadying herself against the tree.

Matt broke from the trees and ran, fuelled by adrenaline. He hurdled bushes and rocks. He stumbled once and almost fell. Another scream, louder now, escaped the building. Leaping the balustrade, Matt could hear a fight in progress.

Two bodies rolled on the floor, one man, one woman. Blood smears distorted their faces, but Matt knew who they were. Annie clawed at Ricky's face. Ricky pawed at her naked torso, trying to evade her vicious hits whilst unable to restrain his excitement.

Matt aimed his boot viciously at Ricky's side. He grunted as a rib cracked and the kick rolled him sideways. Annie rolled the other way gasping for breath, and got on her knee against the wall. Matt kicked again, this time to the side of Ricky's head. Ricky moaned, slumped to the floor with a thud and lay still. Matt stood looking down at the prone figure, panting.

Annie stood slowly and stared at Ricky as he lay on the floor. 'Is he dead?' Then she looked at Matt, shuddered and ran for the door, where she vomited over the balustrade of the balcony.

Matt knelt beside Ricky and watched his chest, relaxing slightly as he saw it rise and fall slowly. As he left the room

Matt stopped, then turned back and stamped on Ricky's outstretched ankle. That would slow him down if he decided to follow them.

Outside, Annie continued to retch. When she stopped Matt asked quietly, 'Can you walk? We really ought to get away from here before he comes round.'

'He's alive then? Pity.' Annie wrapped her arms around herself to cover her nakedness and stood on the wooden boards. Matt suddenly blushed as he realised she was looking at him directly and she was as gorgeous as when he'd first seen her in Peshawar, despite the vicious fight she'd just been through. 'Thank you. I have no idea how you suddenly turned up, but thank you.' Annie smiled at him weakly. 'Don't suppose you've got some spare clothes with you?'

'Of course, sorry. Isabelle's got them.' Matt looked around him and saw Isabelle a few yards away watching them.

'If you killed him nobody would know,' suggested Isabelle.

Matt looked at her, wondering if she was joking, but from the look in her eyes she wasn't. 'Help Annie,' said Matt firmly, as he took Annie by the elbow and directed her towards Isabelle. He wanted to check Ricky again before they left, just to make sure he wasn't dead.

Wrapping an arm round the shaking Annie, Isabelle led her away to the rucksack in the trees and the spare clothes.

A scraping noise in the room behind him startled Matt. Ricky was hauling himself upright in the doorway with a murderous glare in his eyes as he stared at Matt. 'You'll regret this,' he hissed through his pain. 'You won't get away from here alive. I'll kill the lot of you.'

Matt took a step towards him. 'Yeah? Want some more?' Ricky made no reply, nor any attempt to restart the fight.

'Don't leave here for a day or two. If you follow us, I'll kill you.' Matt stared at Ricky, until he lowered his gaze.

Edging backwards along the balcony, Matt watched Ricky closely. At the corner of the building he glanced towards the trees just in time to see Annie and Isabelle reach them, heading for the rucksack.

Ricky's gaze followed Matt and hatred burned in his eyes, but he made no attempt to follow. Matt strode away from the house and caught up with the two women ten metres into the copse. Annie was dressed in his spare shirt and fleecy; the girls were hugging each other.

Matt was shaking himself and craved some physical contact too, but he realised that was not going to happen and he would just have to get on and deal with his post-fight tremors on his own as the adrenalin faded away.

'We better go.' Matt stood a few metres away facing back towards the building, trying to give the girls some privacy whilst checking Ricky wasn't following.

'Thank you.' Annie's weak voice sounded just behind him. Matt turned and gazed into her eyes, one swelling and blackening. She touched him on the arm and smiled.

'No problem,' Matt said. Let's go,' he added gruffly as he closed up the rucksack and heaved it onto his back.

Isabelle and Annie walked ahead of him, helping each other. It was hard to tell which one needed the help most, they both limped so badly. None of them had a watch on, but Matt estimated there was nowhere near enough daylight to get them back over the pass to their hotel before night fell. It was going to be a long night.

*****

Raseem lay on the mattress in his room for an hour, with no intention of following Matt. He was a coward at heart, though he would never admit it. He blamed his current inactivity on the pain in his ribs and the returned migraine that was making him nauseous again.

When he finally remembered the spare joint he had in his pocket, he lit it. By the time it was finished the pain was gone and his courage fortified.

He took the jeep slowly down the road. There was only one road out of Birer and he was sure he would find them if he was careful. There was the pass to Bumburet, but Ricky discounted that as far too difficult an option for the girls.

His hunting knife lay on the passenger seat. He was going to fuck that bitch, even if he had to kill her in the process.

*****

Yaks munched the grass, unconcerned with his presence. Eagles and hawks hovered silently above him in the clear blue sky. A low hill hid the barrier gate and the frontier policeman's hut. The still lake perfectly reflected the snow-capped mountains rising around him. Ishmael was alone in his mountains. He was glad he had not seen any game close enough to shoot; firing his gun would have ruined the peaceful world around him.

His pace was slow and unhurried as he enjoyed the solitude. He had decided to head for the lip of the pass, on both the east and west sides. On the Chitral side he could contemplate the holy mountain of *Tirich Mir* and pray for his family. On the Gilgit side he could look down towards home and send his thoughts to his wife and children with the spirit of the mountains. His wife thought he was mad when he told her what he did, though she smiled with pleasure that he remembered her during his time away. She said he was almost a Kafir, they believed in the spirits too. His tribe had only converted to Islam relatively late, with the encouragement of a sword to help them along, but they still held on to a few of the old traditions.

*****

When it was too dark to continue, Matt called a halt. The two women wanted to keep going and get as far away from Ricky as they could, but Matt reasoned if they could not see, neither could Ricky.

When they found somewhere to stop, Matt tried to reassure them they would be OK to rest properly. 'I'll stay awake all night and make sure you're safe. You get some sleep. There's only two sleeping bags anyway.'

Annie and Isabelle huddled together in a hollow among the rocks. Matt sat on a boulder twenty feet away. He could only see the vague outline of their presence from where he was, and he knew they were there. Their invisibility would make it almost impossible for someone else to find them if they came looking, especially in the dark. It was also likely he would make so much noise they would hear Ricky coming a long time before he arrived.

As the temperature dropped the boulder grew intolerably uncomfortable. Matt moved to some coarse grass nearer the sleeping Annie and Isabelle, and leant against a smooth boulder. The regular breathing of the girls was comforting as he tried to determine the sources of strange sounds coming from the darkness around him.

Eventually, the effects of his exhausting day overtook him, and he too began to doze.

*****

Raseem asked everyone he saw as he drove slowly down the valley, but no one admitted to having seen any foreigners. He was kicking himself now for not watching which way they had gone, instead of hiding in his bed nursing a headache and feeling sorry for himself.

Where the valley narrowed to a gorge he parked for the night and smoked another joint from the handful he had picked up from the restaurant on the way past. The hash made him hungry, but there was nothing he could do about that since he hadn't thought to buy food as well. Despite his hunger and resolution to stay awake so they wouldn't sneak past him in the night, Raseem's head soon dipped and he slipped into a dope induced dream.

*****

'Oi. Sleepy head.'

Matt's head hit hard rock as Annie prodded him gently with her boot and wrenched him from sleep.

'Lousy guard you are,' she said, smiling amiably at him.

'Huh? God, I must have dropped off to sleep a few minutes ago.' Matt rubbed his eyes and scrambled to his feet. 'I've been up all night.'

'I've been awake an hour and you've been snoring all the time.'

'Oops. Sorry,' he said. 'How's Isabelle?'

'Safe, thankfully. She's still asleep. She was exhausted, poor thing.'

'Good,' nodded Matt. 'How are you?' he asked, looking at her puffy eye.

'Not bad, considering.' Annie tested the swelling round her eye and grimaced.

They sat in silence for a few minutes, looking out over the mountains bathed in the early morning light. Annie coughed nervously and glanced at Matt. 'Isabelle told me how you insisted on coming to my rescue as we climbed up here last night. After the way I spoke to you in Chitral I'm a very lucky girl. How did you know he had me anyway and where we were?'

'You passed me on the road, but were going too fast and my jeep didn't keep up so I lost you. Fortunately Isabelle found me and brought me over the pass to show me where you were. If it wasn't for her you'd still be there.'

Annie gazed out over the mountains spreading into the distance. She looked down to the valley and the trees that hid Ricky's house. A single tear ran down her face.

'Thanks for coming. You were right about Ricky.' Annie's voice cracked and she smiled tentatively at Matt. He wanted to reach out and hold her, but did not have the courage.

'No problem. I should have tried harder to tell you what he was really like.' Matt smiled back at her, pleased they were friends again. 'We'd better get going. Isabelle probably ought to see a doctor soon, instead of camping out on mountain tops.'

It took many more hours to reach the crest of the pass. Isabelle was weak and the exertions of the last two days were taking their toll on her already weakened body. Annie was bruised and sore, but struggled gamely on, encouraging Isabelle as much as she could.

Matt followed at the rear as they climbed; the two women felt more comfortable if he was between them and Ricky. As he watched Annie and Isabelle struggle ahead of him he was painfully aware of how little he could do to help them through their emotional trauma. It was good they had each other to lean on.

At the crest of the pass they split the last of the stale bread between them into three mouthfuls and chewed it slowly. There was no sign of Ricky, but none of them could relax and they continually scanned the ground behind them for any sign of movement.

*****

Pain woke Raseem. His ribs hurt and his face hurt where the mark from Matt's kick had turned to a bruise. His ankle ached horrendously too, but he couldn't remember why it hurt so much. The clock on the dashboard told him it was three o'clock in the morning.

The high snow-capped peak of the mountain at the top of the valley where the locals believed the Toad Faerie lived glowed faintly in the dark sky. Raseem tried to ignore it, he didn't believe all that shit, but it seemed to be watching him and it made him nervous in the intense darkness of the gorge. When he couldn't stand it any more, he slowly and carefully drove through the dark to Ayun and parked by the bridge. There was only one road out of the Kalash valleys after all, he rationalised, and they would still have to pass him in Ayun if they took the main road straight from Birer, or had gone over the pass to Bumburet after all.

*****

After careful observation of the backpackers around him, Chris had gone clothes shopping. He was now dressed in hiking boots, canvas trousers and a baggy 'Tin-Tin in Gilgit' T-shirt. The outdoor shops of Gilgit were surprisingly well stocked with all sorts of high quality climbing gear, all second hand. Chris was amazed at what all the climbing expeditions left behind.

Despite his new clothes Chris still felt out of place. His hair was cut too formally, his face too pale and he knew he looked soft. A few of the backpackers said hello to him, but most just eyed him suspiciously when he tried to talk to them.

He was enjoying the food immensely, though it was nothing like the curries available in Pakistani restaurants in London. He had enjoyed an amazing chicken tikka in the bazaar, a whole chicken sliced through the middle and cooked in a delicious sauce of onions, tomatoes and spices he could not identify. His wife would never believe him when he told her he had eaten a real Kashmiri meal; anyway, she had no idea where he went on most of his trips abroad and usually didn't want to know.

The hotel supplied chai free of charge to its guests, hoping to entice then into buying dinner as well. Most of the backpackers did, many seeming nervous of getting too close to the locals, as well as the strange foreign man who could well be a policeman. Chris sipped his chai, all alone at a table in the crowded outdoor eating area of the Tourist Hotel.

'Hi, man. You look better.' The old hippy sat down and bellowed for chai. 'Had a good day?'

'I've had better. You?'

A waiter placed a steaming cup on the table.

'Let's take a walk. I don't want people listening.'

The two men strolled to the grass and sat apart from the crowd with their chai. The hippy started rolling a joint.

'I asked around about your niece. I didn't tell anyone you wanted to know. A few people asked who you were though, so I said you were just some old geezer going through a mid-life crisis.' The hippy smiled broadly at his own sense of humour.

'Thanks' said Chris wryly. That nicely put him in his place. 'What did you learn?'

'Your niece, if that's what she is, was in Peshawar. Caused quite a stir; you never said she was such a stunner.'

'She's my niece, for God's sake. I don't think of her like that.' Chris smiled in spite of himself. There might be an added benefit if he succeeded in this job, rescuing a gorgeous young lady like a knight in shining armour.

'Yeah. Whatever. Anyway, she went to Chitral. You're in the wrong part of the country.'

'Chitral, that's the other side of the Shandur Pass isn't it?'

'It is. You're not as naïve as you look, are you?' said the hippy eyeing him more closely. 'Sure you're not a copper?' The hippy stood and wandered away to join a group of backpackers. Chris lay on the grass and cursed his luck. How the hell was he going to get to Chitral?

*****

Matt and Annie supported Isabelle between them for the last two hours. Exhaustion and hunger had left her almost incapable of walking. She was too ill now to worry about Matt getting close to her.

At the hotel they laid a sleeping bag on a charpoy, placed her gently on top and covered her with the second sleeping bag. The Kalash woman brought tea immediately and soon after, a pot of stew. She sat with Isabelle and nursed her like one of her own, encouraging her to eat and drink until she fell into an exhausted sleep. Matt and Annie gratefully sat outside on the terrace, slowly eating their own food, too fatigued to talk.

Within an hour Annie was asleep on the floor beside Isabelle in the room, while Matt was slumped asleep on the veranda outside the door with only a single blanket, provided to him by their host.

*****

He hated Ayun. The locals were unfriendly, the chai-shop expensive. Everyone stared at him suspiciously, wondering why he was just sitting there and wanting to know what he was hanging around for. Panic cramped his stomach. Pain ripped his chest.

Isabelle, Annie and Matt were out there somewhere. He had to stop them getting to Islamabad; he just knew they would go to the British Embassy and report him. He carried a British passport and desperately wanted to go back to England, but he feared jail, whether in Pakistan or Britain. He was regretting now that he'd made use of his dual nationality and entered Pakistan on his Pakistani passport, as the British Embassy would disown him and that made it more likely he would end up in some stinking Pakistani jail if they got away.

Raseem planned to plant some drugs in their bags and shop them to the police if he found them in time. That would ruin their story and take the heat off him. Failing that, he would get them killed. Hits on foreigners were expensive, but there was bound to be some Afghani in Chitral who would do it for jihad, or the money.

*****

During the evening Isabelle woke up screaming. Annie held her close. Matt loitered uncertainly and sleepily at the door to their room, having been woken from a deep, exhausted sleep.

Only one jeep a day went from Bumburet to Chitral, first thing in the morning. Matt planned to get them all to the government guesthouse, reckoning it would be the safest place in town. It might even have guards to protect the richer tourists from having to mix with the locals. Ricky would hardly be likely to come looking for them there.

Matt wanted to sleep in the next room on the charpoy, but Isabelle wanted him to sleep outside the door again even though Annie had agreed to stay inside on the floor of the room. Matt desperately needed a good night's sleep and wanted to get his head back down and return to his interrupted sleep but the pleading look on Isabelle's face was enough to make him agree. Just as he was settling down with his thin blanket though, the ever hospitable Kalash woman appeared and pulled the charpoy from the room for Matt to use on the terrace. He smiled broadly in thanks, never having thought he would be so relived to be sleeping on a charpoy. Then he settled back down on the terrace for what he expected was going to be another long night.

*****

Late that evening Raseem abandoned Ayun too, to drive to Chitral. He checked into the Garden Hotel and waited for three foreigners to arrive. He reckoned it was the logical place for them to go, since it was where they had stayed before and Annie's bag was probably still there.

It was also more comfortable than his jeep and he didn't fancy another bad night's sleep and waking up with a migraine again.

Chapter Sixteen

Low cloud obscured the sun. It was threatening to rain. 'Thank God we crossed the pass yesterday. I'd hate to be caught up there in bad weather.' Annie nodded tiredly at Matt as he tried to make conversation; she was too tense to think of small talk. Isabelle's face was blank with trauma, shock and exhaustion. Her blistered feet were bootless, protected from further damage by thick socks borrowed from Matt.

'To think Isabelle crossed that pass three times in forty-eight hours. It was bad enough crossing just the once. She's one hell of a gutsy girl,' admired Annie.

It was six o'clock in the morning and they were loading themselves onto a jeep; in a few hours they would be in Chitral. Isabelle wrapped herself in a sleeping bag in the back of the jeep, the exhaustion and shock demanding she cocoon herself against the world. Annie sat next to her and huddled up close, as Matt joined the driver up front. It had taken a lot of money to persuade the driver not to pick up any other passengers and fill his jeep to its normal capacity. It was not just the other fares Matt had been forced to pay: the premium on exclusivity was expensive here.

As they drove through the straggling village without stopping, angry locals wanting a ride shouted at them, gesticulating offensive and threatening gestures. The driver was nervous and edgy, seemingly worried they they might do more than shout and threaten. But the fifty per cent of the money Matt had withheld until arrival must have made the risk worthwhile, because the driver kept going.

*****

Looking out over the Chitral valley towards *Tirich Mir* Ishmael sipped his chai and concentrated on his family. Five minutes earlier he had finished his mid-morning prayers and now it was time to practice the traditions his people had followed for centuries. The two blended into a way of life that in other parts of the Islamic world would have been deemed blasphemous, but in the northern mountains of Pakistan a more mystical form of Islam was common enough in private.

As an afterthought, Ishmael paused to consider the plight of the missing foreigners and ask the mountains to watch over them.

The Himalayas stretched for hundreds of miles behind him. Ishmael drew on their strength and permanence, invoking their immovable presence to protect his family and those in need.

Returning his mind to his present surroundings Ishmael noted that to the south black clouds billowed and signalled the arrival of the monsoon rains. They were late this year and badly needed, though there was always the risk too much rain would fall on the dry land and cause destruction and death as it flowed back to the sea, instead of bringing life and sustenance as it should.

*****

Anxiously, Matt watched for Ricky's jeep. He hoped not to see it, but knew Ricky would be looking for them. The bigger worry was that if Ricky really did have friends here, there was no way they could avoid them.

It was difficult to know if speed was better, to get Isabelle to somewhere she felt safer, or whether to make the driver go slowly to soften the ride. Matt abdicated responsibility and left the driver to decide.

At Ayun the driver stopped to talk to friends, standing with his back to the jeep while he chatted volubly. Matt was convinced it was so he could not see his passengers growing impatient and angry at the delay.

There was no sign of Ricky or his jeep, though. But there were too many buildings he could have hidden the jeep behind for Matt to be sure he was not watching them, hidden from view in a dark chai-shop.

Swaying gently, the bridge carried them back over the river. Matt began to relax; they were away from the Kalash valleys and Chitral with its airport and flights to safety was not far away.

Isabelle was asleep again, buried in her sleeping bag with Annie sitting uncomfortably and protectively beside her. Annie was looking drawn and tired too, sickened by the effects of her own ordeal and the horror of what might have been.

Flying seemed to be the obvious way to get Isabelle and Annie to Islamabad. The flight was quick, comfortable and most importantly would get them far away from Ricky. There was one flight a day from Islamabad to Chitral and back, that took less than an hour each way.

Matt just hoped they would get to the airport in time so they could be on the flight today. The responsibility of looking after Isabelle whilst being so incapable of helping her was draining his energy and making him sick with worry.

*****

Parking his jeep at the end of the bridge, Raseem settled down to wait once more. He hadn't slept as well as he'd hoped at the Garden Hotel. His ribs had hurt all night and the wooden seats in the garden were no better when he finally got up. Eventually the lure of the soft seat in his jeep and the coolness of the air-conditioning had been irresistible.

Raseem knew the jeeps from the Kalash would arrive just before midday, and they always crossed this bridge. Only private jeeps went further upriver and entered town over the second bridge on their way to the PTDC guesthouse and the airport to the north of town. Three white faces on a jeep, amongst those of the local passengers, would be obvious as their vehicle crawled across the bridge. They wouldn't get past him here.

Stubbing out another joint he stepped from the jeep and strolled groggily towards the river, a pair of binoculars swinging from his neck. The hash killed the pain in his ribs and helped settle his anger by making him pleasantly mellow. Without the hash he'd struggled to think straight from the pain, but having smoked a few joints during the morning he was now beginning to find it hard to think much at all.

*****

Chitral was only a couple of miles away; the suspension bridge marking the southern approach to town was in view. A queue of traffic waited to cross the river ahead of them; a few jeeps were idling on the far side too, waiting to head south.

The traffic heading north started moving over the bridge towards Chitral. Matt waited in anticipation of their jeep following them across the water, but they kept going north on the east side of the river.

Matt turned to the driver questioningly and pointed at the bridge. 'Chitral. I want to go to Chitral.'

'*Seedha. Seedha*,' smiled the driver as he waved his hands manically trying to indicate they were going further north before crossing the river.

Matt turned to smile reassuringly at Annie and wave through the window behind his head to show everything was all right.

Annie was staring hard across the river, her face white with loathing. She was gripping the side of the jeep hard enough to turn her knuckles white.

Across the far side of the river, parked behind the concrete brace supporting the bridge sat Ricky's jeep. They'd never have seen it until they got to the far side if they had crossed the river here. Sitting stiffly upright on the bank of the river, holding binoculars to his face, a man watched them.

*****

He wanted to scream. She was close, but still out of reach. Even across the river he'd known it was her as soon as he'd seen the nearly empty jeep with two white women riding in the back.

250

As they'd come round the concrete blocks supporting the far end of the bridge Raseem had focused his binoculars on the two girls.

'Fucking bitch,' hissed Raseem as he confirmed it was Annie. He didn't pay attention to the girl sitting next to her, though she looked vaguely familiar and quite pretty.

Focusing on Annie, Raseem targeted all his hatred through the magnifying lenses of his binoculars. The fucking bitch must be heading for the airport, he thought. She'd get away from him if he wasn't careful.

The slow oncoming traffic stopped him crossing the bridge to follow her. He raced for his jeep and spun the wheels as he pulled away to drive through town and catch them at the other bridge for which they were obviously heading.

People, animals, horses and vehicles slowed his progress. His air horn blared, but no one paid any more attention to him than they did any other vehicle doing the same on the crowded street. The main street was packed with people in no hurry to move.

Raseem fumed and swore. His ribs hurt from the careless charge to the jeep and the reckless driving on his way back to town had caused him more pain as he'd fought with the steering wheel.

Now these stupid people were stopping him getting to the airport before Annie. If she got into the airport building he'd never be able to get her back and he'd likely as not end up in prison. Raseem looked in the rear view mirror to see if he could reverse up and find another way to the airport, but as he'd knocked it when he jumped into the jeep at the bridge all he saw was the big boot shaped bruise on his face. That bloody bastard, Matt. He was going to kill him if he ever got the chance.

*****

Matt tapped his fingers impatiently on the door of the jeep. The sight of Ricky had seriously unsettled him and he was desperate to reach the safety of the PTDC guesthouse and buy three plane tickets to Islamabad from the PIA office there. A two-lane span of concrete crossed the river at the north end of Chitral. The government guesthouse stood a hundred yards past it. The driver pulled up his jeep outside the guesthouse, stopping under the trees.

Pointing at a sign in the window beside the front door announcing *'Airplane Tickets'*, the driver hurried his passengers off his vehicle, leaving the engine still running while he did so. He drove away sharply as soon as they disembarked and Matt gave him the rest of his money, leaving them standing alone in the shade with their bags.

Leaving Annie to sit with Isabelle against a tree, Matt hurried in to the hotel to buy the plane tickets to Islamabad.

'Three tickets to Islamabad, for today. Please.'

An apologetic face looked back at him across the counter. 'Sorry sir, there are no tickets left for today. The flights are very busy and there will be no flight tomorrow at all for bad weather. I have one ticket for five days time and two tickets for two days later. You want?'

'I need to go today. It's urgent. My friends are very ill. They need a doctor.'

'We have doctor in Chitral. Good England taught Doctor. You see him.'

'No. I need to get my friend to Islamabad. Today. I want some bloody plane tickets!' Matt argued. He shouted. He pointed at Isabelle sitting slumped under the tree outside the window. Nothing worked. The concierge shrugged and smiled apologetically.

'You can have a room, sir. We only have one free, but it has three beds.'

Matt looked at him incredulously. The man picked up his paper preparing for Matt's rejection of the offer.

Just about to tell the man where to put his useless offer, Matt glanced out at Annie and Isabelle lying exhausted and scared by the tree, with a growing crowd of children gawking at them.

Turning back to the concierge he capitulated. 'Okay, I'll take it.'

*****

Stuck in a traffic jam half way down the main street, Raseem could not see the bridge crossing the river north of the town, but he could see the PTDC guesthouse in the distance. A cruel smile curled his lips as he saw his prey climb from the jeep and slump beneath a tree with the other, less interesting, girl.

He had her back in his grasp now, she wasn't going anywhere quickly. Matt was obviously going to buy plane tickets to get them out of Chitral as quickly as possible. 'Hah, no chance of that,' spat Raseem excitedly as he looked at the low thunderclouds billowing around the mountain tops blanketed in a fresh fall of late snow. The plane would be cancelled today because of the weather and the Lowari pass would be icily treacherous and coldly slow to cross.

Idly reaching out his hand Raseem stroked the bag containing the packet of heroin. He had his plan all worked out.

It was going to be easy finding some kid to plant the drugs in Matt's bag. The Afghani refugee kids round here were all half starved and desperate for money. A quick phone call to the police and that would be the end of any worries he had that he, the untouchable Raseem, was going to be in trouble.

With any luck the police would let Annie go pretty quickly, too. A foreign male was much easier to put in prison without any of the embarrassing news coverage that went with arresting a pretty foreign girl. The arresting policeman would probably get a bonus too, which made them more amenable to taking the easy option.

Then, without Matt in tow, Annie was going to be an easier target again and with any luck he would get one more chance to seduce her with his undoubted charms.

Abandoning his jeep in a side street, Raseem stepped onto the unmade roadway and strolled casually towards the guesthouse, smiling.

People packed the PIA ticket office. More waited outside. Everyone was shouting and angry. '*No flight 3 days*,' announced a notice tacked to the door.

Pushing his way to the front of the scrum Chris waved his diplomatic passport. At times like this he found it sometimes helped to put on the attitude of an arrogant foreigner. This time he met with failure. The staff member behind the counter did break off momentarily from an argument with another potential customer though. 'Sorry, sir. All flights are cancelled. Bad weather between here and Rawalpindi. There will be no flight for five days, I think.'

The harried man managed to look apologetic, embarrassed and argumentative all at the same time. Abandoning hope of getting on a flight in any timescale that would be useful, Chris pushed his way back through the crowd and out of the office.

Quickly re-checking his map first, Chris headed through the bazaars and went in search of the bus station alongside the polo ground. Muttering impatiently to himself as he went, Chris wondered how he would explain to his boss that he had travelled half way round the world to end up in the wrong town, in the wrong valley, with nothing to show for the expense. He supposedly had total discretion in what he did, but somewhere down the line he had to account for the money he spent by showing a result. He wasn't sure this particular operation would tick enough boxes in potential outcomes to pass muster. 'Bloody accountants,' he announced to the world in general as he reached the bus depot.

Another pack of shouting, frustrated people milled around the compound that was home to the bus station.

'Islamabad. I'm looking for a bus to Islamabad.' Chris said to anyone who looked like they might know what was happening in the chaos, but was met with nothing but shaking heads and smiles.

Finally, he saw a well dressed man looking as out of place and confused as himself. 'Excuse me, I'm trying to get to Islamabad. Do you know which bus I should take?'

The man laughed ironically, 'You'll be lucky. There's been a landslip. The same bad weather as disrupted the flights has broken the road too. I work for the government, I only came up to this awful place for one day. Now I can't get away again.'

'That happens all the time, doesn't it? The road will be repaired soon though, won't it?' Chris was beginning to feel trapped. It might look like paradise despite what this urban civil servant thought of the place, but he still needed to be somewhere else.

The well-dressed man raised his arms and let them fall dramatically. 'No one knows when it'll be repaired. It was a big fall. And there might be more we don't know about yet. The weather is very bad. We might be stuck here for days.'

'So not today then? What about tomorrow?' asked Chris desperately, but the man turned away without answering, leaving Chris to ponder his options alone.

*****

Crisp clean sheets covered the proper beds, a TV with satellite channels stood in the corner. A balcony overlooked the lush green gardens shaded with trees. Most importantly though, the room even had a proper dead-bolt on the inside of the door, that Isabelle made sure was closed as soon as they entered the room.

'I'll go find your bag at the Garden Hotel and then organise some food in the room for us all, so you can stay here,' said Matt. Isabelle was already laid out on the bed furthest from the door, wrapped closely in her sleeping bag.

'Never mind about my bag. Just find us a way to get to Islamabad as quickly as possible. We need to get Isabelle far away from here as soon as we can.' Annie glanced across at the girl lying on the bed. 'God knows what he did to her, but she's spoken less and less since we left that hut of his. She needs help from someone who knows what they're doing, as well as a doctor.'

When the bolt clicked home behind him, Matt slumped. The weight of expectation was exhausting him. He was

255

running out of ideas and could have just as easily curled up in bed himself.

The sight of Ricky watching them across the river had frightened him more than he would have thought possible. The guy just never gave up. But the look of horror on Annie's face had strengthened his resolve to get them all away as quickly as possible.

It was fortunate Isabelle had been fast asleep and not seen Ricky at the bridge, and by unspoken agreement neither Annie nor he had mentioned that that they'd seen her abductor.

In the lobby of the hotel a notice board covered in handwritten notes caught Matt's eye. The *'For Hire'* and *'Jeep Trip'* titles sparked more interest and gave him an excuse not to leave the safety of the hotel and risk meeting Ricky.

'Day-trips to see Kalash'. 'Enjoy Hot Spring at Garam Chasma'. 'Peshawar in Comfort'. 'Luxury Jeep to Gilgit'. 'Treks to Tirich Mir'. The options were wide, but none offered Islamabad as a destination much to Matt's disappointment.

'You want jeep, sir? I take you Islamabad. No planes, I hear you ask. I have good jeep, Nissan Pajero.' A local man in a clean fresh *kameez* and waistcoat stood smiling nearby. Matt looked at him, unsure what to do. The last time someone had offered him a lift it had been Ricky.

'I take tourist to Islamabad all the time when plane cancelled. Best service. Air-conditioning on hot day. Heating on cold day.' The concierge watched them with an encouraging and reassuring smile.

'How much?' asked Matt, finally.

'Three hundred dollar total for three persons. Best price. Leave tomorrow, two day in Islamabad. Nice place stop on way. My brother house.'

'Is that the best price you can do?'

'Oh yes. Only price. Fixed price agreed with hotel.' The man turned to seek confirmation from the concierge.

'Yes. Yes. This man is reliable,' said the concierge.

'Approved price, sir. So tourist not get ripped off,' said the tout.

Recognising the futility of arguing with the combined front of the hotel and driver and, even worse, risk losing an opportunity to leave Chitral the next day, Matt opted to take the man at face value. 'OK, I'll take it. What time do we leave?'

'Nine o'clock, after breakfast. Fifty dollar deposit.'

'I'll give you a hundred dollars before we leave. The rest when we get there. There'll be a fifty dollar bonus if you make good time and get us there safely. And I want to leave at seven o'clock.'

The tout turned to check with the concierge, then nodded at Matt, 'OK. Eight o'clock. Seven o'clock too early. Tomorrow, I see you at front door.'

In the hotel lounge a soft armchair beckoned and Matt sank his tired body into it, postponing the moment when he would have to leave the air-conditioning and go back out into the heat and dust and face the possibility of meeting Ricky.

Outside the window the tout strolled slowly down the path towards the street.

From under the shadow of a tree stepped Ricky. Matt sank lower in his chair hoping desperately Ricky had not been able to see him in the lobby a few minutes ago. That vain hope was dashed when the tout stopped to talk to the man they were trying to escape from.

*****

'The party of three foreigners in there, two women and a man, you know them?' Raseem said casually.

'Yes. I'm taking them to Islamabad tomorrow,' admitted the driver.

'How much they paying?'

'Three hundred dollars and a bonus if I get them there safely. Stupid foreigners all have too much money. They didn't even haggle,' laughed the man.

'I'll give you another hundred if you take them to Drosh and leave them there.'

'Why?' asked the man suspiciously.

'They're friends of mine. I want to surprise them with a stay in the Mir's Palace; he's a friend of mine too.' The lie came easily; he used it frequently in Islamabad when he wanted to impress someone, but he'd never tried it here before.

'I'll do it for two hundred dollars,' said the driver, glad he hadn't mentioned when they were going to pay him. 'They're not going to pay me until I get there. What's the catch?'

'No catch. I was at university in England with them and I want them to see the best of Chitral. All I want you to do is stop at the point where you have the best view of the palace from the main road and suggest they get out to take a photo. When they do, drive away and leave them. I'll be round the next corner so you can give me their bags, then I'll go back and pick them up. Easy. What time are you leaving tomorrow?'

'Nine o'clock. They wanted to go at seven, I agreed eight, but I won't turn up until closer to nine. What's the point if I'm only going to Drosh, eh?' said the man with a smile.

Raseem felt his tension ease slightly as he handed over a hundred dollars to seal the deal. He had caught up with Annie again, his plan was coming together, and soon she would finally be his to play with.

*****

'Shit.' Matt watched the two men talking under the tree. The conversation went on too long for it to be a casual exchange. When the tout turned and waved his arm back at the hotel Matt was convinced they were talking about him and the two girls. When Ricky handed over some money Matt knew his plan was blown and Ricky knew where they were headed.

'You want a drink, sir?' A waiter distracted Matt momentarily and Ricky was gone by the time he looked back through the window.

Indecision kept Matt in his chair for an hour. The three cokes he supped began to make him twitchy. Should he tell

Annie? Should he take the chance and go ahead with their plan to head for Islamabad anyway? How else could they get out of here anyway?

'You're going Islamabad tomorrow?' A man sat in the chair opposite Matt.

'Why?' Matt glared at the man suspiciously.

'I saw you talk to driver. He bad man. Bad jeep, old Suzuki. Price too high.'

'He said he had a Nissan Pajero.' Matt wasn't going to trust anyone any more. But this man might provide a way to escape from Ricky.

'He does, but he won't take you in it. I have old Suzuki, but my prices cheaper. I take you to Gilgit for one hundred and fifty dollar. Nice journey, pretty mountains. You fly Islamabad from Gilgit.'

'How long does it take?'

'Three days. Much fun.'

'It's only two if we go straight to Islamabad and I need to get there quickly. My friend's not well.'

The man shook his head. 'No, sir. The road across Lowari is very bad. Much rain damage road. Tunnel flooded. It take four day now.'

'I thought the tunnel wasn't finished?'

The man laughed. 'It's not. But we use it anyway when we can. You want travel with me?'

Matt considered the man in front of him. It was hard to know who to trust and who to run a mile from. Was this man any better than the other one? But if Ricky thought he had bought off the first man and knew how they were leaving, then it was highly unlikely he would send someone else with an alternative offer. Unless that was Ricky's plan.

'Well?' queried the man. His eyebrows raised.

Matt decided not to over-complicate things and accept the new offer, despite the potentially longer journey and the fact he wasn't really sure how you got from Chitral to Gilgit.

259

'Okay. But we leave at seven o'clock tomorrow morning. If you're late I go with the other man.'

'Seven o'clock too early. I need buy petrol and pump not open before seven thirty. I'll be here before the other man, he's lazy and always late.' Matt accepted the explanation. What else could he do? The man left quickly and Matt finished his Coke in a single gulp.

*****

Secure in the knowledge that he knew when Annie was leaving and that she would be delivered to him in Drosh, Raseem completed his plans.

From Drosh he could have Annie back in his house within three hours, once he'd got rid of Matt and that whore Isabelle, whose name he'd finally remembered.

Ten yards away a small boy waited patiently to be called forward. Raseem was getting fed up with him standing there, even though it had been his own idea to leave the boy waiting for half an hour just for fun. With a nod of his head Raseem called the boy over.

'You must be back here before eight o'clock tomorrow morning. Don't be late.' Raseem glowered at the small malnourished boy standing in front of him. 'I'll give you a parcel you need to deliver for me. It's a surprise though, so nobody can see you deliver it. Here's what you'll need to do.'

The boy took his instructions quietly. Raseem let the ten dollar bill on the table in front of him work its magic. The boy hardly took his eyes off it. Raseem despised poor people. Really, they were hardly human. Scrabbling about in the dirt to scratch a living, desperate to do his dirty work for him in exchange for a few measly dollars, while he made thousands sending a few packets of heroin back to London on his mules, and enjoyed himself with a few of the prettier ones along the way.

Once the boy had made his delivery it would be a simple matter to phone the checkpoint at Drosh and tell them where to look. He might have to encourage the policeman to only let Annie go late in the evening, at a time that suited him. Another hundred dollars would do it easily. Pakistani policemen were another of his pet hates. They treated him like shit unless he paid them to do what he wanted.

'Right. You'll get paid once the parcel is delivered. Now, off with you.' Raseem had no intention of paying the boy ten dollars. The kid might get one if he was feeling generous.

*****

Annie's recovered bag lay at his feet. A room service dinner was ordered to their room for an hours' time. Matt was exhausted and anxious.

'We're leaving at seven thirty in the morning. We're going to Gilgit by jeep.' Matt and Annie stood in the corridor outside the room where Isabelle slept. Annie stood close to him as they spoke quietly to protect themselves from their own paranoia.

'Why the hell Gilgit?' demanded Annie. 'It's a much longer way to get to Islamabad.'

Matt ran his hands through his hair fretfully. 'I know. I booked a jeep for eight o'clock going straight to Islamabad, but Ricky intercepted the driver as he left the hotel and I'm sure he told Ricky about the trip I'd booked.' Matt waited for Annie to point out the problems with his plan. 'That's why I booked a second the jeep to Gilgit for seven thirty, half an hour earlier than the jeep to Islamabad.'

Annie was temptingly close. Matt wanted to reach out and stroke her strained face. She looked back at him trustingly, desperate for him to come up with a plan to get them away from Ricky.

'How do you know the one to Gilgit will be on time and the other won't be early?' Annie's eyes flicked up and down the corridor before she locked her gaze with Matt's.

'I told him we would go to Islamabad with the other guy if he was late. I was hoping the competition would encourage him to be on time.' He hated bending the truth with Annie, but didn't want to add to her stress by letting her know how fine the timing was.

Annie smiled slightly at his reply, 'You're too devious. I'm not sure I should trust you.' Matt felt his stomach clench as she reached out and put her hand on his bare forearm. 'Thanks. You're a star. I don't know what I'd have done without you,' said Annie. Then she glanced nervously along the corridor again before ducking back into the room, leaving Matt luxuriating in her touch before he followed with the rucksack.

*****

At quarter to eight Raseem dragged himself from bed to the noise of the alarm on his phone and shouted for chai. The small boy stood outside his door waiting wide-eyed and expectant for the parcel he was to deliver. Raseem was going to follow Annie to Drosh from the PTDC guesthouse, to make sure the whore of an untrustworthy driver didn't cheat him of the hundred dollars he'd already handed over.

The nauseating prospect of losing Annie again had kept him from sleeping properly until almost six o'clock. Occasional snatches of sleep were broken by disturbing dreams of Annie and Matt that only made him angry too. Now he was sick with tiredness and tense with anticipation and the thought of his long awaited revenge.

As he waited for the chai Raseem handed over the parcel to the boy with one final warning. 'Remember, if you don't do exactly as I tell you I'll find you and thrash you so hard you'll regret it for the rest of your miserable life.'

*****

Matt was pacing, kicking the stones and twigs littering the ground.

Isabelle had slept well and looked better, she had even questioned him closely about the plans for their escape. Now she was sitting still and silent while constantly scanning her surroundings, wrapped in too many clothes with a woolly hat pulled low on her head and a shapeless waterproof coat over it all, despite the early morning warmth.

Annie sat on the grass next to Isabelle, not so heavily wrapped, but with the hood of her hoodie pulled over her head hiding her hair, giving her a strangely androgynous look in the morning light. 'We'll cross over the Shandur Pass, where they play the highest polo match in the world every year. We'll see yaks and be right up in the mountains. Not many people get to see the place it's so remote.'

It was clear Annie was trying to distract Isabelle from obsessing about Ricky, but even so, it was annoying Matt in his impatient state. Isabelle obviously thought it annoying too. 'I know, I was planning to go there myself until Ricky. . .' Her voice trailed off to silence and Annie grimaced because she had done the exact opposite of what she been trying to do.

All three of them lapsed in to silence, watching the gateway to see which driver would arrive first.

It was well past eight o'clock by the time the old Suzuki jeep arrived. 'Where the fuck have you been? You're late,' shouted Matt.

'Sorry, sir. Buying petrol. Big queue this morning and pump not working properly.'

Matt quickly tossed their bags, one-handed, into the back of jeep, hardly noticing the weight that back in London had seen him struggling to hoist his own bag onto his back. All three of the foreigners climbed into the back and were still arranging themselves as comfortably as they could amongst their bags as they pulled away from the guesthouse and began heading north towards the weather-bound airport and away from the town. To the south, towering clouds billowed around the peaks, a physical barrier to any plane ride to safety.

As they left the guesthouse behind Matt intently watched the road behind them, waiting for the second jeep, or Ricky's, to come into view. Chitral stretched up the hill, with early morning traffic beginning to build up as lorries delivered to the shops. Only when the guesthouse had disappeared behind some houses and a few trees did Matt turn back and see Annie watching too.

'That was too bloody close,' cursed Annie. 'It was a good job both drivers were late, otherwise your plan would have been scuppered from the start.'

They made good time for the first mile or so, until the airport appeared. Then the tarmac narrowed as they passed the turn off to the tiny terminal building. The narrowing of the road also signified a drop in quality and the jeep slowed noticeably. The early relief of moving so quickly away from Ricky was replaced by tension among the passengers.

*****

At twenty five past eight, according to the clock on his dashboard, Raseem parked his jeep in the lee of a building at the entrance of the PTDC guesthouse, and waited.

As he'd come down the hill of Chitral main street an old Suzuki jeep had pulled away from the entrance of the guesthouse with three figures arranging themselves in the back. For one frightening moment Raseem had thought Annie was giving him the slip, until he'd seen the shapeless figures of what were clearly teenage boys in the open back of the jeep just before he'd driven into an alleyway.

Three cigarette butts lay discarded in the mud beside the jeep within quarter of an hour. He hated this waiting and could hardly restrain himself from going to look through the windows of the guesthouse to check if Annie was preparing to leave.

Two minutes before nine, his friendly jeep driver waved at him from a rattly old jeep as he passed by and headed for the guesthouse.

Tension knotted in Raseem's stomach as the driver entered the front door of the guesthouse. Within minutes he expected to see the bitch and her friends. His mouth watered at the prospect of seeing her up close again.

He hated her. He hated her so much he wanted her all to himself. He'd make her want him, then throw her away as

264

she'd done to him all those years ago. Then he'd forget her and marry a good, decent wife, someone his father would approve of.

Raseem closed his eyes to bring back the image of Annie standing almost naked in the house at Birer. But all he saw was Matt grinning at him gloatingly.

The door of the guesthouse swung wildly and banged against the wall as the driver scurried through it, bringing Raseem back to reality. He waved at Raseem, who swore at the man's stupidity.

Raseem sat up in surprise as the jeep sprang into life and the driver pulled away from the entrance empty of passengers.

When the jeep reached Raseem the man pulled up close and shouted from his seat without bothering to get out. 'They've gone. They left at twenty past eight and went to Gilgit with someone else. Bloody foreigners, always changing their mind. I want my money. Now.'

'The bitch.' Raseem thumped his fist into the steering wheel and the jeep driver looked at him quizzically.

'I though they were friends of yours?'

'So did I. But they're lying bastards. The lot of them. And you. You can fuck off, you're not getting any money, you haven't done anything. And I want my hundred dollars back too.'

'Fuck off yourself,' said the jeep driver and drove away.

The small boy appeared next to Raseem's window, holding the parcel out in front of him. 'Sorry, sir. They're gone. They were not on that jeep. I cannot deliver the parcel.'

'Give it here, you little shit.' Raseem grabbed the parcel roughly, throwing it into the back seat before slamming his jeep into gear and revving the engine hard as he spun the wheels to pull away from his hiding place.

Chapter Seventeen

Too slowly and more violently than they could have expected, the Suzuki jeep crawled northwards. The road was so potholed it was impossible to go any faster. The driver smoked a joint and Matt was tempted to ask for one too.

Amid a harsh and barren landscape, the road sloped continuously upwards. Cultivation to the north of Chitral had given way to grazing animals and the settlements shrank to single dwellings.

The regular jarring from potholes made it impossible to sit on the metal floor of the jeep for long. Isabelle, not having the energy to stand, had moved forward to the passenger seat and squeezed herself into the corner of the door as far from the driver as possible. Annie and Matt stood in the back hanging on desperately to the roll-bar over the driver's head.

Every few minutes Annie and Matt risked taking their eyes off the road ahead to look back over their shoulders, praying they would not see Ricky chasing up behind them. Isabelle stared blankly through the windscreen ahead of her, looking at nothing in particular.

'I reckon we've got at least an hours start on him,' opined Matt. 'If the other driver was as late as this one and then he took a while before he told Ricky that we'd already left and come this way.'

'Let's hope so,' said Annie looking over her shoulder again.

'If we can keep ahead of him, we'll be fine.' Matt tried hard to sound optimistic.

'I doubt if Ricky could go any faster than this, so we might just do it. We'll also have to make sure the driver doesn't try and stop too early in the day.' Annie was thinking through the problems with Matt's optimistic view of their situation.

'If he does, I'll drive this bloody thing myself if I have to.'

*****

An hour after leaving the guesthouse Raseem finally reached the front of the queue for petrol. His temper was raw and volatile, made worse when he had to argue for twenty minutes until the man agreed to fill his tank. Even then the attendant demanded another fifty dollars on top of the price of the petrol to do so. Petrol was rationed this week because the bad weather had damaged the Lowari Pass and delayed the petrol lorries.

With a stack of bread and two bags of dried apricots on the passenger seat and six, one litre bottles of water in the footwell, Raseem eventually left Chitral. His head thumped from too much nicotine and not enough sleep. He hoped the ounce of hash making a bulge in his shirt pocket would kill the pain and the carton of cigarettes on the dashboard would be enough to last him the next few days.

Hidden under his seat was the hunting knife, loose in its scabbard and freshly sharpened.

He had almost three days to catch them before they got to Gilgit. He planned to kill Matt and Isabelle as soon as he could, probably somewhere on the Shandur Pass, which would be deserted at this time of the year. He'd also have to get rid of their driver somehow, but he'd worry about that when he needed to. Then he'd have some fun with Annie.

The change in road quality caught him unawares. The first pothole past the airport turn-off slammed his head into the roof of the cabin as it threw the jeep into a dangerous lurch, forcing him to slow down. The knowledge that their jeep would have to go just as slowly did little to soften his frustration and burning anger as the prospect of them escaping overwhelmed his excitement.

As he struggled to force the jeep along as quickly as the road allowed him, Raseem mumbled to himself. The memory of Annie, her blouse teasingly open to show a glimpse of her firm breasts, unconscious in his passenger seat on the road to

Birer fuelled his frustration. It took serious effort to control himself from flooring the pedal and abandoning himself to fate, but the terrifying memory of his near miss with death on that same trip just about kept him in check.

*****

Ishmael returned with his measured pace to the prepared campsite in the hollow near the lip of the Chitral side of the pass. He was back to waiting.

To fill his time he decided to write a brief report to send back to Gilgit with the next jeep that passed. He wrote clearly and carefully. Ishmael knew his boss would rather have a brief report saying there was nothing to report, than a long-winded ramble filled with fluff. Though Ishmael deliberately covered his trek around the lake by mentioning his failure to find a second track across the Shandur Pass.

*****

Five hours of driving had exhausted everyone. The road had been tarmaced at some point, but the winter had taken its toll. Stretches of tarmac were missing altogether, loose stones flicking up under the jeep with damaging force if they went too fast. When there was tarmac the road was pock-marked with potholes. The driver called a halt where the river ran close to the road. After dousing his head in the ice cold water, the man stretched out on the grass by the jeep and went to sleep in the poor shade of a spindly tree.

Even Matt realised it would be dangerous to press on without a rest and gratefully stretched out in the shade of the jeep. For the first time in hours he could relax his aching muscles and not worry about being thrown from the vehicle by a sudden lurch.

Isabelle marched across to the river, washed her face, neck and hands, then returned to the jeep. 'I feel safer in here,' she said by way of explanation, then hunched back down into her jacket.

Matt watched Annie stroll to the waterside and remove the loose long-sleeved shirt she kept on to protect her from the sun. The tight singlet she wore underneath accentuated the soft curves of her body, though the bruises inflicted by Ricky were clearly visible.

At the water's edge Annie sluiced the dust from her arms and face, tipping handfuls over her head then squeezing the excess from her hair. She was looking more relaxed than she had done the night before, despite the ever-present tension and constant rearward checks of the day.

He and Annie had enjoyed some lighter moments during the drive as they enjoyed the spectacular scenery. The constant jostling of the jeep threw them against each other companionably as they fought to keep their balance. Riding the open back of the truck was like riding a motorbike, with the wind in their faces and the sun on their backs. It was exhilarating and the constant concentration required to stay upright had occasionally distracted them enough to let them enjoy themselves.

Matt followed Annie to the river. 'How long do you reckon we'll stop for?' said Annie as he squatted next to her and splashed his own face with the ice cold water.

'An hour maximum. That guy deserves a rest, he must be knackered.' Matt dunked his head in the river and sprayed water over Annie as he shook the excess off on the way back up.

'Oi,' she warned, laughing. 'I'll soak you if you're not careful.' She flicked water at Matt then lay back in the sun.

'I'm not sure I'd have lasted so long if it had been me driving.' Annie watched a large bird circle high above them looking for its prey. 'But Ricky will have to rest too, no one could drive all day on this road without stopping.'

'God. I hope so.'

Matt took his boots off and dipped his feet in the water.

'About when we were at Ricky's and I burst in the room. Sorry I stared at you.'

Annie kicked at the stones, then looked at him with a forgiving smile. 'Don't worry about it. How did you find me? I never did get the proper story.'

Matt thought for a moment, wondering where to start. 'Isabelle climbed over that pass all on her own after she escaped and found me in Bumburet. She wanted to head for Islamabad straight away, but not on her own. When I suggested she wait until I got back from looking for you she said she would show me the way. Without her you'd still be there. What happened in Chitral? How did you get there, at Ricky's?'

'I think you're being too modest about your part in it all.' Annie took her boots and socks off too. 'I didn't go of my own free will, you know.' She frowned at Matt, daring him to contradict her.

'Yeah, I know.'

'Oh, yeah. You said you saw me in his jeep. Where was that?'

'Ayun. I was on a jeep going to Bumburet getting away from your bad mood, and Ricky passed us. I saw you unconscious in the passenger seat.'

'Lucky for me you don't hold grudges and decided to come after me.' Annie smiled gratefully, then turned serious. 'He drugged some food and gave it to me.'

'Was that in the Garden Hotel?' asked Matt.

'No, he found me down by the river and very kindly shared his picnic with me,' said Annie ironically. 'I wonder what it was he drugged me with?'

'Probably just sleeping pills, you can buy most things across the counter in the pharmacy here.'

'He turned out to be a bad one didn't he?' murmured Annie. 'Don't say I told you so,' she added with feeling, looking up a him.

'Of course not.' Matt scuffed his feet. 'I wouldn't dare.'

Annie stared out over the hills and spoke so quietly Matt had to strain to hear her. 'I sort of knew him. I was at university with him. His name then was Raseem. He said I was horrible to him at university and he was getting his own back.'

'Were you? I mean, were you horrible to him?'

'Of course not. I hardly knew him. He was just one of those guys most people try to avoid. Mostly, I'd ignore him, if I even noticed him in the first place.'

Matt nodded his understanding. 'I knew some people like that too.'

They both fell silent and Annie dipped her feet in the water beside Matt, whose own feet were now going numb with the cold. Though he desperately wanted to remove them, Matt didn't want to break the pleasant spell sitting with Annie.

After a while Annie spoke again. 'So. Would you stare at me again?' She glanced coyly at him while he blushed deeply, speechless. Then she pulled her feet from the water and returned to the jeep.

Matt enjoyed the guilty pleasure of remembering Annie in that room, her anger up, all ready to attack her abductor. She was one strong minded woman and he really liked her for it.

Even with the blood all over her face she'd looked magnificent.

'A penny for your thoughts?' Annie was back, looking down on him with a bemused look on her face. Matt sat up quickly, conscious of the fact his jeans were fuller than they had been a minute ago.

The driver snored twenty yards away. Annie looked at the river and glanced at Matt. 'You reckon there's anyone else around?'

'Haven't seen anyone since we went through that tiny village an hour or so ago. Why?'

'I want a proper wash.'

'Oh. I'll go over there and keep watch.'

'On me or what?' Annie smiled devilishly at him.

A hot flush coloured Matt's face again. 'You know what I mean.'

'You've seen me once, but don't go getting any ideas, okay?'

Matt nodded meekly, then shook his head, confused and unsure how to respond to her statement. Slipping his feet into his socks and boots Matt scurried away to the jeep without tying his laces. He tried hard, but couldn't help glancing back towards Annie.

She rolled her trousers above the knee and stepped into the water. She slipped off the singlet and bra and dropped them on a rock, and bending from the waist cupped her hands and splashed water over her torso. The curve of her breasts were silhouetted against the sunlit river and her slender back and long neck sparkled as she threw water over herself.

As Annie stood at the end of her wash Matt closed his eyes and pretended to sleep.

'That was bloody good. You should try it yourself. I won't watch, either.' Annie stood a few yards from Matt, looking wryly at his pretended innocence. Her wet hair dripped onto the shirt that clung to her refreshed body and showed the skimpy singlet underneath.

'Uh, yeah. I think I might.'

'Great. You should go for a swim.'

'What?'

'Go for a swim. The water's flowing pretty slow and you'd enjoy it.' She leant against the jeep window and started talking quietly to Isabelle.

The river did look enticing, but Matt doubted it was deep enough for a swim. He strolled leisurely to the water, trying to look casual. Annie was still talking to Isabelle and not looking at him. A small rock offered some cover.

Matt removed his shirt. Annie was still talking to Isabelle. Kicking off his boots and socks again, Matt sat behind the rock and stripped off. The water was freezing, but the cool air it gave off felt so good on his sweat soaked body that he eased forward into it and sluiced himself all over.

No sound came from the direction of the jeep and the driver was hidden by the same rock. He was alone in the world. Matt sat on the gravel riverbed and ducked his head under the water then sat looking at the mountains as the water flowed over him. The cold felt good for a minute, then started him shivering. Hauling himself upright Matt turned for his clothes.

'Is that good?' Annie was sitting on the rock grinning at him.

Matt covered himself, then held his hands up in surrender. 'You got me,' he said laughing.

'I'm not sure whether you look better with your clothes on or off, but the cold doesn't do much for your manhood.' She laughed good naturedly, then walked back to the vehicle.

It was difficult to know whether to be angry or amused. Matt dressed quickly, noticing idly that he needed to tighten his belt one more notch than he had before he left England. Then he too returned to the vehicle, woke the driver, and, ignoring a smiling Annie, he feigned grumpiness as they all climbed back on board.

'What did you do that for?' Matt tried to sound casual as the jeep picked up speed, but failed miserably.

Annie looked at him to make sure he wasn't really grumpy. She said, 'It makes us even.'

*****

The hash almost let him forget his ruined ribs and lessened the stress of driving on the god-awful road. It was common practice among the local tribesmen to smoke while they drove; they all claimed it made them better drivers. Raseem, feeling relaxed, agreed with them now.

Five hours without stopping and he felt he could keep going all day. The supply of joints he had made while waiting for the petrol was going down, with only eight left. They were fairly weak, but one an hour worked well. The bread and water were going down fast though.

He had seen little other traffic all day, but that did not surprise him. Given the time of day he had left town he was not going to meet any jeeps coming in to Chitral from the villages in the immediate local area. Even in the villages he had passed through there were very few people on the streets. The further north he went the more remote it was and the few widely dispersed residents rarely travelled far from their homes.

It was also far too early in the year for the tourists to be heading up this road to Gilgit. They only ever travelled this way in any numbers later in the season when the passes were less prone to suffer from late snowfalls and the road crews had fixed the winter damage.

*****

'Ian? Ian, is that you?' Chris struggled to make himself heard on a badly connected line to the Embassy in Islamabad.

'Yes. Is that you Chris? How's it going?' Ian's voice came through faintly and electronically distorted.

'I'm in the wrong bloody place. I should be in Chitral, but the flights are all cancelled and the road's broken. Can you go to Chitral? I've got a positive sighting of the girl, Annie, who met the guy in Islamabad who might be Ricky.'

'I'd love to, but the airport's closed.' Ian sounded disappointed, even on the bad line, that he was not able to take up the offer of a chance to go to Chitral.

'Can you drive there?'

'Of course, but it'll take three days.' Chris thought Ian sounded distinctly excited at the prospect. As an afterthought Ian added, 'Can't you get your contact to do something quicker?'

'I can only contact him using the secure communications system, which I can't access here. And I can't tell you the passwords over the phone.' Normally, secrecy and steady detective work was to everyone's advantage, but not today.

Not for the first time Chris wanted urgency and the option of being able to dial his contact's telephone number.

'Can I do something? Shall I drive to Chitral?' Ian's voice interrupted Chris's thoughts.

'I'll think about it. I'll call back.' Chris put the phone down and wandered back onto the streets of Gilgit.

A beer would have been good, but Chris had no idea if any of the bigger hotels had a foreigners alcohol licence and he didn't want to trawl round asking. It would make him look like an alcoholic. Instead, he went back to his hotel to find the old hippy. He hoped the man could give him some ideas on how to get to Chitral.

*****

'I wonder how far we'll get today?' Annie leant on the roll-bar above the driver's head and stared forwards along the never-ending dirt road.

'I've no idea. What is there up in these mountains anyway?' Matt stood next to her and not for the first time wondered what she really thought about him.

'Get the map out, maybe there's a village or something that the driver's aiming for.'

Matt struggled with his rucksack and finally extracted the map, while hanging on for dear life with one hand. There was little of interest marked on the road between Chitral and Mastuj, just two villages. 'I reckon we must have passed this first village here.' Matt stabbed a finger at the map. 'There's only Buni and Mastuj marked this side of the pass. At this rate we might get to the Shandur Pass by tonight.' He held the map up to Annie, but she declined it with a shake of the head.

'I wonder if there'll be anywhere to stay when we get where we're going?' mused Annie aloud. 'At least we have three sleeping bags again, if we do have to sleep outside.'

'I guess we'll find out when we get there,' said Matt as he struggled to put the map away again.

The hours passed slowly. The sun burnt their faces and dust ingrained itself in their bodies and mixed to a sticky film on their sweaty skin.

In places the valley was wide, flat and covered in pebbles, with the river meandering backwards and forwards across it. The jeep rolled and lurched over this unstable ground, even slower than on the unmade tracks.

Sometimes rolling hillocks covered the valley floor and the river was relegated to a fixed channel, then the jeep could make smarter progress, though potholes still jarred the passengers.

Only very occasionally, when they passed small, but spectacular, patches of bright green cultivation in cool oases was the colour of their surroundings anything other than beige.

There was still no sign of anything following them and as the day wore on Annie and Matt looked behind much less often. Since their refreshing stop at the river they had relaxed further in each other's company, though Matt remained uncertain of Annie's feelings towards him.

Late in the day the road went through the only sizeable village they had seen since leaving Chitral. As they left behind the lush fields, weeping willows and bleating goats the battered tarmac finally gave out altogether and they hit dirt road. Soon after the road crossed the Yarkhun River, a tributary of the Mastuj, then crossed it again on a second metal lattice bridge slung across a rocky gorge almost totally devoid of vegetation. A crossroads appeared, surprisingly blunt in its appearance after the hours of meandering road without junctions. They stopped in front of a desolate wayside petrol station, abandoned to the elements, sagging and crumbling forlornly.

They were approaching the Shandur Pass and had travelled far to the north of Pakistan. Afghanistan was nearby and Tajikistan closer than Islamabad.

Rusted almost to illegibility a small sign pointed left to Mastuj and a collection of houses could be seen nestling among trees and green fields in the distance. Taking the right hand road the jeep turned away from the valley, and began climbing gently towards the mountains. The temperature dropped suddenly as the sun dipped behind the peaks.

*****

Raseem was pushing his jeep hard. The thought of spending the night in the open frightened him and the further north he went the more he worried about it. He liked the security of crowds and locked doors when he slept in strange places. The wide-open spaces, lack of villages and absence of people made him edgy and nervous. The fear of what might be round the next corner was becoming unbearable.

He had stopped once, where the road passed close to the river and gave him easy access to the cold water, without having to venture too far from the safety of his jeep. The water was icy when he splashed some on his face and he would have loved to dip his feet in it and paddle like a child, but he couldn't ignore the feeling that someone was watching him and relax enough to do so.

Looming over the road, watching him and challenging his progress was the ever-present *Tirich Mir*. He'd always laughed at the village stories which told that it was home to faeries, the mythical demons of history. Now he was approaching it, closer than he had ever been before, it was not so funny. Raseem could see that the mountain had a personality, and it didn't like him.

Tiredness was hitting him hard now and the approaching dusk increased his difficulty driving through the blurring potholes, threatening to leave him stranded and alone in the wide empty spaces of the upper Chitral valley.

If he hadn't come so far he would have turned tail and run back to Chitral. But Mastuj was the closest point of safety where he knew there was a hotel, and it had been for some hours.

Only the knowledge that this was the only road that Annie could possibly have travelled had kept him going earlier in the day. Now it was the fear of spending the night outdoors, alone, in the dark.

A bare thirty minutes after his quarry reached the abandoned petrol station, when Raseem had been passing the village of Buni, Raseem eased slowly to a halt by the rusting signpost. He desperately wanted sleep, food and safety. Annie was too much to contemplate just now.

Following the route indicated by the first sign he had seen in hours, Raseem turned left, towards Mastuj.

*****

'Harchin Hotel,' said the driver. 'We stop here tonight and cross the Shandur Pass tomorrow.' The light had faded rapidly and darkness was now closing in on them.

Three wattle and daub huts, along with a few animal pens made up the hotel. Spread along the road ahead, more huts made up the rest of the village. Willow and poplar trees grew along the river and among the houses. Rough grass grew in the darkened fields. It was nothing like the romantic mountain villages sheltering under the high peaks that Matt had imagined. The poverty was different to the oppressive squalor of Karachi, but as real none the less.

Worn, handmade carpets covered the floor of the single guest room that a veiled woman showed to Annie and Isabelle. 'Only one room in hotel.' The driver smiled apologetically at Matt, who stood outside with the men. 'This my cousin's hotel. I sleep with family. Toilet over there, tap for washing there.' A small wooden hut stood against the wall, the smell evident from twenty feet away. The tap dripped into an animal trough in the middle of the courtyard, where a cow splashed water with its tongue.

Within minutes the host family disappeared and Matt sat alone on a wall in the courtyard enjoying the restful, motionless silence. He wanted to give Annie and Isabelle some privacy in the room, though he wasn't sure why. Perhaps he wanted it more himself after the past few days of constant company.

His peaceful reverie ended too soon when the cousin's wife brought out one small pot of stew, three chapati and glasses of tea on a tray and delivered it to the room. The wife quickly disappeared back into the family quarters and darkness wrapped the village in silence, leaving only the hunger inducing scent of fresh cooked bread lingering in the air to draw Matt into the simple hotel room.

Tired and sore from their long day on the road, the three travellers ate dinner in a circle around the pot of watery vegetable stew. Matt desperately wanted to sleep and raised the matter of bed spaces as soon as the stew was gone. 'Where shall I sleep?' Matt looked around the carpeted room where a sleeping bag was already laid out along the back wall, with Isabelle's rucksack protectively shielding it.

'Over there,' Isabelle pointed to the door.

'Is that inside or outside?' Matt attempted a joke and hoped it wouldn't backfire.

'Inside of course,' said Annie. 'The door opens inwards and you'll stop it opening properly if Ricky tries to break in.'

Isabelle nodded, smiling at Matt choking on the last of his chapati. 'Where are we? How far have we got?'

'Harchin, I think the driver said,' offered Matt. 'We've probably got another two days travelling before we get to Gilgit.'

Nodding thoughtfully, Isabelle looked at the two of them directly. 'Ricky will come after us. You know that, don't you?'

'I don't think so,' responded Annie looking to Matt for support. 'Matt and I have been keeping an eye out for him all day and haven't seen any sign of him.'

'He will. He's got too much to lose if we get away and report him. There was another guy at that place for a while, in a different room. He was a junkie and I used to hear him begging and screaming for heroin. The last I heard of him it sounded like Ricky was dragging his body out to the jeep. That was when Ricky went away and left me.'

'Did you speak to this other guy,' asked Matt in surprise. He had never considered Ricky would lock men away too.

'No. I was too scared to try. Ricky said he would kill me if I tried to escape, or did anything stupid.'

Annie reached out and squeezed Isabelle's hand comfortingly.

'Right, bed,' instructed Isabelle. 'You two must be exhausted standing up all day on the back of that jeep.'

*****

Raseem drove into Mastuj and stopped alongside the first person he saw. 'Where's the hotel here?'

'The Mastuj guesthouse is a hundred metres along the road.' The man pointed briefly in the right direction. In his exhaustion Raseem had not even considered what would happen if he met his prey at the hotel.

There was no jeep parked outside the single-storey building that was the Mastuj guesthouse when Raseem pulled up.

As he checked in Raseem casually asked about other guests. 'No, we have no other guests tonight. You are lucky, next week we are full.'

'This is the only hotel in Mastuj, yes? Some English friends were travelling up ahead of me and I expected to find them here.'

'No, there are a few hotels here. Your friends might gone on to Harchin though, or even be back in Buni. Then again, the drivers often take people to a relatives house instead of bringing them to the hotels.' The helpful response offered by the manager only worsened Raseem's mood.

'Where's Harchin? Where's Buni?' demanded Raseem, fearful he may have taken a wrong turn hours ago.

'Harchin's only an hour away, you should have taken the other road back at the old petrol station. If you are going over the Pass tomorrow you will go through it. Buni is half an hour back down the road to Chitral, you will have driven past it.'

Raseem glared at the helpful manager while he contemplated the prospect of losing track of Annie. It was too dark, and he was too tired to really contemplate driving again. And he could drive around all night looking for them when he had no clue which godforsaken village they had even stopped in. Anyway, all he wanted to do was lock himself behind a door and shut out the frightening unknown of this dark mountain village. He tried to look relaxed as he spoke to the owner again. 'I'll sleep here tonight and meet up with them tomorrow, I'm too tired to drive any more today.'

Chapter Eighteen

Dawn was only just beginning to lighten the sky when a knock at the door frightened Isabelle from her troubled sleep with a muffled scream.

'Who is it?' shouted Matt through the door.

'Chai,' came the answer.

Soon after, one of the ubiquitous chilli omelettes and more bread arrived too. Half an hour after sunrise, while the valley was still in shadow, the group was back on board the jeep.

*****

The sky was still grey as Raseem left Mastuj. He had slept badly, every creak, noise and hoot of an owl causing him to sweat and worry that he was going to be attacked or his jeep was being stolen. He'd only fallen properly asleep in the early hours of the morning again. It was becoming something of a habit and this time he'd forgotten to set his alarm too. It was only the morning noises from the early rising village that dragged him from his exhausted sleep well after dawn.

With the returning light Raseem's fears from the night before lessened and his desperation to catch Annie returned. He was now fearful she would have set off again before the sun came up and be getting away from him. Raseem had spurned the offer of breakfast from the guesthouse manager. Hungry though he was, the thought that these mountain peasants could well drug him, rob him and kill him if he gave them the opportunity encouraged him on his way with nothing but a joint and one stale piece of chapati to take the edge off his hunger.

Passing the derelict petrol station Raseem followed the road to Harchin, lighting his second joint of the day to further calm his overwrought nerves. Three empty cigarette packets lay on the carpet from yesterday and a quarter of his hash had gone. His sore ribs were forgotten, sidelined by the dreamy hash haze and raw nerves made worse by having the malevolent presence of *Tirich Mir* pressing in behind him.

*****

Climbing away from the village the road clung precariously to the side of a gorge as it approached the Shandur Pass. The trees finished abruptly at the edge of the houses and the old road, broken and washed away by the river it followed, crawled along the valley floor.

Snow froze to the mountain peaks high above them, glowing orange in the early morning sun. Whining and protesting, the undersized engine dragged their jeep higher into the thinning air of the twelve thousand foot high pass.

Isabelle was back in the cocoon of the enclosed cab. Annie struggled to snap photos and take in the magnificent scenery around her as the bouncing jeep did its best to distract. The jeep was going so slowly Matt took the opportunity to try sitting on his rucksack as he stared back down the valley, to relieve the pain in his legs still aching from standing for twelve hours the previous day. His sunburnt arms itched painfully, competing for attention with the numbing, gnawing tension in his stomach that convinced him the day was not going to be a good one.

Matt raised his eyes from their vigilant watch for Ricky and was drawn to *Tirich Mir* across the valley. He contemplated its reassuring presence and found it comforting him with its aura of permanence and imposing strength. Jo would have loved it, he thought, and smiled.

*****

The noise of a whining engine rose up the pass towards Ishmael. He saw the rising dust first, then watched the Suzuki jeep and its tourist passengers climb slowly towards him. Not that it would be much use, but he would talk to the tourists to see if they had heard anything about this Ricky. At least it would give him a chance to practice his English, an opportunity he never passed up.

*****

A shepherd stood by his goats at the roadside as Raseem pulled into Harchin and he had the presence of mind to stop and ask if his prey had stayed there the night before.

'Yes. Your friends stayed here last night. They left in a hurry half an hour ago with my cousin.' The shepherd eyed him warily. 'My cousin never mentioned they were travelling with anyone. How do you know them?'

'From England,' replied Raseem evasively. Then, without acknowledging the answer to his original question, Raseem sped away through the village. The shepherd watched him depart, noting the registration number to report to his cousin Ishmael next time he passed that way looking for strange men who spoke English with foreigners.

Through his windscreen Raseem could see the road climb out of the trees, cross a spur of mountain and enter a gorge-like valley at the start of the pass. Raseem gunned his engine and pushed his jeep dangerously fast. The timing was perfect; he'd have the deserted Shandur Pass on which to execute his plan. And Matt.

In five minutes he reached the crest of the spur and saw an old Suzuki jeep slowly crawling up the roadway ahead of him. Raseem smiled and concentrated hard on the distant figure of Annie standing in the back of the jeep. She had been holding on to the roll bar, watching the road ahead, but then she turned and sat next to Matt. They were looking back down the pass towards him. It was clear they now knew he was close on their tail.

'You thought you could get away from me, did you? You stupid fucking bitch!' he shouted to the mountains.

*****

'Annie.' Matt kept his voice low. 'Annie. Don't say anything, just sit down here next to me.'

'What?' Annie looked questioningly at Matt, then sat carefully on the bag next to him when she recognised the serious look on his face.

'See that jeep down there on the road behind us? It looks like Ricky's.' Though he kept his voice low, Annie could sense his tension. His muscles were taut, preparing to finish the fight he had started back in Birer.

'His name is Raseem,' said Annie shortly, leaning into him for her own comfort as much as his. 'But yes, it does look like his jeep. What are we going to do?' Her face had gone pale beneath the sun-washed colour it had gained on the previous day's drive.

'I don't know. I guess he's about half an hour behind us, but he's travelling faster than us. He'll probably catch us up somewhere on the top of the pass.' Matt could feel his heart rate picking up and wanted to shout at the driver to go faster.

'Shall we tell Isabelle?' Even though she asked the question, the doubt in her voice made it clear she thought they should not.

'No. It'll only frighten her. Let's leave it until we're sure.' But when Matt looked over his shoulder he saw Isabelle staring back down the pass at Ricky's jeep, with hate-filled eyes.

Annie hugged her knees to her chest and rocked slowly, glad to have Matt's reassuring presence alongside her. Matt chewed his lips and wrapped a comforting hand around Annie's knee while shading his eyes with the other. Annie placed a hand on his solid forearm and squeezed the noticeably firmer muscle that Matt had acquired since he'd sat flabby and scared in the Karachi hotel room.

*****

Ishmael's interest was growing. He was not sure, but it looked like the second jeep was trying to catch up with the first. The following jeep was certainly driving somewhat recklessly, snaking dangerously around the sharp bends and potholes.

From the way the tourists were watching so intently it seemed they thought so too.

Ishmael felt tension washing up the slopes towards him. His ability to feel the emotions of those around him seemed to work as well with foreigners as it did with his countrymen.

As the distance between the two jeeps inexorably shrank, the two foreigners grew correspondingly less happy.

Given their respective speeds and positions, Ishmael reckoned the second jeep would catch the first while it was stopped at the barrier gate. It made no sense to stop them beforehand, and he might need help if the situation turned out as bad as he was sensing.

Ishmael left his viewpoint and began walking towards the hut where the real frontier policeman was dozing uselessly in a patch of sunshine sneaking through a gap in the mountains.

*****

No matter how hard he tried to convince himself otherwise, Matt knew it was Ricky and that he was catching them up.

Less than an hour after they had left Harchin, Ricky was only a few hundred yards behind them as they crested the pass and he briefly disappeared from view. Their jeep picked up speed on the gentler road that crossed the wide, flat, mile long valley that was the Shandur Pass.

Yak grazed unattended on sparse green grass. Fingers of snow reached down the gentle slopes of the glacial valley. A flat calm turquoise lake perfectly reflected the towering mountains. In other circumstances the scene would have blown them away with its beauty. Now they hardly noticed it.

The Suzuki pulled off the road and stopped on the grass twenty feet from the water's edge. 'Need water,' smiled the driver as he leapt from the cab and strode to the lake with a bottle in his hand, blithely unaware of how desperately his passengers wanted to continue and get away from the jeep that had followed them up to the pass. Steam hissed and rose angrily from the bonnet.

*****

The hippy had not appeared the night before, though Chris had sat on his balcony until late into the night. This morning he had slept late, the rigours of travelling and the challenge of acclimatising to Pakistan exhausting him more than he realised.

By the time he dragged himself to a table on the hotel terrace where he could watch almost all the hotel and camp-site and revive himself with fresh tea and another peppery omelette, it was getting on for late morning.

Unable to sit doing nothing, Chris borrowed a book from the hotel library and ensconced himself to read Nick Danzinger and educate himself while he waited for the old hippy to reappear. Chris had a nagging doubt he might not see the man again, but for once in his life he wasn't sure what else to do but sit and wait.

*****

Ricky's jeep crested the pass and sped towards them.

'Get Isabelle and keep her on the other side of the jeep to Ricky. Keep moving if he tries to get near you.' Matt ordered tersely, walking forward a few yards to meet the oncoming vehicle. An overload of adrenalin made him shiver and he wanted to throw up.

Isabelle refused to hide and stood with Annie by the side of their jeep a few yards behind Matt.

It looked like Ricky would try to run Matt over. Then all four wheels locked as Ricky braked hard and slid to a stop inches from Matt, as if he'd realised he'd wreck his own vehicle when he hit the Suzuki as well if he drove straight into Matt. With his feet planted firmly in one spot by fear, Matt stared at Ricky through the windscreen and readied himself for a fight.

Breaking clear of the mountains the sun suddenly flooded the valley with light. Ricky jumped from his jeep, leaving the door wide open. A flash of light bounced off the knife in his hand.

Matt!' yelled Annie, panic in her voice.

'Watch the bastard, he's got a knife,' shouted Isabelle angrily.

'I can fucking see that!' Matt moved to block Ricky's direct route to Annie and Isabelle, holding out his clenched fists to ward off the knife.

Slowly and menacingly Ricky approached Matt. 'You're gonna be very sorry you ever met me. The girl's mine, but you're gonna pay for what you did to me first.' Even in his fear, Matt thought Ricky sounded like a terrible B movie villain he couldn't quite place, and unwittingly smirked.

The two men eyed each other warily, ten feet of loose earth separating them. Sweat soaked Matt's shirt. Ricky grinned manically with bleary, bloodshot, drug-filled eyes.

*****

Lunch passed and Chris was becoming increasingly anxious that he might need to come up with another plan.

At four o'clock the hippy finally entered the gate, strolled into the restaurant and ordered chai from the waiter. Chris waved, indicating the empty seat at his table.

'Hi. Have a good night?' Chris felt he had to make an attempt at conversation before he leapt into his questions.

'Yep. And a good day. Met this really cute chick.' The old hippy stretched and smiled knowingly.

Too impatient to wait any longer Chris asked the question he was desperate to have answered. 'I need to get to Chitral, but there's no flights and the road to Islamabad is blocked. Can I get there any other way?'

'Of course. But what's the hurry? You were chilling nicely yesterday, don't spoil the vibe, man.'

'Yeah, yeah. Whatever. How do I get there?' Chris was losing the will to control his temper, having to remind himself the man was under no obligation to help him.

The old hippy looked at him carefully and shrugged. 'Over the Shandur Pass. It's at least two days, maybe three to Chitral.

You still want to find your niece?' The hippy started rolling another joint and Chris wondered how much the man smoked every day.

'Yes. I really think she's in some kind of trouble. So I just want to make sure she's all right and put my mind at rest.'

'Can't blame you. There are all sorts of stories coming out of Chitral. People supposedly go in and never come out,' said the hippy without any noticeable concern.

'How do you know those aren't just travellers' tales? How can you tell if there's any truth in them?'

'You get the same story too often for it to be just travellers' tales. You start to get a feel for these things when you've been on the road as long as I have.' The old hippy shrugged with resignation. 'It's not always a good experience travelling in this part of the world. It can be a dangerous place, man.'

'Is there a bus or something that goes to Chitral?' Chris tried to hide his heightened concern that the disappearances were frequent enough to be part of backpacker lore, with pretended excitement at the possibility of getting to Chitral.

'Nah. You'll need to hire a jeep. You look like you've got the money to get one all to yourself, too. Ask the guy that runs this place, he's bound to know someone with a jeep you can rent in a hurry.' The hippy considered him for a moment, then seemed to make a decision. 'I like you, though I probably wouldn't approve of you if I knew what you're really up to. So I'll give you some friendly advice. The fare is usually $200, so don't make it too obvious you're in a hurry or they'll charge you double.'

*****

Ishmael was half way to the barrier gate when the first jeep came into view. He kept walking, reckoning he would get there just after they did. When the first jeep stopped by the water and the passengers disembarked he slowed his pace to watch them.

Steam curled from the bonnet as the driver went to fetch water.

The tourists all seemed rather nervous and one limped badly, needing support from her friend as they moved to the side of the jeep. The man stepped forward to face the point where the road crested the pass and steadied himself for a fight. Ishmael changed path and picked up his pace as he headed straight to their parking place across the grass.

When the second jeep approached them fast and slid harshly to a halt Ishmael quickened his pace further. There was definitely something wrong. He was a hundred yards away when the girls shouts echoed round the hills. A knife flashed in the sun. Ishmael unslung his gun and started to run.

*****

The knife slashed at Matt's chest. It missed, just. A second swipe came closer and Matt stumbled backwards. Ricky lunged again. Matt blocked the knife with his forearm and blood oozed from the gash. Matt swore at the sight of his own blood.

Kicking desperately, Matt caught Ricky on the knee. Ricky hardly seemed to notice, the hash and adrenaline killing all sensation of pain. He lashed out again with the knife, and this time it grazed Matt's chest and ripped his shirt. Sudden sharp pain blocked out all sound as the knife nicked his shoulder.

Instinctively, Matt stepped forward inside the knife as he fought for his life. His fist connected with Ricky's shoulder, but the butt of the knife smashed into his temple as Ricky brought it back down on his head.

Matt buckled and fell to the ground as his foot slipped on the grass.

A boot knocked the air from Matt's lungs as Ricky kicked in revenge for his own broken ribs. Matt passed out. Ricky kicked again as bloodlust took him.

Unseen by Ricky, Annie launched herself towards him and hit him full in the face with a clenched fist. He swung back wildly and knocked her sideways to the ground. She screamed at him and scraped a handful of dirt with her fingers. Ricky stepped towards her as she dragged herself onto her knees and threw the dust in his face.

The knife fell from Ricky's hand as he clawed at his streaming, grit filled eyes. Ricky kicked out blindly and caught Annie in the chest. A lung-full of air sighed from her lips; she whimpered, hit the dirt and rolled unconscious into Matt where he lay motionless and bleeding.

Isabelle walked as softly as she could from beside the Suzuki. Still reeling and disoriented with the burning grit, Ricky crouched to the ground swiping at his stinging eyes.

The knife clinked on a stone as Isabelle picked it up. Ricky whirled round and stood as he did so. He eyed her blearily like she was a small dog that might try to bite him. Then he smiled in his most charming way. 'What you gonna do with that, sweetheart? You're not gonna hurt *me*. Think of everything we did together. I'm your lover, we made love together. We have a connection.' Ricky moved slowly forward, one hand over his heart, the other held out for the knife.

Isabelle stared at him silently. Her arms hung limply at her side. The knife dangled loosely in her hand. She watched him from hooded eyes.

'That's right. I'm your boyfriend. You love me. Give me the knife. You've nothing to fear. I'll rescue you from this pathetic specimen of a man, it's him you should worry about.' Isabelle's eyes flickered to where Matt lay on the ground and Ricky lunged, bellowing incomprehensibly. Isabelle screamed and her arms tensed reflexively. The knife, still low at her side, pointed towards the attacking man. Ricky saw the knife rising towards him as he surged closer, his hash-subdued reflexes unable to slow his attack. His bellow faded, then changed to a howl as the two bodies, locked in a violent embrace, crashed to the floor and rolled in the dirt.

Overhead an eagle screamed. Four bodies lay still. The driver stood motionless and horrified by the lake, his mundane drive now a horror show of violence like some Hollywood movie.

A solitary soldier stood transfixed on a hillock fifty yards away staring in disbelief. Then he started running with his gun held at the ready.

Isabelle rolled Ricky away from her and crawled towards Annie and Matt. Annie moaned to herself. Matt did not move. The driver walked slowly towards his jeep, timing his arrival to make sure the soldier got there first.

Lying sideways in the dirt Ricky groaned and tried to rise. Blood oozed from his trousers. The knife was still caught in the material.

The soldier arrived and prodded Ricky with his boot, all the while pointing the gun at his head. With his hands clasped around the handle of the knife Ricky passed out. Buried to its hilt, the knife had entered the cloth of his trousers just where the legs came together. The point of the blade protruded out from the back, just below the rear pocket.

Isabelle reached Annie and fainted.

Annie opened her eyes to see a soldier walking slowly and carefully towards her. He lifted Isabelle's shoulder gently and checked her for blood, then quickly moved on to the unconscious Matt. 'Is he going to be all right?' asked Annie.

'I hope so. I have seen worse.' Glancing at Annie, Ishmael decided more reassurance was needed. 'I am Ishmael, I am a trained battlefield medic. He is not bleeding from an artery. I will patch him up as best I can. Then we will get him to a doctor.'

Annie began to relax, reassured the soldier was on their side, or at least not on Ricky's. She took Matt's hand in her own and squeezed it.

The soldier pointed at Ricky and on a hunch asked, 'Is that man over there called Ricky?'

'Yes. Do you know him?' Annie stared warily at the soldier, suddenly unsure whose side the soldier would really be on.

'No. But I'm looking for him. Are you all right? Do you have any pain or broken ribs?'

'I don't know. I hurt all over. Take care of Matt first, please. He looks bad to me.' Annie moved closer to Matt and stroked his hair as she sat beside him.

*****

'It doesn't matter how much you offer to pay. It's too late to leave today, but I can get you a jeep for tomorrow morning. It'll take time to organise and you need to leave early so you can cross the Shandur Pass before dark. I can tell you're in a hurry so it'll be a good jeep.'

Chris had ignored the old hippy's advice and gone for broke, asking the manager to arrange a jeep to Chitral as soon as he could. 'Today. Now, if possible.'

Despite his entreaties the manager had refused to change his mind about leaving today. Now came the crunch bit and Chris was prepared for the worst. 'How much will that cost me?'

'As I said,' smiled the manager. 'It'll be a good jeep. That costs money. Four hundred dollars, okay?'

The old hippy sat grinning as Chris did everything he'd been told not to do.

Chris resignedly nodded agreement. 'Make sure it's here promptly and it's not full of every bloody traveller in Gilgit. I want speed and since I'm paying top price for it I'll expect it.' Chris put on his sternest face for emphasis.

The manager smiled. 'Yes, yes, sir. Of course. It will be here for you tomorrow morning. First thing,' he emphasised and wandered away to another customer.

'Shit,' muttered Chris. He needed to use a phone and didn't fancy queueing at the Post Office or speaking in the too public lobby of the hotel.

Chris strode quickly from the garden and headed for his room, leaving the amused hippy with his extremely late breakfast and joint.

*****

The solitary guard at the checkpoint had nervously come to see what was happening, but had quickly gone back to his post with relief once Ishmael had made it clear he needed no help.

Having introduced himself in impeccable English, Ishmael had been kind and gentle as he expertly dressed the unconscious Matt's wounds. Butterfly stitches and field dressings now covered the ugly gashes, but shock chilled Matt's body.

Isabelle lay shivering in her sleeping bag, too.

Annie sat between them, in the army tent Ishmael had brought over, as the weak sun attempted to keep the cold at bay. Wrapped in her own sleeping bag, Annie was trying not to move and disturb her damaged ribs.

All three of them were suffering from shock, as well as their injuries.

With Ricky the soldier had not wasted sympathy as he closed the wounds of the slashed scrotum and penis with more stitches. 'I wish I could have done the cutting, not the stitching,' were his only words once he'd finished the job. Ricky, having recently recovered consciousness, promptly fainted again. He now lay handcuffed to the towing eye of his jeep.

The Suzuki had left once Ishmael had tended the injured and written a report. The driver grateful to get away and happy to take the message down from the pass to the nearest army base with a secure phone. He had explicit instructions to make sure it reached its intended recipient as soon as possible.

*****

The pain in his crotch was horrendous. When he had woken up after the bastard soldier had closed his wounds the man had come over, pointed at his crotch and hissed at him in Urdu, 'You're going to live, but I don't think it will ever work again. You are a disgrace to your family.'

Raseem knew he was in trouble. He desperately tried to think of a bribe that would work on this soldier and keep him out of jail. Nobody had looked in his jeep yet, but there was a packet of heroin lying somewhere in the back that could put him away for a long time if he didn't find an answer to his problems soon.

The hash in his pocket taunted him, but he had nothing within reach with which to make it into a joint and kill his pain. Now the last joint was wearing off, his ribs were hurting almost as much as his balls and his fear was making him sweat as much as his pain.

Despite all his problems and pain, one emotion overrode everything: a need for vengeance.

*****

Chris dug through his bag for the mobile phone he had shoved there before leaving London. He never used it abroad because protocol said it wasn't secure, but this was an emergency and protocol said he could use it once only for an emergency. He shifted uneasily from foot to foot as the phone booted up. There was always the chance there would be no reception and he was anxious to phone Ian and get some more information on Chitral.

*****

A quiet cough announced the soldier's return. 'More chai? Would you like something to eat?'

Annie shook her head. She felt nauseous and wanted to sleep, but she also wanted to stay awake in case Isabelle or Matt needed her.

'I have sent the driver down to Teru. It is at the bottom of the pass. There is an army barracks there. They will send a message to my boss. He will send a helicopter to collect you tomorrow. Sorry it will take so long.'

'Thanks, you've been wonderful. Where will the helicopter take us?'

'Gilgit. There is a fine government hospital there for your friends and you can stay with my wife. She lives next door so you can be close. Try and sleep, it will help. I will be just outside if you need me.'

The tent flap closed as the soldier retreated. Annie lay down, just for a rest she assured herself, and slipped quickly into sleep.

Chapter Nineteen

The phone pinged as it picked up a network and text messages streamed in. Chris ignored them and selected a number from the contacts list.

'Ian? It's Chris. I've got a jeep to take me to Chitral tomorrow. I'll be there in three days. I met a guy who told me there are loads of stories of foreigners disappearing there. What do you know about the place? Where should I start looking?'

'Hang on a minute. Where are you? London keeps calling demanding to know where you are.'

'Sod London,' snapped Chris. 'What about Chitral?'

'Chris. There's an envelope here for you too. It just arrived. Hand delivered and marked personal, urgent and confidential. It's addressed to, *The man from London visiting Ian Davies*. That has to be you, doesn't it? You might want to hear what it says first. Shall I open it?' asked Ian nervously. Chris never usually shouted at people.

'Who's it from?'

'Doesn't say. Perhaps it will inside.'

'Okay. Open it, what's it say?'

'Slow down. I filed it somewhere.' Chris could hear papers shuffling on the surprisingly clear line. 'Ah, got it,' said Ian in a frustratingly relaxed tone.

'Hurry up, will you? I doubt this signal will last long.'

'Right. Here goes. It's unsigned.' Ian took a deep breath and read slowly.

'Your man is on the Shandur Pass. There are three foreigners with him, one male and two female. Three of them are injured, two seriously. One woman is unhurt, but very ill.

297

A helicopter will fly them to hospital in Gilgit tomorrow.' Ian stopped reading.

'What else? What else does it say?'

'Nothing. That's it.'

'Shit.' Chris thumped his hand on the wooden wall of his room. An answering thud came back from the adjoining room.

'You OK?' asked Ian.

'Yeah. Fine. Right. I'll stay here. Don't leave the office. I'll be in touch.' Chris hung up abruptly and sat heavily on his bed to think.

*****

Isabelle screamed in her sleep and woke Annie. The soldier's face appeared at the tent flap. Matt moaned fitfully, sweat trickling down his forehead. Annie crawled from the stuffy tent and accepted a mug of chai from the soldier. They sat by his fire and watched the shadows creep across the pass.

'How come you were looking for Ricky?' murmured Annie.

'I can't really say. But we heard reports of foreigners going missing in the mountains and here I am. Ricky's name was mentioned as someone of interest,' explained Ishmael in a calm, reassuring voice.

'What'll happen to him?'

'That depends on his story and if he has any important friends.'

They lapsed back into silence as Ishmael began preparing food.

*****

Chris stood outside Gilgit hospital. He wanted to know where he was going before the helicopter arrived, but now he did he was at a loss to know what to do next. There was no point going in yet; he doubted they knew there were patients on the way.

On an impulse he went to the nearby Commissioner's Office.

'Exactly who are you and what function do you have in this country?' A typically arrogant clerk sat importantly behind his desk being awkward.

Just like civil servants everywhere, thought Chris as he summoned up his best smile and prepared to answer.

'I'm a Customs Officer from England, but I'm just on holiday at the moment. I was speaking to a friend at the Embassy and he told me that some British citizens would be arriving at the hospital here tomorrow and he asked me to check on them and make sure they were okay.'

'What exactly is wrong with these people? And where are they coming from?'

'I'm not sure what's wrong. I think their jeep crashed on the Shandur Pass.' Chris tried to make it as uncomplicated as possible. He wanted to get them out of the country as soon as he could and leave his contact in Karachi to sort out the complications that Ricky would bring to the scenario.

'Well, I'm sure the hospital will look after them satisfactorily. We can't give people special favours, just because they are British. Our own people need treatment too.'

'I'm not looking for special treatment. I was just hoping to make sure everything was ready for them when they arrive.' Chris wondered if it would be politic for a holidaying British official to offer a bribe, and decided against it.

*****

As Ishmael and Annie enjoyed a quiet meal together Raseem glared at them. The soldier had offered him some food, but that was the last thing Raseem wanted. Pain muted his hunger but fired his thirst for revenge.

It was obvious now that Annie and Matt were more than just friends; no man would defend a woman that fiercely if she wasn't his whore.

The way she tended to him now confirmed it, and just like the old days she was cruelly flaunting her latest boyfriend in front of him.

Slowly and vengefully, Raseem developed a plan from the depths of his anger.

*****

There was nothing to do now but wait. This was always the worst part of being on active duty. Chris liked to think of himself as a soldier on the front line, defending people from dangers they knew nothing about. It kept his mind alert and on track on the occasions when he was sitting waiting for hours and days on end for a moment of intense, sometimes dangerous, activity.

To pass the time he wandered around the small town, admiring the sights of Gilgit and enjoying a walk along the river where the air was cooled by the fast flowing melt-water from the mountains.

His impatient anxiety about the anticipated events of the next day was hard to ignore though, and the China Trading House and the Bazaar held little charm for him today. He hated shopping anyway and he wasn't supposed to take anything home with him that could identify where he'd been. Which made shopping for souvenirs a pointless exercise.

When a stand of bicycles for hire presented itself outside a shop, Chris decided to rent a mountain bike. A cycle ride out of Gilgit and along the river would be good exercise and alleviate his tension.

Four miles out of town he found the serene image of a Buddha, carved into the rock face. He sat in the shade of a rock to contemplate the image, but it failed to calm him. He remounted the bike and kept pedalling along narrowing lanes and footpaths that eventually returned him to town where he found himself outside the British cemetery.

As he pushed his bike amongst the graves of soldiers who had died so far from home he thought about the waste of young lives given for a cause that today was thought of as a piece of history that should never have happened, if it was ever thought of at all. The melancholy of the place and its history prompted doubts about the value of his own cause and he wondered again were the drugs he fought against a symptom or a cause of the problems the users endured.

*****

Matt had not woken since the fight. Isabelle had done little more than sleep, though occasionally she woke moaning or screaming, took a drink of water, then lapsed back to unconsciousness. Both were suffering from fevers and had discarded their sleeping bags as their temperatures rose ever higher, even when the air chilled through the evening.

Annie and Ishmael fretted over their patients until exhaustion demanded they too retire for the night and re-coup their own strength.

Ishmael put Ricky inside his own jeep and handcuffed him to the steering wheel. Ricky could hardly walk, but Ishmael was always prudent. The last thing he wanted was for his prisoner to get hypothermia and die on him. Then Ishmael removed the keys from the ignition where Ricky had left them and settled down out of reach in the luggage compartment at the back, as an extra precaution to prevent Ricky escaping in the night.

Annie, Matt and Isabelle shared the small tent, their closeness and the sleeping bags keeping them warm. Annie stroked Matt's fevered brow and held his hand, worrying herself to sleep with the guilt that her naivety in Chitral had resulted in his current state.

*****

'You want a drink?' The hippy approached Chris as he sat reading outside his room.

'I'd love a beer, but I doubt you can get one round here.'

'Come with me, my strange friend. Where there's a will there's a way.'

Chris stepped warily inside his neighbour's room.

'It's not like anything you'll have tasted before, but it's alcoholic and strong.' Cloudy green liquid poured from a dirty bottle into two travel-stained mugs.

'What the hell is it?' Chris stared at the liquid with a look of horror on his face.

'Hunza Water. When the locals converted to Islam they kept a few old habits. They brew it from mulberries. Cheers.' The old hippy grinned like a schoolboy as he watched Chris sniff the unappetising looking liquid.

'Cheers,' said Chris as he eyed the brew suspiciously and watched as his host drained his own mug. With a deep breath, Chris followed suit. The sweet liquor was passable and as he lowered his mug it was quickly refilled.

Chris sat listening in disbelief to tales of parsimonious travel in Asia as he sipped the next glass and wondered why anyone would want to travel so cheaply in a region that was cheap enough anyway. There were better hotels in town than this one and they cost almost nothing compared to what he would happily pay in Islamabad. If he had been here for pleasure Chris would not have hesitated to pay three times as much for a room with a real bed in a hotel with more substantial food on offer.

'Why do you do it? Try so hard to spend so little?' asked Chris, hoping to get some insight into the world of long-term travellers.

'That's easy. So I can stay on the road longer. The less I spend the less often I have to go back to the materialistic rat race most people call the real world and earn some more money so I can come back here.'

As far as Chris was concerned there were few redeeming feature of this style of travel, and the size of the still sore lump on his head was a niggling reminder of how hard it could be. He would have a few tales of his own to recount in the canteen at work after this trip though, which was the only place he could ever talk about his trips.

When the bottle was empty Chris stumbled back to his room. There was no electricity in the hotel and he had forgotten to buy any candles. He undressed in the dark and retired to the rickety bed and its coarse blankets, more than mildly jealous of the expensive sleeping bag lying on the charpoy of his new friend. There was obviously an art to travelling cheap and staying comfortably in basic hotels.

His last thought of the day made him laugh, somewhat drunkenly, that he had started the day chasing a drug dealer and finished it getting happily drunk with one instead.

Chapter Twenty

Ishmael woke before sunrise. He liked the first light of dawn and the solitude of praying in the mountains, though with any luck he could hitch a ride down to Gilgit on the helicopter and visit his family today too. His children would be overjoyed to see him so soon. His wife would be calmer and just make his favourite food to welcome him home and show how pleased she was to see him.

Ricky sat on his seat wide-awake and it was difficult to tell if he'd slept at all during the night. At least he was still alive, even if he did look extremely pale. In the tent, all three foreigners were asleep, if that was the right word to describe it. The man's fever was still up and the ill woman twitched and shook as she had the night before. Only the one in the middle was properly asleep, holding the man's hand in her own.

With his prayers finished Ishmael rebuilt the fire and prepared breakfast. Annie joined him just as the chai had brewed to perfection and the soft light of dawn gave way to daylight easing into the valley.

'Good morning. Did you sleep well?' said Ishmael as he handed Annie the first mug of chai. She clasped it in her hands and blew on the steaming liquid.

'Yes, I did thanks. Knowing you were just outside the tent was wonderfully reassuring. Where did you sleep?' Annie sipped at her chai as she watched Ishmael preparing porridge.

'In the back of the jeep. It was quite comfortable and warm.' Ishmael spoke calmly and carefully in his most reassuring voice, choosing his words carefully to make sure his English was correct. 'How are your friends? Their sleep was not restful, no?'

'No. They slept badly. I'm really worried about them. When will the helicopter arrive?'

'It has to fly up from Gilgit, so it could be here about an hour after sunrise.' Ishmael did not add that one would only arrive if the person in charge agreed that it was the emergency he had stated in his letter, or had the wit to phone the number he had included to confirm the story.

Annie enjoyed her bowl of steaming porridge, that warmed her through and revitalised her tired muscles, though it was not quite what she was used to at home being made from barley and water only, and lacking salt, milk and sugar.

Thirty minutes after sunrise Annie took two mugs of hot chai back to the tent, hoping to find her patients improving and ready to face the coming day.

Ricky accepted his mug of chai and bowl of porridge from a watchful Ishmael with a curse. 'You won't get away with this. I'll teach you not to manhandle and handcuff an innocent British citizen like some sort of criminal.'

'We'll see,' smiled Ishmael. 'We'll see,' then returned to eat his own breakfast now his charges were fed and watered.

*****

His head hurt and his mouth was dry. The rough liquor was making him pay for the enjoyable night before. Nausea welled in his stomach. Chris did not know whether to stay in bed and recover, or go for a walk to clear his head. Apathy won and he stayed where he was hoping to be recovered by the time he needed to venture forth to the hospital.

As he lay uncomfortably on his charpoy he cursed himself for being so stupid as to get a hangover in a Muslim country on the day he was supposed to meet some injured people at a hospital.

*****

Ishmael heard the faint clatter of helicopter blades first. The thin air made flying difficult up here and he always held his breath as the old Hueys tried to land. He smiled to himself as he waited for the helicopter to rise above the lip of the pass: with any luck he might be on it when it left.

The noise increased suddenly as the helicopter came into view. Annie appeared at the door of the tent excitedly. 'Is that ours?'

'I hope so. We'll find out soon,' shouted Ishmael as he stood, outwardly calm, watching the helicopter approach.

Sliding low over the grass the helicopter approached fast. Both doors were open and soldiers sat ready for a combat exit, their guns at the ready. The aircraft flared harshly and bumped onto the ground fifty yards away, spraying up stones and dust. The pilot watched Ishmael and Annie closely as three men leapt from the cabin and spread themselves around the campsite, alert and facing inwards.

Once the soldiers had secured the campsite the pilot relaxed as he wound down the engines and waited for the rotors to freewheel to a halt.

A sergeant jumped from the passenger seat and strode purposefully across the grass as the whining noise of the engines died and the blades slowed. 'Are you Sergeant Ishmael Khan?' he demanded, saluting.

'Yes,' responded Ishmael with a salute of his own.

'I have orders for you,' stated the new arrival with military precision. 'My orders are to collect these foreigners and deliver them to the authorities in Gilgit. Yours will confirm that.'

As the newly arrived sergeant spoke, a medic hopped from the helicopter and headed for the tent. Ripping open the envelope handed to him Ishmael read the brief paragraph ordering him to hand over the foreigners and remain where he was until further notice. It was not going to be his day after all.

Annie loitered by the tent door, excluded by the presence of the medic. A soldier kept his gun pointed at her. 'Those are my friends in there,' she said in exasperation, pointing at the tent. The soldier motioned her back with his gun, not understanding what she said.

As she stood frustrated in the sunshine Annie heard Ishmael briefing his colleague behind her. Orders echoed around the pass and a soldier ran for the jeep to cover Ricky with his gun. Ricky smiled tiredly at his guard and began talking quietly to him.

Five minutes after the medic entered the tent he reappeared and shouted instructions. Ishmael and the sergeant collected collapsible stretchers from the helicopter cabin and brought them over.

Only semi-conscious, Matt and Isabelle were transferred to the stretchers and carried to the helicopter. The sergeant carefully strapped his patients to the floor of the cabin and waved Annie to sit between them against the bulkhead at the back. A few moments later Ricky appeared and was lifted less carefully inside. His handcuff was attached to a metal ring on the cabin floor. All the while he continued talking quietly to the soldier escorting him.

*****

With blurry, sleep clogged eyes Chris finally focused on his watch. 'Oh shit,' he muttered. The dial of the watch his wife had given him many years before read nine o'clock. He'd slipped back to sleep when he least expected it. Groggily, he rolled to a sitting position on his charpoy. The pounding in his head was no better. His stomach still felt queasy.

Trying not to make any sudden moves, Chris dressed slowly. As he opened the door of his room sunlight stabbed sharply through his eyes to the back of his head. Automatically, his hands rose to shield his eyes while he struggled to settle his sunglasses protectively on his face.

'You look rough. Want a joint? Guaranteed to soothe a hangover.' The hippy sat in the sun smiling happily at Chris.

'You must be joking. Got any headache pills?'

'Yeah, sure. But I only use the local type, they're raw opium, so I doubt you'll want one of them either.'

'You're right. I don't.' Chris grimaced as he leant gingerly on the door frame of his room and tried to prepare himself for the day ahead.

'Go get a can of coke and some food. Make it something with a lot of sugar and salt in it. It won't be as good as the hash, but it might help.' The old hippy seemed genuinely concerned, maybe even guilty that his generosity had caused what was obviously a major hangover.

With a wave of his hand Chris stepped from the veranda and placing his feet as softly as he could, headed for the hospital. He had no idea whether the helicopter would arrive at the airport or the army base, but they were certain to be moved to the hospital soon after they landed.

A hawker sold him a can of coke and a Mars bar and a chemist supplied him with a pack of Panadol. Chris dropped four pills down his throat and washed them down with the drink. He would save the Mars bar for when his stomach felt more able to receive it.

In the shade of a tree in the quiet garden of the hospital, just ten feet from its front door, Chris lay down and closed his eyes. He hoped the pain in his head would stop him sleeping and the noise of any jeep would alert him when the patients arrived.

*****

Ishmael pulled a small envelope from his pocket. One of the soldiers had surreptitiously slipped it to him when nobody was looking. The man was an occasional messenger for his boss and his family received a small income for it, but no one at the base knew.

The code was simple and prearranged. A simple message, which would not arouse suspicion if someone else read it, told Ishmael what to do. His boss wanted a full report of the events on the pass. A jeep would cross over later that day from Mastuj to collect him and continue on to Gilgit, as if it was on a normal run to collect supplies.

308

Even Ishmael did not know what happened to the reports once he handed them over. Only the boss knew everyone in the chain, but occasionally he was able to link a report of his to a raid nearby and the knowledge he was making a difference made him content.

*****

Twenty minutes after landing on the Shandur Pass, the pilot began restarting the engines of his helicopter. The shrill whine of the auxiliary motor hurt Annie's ears. Isabelle opened her eyes, saw Ricky smiling at her and screamed. Annie leant over to comfort her, before the rising engine noise drowned out her words.

The last of the soldiers climbed aboard. Ishmael waved a silent farewell. Annie smiled a very grateful thank you back. In all the activity to get them aboard she had not had the chance to say a more personal thank you and goodbye.

Rising to only a few feet above the ground, the helicopter spun on its axis and moved forwards towards the lip of the pass. Without climbing away from the ground the aircraft gathered speed, its engines whining protestingly and the rotors chopping alarmingly at the thin air.

Through the open doors cold air battered the passengers. The lake passed behind them, grass flashed past in a blur. Then the ground fell away and the helicopter dropped sickeningly downwards.

Annie held on tight to Isabelle and glanced over to Matt. His eyes were open, but they stared blankly at the cabin roof. A few seconds later, they closed again.

The helicopter dove down the pass, picking up speed as it fell. Slowly it levelled out and rose away from the ground, letting Annie relax enough to look through the gaping doorway beside her and watch the passing landscape.

Much of the ground below was bare and rocky, despite the river forcing its way across the hard ground. Occasionally, an oasis of willows, pools and grass splashed colour on the harsh brownness. Beneath the weeping branches of the trees, villages nestled in the shade. Little Kashmir passed below the helicopter as it sped downwards to Gilgit and a hospital. In different circumstances, Annie would have been thrilled at the aerial view offered by the open doors of the helicopter, but her concern for Isabelle and Matt killed any enjoyment.

Feeling the eyes of the soldiers on her Annie turned her gaze to the inside of the cabin. The soldiers kept their suspicious and curious eyes fixed on her. There was not a friendly gaze among them and Annie began to feel less confident than she had over breakfast that their troubles were over. The soldier sitting between Ricky and the sergeant turned to shout in the sergeant's ear whilst continuing to watch her, but Annie could not hear his words nor would she have understood them anyway.

The two men kept glancing at her as they talked. When they finished the sergeant placed a headset over his ears and began talking to the pilot, watching her evenly as he did so. The soldier turned to nod at Ricky, then continued his monitoring of Annie. Uncomfortable under their scrutiny Annie turned her attention back to Isabelle and Matt, though there was little she could do for them. They both lay unaware of their rapid descent from the mountains.

Ricky watched her as a satisfied smile spread across his face.

*****

Patients arrived continuously, forcing Chris to constantly open his aching eyes. Abandoning his attempt to recuperate, he sat up straight and watched the comings and goings of the patients and their families, while he slowly ate the sticky, melting Mars bar hoping it would do him some good.

*****

The valley grew greener as the journey progressed. Fields and orchards patterned the ground and traffic grew more dense on the road. Gilgit was definitely busier and wealthier than Chitral.

After an hour in the air the helicopter slowed and circled what was obviously an army base, to one side of which, separated by a fence, stretched a runway. Shacks, tents and people littered the brown grass around the tarmac.

As the helicopter bumped to the ground the soldiers prepared to disembark; one loosened Ricky's lap-belt and helped him slowly away to a white painted hut. A second soldier attempted to usher Annie after him, pushing her roughly when she resisted. 'I want to wait for my friends,' she pleaded.

Behind her the sergeant shouted. 'You can't. Go with him now.' The sergeant looked almost angry. Annie took one last look past the attentive medic at Isabelle and Matt, then walked worriedly after Ricky with a soldier following threateningly close behind her.

A line of prefabricated huts, roofed with corrugated iron and painted scruffily in white, made up the army base. A hangar for the helicopter complimented the office blocks and dormitories. A larger hangar along the runway suggested bigger aircraft used the base too. A large red crescent decorated the door of one building and a doctor trotted away from its door, aiming for the helicopter.

Two ancient cannons guarded the door Ricky entered. A flag hung limply from a flagpole on its roof. It was smarter than the other buildings and Annie guessed it was the headquarters building. As she followed Ricky through the door the engine noise finally died behind her and she glanced backwards to see two stretchers being carried towards the hospital building.

'In here.' A voice ordered Annie into a small room, furnished only with a desk and two chairs. A policeman sat behind the desk already. 'Sit down,' he barked.

'What will happen to my friends?' asked Annie desperately. She was worried now they would be taken away and she wouldn't know where to.

'Sit down,' ordered the soldier. Then more gently, 'Do not worry your pretty little head with that. They will be dealt with in an appropriate manner.' The policeman eyed her up and down as he spoke. Sudden dread filled Annie as the man licked his lips and nonchalantly lit a cigarette. 'Want one?' he said.

'No. I want to see my friends.' Annie stayed standing.

'But that may not be possible. You have broken the law. You have assaulted one of my countrymen in a most indecent manner and your friends tried to kill him.'

'What have I done? Ricky, Raseem, whatever his name is, he abducted me and attacked me.' Annie used her hands to emphasise what she was trying to say. 'He kidnapped and attacked the other girl, Isabelle, too. My friend Matt rescued us. He's a hero.' Annie could feel the tone of her voice rising. 'Ricky was the one who broke the law.' Annie was alarmed now at this turn of events.

'Do you have witnesses? The word of a woman is worthless compared to that of a man. Your friend, Isabelle, I think you said. She had sex with my countryman. Sex before marriage is illegal in Pakistan. She should go to prison for seducing him and leading him away from the teachings of Islam.'

Annie stared at the policeman in disbelief, then spat, 'He raped her!'

'That is a serious charge. Do you have witnesses? Can you prove it?'

Annie was lost for words. All her life she had thought policemen were there to protect people, but this man was accusing the victims of being in the wrong.

'Matt saw Ricky attacking me. He's a witness. He'll tell you what happened,' she said desperately.

'Ah, Matt. Raseem says that you were his girlfriend. That you agreed to have sex with him and Matt attacked him and kidnapped you in a jealous rage. He assaulted Raseem, stole his woman. That is a crime.'

'It's not true! When did he tell you this?'

'He told the soldiers who brought you here in the helicopter, they radioed the news to me.'

'What about the soldier who called for the helicopter? He saw what happened, he knows Ricky attacked us.' Weak hope raised Annie's spirits a fraction.

'That man will never testify on your behalf. He is not really a soldier. You will never see him again.' The man laughed and puffed on his cigarette.

*****

As they transferred him to a bed Matt woke. The men were none too gentle with him and he felt his wounds stretch and the stitches pop. Pain seared his arm and chest and warmth seeped from his wounds. A policeman entered and pulled his good arm above his head. Cold metal clicked as one cuff clamped tightly on Matt's wrist, then it rattled as the second cuff caught on the metal bedstead.

'What's happening?' he asked feebly. 'Why are you doing that? It's the other guy you want, not me.'

A hollow laugh frightened him. 'You tried to kill a man. You're lucky you're in hospital. I could have put you straight in prison.'

'Where are my friends? What have you done with them?'

'That's no concern of yours. They are immoral women, they will be dealt with.'

*****

In a room not far from Matt's, Isabelle lay curled up into a protective ball on the bed watching the policeman standing nearby. She had come round as they handcuffed her to the bedstead, tired, but no longer too exhausted to even think. The policeman was haranguing her. 'You are an evil woman. You tempt a man. You sleep with a man. Then you try to kill him. You will not get away with it. Immorality is a serious crime.'

313

She felt remarkably composed given the frightening twist of events. 'I didn't sleep with that bastard,' hissed Isabelle. 'I wish I had killed him, but it was self-defence.'

'Lies! You are a woman. No one will believe you.'

Isabelle decided not to waste her breath responding to this pig of a man. She held his gaze, suppressing the fear she felt in an effort to intimidate him and make him look away.

The policeman considered her. 'I can see how you would tempt a man,' he mused. 'It is a woman's responsibility to refrain from leading a man astray. You foreigners think you can do want you want in this country, but you can't. You have no respect for our culture. I'll be back for you later.'

*****

Raseem lay on a bed sipping chai and trying to look strong. A senior policeman sat on a chair beside the bed anxious to hear Raseem tell his story. 'The pilot radioed down with some details about what happened, can you fill me in on why these foreigners attacked you?'

'I met this girl, Annie, in England. We were at university together. We were lovers. She tempted me and seduced me. She was supposed to be helping me with my work, but she just wanted sex. Then she threatened to tell my family if I stopped sleeping with her; she blackmailed me in return for sexual favours. These English girls are so depraved. I almost failed my degree because of her.' Raseem frowned and sipped his chai. He was going to have to concentrate hard to keep the policeman on side without making himself look like a weak willed fool.

'That is indeed a problem. Did your family know about this woman?' The policeman was frowning disapprovingly, though Raseem could not tell if it was aimed at him, or Annie.

'No. My father would have been very angry. He is a devout man.' Raseem took a sip of his chai and looked down respectfully at the mention of his father. 'I came to Pakistan to get away from her, but she followed me here. She came up to the house I rented in Chitral and told me she was carrying my child. I promised to do the honourable thing and marry her. A few days ago we were messing around, we were going to have sex, she wanted it all the time. I had to do it five times a day to keep her quiet. Then this guy, Matt, he burst in and attacked me. I think he wants the girl for himself. He beat me up and took the girl with him, she was screaming and crying, but he dragged her away.'

'What about the other girl?'

'I met her in Peshawar. She wanted me too, but I turned her down. She's just jealous, she helped Matt abduct my fiancé.'

'Do you want to press charges?' asked the policeman. 'He will go to prison for a long time if you do.'

'Yes. That guy is dangerous, he should be locked up before he kills someone.'

'He will be. Don't worry.' The policeman looked serious for a moment then smiled broadly. 'What about the girls? You want to keep them both? That could be fun if you had the energy.'

'I want that other girl charged. But not Annie, she is carrying my son so I will have her.'

*****

There was no sign of any foreigners arriving and Chris was getting worried. Perhaps there was a hospital at the army base. He climbed the steps of the hospital to find someone in charge who could tell him what was happening.

'No. We are not expecting any foreigners. Who was it that told you they were coming here?' The senior doctor was being as helpful as he could be, but knew nothing.

'A colleague at the embassy was told that the army was flying them here in a helicopter.' Chris explained for the second time why he thought the three foreigners would be there.

'Ah. The army has a hospital of its own. Your friends are probably there.'

'Where is it? How do I get there?' Chris demanded, annoyed that he had not thought of checking whether there was another hospital in Gilgit.

'It's by the airport, but the army will not let you in,' offered the doctor apologetically.

Disconsolately, Chris left the hospital and trudged towards the Commissioner's Office. Having to go through official channels would be time consuming. Armies were notoriously slow in issuing permission for foreigners to enter their bases, especially when they had other foreigners there already.

Chapter Twenty One

Raseem was recently returned from the operating theatre. The local anaesthetic had yet to wear off and he felt no pain in his groin. The doctor stood at the end of the bed with a serious look on his face.

'You have two broken ribs, but they will mend in time. As for your other injury, the soldier who stitched it did okay on the outside, but there will be permanent damage on the inside. You will never have children and it will probably never work properly again at all. The knife severed some important parts. You may have to have your testes removed too. Take the pills you have here every two hours to reduce the swelling and the pain, I'll arrange for you to see a specialist in Islamabad.' The doctor had examined him intimately, much to Raseem's horror and embarrassment, and now he had delivered the worst possible news as dispassionately as if he was a mechanic reporting on a problematic jeep.

'The fucking bitch.' Raseem thumped the bed, the aggression sending pain searing from his broken ribs.

Last night and this morning there had been nothing more than a dull ache, but on the helicopter his balls had started to swell and the pain had grown continuously since then. The medic had given him some strong painkillers during the flight, but their biggest effect was to make him lethargic, not kill the pain.

Raseem had hidden the discomfort as best he could while he told his story to the policeman; he had wanted to look like a real man and make sure he got himself out of trouble as soon as possible. Now he wanted to kill someone. That bitch had left him no man at all.

*****

317

'It is impossible. You cannot enter the base without permission from Islamabad and they never give it to a foreign civilian. Your military attaché may get permission, but it will take a long time. These things must be arranged weeks in advance.' The Commissioner was firm in his pronouncement.

'But there are injured British nationals there, I must have access to them. It is agreed under international law that a representative of the diplomatic service must be allowed to visit their nationals in hospital.'

'If they are transferred to the civilian hospital you can visit them then, but that is not likely to happen.'

'Why not? Are they seriously injured?' Chris was growing more concerned by the minute.

'No. They are under arrest. It seemed they tried to kill someone. The women are also in trouble because of immorality.'

'What? This is ridiculous! I demand to be allowed to see them.'

'You are in no place to demand anything.' The Commissioner shouted angrily and thumped his desk now. 'This is Pakistan, not London. We do things our way here, not yours. The British Raj no longer rules the world. Now leave, before I have you deported.'

'I will call my ambassador,' said Chris stiffly. 'There will trouble over this.'

'Yes. And you will be the one in trouble. What would your British press think if a Pakistani was arrested for attempted murder in London, and we demanded his release?'

'What would you think if we tried to frame a Pakistani to cover up for a British citizen, eh?' Chris glared at the Commissioner.

The Commissioner spoke very slowly, with menace in his voice. 'I advise you to leave while you can. There will be a plane leaving today, or maybe tomorrow. I will leave instructions that you be issued a ticket for the next plane to

Islamabad.' The two men eye-balled each other. 'If you are not on it, I will arrest you.'

Chris slammed the door as he left without saying another word to the Commissioner, worried about what might come out of his mouth. He almost ran back to his hotel to retrieve the mobile phone hidden there.

It took twenty minutes for Chris to reach the hotel and re-boot the phone. It might be a breach of protocol but this was too serious a situation for Chris to worry about it. 'Ian, there's trouble,' he said without preamble.

'I know. I got another message from your friend. I'll read it. 'Three British citizens are under arrest for attempted murder and two of those for immoral behaviour as well. They will be transferred to Islamabad prison as soon as practical.'

'Is that it? When did you get the note?' Chris shouted and travellers in the garden turned to look at his room.

'Ten minutes ago. You'd better get back to the embassy as soon as you can,' Ian begged. 'The ambassador is screaming. He wants to know why you did not advise him of the situation.'

'Who told him? Was it you?'

'Yes. I had to. I couldn't contact you. I had to do something. Sorry.'

'What's he going to do?' Chris was trying to calm himself and not attract attention. He sat on his bed and breathed slowly to control himself.

'He's meeting with the Minister of the Interior in an hour. He has issued instructions that you are to be put straight through to him if you call. And on a plane to London if you appear at the Embassy.'

'No. Don't tell him I called.' The last thing Chris wanted was someone ordering him back to Islamabad just at the moment. He would go in his own time, or not at all if the Commissioner had anything to do with it.

'Why not?' A second, more commanding voice came on the line.

'Who's that?' asked Chris quietly.

'Who do you think?' A click on the line signified Ian had put his handset down. 'Now, why don't you tell me what the hell is going on and who this contact of yours is?'

'It's a long story.'

'I know, Ian very kindly told me everything he knows. It's a right mess and I want to know everything else. Now.'

Briefly, Chris told the ambassador everything he knew about Ricky.

'Who is this contact of yours?' demanded the ambassador again.

'I can't tell you. Officially he does not exist and this is not a secure line.'

'All right. But when you get here you will tell me everything. This is my embassy and I am responsible for it, even if I do have to let people like you come in here and cause me problems. I could probably order you back, but I don't want you to disobey an order, so I won't. When are you planning on coming back to Islamabad?' The ambassador was sounding less angry now and more like a General planning his battle.

'Probably as soon as I can, now Ian has passed on the message. I don't think there is much else I can do here. I seem to have outstayed my welcome in Gilgit.'

'Good. I look forward to meeting you. One of my staff will arrange for you to receive a VIP ticket on the next flight out of Gilgit and you had better be on it.' The line clicked dead.

*****

The room was a lot like the one at Ricky's house and Annie kept expecting him to enter the door. Bare boards, dirty walls and a dusty, barred window were all she could see. Black stains marked the floor beneath her and she tried not to think what had made them. A handcuff secured her to a metal ring bolted to the wall. It was obviously the army lock-up.

Blood stained Matt's bandages. A doctor had re-stitched his arm and chest and given him some penicillin, but no painkillers. The handcuff held his arm painfully above his head, making it impossible to get comfortable.

The policeman had not returned.

*****

Isabelle shivered, in spite the heat. Though she had faced down the policeman, fear, pain and shock clouded her thoughts. She felt too exposed with her hand chained to the bed. The nightmare should have been over, but it was getting worse. Occasionally a soldier or policeman would come in and stare at her. Once, two came together and stood staring at her while they made suggestive comments in Urdu. She lay in the corner ignoring them all, while watching them in her peripheral vision.

*****

Hundreds of people crowded the airport office, all waving tickets at the harassed clerks. Chris kicked his way through the mêlée, in no mood to wait politely for people to move out of his way. No one complained; they took one look at his angry face and eased aside to let him pass.

'There should be a VIP ticket for me. For the next flight.' Chris stared at the clerk, challenging the man to make him wait.

'Name?'

'Christopher Sinclair. British Embassy.'

Without checking the man answered. 'No. There are no VIP tickets in that name.'

'Check.' Chris snarled and laid his hands flat on the counter. The man picked up a short list and waved.

'The name is not on the list. Come back tomorrow.'

'I'll wait.' Chris put his shoulder into a man trying to force his way to the counter.

The persistent man leant past Chris and the clerk took his proffered ticket, read another list and handed it back. 'The flight is full today. Come back tomorrow,' announced the clerk.

A murmur rose from the crowd. The clerk picked up his telephone and leant back in his chair as he spoke quietly into the mouthpiece. When he finished the call he started reading his paper and ignored the angry shouts aimed at him. Ten minutes later policemen began forcing their way into the room and pushing people out.

When the room was almost empty an officer strolled to the desk and handed a form to the watching clerk who bent over his desk to read it. Without looking up the man signed it twice and handed it back. Chris watched with interest, until the policeman turned his gaze towards him.

A computer on the clerk's desk beeped with the familiar sound of an email arriving. 'You must leave. There are no tickets left. Come back tomorrow.' The policeman stared menacingly at Chris.

'I'm waiting for a VIP ticket.' Chris tried hard to sound calm, but with three armed policemen backing up the officer it was not so easy.

'There will be three dangerous criminals on the flight. There will also be an injured man aboard. There will be no other passengers, including VIPs.'

'What did you say your name was?' The clerk was sitting up straighter behind his counter with a worried look on his face.

'Christopher Sinclair, British Embassy.'

The clerk swung his screen around and pointed for the policeman to read it. He did, slowly, then looked up angrily. 'It seems you have important friends. The flight leaves in one hour, it won't wait.'

*****

'It's time to go.' A policeman un-cuffed Matt from the bed, then locked the spare cuff to Matt's other wrist.

'Where to?' Matt struggled to rise from the bed.

'Prison. Where you belong.' A second policeman appeared and escorted Matt from the building to a waiting lorry, forcing him along by the elbows and stretching his stitches once more. Two soldiers pushed him up on to the flatbed as blood began leaking from his wounds.

*****

'Get up. You're leaving,' the soldier shouted at Isabelle as he released her from the bed. He pulled her along by the loose end of the handcuff. Isabelle stumbled after him, her stiff legs and sore muscles screaming in agony.

Bright sunlight blinded her as they stepped through the door. She covered her eyes and tripped. The ground was hard and a policeman laughed as he took over from the soldier and dragged her roughly upright and pushed her towards a lorry.

'Isabelle. Are you all right?' Relief washed over her as she heard Matt's voice.

'Yes. You? What's happening?' Carefree hands wandered onto Isabelle's backside as they loaded her on the lorry with Matt.

'I don't know. Ricky must have convinced them we attacked him. The bastard,' hissed Matt, who was so pale it was the only thing Isabelle noticed about him as he moved closer to her.

Isabelle and Matt sat close to each other and only then did Isabelle notice the damp blood soaking his shirt. She placed her hand comfortingly on his knee and scowled at the men standing by the open tailgate.

Annie's voice sounded angrily nearby. 'Get your fucking hands off me!'

'Annie,' shouted Matt. 'We're in here.'

'Thank God for that. What's happening? Are you two all right?' Annie positively flew into the back of the truck and sprawled in the dust.

323

'Just about. I don't know where they're taking us though.' Matt didn't want to mention prison, he was still hoping it was only the policeman trying to frighten him. 'What's been happening to you?' Matt feasted his eyes on Annie. She seemed okay and that gave him strength.

'They accused me of being an immoral woman and seducing Ricky. They said you attacked him and abducted me. Attempted murder, I think they said.'

'Fucking bastard. I will kill him if I get hold of him again.' The exertion of transferring from the bed to the truck had exhausted him and Matt slumped against Isabelle.

Annie sat the other side of Isabelle and the three of them sat quietly awaiting their fate. Four policemen climbed aboard and watched them carefully, but their guns were not drawn like those of the soldiers.

*****

Out of breath, Chris arrived back at the airport. He had his few possessions stuffed in the hold-all. He had left his business card for the old hippy, with the telephone number of the embassy and a note scribbled on the back. 'Thanks for your help. If I can return the favour, call me.'

A smile curled Chris's mouth as he pictured the hippy's face, when he realised he had been smoking dope and drinking illegal booze with a customs officer.

The departure lounge was basic and the air-conditioning in the concrete built building was ineffectual, or off. No other passengers were present, just a crowd of inquisitive staff waiting for something exciting to happen. At the check-in counter he had to produce his diplomatic passport and supporting identification. It always amazed him when it took more than his passport to prove who he was.

'Wait there,' said the official. He pointed to a solitary row of plastic seats. Chris took a seat and prepared to wait. Through the windows he could see the same plane he had arrived on; it looked too flimsy for his liking but was still a better option than making the trip by bus. Beyond the plane mountains soared to snow-capped peaks, hemming the town in. Chris had seen the buses at the depot and was grateful he was not facing the long and dangerous journey by road in one of the over-worked vehicles.

An army jeep pulled up by the steps of the plane and a man awkwardly dismounted from the passenger seat and slowly climbed up to the aircraft cabin, gently assisted by the driver. A police officer followed them, before the driver returned to his jeep and departed.

'You!' shouted the official. 'You board now, hurry.' The man opened a door and waved Chris to the plane. He handed over a voucher as Chris left the building.

*****

The lorry rumbled past the base buildings, through a gate in the main fence and across the tarmac of the runway. 'We're leaving. They're letting us go. They're going to put us on a plane and send us home.' Annie looked excitedly at Matt. 'They were just frightening us to see if his story was true.'

'Let's hope so. I guess we'll find out soon.' Matt was not yet convinced.

'Don't be so pessimistic. Ishmael saw what happened on the Shandur Pass, he'll vouch for us.'

'But he's still there. He can't help us now.'

The lorry slowed then turned sharply and a civilian aircraft appeared alongside them. When the Pakistan International Airlines emblem became visible Annie smiled happily, 'I told you. They're letting us go.'

*****

At the back of the plane the policeman and the other passenger were talking quietly together when Chris entered the cabin. They looked up at him and continued talking while they watched him show his voucher to the steward.

'Please sit at the back, the prisoners will be arriving shortly,' said the steward as he pointed Chris along the aisle.

As he walked towards the back of the plane the officer scowled, but the other man smiled and started to talk.

'Hi, I'm Raseem Hasni. My friend here told me you are with the Embassy, I'm British too. I'm pleased to meet you. I might need your help to get me back home. I was attacked on the Shandur Pass and I've lost everything, I'll need a new passport.' Raseem rearranged himself on the seat, obviously in pain. Sweat stood out on his forehead.

Chris stared at Raseem, not sure what to say. The name was wrong, but the story was right.

Raseem carried on. 'I'm rather worried though, and a bit scared too. The people who attacked me will be on the plane with us.' After a slight hesitation Raseem added, 'Only in Pakistan, huh?'

Staring hard at the man, Chris forced his voice to remain steady as he spoke. 'Raseem Hasni? Did you say your name was Raseem Hasni?'

'Yes.' A concerned frown creased Raseem's forehead. 'Why?'

'I think you go by the name of Ricky too. Don't you? If you are the man I'm looking for, I doubt if Her Majesty's Government will be very keen to issue you a new passport.'

'Why? What's wrong?'

'There is a warrant out for your arrest if you ever get back to England.' Chris stretched the truth. If there were not one issued by now, he would make damn sure there was as soon as he got back to the Embassy.

'Not me, mate. Must be someone else you're looking for,' smiled Raseem, a little tensely thought Chris. A noise at the doorway attracted their attention and they all looked towards it.

A policemen entered, followed slowly by three foreigners, all of whom looked to be ill or in pain. Two more policemen crowded after them and pushed them towards separate rows. The three foreigners glowered at Raseem, while he arrogantly gazed back at them. A policeman sat next to each foreigner, the fourth sat behind them.

'Who are they? What nationality are they?' asked Chris loudly of the officer near him. One of them could have been Annie MacDonald, but it was hard to tell. Thousands of people would fit the description Dominic had given him. The young man glanced in his direction and smiled hopefully.

'They're all British. They will undoubtedly want your assistance when we arrive in Islamabad.' The policeman sounded pleased with himself.

'What have they done?'

'They are accused of attempted murder. The women are also charged with improper sexual conduct. The gentleman here is their victim.'

'They are the ones who attacked me,' said Raseem, rather louder than necessary.

'Can I talk to them? Now,' said Chris, ignoring Raseem.

'When we have taken off, yes. But not for long.'

The aircraft door slammed shut and the engines started. Once the aircraft was airborne Chris unbuckled his seat belt and moved forwards. The man looked to be in pain and a bloodstained bandage showing beneath his ripped shirt confirmed why. One girl lay back in her seat with her eyes closed. The second girl turned to look at him hopefully as he approached.

'Hi. I'm Chris Sinclair, from the British Embassy. Is one of you ladies an Annie MacDonald?'

'Yes. That's me. Why?' Annie sat up looking unsure of herself. Hope mixed with fear as the stranger looked at her.

'I'm from the Embassy. I met a friend of yours, Dominic Renard. I've been trying to find you. I've also been trying to find a man called Ricky. Is that him? What's happened to you?' Chris stopped himself asking all the questions he had, so he could get some answers.

Annie stared at the floor for a moment then took a deep breath before she replied quietly. She stared directly at Chris as she talked steadily, clearly trying to give him as much information as she could in a short time. 'Yes, that is Ricky, also known as Raseem. He abducted Isabelle and me. Isabelle escaped and found Matt. They rescued me and we tried to escape over the Shandur Pass. Ricky caught us up and attacked Matt when he tried to protect us. After a fight when Matt was stabbed, Isabelle and I joined in. Isabelle stabbed Ricky in the balls, which he deserved after what he did to her, the fucking bastard.'

'Why have you been arrested?' asked Chris quietly.

'Because that lying little shit is a smooth talking bastard.' The other girl opened her eyes and looked up at Chris. 'Be careful what you believe when you speak to him. There was another guy at the place where Ricky imprisoned me. I think he killed him.'

'No. The guy made it back to London. It was him who told us about you.' Chris smiled. 'Thank God you're OK.'

'She's alive, at least,' muttered Matt.

'Only just,' added Annie. 'And now it seems that bastard Ricky says Isabelle and I seduced him and then attacked him. The police believe him, not us. Can you help us, please?' She almost started to cry and wiped her face fiercely with the back of her hand whilst glaring a challenge at Chris.

'I hope so. That's why I'm here. The Ambassador knows about you, he has a meeting with the Interior Minister this morning.' Chris tried to sound reassuring, though he was unsure what he could do if the Pakistani authorities did decide to press the charges they were threatening.

'That's enough. No more talk to criminals.' The policeman called Chris back to his seat in the rear of the plane.

As he moved slowly back to his seat Chris vowed silently to himself that he would never let his own beautiful daughter travel alone.

Chapter Twenty Two

'Mr. Ambassador, it is always a pleasure to meet you.' The aristocratic looking Pakistani gentleman stood as the Ambassador was shown through the door.

'Mr Interior Minister, likewise.' The Ambassador strode forwards and offered his hand. The two men shook hands firmly.

The Minister waved his visitor to a seat and returned to his own. Bright sunlight coming through the window behind the Minister made it hard for the Ambassador to read the Minister's face as he started to speak. 'I cannot remember when I last received such a sudden visit from Her Majesty's Ambassador. Tea? Or coffee maybe?'

'Coffee, thank you.' The Ambassador was used to the necessary preamble that allowed such a meeting to take place without causing an incident, but he hated the waste of time.

The two men watched as the secretary prepared two bone china cups of coffee and delivered them, without spilling a drop, to the Minister's desk and the small table ideally placed to one side of the Ambassador's chair.

'Will you be returning to the UK for the summer holidays, Mr Ambassador?'

'I will be returning to London, but it will be mostly business. As usual.'

'For a month? Meetings in London must be very long.' The Minister almost smiled as he gently teased his visitor. Then without warning switched to business. 'How can I help you? My secretary said you told her it was urgent and of vital importance. It must be for me to have the pleasure of a personal visit from you.'

329

With the Minister having given him the opening he needed the Ambassador launched into his prepared speech. He knew he had only moments to catch the Minister's attention and secure the help he needed.

'I assure you I would not waste your valuable time for something that could be dealt with in any other way.' The Ambassador held the gaze of the Minister. 'Our police in London have learnt that a British citizen of Pakistani origin, by the name of Raseem Hasni, also going by the name of Ricky, has been kidnapping young foreigners, including British citizens, and forcing them to smuggle heroin to England for him.'

'Force? How can he force them? As soon as they get on the plane to London they can do what they want.' Scepticism was ripe in the Minister's reply.

'He drugs them, injects them with heroin until they are addicted, threatens to harm their families and tells them that customs officers are in his pay at Islamabad airport, so there is no point turning themselves in because they will go to prison if they do so.' The Ambassador felt himself losing ground, his last sentence had been too long and made him sound desperate.

'Very interesting. But do you have evidence to back up these claims of corruption in our fine customs service?'

'No.' This was definitely not going according to plan. During all his years as a diplomat it had been drummed into him by senior colleagues to never say no. It was too definite an answer for a diplomat.

'Well then. How can I help you? Accusations without proof are slanderous and our government will object in the strongest terms if these accusations are made in public. It seems that the main issue here is with your own citizens.'

The Ambassador saw a chance to redeem himself. 'That is true. We have a witness who will testify against this Raseem, a British citizen, if he is caught. We do, however, believe that three more of our citizens will be able to do the same once we can interview them. We will be happy to deal with our citizens and leave Pakistan to investigate its own.'

'Where are these other three people?'

'They are currently under arrest for attempted murder.'

'Very unreliable witnesses then.' The Minister almost smiled; the Ambassador could see the man's face twitching with amusement.

'They are accused of attacking this Raseem Hasni. On the Shandur Pass. They have been arrested by the fine Pakistani police.'

'I am sure that their case will be tried appropriately. Surely, you cannot be asking me to interfere with the rule of law, Mr Ambassador?' The Minister did smile this time; it was usually British diplomats accusing so-called third world countries of interfering with the rule of law, not asking for it to happen.

Feeling he had little left to lose, the Ambassador decided to push harder. 'Of course not. I just wanted you to be aware that we will be issuing an arrest warrant shortly for this Hasni fellow. There will be at least one count each of kidnap and assault. When we have talked to our citizens whom your fine police have arrested, I am sure there will be more charges to follow. We will of course ask for his extradition in the most public manner.'

'What are you saying, Mr Ambassador?' The meeting was distinctly less friendly than when it had started out.

'All I am saying is that people may not look too kindly on a case where four people are variously accusing one man of assault, but three of them are on trial for attacking this one man, when they themselves are under medical treatment for wounds inflicted on them.' The tide was turning and the Ambassador began to feel more confident again.

'Our judiciary and police force are independent, I cannot interfere.' The Minister picked up a pen and began to play with it while he stared at his desk. Then he glanced at the Ambassador and said, 'That, of course, is the official position.

However, I will make sure that the case is investigated quickly and correctly.'

'I understand. Thank you for listening and for your time.' The Ambassador relaxed. This was about as close as he could get to a commitment that the Minister would release the three prisoners promptly.

Having made his decision, the Minister placed his pen back in its place and resumed his confident demeanour. 'Do you know where these people currently are?'

'I believe, sir, that they are on a plane in transit from Gilgit to Rawalpindi. A member of Her Majesty's Diplomatic Corps is on board too. He just happened to be in the area.'

'Very convenient, I'm sure,' smiled the Minister wryly. 'Thank you for your visit. It was a pleasure to meet you again. Come again soon.' The Minister rose and held out his hand. The meeting was finished. The Ambassador had done all he could and it was out of his hands now.

*****

As the police officer escorted him to the door of the aircraft Raseem grinned at his vanquished enemies, despite the pain in his groin. Isabelle and Annie stared defiantly at him, despite their concern at the unexpected turn of events. Matt glowered and it was clear to Raseem that he was thinking of all the things that he would like to do to him if he ever got the chance.

Fortunately, it looked very likely that it was Matt, Annie and Isabelle who were going to prison, not him. They were under arrest, he was being sent to see a specialist surgeon in an Islamabad hospital. A wheelchair waited for him at the bottom of the steps and with the pain that was spreading down his legs and up into his stomach now, it would be a relief to get back to a hospital and get some more painkillers inside him. Raseem really wanted some hashish, but he didn't think it would help his cover story if he asked a policeman for a joint.

'Please sit here, sir. We will take you to the military hospital, it has the best surgeons in the country. The frontier police authorised you to receive treatment there.' The waiting orderly wheeled Raseem to a shiny white ambulance, and with the help of a second man rolled the wheelchair up a ramp into it, before quickly strapping Raseem in safely for the impending journey.

Alongside the ambulance stood a forbiddingly grey prison van.

*****

'You three, move.' The police officer spoke harshly to his three prisoners, who stood obediently and moved apprehensively towards the door. All three glanced back towards Chris, who smiled encouragement at them. He had been ordered to remain in his seat until the prisoners left.

Through the window he saw the three prisoners shuffle dejectedly down the steps and enter a grey prison van. The doors slammed shut behind them and the van drove away quickly. 'All right, you can leave now.' The police officer spoke curtly to Chris and nodded at the door.

A member of the ground crew directed Chris to a police car newly arrived near the steps and he started towards it. 'You can walk,' said a sharp voice behind him. 'That's for me.' The police officer brushed past Chris and as he approached the car a driver opened the rear door for him.

With one foot already in the car the officer lifted his gaze to a bemused Chris, standing lost on the tarmac. He pointed across the tarmac to a line of buildings a few hundred yards away. 'See that white building over there, that's where you should be. Have a nice day.'

'Bastard,' swore Chris angrily as the police car drove off. If the police were treating him like this, then he knew the three prisoners were definitely in trouble. Chris started walking towards the terminal, quietly fuming to himself and sweating in the clammy heat of Rawalpindi.

At the door of the arrival's building an official looked at Chris's voucher and passport and quickly waved him to an exit. Sweat soaked the customs officer's shirt and plastered his hair flat on his head. He wanted a cold drink and some air-conditioning.

'The British Embassy, Islamabad,' said Chris tiredly as he sank onto the sticky plastic seat of the taxi hoping the journey from Rawalpindi would not take too long. His day was not getting any better though. 'Sorry sir, air-con broken,' apologised the driver as he pulled away.

*****

Dirt covered the tinted windows, allowing only a little light inside the van and a very blurred view of the outside world. Matt gave up trying to see where they were going and sat back down. Annie and Isabelle sat near each other on the bench opposite him. All three of them were soaked in sweat; the metal sides of the airless van oozed heat.

Potholes shook them and corners threatened to throw them across the van. Too hot and scared to talk, the three prisoners sat in silence.

Almost an hour after setting out the van slowed to a halt outside metal gates set in a thick wall, but the solid metal barrier swung smartly open and the vehicle entered quickly. All three prisoners shivered as the metal clanged shut behind them, sitting lost and scared in their own thoughts.

The prison van doors opened and the outside air seemed cool in comparison. A straggly tree wilted with sympathy in the heat. Shouting policemen hustled them inside the building.

A police officer directed Annie and Isabelle to the left whilst Matt was dragged to the right by another aggressive guard. The three had no time to say goodbye as they separated and staggered through double doors to separate sections of the building.

*****

Clean and efficient, the military hospital impressed Raseem. An orderly took him to an officers' room, with a solitary western style bed, clean sheets and pillows; a jug of chilled water, sitting in a puddle of condensation, stood next to it. A second orderly arrived with a strong painkiller and informed him that the doctor would arrive shortly.

The lack of hashish stopped troubling Raseem as he lay back on the soft bed. Reality was a dream and his pain was gone as he slid down into the warm wrap of an opiate induced haze; he had never taken anything like that before, but he was enjoying the experience.

The fact of his lost manhood failed to anger him any more as the ecstasy of his own money-making poison took over. Raseem wallowed as the room changed shape around him and he drifted in and out of consciousness.

*****

Isabelle and Annie were hurried along a corridor and out into a courtyard through another set of doors. Cages lined the wall of the courtyard, where women lay on the bare floors or leant on the bars. 'You can live with the rest of the whores,' laughed a policeman. 'It's not a bad living and you two will be in demand.'

Inquisitive faces stared at the two foreigners as the guard opened a cage. 'Inside, quickly.' A hand shoved Annie into the cage and she only just managed to stop herself tripping as her eyes adjusted to the gloom. She recoiled from the squalor around her. All her hopes of release were rapidly slipping away.

Isabelle hurried after Annie but a guard tripped her as he pushed her into the cage and she fell in a crumpled heap on the dirt encrusted floor. The clang of the cage door slamming shut echoed round the courtyard and drowned out the guard's laughter.

*****

Dark dank cells, frighteningly similar to those in Sukkur, lined the corridor. The smell of urine and faeces filled the air. Screams and moans, from men chained to the walls, echoed eerily in the concrete block. The only light entered through the single small window above the orderly's chair at the far end of the building.

A guard opened the grill in the doorway of a cell. Matt shrank back from the horror inside. Three soiled men lay in their own waste, fastened by chains to the wall. A fourth chain lay unused on the floor.

'This one's for murderers, you should feel at home in there.' Matt resisted, but strong arms propelled him forward. He started fighting when a guard picked up the loose chain. Two other guards sat on him as the shackle was locked to his leg. They leapt clear and moved out of reach once the lock clicked.

Matt tried to follow them and prolong the fight, but the short chain stopped him and he fell to the floor. The guards laughed as they closed the door leaving him in darkness with murderers.

As the acrid smell of ammonia filled his nose and lungs, Matt retched and vomited; the other prisoners kicked him and tried to move him away from them. No matter where he moved, someone hit him.

Anger and frustration overwhelming him, Matt lashed out. He caught one prisoner on the side of the head and sent him flying. He kicked another with his free foot and heard the man gasp in surprise. The third prisoner moved out of range and Matt was left with floor space to himself.

*****

The chowkidar made Chris walk from the front gate of the embassy. 'Only official embassy cars allowed inside. Security,' said the man officiously. However, he did condescend to telephone Ian directly to announce Chris's arrival.

The driveway seemed much longer now he had to walk up it. Ian met him in the lobby, just inside the door of the building, not wanting to leave the comfort of the air-conditioning. 'Glad you're back,' he grinned. 'You can see the Ambassador from now on and tell him what's happening.'

'You haven't told him I'm back, have you? I was hoping to freshen up before I see him.' Chris looked questioningly at Ian.

Ian completed the necessary registration process, ignoring Chris's last question. 'We were told there were no passengers on board the flight, otherwise we would have collected you. Sorry.'

'That doesn't surprise me, the way my day's gone so far. What's happening? Where are they?'

'The Ambassador met the Minister this morning. He's not hopeful of a quick solution, though he thinks something will happen eventually. But we don't know where they are at the moment.' Ian took a visitor pass from the receptionist, then waved his own electronic pass to open the security doors. 'Have you got any news? The old man wants to see you immediately,' said Ian as he led the way into the embassy proper.

'I met them all on the plane. It was just them, their guards and me. That smug little bastard Raseem has charmed everyone into thinking he's the innocent party.' Recounting the story rekindled Chris's anger and his voice rose. 'An ambulance took him off to hospital and a prison van whisked the other three away to God knows where.'

'Come on, let's get you upstairs,' said Ian as he took the steps two at a time.

'I need a shower first,' complained Chris, without following.

Ian laughed. 'You must be joking, the Ambassador said straight away and I'm not going to get into any more trouble just so you can have a wash.'

With a grunt of disgust, Chris followed Ian up the stairs to the wood-panelled office of the boss.

'Ah. Mr. Sinclair. The man I have heard so much about and not had the pleasure of meeting before. You look like you could do with a drink, what would you like?'

'A beer. I've heard you have them in here somewhere.'

'I do, but you will have to go and see some important people later, so you will need to have something soft for now.'

337

'Coke then, a large one. With ice. Please.' Chris was too tired to be overly polite. He disliked people who tried to pull rank and demonstrate their power without due cause. Chris considered it an abuse of power and ultimately a sign of weakness. Especially when the man did it in his own office.

The Ambassador nodded at Ian. 'Get my secretary to bring in the drinks when you leave; tell her I'll have my usual.'

Dismissed, Ian left with disappointment etched on his face. Chris perched on the arm of a low-slung sofa, refusing to put himself two feet lower than the man behind the large oak desk. He held the Ambassador's gaze, willing him to speak first. Chris won.

'Tell me what's happening. Don't leave anything out.'

'Ian has probably told you everything I know up until the last time I phoned from Gilgit. I just came back on a plane from there with four British citizens. Three of them are accused of attempted murder and two are also accused of immoral behaviour, which seems to be the worst offence in this country.'

A secretary entered with their drinks. Two small glasses of coke for Chris, and a whisky on the rocks. 'We only have small glasses, sir,' said the woman as she handed Chris his glass. 'So I brought you two as Ian said you were really thirsty.' Chris nodded his thanks, taking a glass in each hand.

'Thanks Portia,' said the Ambassador as he took his own drink.

The men waited, watching her leave, then the Ambassador smiled, 'She has a Masters from SOAS and speaks four Asian languages fluently. She's the best source of local information I have. It's amazing what people say in the waiting room in front of what they assume is a lowly secretary.'

Looking back at Chris the Ambassador raised an eyebrow for the story to continue.

Following a long draught of ice-cold Coke, Chris restarted. 'Three were taken off the plane, in chains and put in a prison van to God knows where. Ricky, or Raseem Hasni as we now

now him to be called, is being looked after like a king, taken off in a military ambulance, presumably to the military hospital in the cantonments. What happened in your meeting with the Minister?'

An eyebrow rose in surprise on the Ambassador's face. He was obviously unused to such direct and impertinent questions. 'He was polite. He emphasised the fact that the judiciary is independent and he cannot interfere.'

'Bollocks. That's not true in England, let alone here.'

'I know, but I am a diplomat and these things have to be done gently, through official channels. It is the way it works.' The Ambassador sipped his whisky.

'You mean by lies and insinuation.' Chris drained his first glass and put it on the polished wood of the big desk in front of him. The Ambassador winced as condensation ran down the glass and pooled on his immaculate antique.

'I wouldn't put it like that.'

'I'm sure you wouldn't. You're far too diplomatic.'

'The Minister gave the strongest indication, within the constraints of his office, that he would look into the matter. I expect to hear they have been released in a day or two.'

'A day or two? They need doctors, now.' Chris could hear the tone of his voice rising again and took a sip from the second glass to calm himself.

The Ambassador watched him, bemused. 'You seem very . . . involved in this case.'

'It is particularly disturbing,' allowed Chris. 'Anyway, I'll believe the two days when I see them on a plane out of here. If you have nothing else to ask, I'll be getting along. I need a shower and then I must see if I can get my contacts to do something.'

'Ah, yes. Your contact, who is he? I am in charge here and all official contact with the Government of Pakistan must be authorised by me.'

'Oh well, this doesn't count then. It's unofficial. Goodbye.' Chris pointedly placed his second dripping glass besides the first, then left the office, leaving the door open behind him. He could feel the calculating gaze of the Ambassador on his back.

Chapter Twenty Three

A single pot of food entered the cell though a hole in the bottom of the cage door, a pile of bread landing on the dirty floor next to it. The six women in the cell with Annie and Isabelle pulled bowls from their clothes and moved towards the food. There was a definite order in which the women approached and poured their food for the communal meal.

When the other women had taken their food, there were two pieces of bread left and a little amount of curry in the pot. One of the women nodded at Annie and then the food. Isabelle glanced at her and they retrieved the pot and bread to share between them.

Isabelle scooped thin curry to her mouth with a scrap of bread, just as their cell mates were doing. Annie glanced in the pot and shook her head, unable to face the greasy food. She took a piece of bread and ripped off a small piece to chew on.

'I couldn't. It looks horrible,' grimaced Annie as Isabelle tucked in.

'It's better than what Ricky ever gave me,' said Isabelle shovelling more curry to her mouth.

'Is there anything to drink?' said Annie, to the cell in general. The women looked at her, then one shook her head and spoke slowly, struggling with her English.

'One time a day, in the morning, they open door. You get water then. If you want water other time you need to keep it in bowl, or pay guard.'

Annie looked through the bars of the cage; there were no guards in sight. She closed her eyes and thought of how badly her dream trip had gone awry. It was just like Dominic had said could happen. She was stuck in prison, not having done anything wrong.

*****

Two pairs of hands lunged for the pot as it hit the cell floor. The third prisoner was chained out of reach, though he watched to make sure he would still get his share.

When bread flew after the pot the men tried to catch it before it landed in the filth on the floor.

Food was the last thing on Matt's mind. He knew that living like this for long would kill him. The other three men in the cell with him were covered in sores, their lips cracked and suppurating. One of them had hardly moved since Matt arrived and kicked him in the fight; he was stick thin and looked more dead than alive. There was bound to be cholera, dysentery, or some other hideous disease living in the muck all around him.

Curry splashed to the floor as the men fought, until one hit harder than the other and won the pot to himself.

Matt wondered what Chris was doing. The embassy should be trying to arrange a visit, though it was doubtful if they even knew which jail he was in. Then there was Annie and Isabelle too; at least they were probably still together, though their conditions were unlikely to be any better than his.

Matt lifted his leg and slammed the manacle into the concrete floor. 'Fucking bastard!' he shouted. If he could get hold of that shithead Ricky, he would kill him slowly; the thought of inflicting pain on the man was intensely pleasurable.

The other men looked at him fearfully and the weakest looking one held out a piece of bread to him. 'Fuck off,' growled Matt. The man flinched back and stuffed the bread into his mouth, before Matt could change his mind.

*****

'Do you want the good news first, or the bad news?' The doctor spoke as he washed his hands in the bowl held by an orderly.

Raseem carefully settled himself on the bed. He hated the indignity of a man handling him; it made him feel angry and embarrassed. 'The good,' he finally muttered to the doctor.

'You're lucky. I won't have to remove anything.' The doctor smiled encouragingly at Raseem but could not hold his gaze.

'Great. What's the bad news?' The drugs in his bloodstream stopped Raseem from noticing the doctor's discomfort.

'It'll never work again. There was too much damage caused by the knife. Sorry.' The words came out in a rush and the doctor took a step backwards.

Raseem's drug-slowed brain tried to decipher what the doctor had told him. Slowly it dawned on him that the doctor in Gilgit had been right after all, he would never have sex again, ever. Sitting up he shouted at the doctor. 'You're lying! Fuck off! I want to see another doctor! I want to to go home.' He gasped for breath and fell back on his pillows as the movement stabbed pain at his balls and tore at his ribs.

The doctor moved towards the door. 'That's it, fuck off!' screamed Raseem. An orderly appeared at the door.

'That fucking bitch should rot in jail for ever for this. What did I ever do to her?' His tantrum hardly helped, nor did remembering how he had dominated her before; it only reminded him of what he would never do again.

As the doctor watched him indifferently from the door he muttered, 'I'm sure she will rot in jail.' Then more loudly, 'I'll see you again tomorrow. You might be able to leave here tomorrow if the stitches hold well, sit still as much as possible. Take the pills the orderly gives you, they'll help you sleep. He'll come back in an hour with the next one.' The doctor turned on his heel and left Raseem to his own private hell.

The pain between Raseem's legs soared again and he sank to the pillow, 'Orderly, I want more painkiller.' He needed the pleasure of the opiate again. 'Now.'

'You'll have to wait for the pills, like the doctor said.' The orderly shook his head with a slight smile as he settled Raseem and straightened the IV drip. He looked at Raseem contemptuously. 'What was is it you did to the girl that she chopped off your manhood anyway?'

*****

As Chris dressed after his luxurious shower in the basement of the embassy, Ian came running in. 'Hurry up, I've got something you'll want to see.'

'What is it that's so important a chap can't get dressed in peace and quiet?'

'We got an email from London. There was a photo of Ricky on David's camera and he positively identified him as the man who kept him prisoner and gave him the drugs to carry home.'

'Have you printed it off?' Chris pulled on the rest of his clothes quickly.

'Of course. The old man is going back to the Minister in an hour.'

'Email me a copy of the photo and the statement. I'll need a computer too. Hurry man, hurry.' Ian turned and hurried from the room, Chris following soon after.

*****

Chris opened the email London had sent. The photo was surprisingly clear and easily good enough for identification purposes. A brief note confirmed it was the man who had sent David back to Heathrow with the heroin.

Entering an additional password on the secure email system Chris accessed the obscure series of letters and numbers that were the email address of his contact, so he could forward on the photo. A few seconds later the delivery receipt appeared.

Chris sat back in his chair wondering what to do next. Ian sat at another desk watching him expectantly.

The phone on Ian's desk rang. The two men looked at each other, then the phone. 'Go on, then. Answer it,' said Chris impatiently.

'Yes,' answered Ian guardedly. He listened for a few moments before speaking again. 'Who is this?' Ian looked at Chris quizzically, then leant forward and transferred the call to Chris. 'He asked for the man from London looking for Ricky, but wouldn't tell me who he is. What's going on? How did he know to ask for me?'

Chris picked up the phone without answering Ian. 'Yes,' he said into the phone.

'I've been expecting to hear from you, what took you so long?' Chris heard the unmistakeable voice of his contact over the phone line. 'I like the photo you sent me. It'll look good in the album.'

'Glad you like it. How did you know I was here? asked Chris. Impressed with the detective work.

'It's great, it'll go well with the postcard I received this morning from my nephew. He met up with your niece and her friends.' Chris smiled wryly at the unsubtle indication his contact had been keeping an eye on him in Gilgit when he had been looking for Annie. Then he returned to the serious matter at hand.

'What's it say? Will my niece be OK?' Chris hoped it was something that would get the three prisoners out of jail. He held his breath, waiting for the man to give him some good news. He was not disappointed.

'I believe your niece and her friends will be able to visit you soon. I hope you enjoyed your trip to Gilgit, now I must be going.'

The line went dead before Chris could think of an adequate response.

'What the hell was that all about?' demanded Ian. 'Who was it? He asked for me by name. Was it the same person who sent you those letters? What's your niece got to do with anything?'

'That was proof we are not the only ones who are good at detective work,' smiled Chris.

*****

The man sat up suddenly; it was the most he had moved since Matt's arrival. Three pairs of eyes watched the man. He sat holding his stomach. For two minutes there was silence in the cell. Then he vomited blood and fell over. It was clear to Matt that he was dead. Matt vomited too and knew he was facing death himself if he stayed here much longer.

*****

A special messenger handed an envelope to the Minister only a few minutes after his visitor had arrived. It was marked with one of the special codes that meant it was delivered to him, unopened, as soon as it arrived.

He was already vaguely annoyed that the Ambassador had returned so soon. He had made it clear he would do what he could and he hated being hurried, especially by arrogant British Ambassadors. And a message marked as important as this was bound to be trouble.

Taking the opportunity to make the Ambassador wait and make it clear to him there were more important things in life than an Imperial servant, he looked up and said, 'Excuse me one moment, Mr Ambassador. Urgent affairs of state.'

The Minister rose and walked to the window. He rarely received anything this urgent from the secret anti-narcotics bureau he had established. He left them to get on with their work in any way they thought best and only ever expected a briefing every six months to keep him abreast of their efforts. Their main task was to collect information and pass it on to foreign governments, to make sure the smugglers and their distributors around the world were caught and stopped somewhere outside of Pakistan. Locking up foreign drug smugglers in his filthy jails did not make for good international relations.

A photo and two pieces of paper slid into his hand. The minister read them quickly and frowned. So, the Ambassador was right and probably wanted to gloat. He returned to his desk and began speaking immediately.

'Since you are here I might as well tell you that three of your nationals will be released as soon as the paperwork is completed. Raseem Hasni will be arrested and charged with kidnapping, attempted murder and smuggling narcotics. Now, how can I help you?'

It was hard work not smiling. The Ambassador's eyebrow twitched as he digested the sudden announcement. The Ambassador began speaking, trying to regain his position as he did so. 'I had some information and a photo regarding this case that I wanted to give you.'

'I've already got the photo of Raseem Hasni and I have a statement from one of our policemen regarding Raseem's attack on the three British citizens on the Shandur Pass. Is there anything new you have to assist our investigation?' The Minister was almost brusque; he was enjoying himself immensely.

'No. Thank you. I see you have everything under control.' The Ambassador was fuming that the Minister had scored a victory over him. He viewed diplomacy like a game of chess, and he was losing this week.

'I hope you will be able to report to your Minister in London that Pakistani justice is efficient and competent. Not corrupt and incompetent as is so often reported in the papers of your country.'

'My report will contain all the relevant information,' allowed the Ambassador as the two men took their leave of each other. The Minister did not try overly hard to hide his pleasure at having pre-empted the Ambassador's news.

Chapter Twenty Four

It was late afternoon when two policemen entered the room. They smiled at Raseem and asked how he was. 'The doctor told us you would leave hospital tomorrow, but he said it would be all right for you to come with us now.'

'Where are we going?' Raseem said warily. He had not expected any policemen to take him anywhere and he didn't want to miss his next dose of painkiller.

'The Islamabad police would like to provide you with some hospitality, as you have been so helpful with our enquiries,' said the senior man with an ingratiating smile.

'Will I be able to have my next dose of medicine,' asked Raseem plaintively.

'Of course,' smiled the policeman.

Relaxed by their reply, Raseem dressed slowly and carefully. He followed them gingerly to the car park and climbed in the back of their shiny new Nissan jeep. It was cool inside as the driver had kept the air-conditioning running while he waited.

Traffic cleared from the road in front of them as they drove through the suburbs of Islamabad. Raseem smoked a cigarette proffered by one of the policemen and watched the mountains glow red in the sunset as he wondered which hotel they were taking him to. No one spoke; the driver had Hindi-pop blaring loudly from the stereo that made conversation all but impossible.

A high fence and sentries announced their arrival at what looked like a concrete fortress. Large gates swung open before they had time to stop completely. The jeep swung inside and the gates closed behind them.

'We wait here for a while.' The policeman smiled at Raseem and handed him another cigarette.

*****

In all the cells around the courtyard the women had moved as far to the back as possible. All conversation had stopped and only an occasional whisper broke the silence. The noise of the city crept over the surrounding buildings and a gate crashed open somewhere nearby. Annie and Isabelle had moved back too; it seemed only sensible to follow the lead of the other women, but they had no idea why.

Five policemen burst into the courtyard. Collectively the women sank back further into their cells. The men laughed raucously and Annie knew from their demeanour they were telling coarse stories. She had seen the guys at university behave exactly the same way when she worked in the union bar. There was something about the way they strutted and leered that made her and Isabelle shrink even further back in the cell.

The men looked around the cages, looking for someone in particular. When one of them saw Annie and Isabelle he shouted to his friends and they descended on the cage in a pack.

A key appeared and unlocked the door. Two men strode inside and roughly pulled the foreigners back outside.

'We have fun tonight? Yes?' The leader grinned at Annie and slapped at her backside.

'No!' Annie slapped his hand away.

The men cheered and the leader grabbed at Annie again. 'You are whore. You are in prison now. You do what I say.'

Isabelle yelled, as two men grabbed her. 'Fuck off! Leave me alone!'

Two more grabbed Annie and the leader waved them all angrily back towards the doors of the building. Fighting hard the two girls resisted strongly, but slowly and steadily they moved closer to the building.

A second jeep entered the courtyard; it was newer and cleaner than the one Raseem was sitting in. A senior officer waited in the back until his driver hopped out and opened the door for him. Raseem watched in idle curiosity as the man stepped out regally and saluted with his swagger stick. The officer glanced at Raseem, who nodded politely to him. Holding his gaze, the uniformed man stared fiercely at Raseem until Raseem dropped his eyes.

Once Raseem dropped his eyes he heard orders being shouted and his heart began pounding in fear. Something was wrong. The door next to him opened suddenly. 'Out, get out! Quickly!' shouted a policeman.

Taking care not to stretch and twist too much, Raseem eased himself from the jeep. 'Follow me,' said the newly arrived officer and turned towards the building only a few feet away.

Raseem rolled up the steps like a constipated horseman, keeping his legs wide to lessen the amount his balls came into contact with his thighs. A finger jabbed his back to hurry him along. He could hear a lot of noise over the walls of the courtyard; women shouting and men laughing harshly.

The officer entered the doors first, his body language angry. Raseem followed a few seconds later and saw Annie being dragged by her hair across the room. Then he swivelled his head in the direction of someone yelling in English. 'You bastard! You won't get away with this.' Isabelle spat at him.

Raising his swagger stick the officer stepped forward. The policemen loosened their grasp on Annie and Isabelle, staring in surprise at the senior officer. Annie pushed herself free and stepped forward as if to speak. Isabelle flew across the room and attempted to knee Raseem in the groin. The officer slashed his stick across a table as Isabelle knocked Raseem to the floor. A sharp crack echoed round the room.

Silence settled over the scene. Everyone stared at the officer. The five policemen hung back at the edges of the room. Isabelle stood over Raseem as he lay groaning on the floor.

'Are you two ladies all right? I hope these policemen did not hurt you.' The officer spoke in perfect English with a clipped accent. Then he raised his head and shouted orders in Urdu. People scurried away as he looked dispassionately at Raseem.

'Are you Raseem Hasni?'

'Yes, sir,' responded Raseem carefully as he regained his feet. He didn't like this new turn of events, he had the feeling he was going to have to go over his statement again. And he'd need a better story to convince this man he was the aggrieved party.

Reverting to Urdu the senior officer looked towards the policemen around the room and quietly gave his instructions. 'Take him away and lock him up. By the end of today I want to know who he is and everything there is to know about this worm. And I don't care how you find out.' Raseem's legs sagged, but a policeman grabbed his arm and hauled him away.

Annie watched, shocked. A pale Raseem tottered as two escorting policeman dragged him across the floor and through the doors Matt had disappeared through earlier.

*****

An hour's shouting to the orderly at the end of the corridor had finally resulted in a guard arriving to take the body away, but he made no attempt to clean up the congealing blood on the floor. Now the loose manacle lay open and abandoned, waiting for its next occupant to arrive. Matt idly wondered if the previous occupant of his own manacle had died in it too.

The death of his cell mate reinforced Matt's conviction that his life was in danger just from being there. If he was going to survive long enough to get out alive, he was going to have to have a survival plan. He wished he'd read the book, as well as watched the film, of *Midnight Express*. He had to be strong. Weakness would kill him by starvation if the last mealtime was anything to go by.

Not twenty minutes after the body was removed, guards noisily entered the corridor, a prisoner with them whining and pleading. Matt waited expectantly for the prisoner to arrive at his cell and fill the vacant space, wondering if he was going to be a threat to his own survival, or another wretch ready to die.

The cell door opened and two policemen kicked their frightened prisoner inside. Urine and blood soaked the man's trousers. Tears dripped from his nose. The chain clanked on the floor as the manacle was placed on the prisoner's leg. When the guards moved away Matt recognised Ricky cowering and snivelling in the corner.

Only once the police had locked the door and left did Ricky look around the cell. His gaze reached Matt last. His face froze under the fierce glare of his worst nightmare. His jaw dropped. Fear squeezed his bowels and the stench of faeces grew stronger in the cell.

*****

'You two are Annie MacDonald and Isabelle Jones?' They were now sitting on soft seats in a clean office and the man Annie viewed as some sort of guardian angel had ordered hot food and chai for them.

'Yes. We are. What's happening?'

'You will be released on bail pending further investigation of the case. You had a male friend with you, didn't you?'

'Yes. We all came here together, but they took him away through those doors where they took Ricky, the man that you called Raseem. Is Matt being released too?'

'When I have located him, yes.' An orderly arrived with three passports and the officer flicked through them quickly to the back page with all the personal information until he found what he was looking for.

'Your friend?' He held up the photo of Matt.

'That's him,' confirmed Isabelle.

The officer looked up at the orderly. 'Fetch the man called Matthew Peterson. Hurry.'

*****

Matt stood and moved closer to Ricky, who cowered as far into the corner as possible. The chain stopped Matt moving as close as he wanted. Leaning on the wall for extra balance, Matt swung his boot as if he was going to kick a penalty. A pitiful scream broke from Ricky's mouth as the hiking boot connected with the same ribs Matt had broken in Birer.

The noise of a key in the lock stopped Matt kicking again and saved Ricky from further pain. He was still standing over Ricky when the guard entered the cell and looked at them questioningly, then the guard bent and unlocked the manacle on Matt's ankle. '*Chelo,*' said the man and signalled Matt to leave the cell.

*****

Chai, fresh curry and chapati arrived a few seconds before Matt. Annie hugged him hard as he looked around the room, confused by the latest turn of events. 'What's happening?' he asked suspiciously.

'They're letting us go,' said Annie as she took his hand and led him to a seat.

'That's great,' responded Matt cautiously. He would believe it when it happened, and he wished they'd left him for just a few more minutes with Ricky.

Chapter Twenty Five

'Sorry about your luggage, it seems to have got lost somewhere along the way.' The officer held out no hope that they would see it again and none of them were that concerned about it. All they really wanted to do at the moment was to get away from the place as quickly as they could.

To their great relief though, he handed over their passports. Surprisingly, he also handed over their money belts. There was no cash in any of them, but the credit cards and bankcards were amazingly still there. At least they would have access to their money if they could find a bank that accepted them.

'Good luck,' said the officer as he formally shook their hands. 'You are free to go. You will be taken to the British Embassy. Do not get out of the jeep anywhere except at the Embassy. I will inform them you are on your way. I am sorry that your stay in my country has not been as enjoyable as it should have been.'

An air-conditioned jeep whisked the three tense foreigners away from the police station. None of them really believed they were safe as they sped through the darkened streets of Islamabad.

'We're getting close,' whispered Annie. 'We've just passed the French Embassy and the British Embassy is not far from here. We'll be safe soon.'

'Don't tempt fate,' murmured Isabelle quietly.

The jeep swung into the entranceway of the British Embassy building. A light shone above the guard house, but there was nothing to see inside the extensive grounds.

Matt eased himself out and knocked on the window of the little office. His muscles ached and he wanted to lie down and sleep.

'The embassy is closed. Come back tomorrow.' The chowkidar was friendly, but firm. He would not let them in.

Annie and Isabelle joined Matt at the kiosk window.

'It's urgent. Please call the Ambassador, he is expecting us.' Matt tried to sound important, but it was difficult when he looked so scruffy and blood stained his shirt.

'The Ambassador is not here. He is out on official business.' The man smiled smugly, knowing Matt could not argue with him on that point.

Behind them the gears of the jeep crunched as the driver revved his engine and left them alone in the darkness, on the wrong side of the embassy gates.

Isabelle stepped past Matt and leant forward to speak with the chowkidar, her face stern in anticipation of an argument. Before she could speak the phone on his desk rang quietly.

The man stood up as he fell silent and listened. 'One moment, sir,' he said into the handset. Then he looked at the three faces looking at him hopefully, 'What are your names, please?'

'Matthew Peterson. Annie MacDonald. And I'm Isabelle Jones.'

They held their breath, safety tantalisingly close again, having almost slipped away.

'Get in here immediately,' instructed the man as he put down the receiver and unlocked the door of his office.

Matt ushered the two girls into the office as he watched the street, fully expecting someone to arrive, announce it was all a mistake and return them to a prison cell.

He heard running footsteps and scanned the darkness looking for danger as he stepped into the office and the chowkidar slammed the door behind him. As the runners drew nearer it became clear they were inside the embassy grounds, not outside. Two men came into view and ran up to the office. 'It is you. Thank God,' said the man Matt recognised from the plane.

'I'm Chris, remember? From the plane? This is Ian,' he added as he ushered them from the office through a second door on the right side of the embassy gates, and directed them towards the Embassy building. Ian fussed around excitedly. 'I'm so glad to see you. I thought we'd lost you for a while.'

*****

'I want you out of the country as soon as possible. Quite frankly it's all been rather embarrassing and used up too many favours getting you out of prison. The Embassy will arrange and pay for your flight home, but you will be sent the bill later.' The Ambassador had not really wanted to talk to them before he went out for his dinner; they reminded him of his losing encounter with the Minister and his grumpiness was clear for everyone to see.

'Never mind him, he's just annoyed because I won't tell him how I did it.' Chris was happy and had secured a bottle of malt whisky from Portia. He poured five glasses as soon the Ambassador left. Matt never normally drank it and was dubious about taking a glass, but Annie and Isabelle held their glasses up for a group salute and they all clinked glasses. Matt watched as the girls, Chris and Ian all knocked back their drinks, leaving him little option but to do the same himself.

'I think that's enough of that,' said the embassy nurse from the doorway. 'I need to check these guys and make sure they're fit to fly.'

'Just you try and stop me,' laughed Isabelle, the neat whisky going straight to her head. 'Have you booked my flight yet, Ian?'

'I hate to break up the party,' interjected Chris, 'but there's a lot to do if we're going to get you lot home tomorrow. Isabelle, you go with Nurse Jenkins. Ian, go and book the flights. Annie and Matt, you have a lot to tell me.'

*****

356

Isabelle weakly waved goodbye from the top step, the accompanying nurse standing next to her. Ian had secured the last two seats on the British Airways flight to London and no amount of begging or threats could get two more.

The nurse had insisted she travel with Isabelle, to provide constant care on the flight home. The emotional and physical trauma of the past few weeks had hit Isabelle hard overnight. She was running a fever and had lost all her energy. 'It's not uncommon for people to keep going until they reach safety, then collapse,' explained the nurse. 'She's exhausted, malnourished, needs counselling and the comfort of her family. The best thing I can do for her is get her back to England as quickly as possible.'

Chris and Ian had accompanied all four of them to the airport and helped speed their way through the bureaucracy of dealing with Isabelle's expired visa. Ian had bought them drinks and snacks while they waited in the VIP lounge for the flights to be called and Annie idly wondered why the Ambassador could not have been so nice too.

Matt and Annie waved back to Isabelle from the windows of the terminal building. Their own flight left in an hour, for Paris. It was the only other direct flight to Europe that day with seats available and Chris wanted them to get away as quickly as they could. From Paris it was an easy hop to London.

Forty anxious minutes later they left the terminal building and entered the Air France plane from the walkway. 'Courtesy of the French Government,' smiled the stewardess who surprisingly directed them left to the business class section. 'The Ambassador personally called to insist you were well looked after, and wish you *Bon voyage*.'

With the door of the Airbus aircraft closed and the engines started, Annie and Matt finally began to relax. When the plane taxied away from the terminal building their excitement grew further. At the end of the runway as the plane prepared to take off, Annie grabbed Matt's arm and held it tight, her cheek on his shoulder.

Pakistan sped past the window as the plane accelerated along the tarmac. Annie and Matt peered through the small window and held their breath until the plane left the ground.

They sat back in their seats and smiled happily at each other. 'Paris. I went there once,' said Annie to Matt. 'It's very romantic.' Then she leant over, caught his face in her hands, and kissed him hard.

20231226R00195

Made in the USA
Charleston, SC
01 July 2013